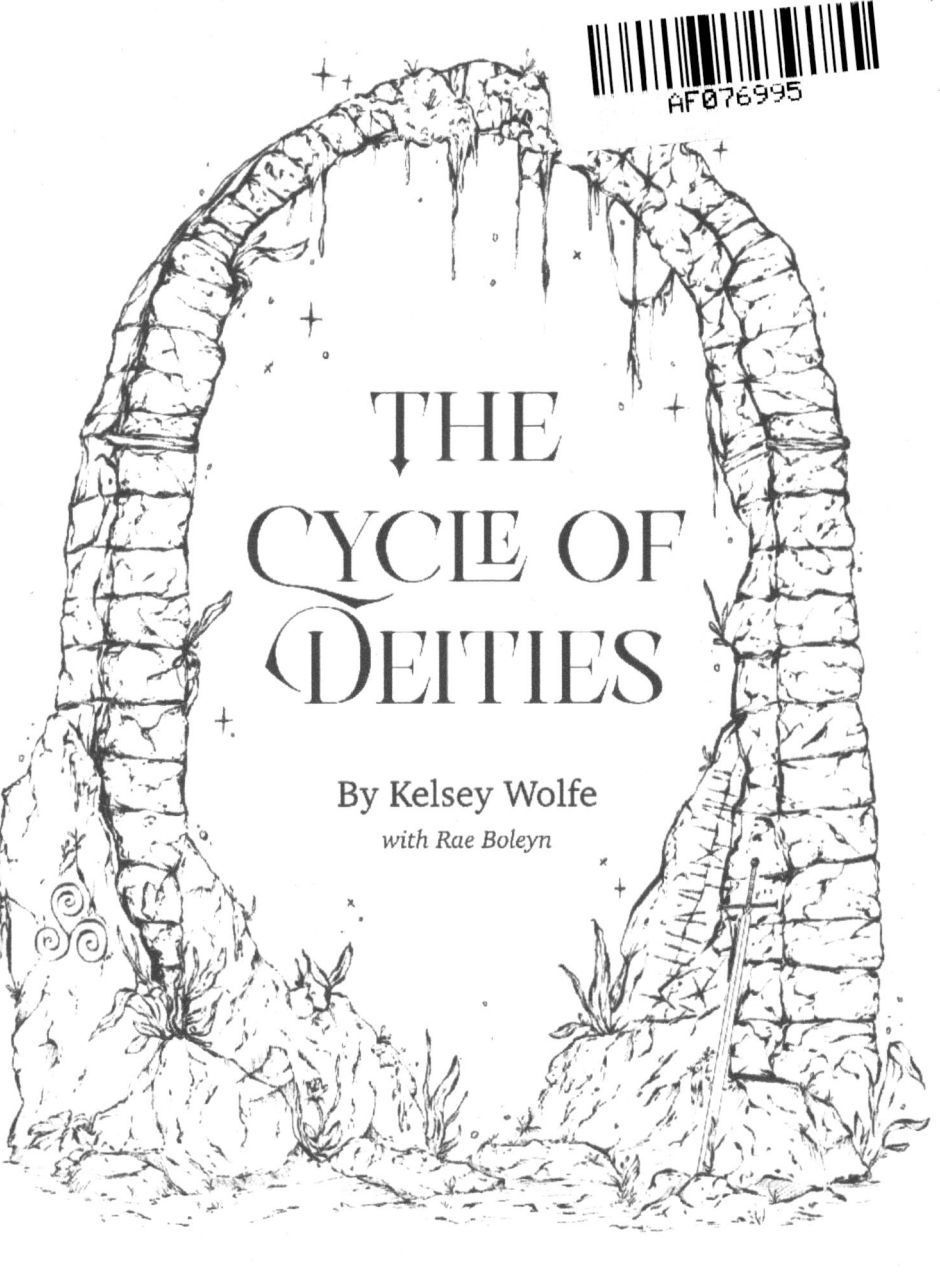

THE CYCLE OF DEITIES

By Kelsey Wolfe

with Rae Boleyn

FIRST EDITION

Copyright © [2026] by [Kelsey Wolfe]

All rights reserved.

No portion of this book may be reproduced in any form without written permission from the publisher or author, except as permitted by U.S. copyright law.

ISBN PRINT: 979-8-9997897-0-9

ISBN E-BOOK: 979-8-9997897-1-6

Cover Artist: Jennifer Inkwright

Internal Artist: Marta Riva

NO AI TRAINING: Without in any way limiting the author's [and publisher's] exclusive rights under copyright, any use of this publication to "train" generative artificial intelligence (AI) technologies to generate text is expressly prohibited. The author reserves all rights to license uses of this work for generative AI training and development of machine learning language models.

Side Note: This book was created by human writers and human artists. NOT by our future evil cyber overlords. We can't force you to support us, but we do hope that you support human authors and artists, as the literary and art world is currently being muddled by AI slop. Thank you!

This book is for my first anam cara, Laura.
This story would have never seen the light of day without your friendship, sisterhood, encouragement, & love over the past three decades.
The Cycle exists because of YOU.

Prologue

She hadn't moved from her chair in over an hour, completely absorbed in the book before her. Most people would have found watching her uneventful, but I found it fascinating. Every so often, when the pages stuck together, she'd wet the tip of her finger and delicately separate them, never once breaking her focus.

I pulled my jacket tighter against the damp cold, resisting the urge to step inside and warm myself with something hot.

Just one cup.

One excuse to be closer to her.

But I stayed where I was... watching as another page turned, another sip of coffee was taken, the cycle continuing as effortlessly as the rhythm of her breath.

Could she sense how close I was?

I wondered what book had her so enraptured. She never kept dust jackets on her books, insisting they only got in the way.

It was ironic, really.

She was stripping away their protection in order to keep them pristine. Another little habit of hers I'd come to know. Another detail I couldn't help but admire.

I was ignorant about many things in this world, but there was one thing I knew without a doubt.

Adair Hanlon must be protected.

No matter the cost.

Chapter One

Adair leapt back as a car sped past her, the driver hurling an obscene gesture before racing down the busy street. The light had *clearly* been red, but in Seattle, it seemed that no one cared about such trivial things as human life. With a sigh, she glanced up the road to ensure she wouldn't become roadkill, before continuing her journey to the bookstore she considered a second home.

Stepping into the vestibule of *Walmsley's Bookshop & Bindery*, she began to fish through her purse in search of her keys. Each item she encountered seemed to mock her—lip balm, receipts, a tangled pair of earbuds—anything but the one she needed. With a soft curse, the umber-haired woman surrendered her purse to the door handle and plunged in with both hands. At last, her fingers brushed cool metal, a sigh escaping her lips as she savored the minor victory.

"Excuse me, miss?"

Caught off guard by a gravelly voice with a British lilt, the keys slipped from Adair's fingers, clattering loudly to the ground beneath her feet.

Dammit.

"I apologize. Did I startle you?" A lanky, grey-haired gentleman with a weather-worn face peered down at her.

She opened her mouth to respond, but nothing came out.

As the unknown man stooped down to retrieve the keys, Adair quickly realized that this stranger now had her cornered, her only means of escape dangling between his long, slender fingertips.

"O-oh. Um, no. Not at all, sir."

Flashes of axe murderers and true crime documentaries filtered through her mind as she wondered where exactly her body would be found. Who would be the one to discover her mangled corpse stuffed in the bookshelves she once found solace within? What would they say about the young employee who still had so much life ahead of them? Her palms began to sweat, but she tried to remain affable.

"S-sorry, but we don't open until seven," Adair stammered, her eyes fixed on his expensive black leather shoes. Being a thin wisp of a girl, she knew there was nothing to do now but wait for her inevitable demise.

A jingle brought her back to reality as the British gentleman held out her keys to freedom.

"Yes, I am a bit early. I have a meeting with Mr. Walmsley this morning."

She finally met his regard, his deep brown eyes locking with hers. Adair found nothing but an endless pit of darkness in his gaze. She felt momentarily out of place as a sudden wave of emptiness washed over her body, his pronounced features doing nothing to ease the fearful fantasies racing through her mind.

"Oh, well…" She smiled shakily. "You're welcome to wait in the shop?"

She reached out to touch the bundle of metal the man held out before her, but his grip remained firm. As much as Adair wanted to look away, she couldn't find the strength to escape his stare. Something briefly flashed behind his eyes, causing her to brace as she prepared for the worst.

Instead, the gentleman surprised her, releasing her keys with a smile as he stepped back.

"Where are my manners?" The man chuckled darkly, shifting a package that she had failed to notice earlier to his left hand, as he reached out with his right. "Grey Ainsworth is the name. Longtime friend of Mr. Ian Walmsley."

Adair hesitated while she gauged the authenticity of his statement. Finally, she took his hand, amber eyes never leaving his. "Nice to meet you, Mr. Ainsworth. I'm Adair Hanlon."

She stared at him suspiciously, racking her brain for any mention that Mr. Walmsley would have made of this so-called 'friend.' She was typically adept at remembering the people important to her employer, but nothing about this man's name or stature rang a bell. They had their similarities, of course. Both men dressed sharply and moved with the poised confidence of royalty, but that did little to soothe the unease prickling beneath her skin.

"Please, come in." She swiftly unlocked the door behind them and moved inside the cluttered bookstore.

At once, the rich, earthy scents of vanilla and weathered parchment greeted Adair like an old friend. She took a moment to inhale deeply, a ghost of a smile playing over her lips. She flicked the switch by the door to make the Edison bulbs overhead blink to life, casting a warm glow over the cozy bookshop.

As Adair slipped into her familiar morning routine, she remained subtly attuned to Mr. Ainsworth's every step. The soft chime of bells halted her darkening thoughts, announcing the man's arrival before his contagious smile and warm voice filled the small space.

"Good morning, Miss Hanlon!" Ian announced, his mustache bouncing happily on his face as he spoke. His gaze moved from Adair to the gentleman standing to her left, his brows quickly rising in evident surprise.

"Grey, my good man!" Ian chuckled, striding over to his friend. "You are far earlier than I expected." With a mischievous twinkle in his eye, Ian grasped his companion's hand and clapped him on the shoulder.

"It's good to see you." The man rasped, a grin forming on his face.

Observing the interaction, Adair smiled meekly at the scene before her. It would be evident to anyone that these two men had a long history of friendship. Chiding herself for her glaring overreaction, she cleared her throat.

"Your usual this morning, Mr. Walmsley?"

Releasing his friend, the shop owner turned to face her. "Yes, thank you. One for my companion as well."

His eyes crinkled behind his glasses, and Adair could feel her own smile spread in response to his delight. Ian was a man whose positivity was effectively infectious. She set about brewing the black teas as the two men made their way towards the heavy, ornate, wooden door at the back of the shop.

Once they had vacated the main room, Adair suddenly felt foolish as the adrenaline wore off, and all her earlier anxieties flooded back. Ian Walmsley had taken her under his wing and treated her like a daughter. For her to doubt his choice of company felt like a betrayal of the man she so admired. She promised herself she'd be more open-minded in the future, no more inventing villains out of shadows. Balancing the tea carefully, she made her way to the back, determined to be useful.

The workshop door had been left ajar. Adair carefully nudged it open and paused at the threshold, taking in the sight before her. The two men hunched over a long table, smoke curling from their pipes as they examined a weathered book laid reverently on the surface. As the woman drew closer, the ornate cover became visible, and she suddenly felt a strange urge to cry. It was apparent from first glance that the binding had let go; a beautiful old thing, but the First Edition *Sherlock Holmes* had clearly seen one too many adventures.

Determined to make a better impression, Adair looked up at Grey and offered a strained smile. Carefully placing the cups and saucers on the wooden table, she made her way towards the exit, leaving the men to their essential work.

"Oh, Adair?" Ian spoke around the stem of his pipe.

She paused halfway to the door and turned with expectation. Any request from Ian was usually an opportunity in disguise. Sometimes he invited her to help with rebinding projects or let her sit in on his consultations, each moment an apprenticeship of sorts, a slow honing of her skills.

"Isn't the poetry reading at the park tomorrow?"

Adair let the disappointment slide off her shoulders as she toed the edge of a loose floorboard. "It is, but I didn't want to leave the shop unattended."

Ian removed his pipe, watching her intently. With a flourish, he produced two items from his tweed coat. A satisfied smile graced his features as he held the tickets out for the girl to take.

Adair's face lit up. She felt her hand rise instinctively, but then halted, shaking her head as she breathed out a sigh of disappointment. "No, I couldn't possibly."

As she wrapped her arms around her body, she felt warm hands softly grip her shoulders. She looked up to find steel blue eyes staring intently into her own with a look that nearly melted her heart.

"Adair, you work far too hard for a young woman of your age," Ian said decisively. "Take a day off."

It came across as a command, yet there was an unmistakable hint of pride woven into the statement.

"Take a look. They have yours and Nadia's names on them." He pointed to the tickets, then held them out to her once again. "That means there are no returns and no exchanges. So also, no point in arguing, my dear," he chuckled. "Before you start on that nonsense about how I couldn't possibly manage the store without you, please remember that I am thirty years your senior, and I refuse to be talked back to."

The pair smiled and shared a laugh while Adair used her oversized sleeves to wipe the tears from her eyes.

"Thank you. Thank you so much, Mr. Walmsley." Her voice cracked on the words.

"A new series just arrived, and I need you to shelve them. Now, off with you." Ian gave her a playful shove as he placed his pipe back into his mouth.

Adair spared the men one last glance, a grateful smile on her lips, before getting back to the tasks at hand.

Ian turned back toward his friend, who was typing furiously on his phone. "On to business, then?" He walked back to the table as Grey pocketed his device.

The lightheartedness of the earlier conversation was snuffed out in an instant as the two men turned their full attention back to the book, with its fading pages and well-worn binding.

Adair closed her hardcover copy of *The Return of the King*, slipping a bookmark between its pages before setting it aside. Instinctively, she rose to greet an approaching figure, expecting an unfamiliar customer, only to find her employer stepping back in from the street, the faint scent of rain clinging to him after having bid farewell to his old companion.

"Sit," the ashen-haired man said, pointing toward her with mock severity as he folded his wet, black umbrella. Ian wiped his muddy shoes on the mat, his eyes gleaming with playful authority.

Adair obeyed with a sheepish grin, settling once more on the tufted stool behind the counter. She let out a quiet sigh as she reopened her book, eager to disappear into the grand adventure waiting on the page.

Much to Mr. Walmsley's feigned annoyance, she genuinely loved her time in the shop. "*You spend enough time here. Why don't you go out with friends and get into a little trouble?*" he had teased. But unlike many of her peers, Adair had no interest in trouble. She was happiest tucked away in the company of hobbits, wizards, and great sweeping tales of love and loss.

The bells over the front door chimed again, and a plump elderly woman in a bright floral dress swept into the shop, her smile broadening the instant she spotted the owner. Adair glanced at Mr. Walmsley, who waved her off in silent assurance as he approached the customer with a matching grin.

After a brief exchange, Ian led the woman toward the romance section tucked into a cozy corner near the back. His warm British cadence threaded through the shelves, each word deliberate without losing sincerity. Adair was not surprised at the authentic passion she heard there. It was no secret that intimate stories were not Mr. Walmsley's preferred reading, yet his love of literature had always outweighed his biases.

When Ian returned, he caught her gaze. "To each their own," he remarked with a knowing smile as he made his way back behind the counter.

Adair laughed and lifted her hands in surrender. "I've spent plenty of time in that section, so no judgment from me." She tucked back into her book, feeling the familiarity of the words wash over her. The rain outside was tapering into a soft drizzle as she continued her journey through the misty mountains and fantastical realms.

Time seemingly sped past as she found herself reaching the final page, and a sigh escaped her lips as she shut the book, an ache of bittersweet nostalgia tugging at her heart. Placing the closed tome to her nose, the young woman inhaled the scent of the pages, taking a moment to enjoy their faint musk. Reluctantly, she returned the daring journey to the shelf from which she had borrowed it, her fingers dragging across the leather spine as if bidding farewell to a beloved companion.

"That's that, then?" Ian asked, peering at her over the rim of his glasses.

"Yes," she said with a wistful smile. "It was the last one in the series."

Part of her ached to experience it all again for the first time. These stories had always been her escape, carrying her to worlds where courage and companionship overcame impossible odds.

Ian bit down thoughtfully on the stem of his pipe. "Then I suppose it's off with you for a wild night of drinking and drugs?"

"You know me better than that, Mr. Walmsley," Adair chortled with a lighthearted roll of her eyes.

"One could only hope Nadia might drag you into drunken debauchery. Isn't that what friends are for?"

"As much as she tries, I would never let that happen." Adair lifted her chin in mock defiance, though a fondness for her friend stirred warmly beneath the banter.

"Oh, I know that all too well." Ian chuckled, smoothing his mustache with a free hand.

Adair responded with a simple laugh, shaking her head as she approached the front counter. After clocking out and retrieving her bag, she smiled up at her employer one final time. "See you tomorrow, Mr. Walmsley."

"Are you not forgetting something?" Ian asked, with a glint in his eye.

Adair stopped moving towards the exit and began to run through her mental checklist, but a chuckle from Ian interrupted her apparent confusion.

"You have tomorrow off, my dear."

Adair paused, then broke into a wide grin. "Oh. I completely forgot. Thank you again for the tickets! They've been sold out for weeks, and I'd given up hope of going. I don't even know how you managed to get *two* of them." She knew she was rambling, but excitement overpowered her restraint.

"I have my ways," he said with a mischievous lift of his brows. "Enjoy the market and the vendors. See if you can find something worthy of my collection."

Adair nodded, though in truth the shop was already brimming with oddities, yet their presence was part of what gave it such charm. Her fingers tightened around the strap of her bag as a familiar unease crept in. Saturdays were always hectic, and she hated the thought of her employer shouldering the work without her.

"Are you sure about me taking tomorrow off? There will be other events. I really don't have to go." Her gaze strayed to the bright floral dress of the elderly customer, now making her way to the counter with a basket piled high with books.

"I trained you, lest you forget," Ian responded, fixing her with a look over his glasses that made her grin despite herself. "I will not allow further argument. I will see you Sunday, Miss Hanlon."

Adair nodded and slipped out the door, the soft chime of bells drowning out Ian's conversation with his satisfied customer.

As the sun slowly sank beyond the horizon, the sky transformed into breathtaking shades of pink and purple. Adair glanced both ways, ensuring no cars were coming before crossing the street towards her destination.

Each step she took away from the store felt lighter than the last. The day's cares slipped away as Adair inhaled the fresh scent of rain-kissed pavement and blooming flowers, her heart fluttering at the prospect of an evening spent in solitude.

Pulling her keys out of her bag, Adair pressed the button on the fob, listening for the soft trill that would lead her to her olive green *Subaru Outback*. The sound echoed in the stillness of the parking lot, guiding her through a row of vehicles until she reached her parked SUV. She opened the door and slid easily into the driver's side, tossing her bag onto the adjacent seat with a relieved sigh.

With a turn of a key, the car roared to life, a rush of cool air from the vents hitting her instantly, easing the sweat that had formed on her brow. Music played through the speakers, and she found herself humming along, the rhythm lifting her spirits as she buckled herself in and navigated the route home. Traffic was light, and the drive felt almost meditative as she maneuvered her way down the tree-lined road.

As twilight descended, the vibrant colors of the sunset gradually faded into deeper hues, transforming the sky into shades of lilac and indigo. A small spattering of light filtered through the trees as they grew denser, cloaking the road in a soft, muted glow. The dew left behind by the rain glistened on the winding road's greenery, catching the light and dancing like diamonds amongst the pines and ferns. The turn into her descending drive appeared around the next bend, and she felt a sense of familiarity wash over her as her destination came into view.

The old house rested halfway up the hill, its weathered shingles silvered with age, its wide bay windows gazing upward over the street like a quiet sentinel. In the soft light of evening, the garden surrounding the terrace seemed to curl protectively around it, a scatter of blooms and greenery that bore Laura's loving touch. Adair could picture her aunt sitting on the small patio now, cradling a warm mug of tea, her gaze lingering on the passing world as if she could catch and hold the fading day.

Built into the hillside, the upper part of the dwelling was her aunt Laura's domain, while the lower level, formally a music room, had been transformed into Adair's little apartment. This sanctuary offered the young woman privacy, without losing the comfort that came from having family nearby.

As Adair reached the foot of the steep drive, the sight of a familiar car beside her aunt's made her groan aloud. She shifted into park and leaned against the headrest.

"Just one peaceful weekend," she muttered. "Is that too much to ask?" Ian's earlier words about finding some trouble felt suddenly prophetic.

Her bag sat on the passenger seat, and she rummaged through it with tense fingers until she found the pill bottle buried deep inside. The lid resisted before giving with a soft click. She tipped one small blue tablet into her mouth, the bitterness fading instantly beneath a gulp of water.

One pill remained. She made a mental note to call in a refill, but not tonight.

Adair steeled herself as upbeat music spilled from the house, its rhythm pulsing against the quiet of the evening. She pushed open the door, plastered on a smile she hoped would mask her discomfort, and stepped inside the inconveniently occupied dwelling.

Chapter Two

Adair had no idea what she would encounter when entering the front door of her typically peaceful apartment. Still, the sight that greeted her was as familiar as it was jarring. Nadia had pushed the coffee table toward the fireplace on the far wall, creating an open area where she danced, her movements fluid and exaggerated. The soft glow of a ring light cast a halo around her companion as she moved, illuminating her curves and vibrant energy.

A phone on a tall silver tripod clued Adair in to the bizarre scene's purpose. Nadia was in the process of filming another social media post for her adoring '*fans,*' and for some unimaginable reason, she felt the need to use *her* home to do it.

Adair wished she felt more shocked at the revelation.

She had only a moment to take in the view before Nadia's eyes lit up in the camera, signaling her knowledge of Adair's arrival. The woman spun gracefully, her laughter ringing through the small space.

"Addie, you're finally home!" Nadia elegantly floated around the sofa and towards her friend. "It took you long enough!"

Adair felt a mix of affection and exasperation as she plopped her bag on the dining room table, the thud echoing darkly in the otherwise cheerful ambiance of the room.

"I just got off work. What are *you* doing?"

"Oh, nothing. Just a little dance to celebrate your return!" Nadia twirled, her hair streaming behind her like a curtain of pink silk. "Come join me! We shall have a fabulous weekend, whether you like it or not!"

Adair couldn't help but laugh at her friend's antics. She was still yearning for solitude after the events of the day, but the warmth of Nadia's enthusiasm was beginning to chip away at her resolve.

"Nadi, I—" Before Adair could finish her sentence, her friend enveloped her in a massive hug, lifting her off the ground.

"Sorry! Let me turn it down!" Nadia's cheerful British accent cut sharply through the blaring music as she cleared the end table before spinning the knob on the receiver, lowering the volume to a more manageable level.

"Nadi, I don—"

"Nope!" She spun around to face Adair, her cotton candy hair swaying in rhythm. "Don't start. I'm not here to ask you to go out tonight."

Adair's shoulders sagged, a wave of relief washing over her face. "Thank God. I thought you were here to drag me to that club opening you keep raving about."

"Oh, that? That's tomorrow night!" Nadia declared, a glint of mischief in her hazel eyes as the Pakistani girl moved the coffee table back into the center of the plush rug. "Tonight, it's a night in, complemented by cocktails and that fantasy show you like so much."

"But you hate fantasy shows..." Adair eyed Nadia with distrust as the woman glided into the kitchen and began to mix drinks.

"Pish posh. A woman can change her mind," Nadia said, flipping her vibrant hair over her shoulder, obscuring the dual stars that mirrored the pair adorning the back of Adair's neck.

The tattoos were an act of solidarity acquired on a night full of silly antics and drunken bravado. Still, they were a stark reminder of the connection that the two girls shared despite their glaring differences. Where Adair was a cozy Autumn, Nadia was the bright Spring. Adair was the anxious and hesitant one, while Nadia was confident and expressive. Like an old city library, Adair felt muted and quiet, while her best friend was the explosive color found in an underground art showcase. Nonetheless, the girls had been inseparable since middle school.

"Oh... I know what it is..." Adair chuckled softly. "It's because of the nudity, isn't it?" She arched a brow at her companion.

The bronze-skinned woman spun towards her, a hand to her chest in mock offense. "How dare you? I am a woman of substance." Perfectly manicured digits picked up the glasses from the counter and passed one to Adair. "I can appreciate the female form from a purely *artistic* standpoint." With a wink, she took a sip, while her best friend burst into a fit of giggles.

"Pretend all you want. As if we haven't been friends long enough for me to see right through you," Adair said, wiping her eyes of the laughter-induced tears.

Speaking of seeing...

Adair opened her purse, digging deep until her fingers found the plastic contact case she kept in the bottom. Her vision wasn't poor enough to keep her from recognizing faces, but without the extra assistance, the world lost its edges, softening in a way that wasn't ideal for shelving books or reading tiny price tags.

She'd ruined or misplaced enough glasses over the years to make peace with contacts for daytime use. Even so, she always looked forward to slipping back into her tortoiseshell frames at night, the faint weight on the bridge of her nose a familiar anchor at the end of a long day.

With practiced care, she removed each contact lens and placed them carefully into their separate compartments before reaching toward the green leather case she'd left on the side table. She popped the case open and slid on the pair of wide-rimmed glasses that had been lying neatly inside. After ensuring everything was back in order, the woman melted into the couch, reclaiming her drink with an exaggerated sigh.

Adair lifted and stared into the swirling glass, a constellation of colors mingling with some kind of edible glitter. Tentatively, she took a sip, her eyes widening in surprise. "This is amazing!"

Nadia playfully pinched Adair's cheek, which prompted an annoyed smack to her hand in response.

"Don't look so astonished. I told you I would be practicing, so it wouldn't be as horrible as last time." She flicked on the television, deliberately ignoring the dramatic roll of Adair's eyes as she nestled in beside her, tugging the other half of the blanket securely across her lap. "How about a fire to set the mood?"

Adair balked, her brows furrowing in disbelief. "Are you serious? It's like ninety degrees out."

"Spoilsport," Nadia pouted, her expression a mix of disappointment and playful teasing.

Adair chewed her bottom lip, glancing at the fireplace. She knew that the fire would be far too warm for the spring evening, but she felt torn between wanting to indulge her friend and the instinctual need for comfort.

Sensing the abrupt shift in the atmosphere, Nadia gently placed a hand on Adair's shoulder. "Oh, stop. It was a joke," she said softly, her tone laced with understanding. "We can compromise."

Nadia quickly popped off the couch and grabbed the container of matches from the mantle before lighting a large candle in the center of the coffee table. The warm glow flickered to life, casting soft shadows across the room. While the flame danced, she noticed Adair's throat bob, her friend's eyes growing distant as she became lost in her thoughts.

"Did you take your medication?" Nadia asked curiously, not an ounce of judgment in her tone.

Adair's jaw tightened at the imagined accusation, the stillness stretching between them like an invisible barrier, and Nadia could read her friend's guilt in the silence. With a swift motion, she whipped the wool blanket off the couch and wrapped it around the woman, cocooning her in warmth.

"I wasn't judging, love. I just... I didn't realize you were struggling again."

Adair was thankful that the blanket concealed the nail of her thumb, which was currently digging sharply into her opposite hand. She focused on the bite of pain in an attempt to distract herself from the shame she felt about her condition.

It wasn't the anxiety or the depression that caused her the most pain. It was the knowledge that her fears and insecurities were negatively impacting the people she cared about most, and she was tired of feeling like a burden.

"Addie," Nadia said softly, "You know you can tell me anything, right?"

A slight dip of Adair's head was her only acknowledgment, and Nadia's heart ached at the sight. She lunged across the couch, enveloping the woman in a tight hug.

Tears pricking at her vision, Adair leaned into the embrace, finding solace in the love and understanding radiating from her best friend.

Logically, she knew the prescribed medication was there to help her control these feelings, but the negative stigma attached to the drug made it difficult to accept her reliance on it. Nevertheless, she could feel the little pill doing its job as the manufactured calm helped her wrangle control over her unbridled thoughts.

Once her heart rate had stabilized, Adair pulled away from her friend, her mask slipping back into place. She shook her arms out as her practiced smile returned.

"I'm fine. Really. You don't need to worry about me, Nadi."

Nadia's eyes scanned Adair's face for any cracks in the facade. After a moment, she gave a little nod to indicate she was choosing to believe her friend's assessment… at least for now.

Snatching the remote and her glass off the table, Adair tried to change the subject. "How about pizza for dinner?" she ventured, her tone brightening as she flicked through the streaming platform.

Nadia swiped through her phone, likely checking how many reactions she had received on her most recent post, and shook her head with a playful huff. "We should order from that Italian place so we can each get what we want."

Adair knew her friend had phrased it that way intentionally, a subtle nod to their differing tastes in food. "You aren't still on that diet, are you?" she asked, wrinkling her nose at the idea of enduring the sour aroma of kombucha and boiled greens all night.

Nadia shot her a glance, her perfect cat eyes narrowing as she schooled her expression into a teasing smile.

"Not all of us can eat whatever we want and not have to pay for it later."

Adair lifted the remote defensively as she contemplated the many types of treats she indulged in daily without an ounce of extra weight to show for it.

"Hey, I take offense to that. Toxic body culture goes both ways, you know."

"Yeah, but *Laura* doesn't comment negatively about your weight," Nadia shot back, taking another large gulp of her cocktail. She attempted to laugh off her own comment, but the vulnerability and insecurity in the statement did not escape her companion.

Adair knew she was lucky to have such a kind and understanding parental figure in Laura.

Nadia, on the other hand, was not afforded the same luxury.

"Where is your aunt, by the way?" Nadia asked, attempting to steer the conversation into lighter territory.

"Oh, she left for some conference this morning. She won't be back until the end of the week."

Adair tried to stay nonchalant, but she knew what her friend was thinking. Laura was a well-respected sex therapist who traveled the country sharing her many varied and occasionally graphic views on the subject. Nadia poured more alcohol into her glass, a flicker of something unreadable passing over her face.

"Damn, I wish I could go to a conference and just talk about sex for a week straight," Nadia said with a chuckle. "Here, place your order." She held out the phone and took the remote in trade.

After Adair ordered her meal, Nadia took back the device to place her own. "Where the fuck is the button for a salmon salad without any croutons or cheese? I don't want to have to pick them off, you stupid app."

Hearing Nadia's additional request, that familiar ache filled Adair's heart once more. Nadia's mother, Nasreen, had always been overly critical of her daughter. Their relationship was like a tightrope walk, perpetually strained and fraught with tension, and it pained Adair to see the destruction that type of upbringing had wrought on her best friend's self-esteem.

Nadia was the most beautiful woman she had ever known, both inside and out. She only wished her friend could see it as plainly as she did. Parental trauma was yet another thing the two women had bonded over through the years. While Nadia struggled to meet unattainable and unfair expectations, Adair was mourning the loss of a mother she never knew. Her mother had died in a car accident when Adair was very young, and the only memories now associated with the woman were the consequences of her passing.

Her father, Michael, unable to bear the reminder of his wife, had sent Adair to live with her aunt, leaving her feeling like an afterthought or an unwelcome burden. Adair and Nadia had spent many nights curled up in their shared grief over their distinct but equally damaging experiences.

Adair reached over, grabbing Nadia's free hand "You know you're more than enough, right? You're stunning, smart, and hilarious. Anyone would be lucky to have you."

Nadia looked down, a faint blush creeping up her tawny cheeks. "Thanks, Addie. I appreciate the sentiment. I just wish that I could believe it."

Adair gave Nadia's hand a gentle squeeze. "You'll get there. But until then, I'll keep reminding you. I will tell you *repeatedly* until you can't help but believe it."

Letting out a small laugh, Nadia's expression softened. "Well, don't stop then. Flatter me with your words." She squeezed Adair's hand back before letting go, her posture relaxing into the couch once more.

"I am glad you agree because you're stuck with me." Adair stuck her tongue out, causing Nadia to snort a very unladylike laugh.

"You're right, I am," Nadia replied, glancing down at the plain, gold bangle adorning her wrist with a grin. "I truly wouldn't want it any other way."

"Me either," Adair said, reflecting the smile. "I don't know what I would do without you."

"Well, if you love me *so much*, then maybe you should come with me to one of those *special* conventions to visit your Aunt Laura," Nadia said, wiggling her eyebrows.

"I am *positive* they are not as great as you think they are," Adair muttered, twiddling her thumbs in discomfort.

Nadia threw her head back in laughter, her pink hair bouncing with each chuckle. "Oh, come on. It's all very *freeing* and *empowering*, isn't it?"

Adair rolled her eyes at the thought. "That would be utterly mortifying. Having *the talk* with Laura was bad enough. I have managed to dodge any other therapy she has attempted on my sex life, or lack thereof." She shuddered, cringing at the memory before leaning into her best friend, her hand resting under her chin. "I still think you should try one of *my* conventions. I am so sad, going all by my lonesome. It would be so much better with a friend." She jutted out her bottom lip in a pout.

Nadia pushed her away with a laugh. "Don't start. I know you love *your* cons, but switching venues might do you some good. Break you out of your comfort zone a little. Stretch those boundaries." She reached out and twirled a lock of Adair's hair with a smirk.

"I like my boundaries," Adair replied stubbornly, using one hand to shoo away her friend's teasing fingertips. "They're safe, cozy, and most importantly, private." She pulled her arms over her chest as if they could protect her from her friend's daring request.

Nadia sighed dramatically, her dark eyes still playful. "You can fight all you want, but we are going to one of those conventions someday, even if I have to *drag* you."

"Tell you what," Adair responded, settling into the cushions, "I'll go to one of *your* conventions if you go to one of mine. Deal?"

The thought of her friend joining her for a day of costumes and day drinking made the idea of a sex-related convention *much* more bearable.

Nadia squinted at Adair suspiciously, but then surprised her by nodding and extending her hand. "You have yourself a deal. But you had better not back out when I find one with a panel on... well... you know." The woman wiggled her eyebrows suggestively.

Adair groaned, pushing her friend's hand away. "You're incorrigible."

"And you love it," Nadia shot back, smiling widely.

Shaking her head, Adair aimed the remote towards the TV and selected the fantasy series they had planned to watch. "You're lucky that I love you so damn much."

Nadia grinned, pulling her legs under her as the intro music began. "I know." Her golden skin glowed in the candlelight, but it did nothing to soften the sudden sour expression on her face. "I just don't see it," she muttered. "Sweaty nerds at a convention versus a weekend full of sex advice? Totally different ballparks."

Adair chuckled quietly. "I feel like one of those conventions would have a lot more sweat-related activities, and it *isn't* the one with comic book signings."

Nadia sighed, eyes drifting toward the ceiling. "Well, some 'activities' are more fun than others. I bet after the sessions, they have, like, wild orgies or something." Her eyes snapped to Adair. "Oh my god, what if they just do it right there in front of everyone instead of using a PowerPoint or something?"

Adair wrinkled her nose in disgust. "Ew, Nadi!" She tucked her legs under herself and reached for the remote cleverly hidden beneath her coffee table, flicking on the electric candles. "You've got to be really repressed if you're imagining old people going at it at a convention."

Nadia laughed, her arm stretching across the couch to poke Adair. "And here I thought I'd found all your clicker hiding spots!"

Adair smirked, her lips tugging upward as she stashed the remote back in its place. "It's all about maintaining *aesthetics*."

"Ass-thetics," Nadia giggled to herself, snuggling under the blanket.

Adair wrapped her half tighter around herself in an attempt to warm up. "Girl, you did not just... Wait. Did you mess with the thermostat?"

Her eyes flicked to her friend.

Nadia's face remained innocent. "I have no idea what you're talking about." She looked everywhere but at Adair. "But I *do* know that Laura's conventions are probably even better than I imagine." The woman sighed dreamily.

Adair rolled her eyes and flung a pillow, but Nadia batted it away effortlessly with a laugh. As the two girls nestled closer on the couch, Adair felt Nadia's legs overlap her own. She raised an eyebrow, her playful grin never faltering. "And you accuse me of being touch-deprived." Her eyes flicked over the rim of her glass to her friend to find a sly expression on Nadia's face.

"Hey, that's what happens when you lock it down long distance."

"Wait, what? You and Amelia are official now?" Adair's mouth hung open in disbelief.

Nadia gave a playful roll of her eyes, clearly pleased with the reaction. "It's nothing official yet. Just... you know, kind of implied."

Adair grabbed the TV remote to pause the show and pointed it at Nadia like a spotlight. "Implied?! You don't drop a bombshell like that without giving me the full story. Details, now!"

Laughing, Nadia quickly plucked the remote from Adair's hand and pressed play. She pretended to ignore her friend's interrogation, but the girl was determined not to let the new information slide.

Adair tussled for the device, smashing the pause button once it was firmly back in her grasp.

"Nadi! Spill. When did this happen?" she asked.

Clearly enjoying the moment, Nadia finally gave in. "Okay, fine! So, Amelia and I have been talking more. A lot more. Not just texting but actual phone calls, FaceTiming, the whole deal. She's even hinted about me coming to visit next month."

Adair leaned in. "Wait, seriously? That's amazing. So, are you staying with her? Is this going to be, like... serious?"

Nadia took a slow sip of her drink, looking thoughtful. "Honestly? I think it might be. I mean, we're both on the same page about a lot of things. She's got this special energy, you know? Like, she just *gets* me. Plus, the distance helped force us to talk about real stuff, not just the physical part."

A warm smile spread across Adair's face as she watched her best friend light up. "That's *huge*! I've seen you in relationships before, but this? This feels different, Nadi. You seem...grounded."

"I know, right?" Nadia chuckled, her fingers idly playing with the hem of the blanket. "I still can't believe it, though. You know me, I'm not the 'long-distance' type. But with her, it feels... different. Easy."

"Good for you, honestly. You deserve it."

Nadia's playful smile returned. "Well, enough about me. What about you? Anyone special in your life? Well... Besides me, of course."

Adair groaned and leaned back into the cushions. "Trust me. If I had someone special, you'd know it."

"Still? No cute, brainy academic catching your eye?"

The woman shook her head. "Nope. Between work, reading, and keeping up with you and Laura, I barely have time to *breathe*, let alone date."

Nadia raised an eyebrow. "As far as reading is concerned, you could always find someone who shares your interests. Find a hottie with a body and go on the most epic of quests together." She threw her hands out with a wild look on her face.

Adair let out a laugh. "If I could find someone who loves hobbits and wizards as much as I do, I would do just that."

Nadia gave her a knowing look. "You're a romantic at heart, Addie. You'll find someone. I am certain of it."

"Maybe. But for now?" Adair lifted her glass and took a sip. "I am perfectly happy where I am and who I am with." She pressed play on the remote once more.

The two friends shared a comfortable silence for a moment, while the fantasy show played softly in the background, its grand landscapes and mystical creatures mirroring the magic of their friendship.

"So," Adair began, her voice playful, "When Amelia comes to visit you... are you gonna take her to one of Laura's conferences? You know, to spice things up?"

Nadia snorted, nearly spilling her drink. "*Absolutely not.* I am not traumatizing her with Laura's sex talks. I was thinking... a quiet weekend in, just the two of us, somewhere cozy."

Adair smiled and shook her head. It was comforting to listen to her friend talk about a healthy relationship, especially since she had only seen toxic ones in Nadia's past. Her sharing this information with her was a testament to their close relationship, and for the first time in a while, she felt truly at ease.

The room settled into stillness, the flickering candles and the soft glow from the screen wrapping them both in comfort. Although hesitant at first, she was content to spend her Friday night at home with her best friend, far from the chaos of the world outside.

As the show played on, Adair found herself glancing at Nadia now and then, grateful for the way she balanced her out.

The calm to her storm.

They might not always see the world the same way, but together, they created a space where both girls felt at home.

Chapter Three

"Maybe you should ease up on the caffeine?" Adair glanced at her best friend with a healthy mix of concern and amusement.

"I'm fine. I've only had one cup today." Nadia replied, leaning back on the vibrant blanket spread beneath them.

With an arched eyebrow, Adair looked pointedly at her friend's leg, which was bouncing rapidly, before meeting her eyes in silent accusation.

"Okay, maybe two cups?" A playful smirk tugged at Nadia's lips.

Adair gestured toward the woman's quivering palm. "And *that*?"

Nadia let out an exaggerated sigh, setting her coffee mug down on the grass beside them.

"Okay, fine, but what do you expect? They've had events running all day. How am I supposed to get through that without a little boost?"

"A *little* boost would have been a single serving, not their entire stock," Adair teased, nudging her with a shoulder. "Caffeine overdose aside, thank you for coming with me."

"No thanks needed, babe." Nadia waved her off. "Besides, I scored tons of swag. And better yet? I scored that hot barista's number," she whispered, casting a sly glance at the slender woman crafting drinks with effortless precision at the nearby kiosk.

Adair chuckled, glancing over at the stunning brunette. "Yes, you did." She wondered whether Nadia's twitchy energy came more from the caffeine or the high of her latest romantic conquest. "Are we worried about how Amelia would take this recent development?"

"You gotta play the field in case shit doesn't work out." Nadia winked, prompting an eye roll.

Adair loved most of her best friend's quirks, but her tendency to self-sabotage was not one of them.

Nadia glanced at her phone, her expression shifting as she noted the time. "I do have to head out soon, though. The new club is opening tonight, and I promised I'd make an appearance."

Adair's smile faltered. "Oh... okay. That's fine," she murmured, a quiet heaviness curling in her chest.

"Don't give me that look. You know I have to go. Plus, we've been here for almost *six fucking hours*," Nadia whined.

"I was hoping you'd at least stay for the headliner," Adair said softly.

Nadia's guilt flickered for only a moment before she grinned. "As much as I would love to remain your hostage, I have to be there, or Darren will kill me. Sorry, babe."

Adair was prepared to give a halfhearted argument when movement across the grassy area caught her attention.

A tall, impeccably dressed man had removed his blazer with a flourish. The dark-haired stranger effortlessly draped the garment over the back of his chair before sitting down, his powerful presence preventing her from looking away.

As he slipped off a pair of leather gloves, his eyes casually scanned the green, landing briefly on Adair. Startled by the contact, she quickly averted her gaze, her heart racing with an unfamiliar thrill.

"Earth to Hanlon," Nadia teased, waving her hand in front of Adair's face. Curiosity piqued, she turned to follow her friend's line of sight and quickly grasped the reason behind the distraction. "Oh, I see. Interesting. *Very* interesting."

Adair remained silent, her fingers absently tracing the edges of her notebook.

Nadia gave her a playful nudge. "You should go ask for his number."

"No way," Adair replied, a warm blush creeping up her cheeks as she pulled her knees to her chest.

Nadia stood and tugged at her arm. "Come on, what's the harm?"

Adair twisted free, shaking her head. "Absolutely not." She yanked her friend back down before she could make trouble.

"Face your fears, Addie. You can't get a number if you don't ask for it." Nadia whispered, a smirk dancing on her baby pink lips.

Adair shot her a sharp glare. "Right, but if I don't go over there, I don't have to face rejection either." She risked another glance at the stranger, noting that his penetrating gaze remained fixed on them.

"I know men aren't really your thing," Adair mumbled, absentmindedly picking at a blade of grass. "But I think that particular one has taken a liking to *you*, not me."

Nadia's head snapped around, carefully assessing the situation.

"You're right on one account," she replied. "Men? *Never* my thing. But that doesn't matter, because you are utterly wrong about which one of us that man is currently eye fucking."

Adair shoved Nadia in the shoulder. "Nope. Your evil mind tricks won't work on me, temptress." They locked eyes for a beat before bursting into a fit of giggles.

Nadia dabbed at her under eye and nodded toward a figure to their right. "I think *that* guy may be a bit more your type, anyway. I say go for it."

Adair followed Nadia's gaze to a slender young man with bright blue hair, large, wide-rimmed glasses, and jeans a few sizes too tight, currently engrossed in a spiral-bound notebook plastered with anime stickers.

Successfully distracting Adair, Nadia snatched her friend's half-eaten pastry and stuffed the entirety into her mouth, cackling maniacally as she chewed.

"Hey!" Adair protested.

"Now, now. Don't get your knickers in a twist. I'm running late, and I need something in my stomach before I start drinking," Nadia said through a mouthful, licking her fingers without apology. She stood, purse in hand. "Sorry, love."

Bending for a quick hug, she paused halfway through and looked at Adair. "You know, you could always come out with me tonight."

Adair's head was already shaking. "Sorry, love," she said, mimicking Nadia's posh accent. "I have better things to do. First, I need to get hit by a car at seven, and then I have that root canal at eight. Plus, I simply *can't* miss my appointment to have glass shoved under my fingernails again. Be an absolute shame, it would."

Nadia snorted and rolled her eyes. "Fine. I get the picture, but you won't know what you are missing until you join me. Still love you, though!" With a whirl of pink hair, she was gone.

"Love you, too," Adair murmured, watching her friend vanish

before focusing back on the woman on stage, finishing a spoken word performance to thunderous applause.

As Adair clapped, her eyes slid to the well-dressed man from earlier, who sipped from his cup while scanning the crowd. Something about him held her attention in a way she couldn't name. Their eyes met again, and she quickly looked down, pretending to write.

Even in Nadia's absence, she assumed the stranger's interest lay with her friend. When she risked another glance, however, his gaze locked with hers a second time, causing her heartbeat to stutter.

The man rose smoothly, buttoning his blazer without breaking eye contact, then began to make his way toward her. Her mind raced with disbelief that he might actually be coming to speak to her.

Their connection was abruptly severed, however, when a towering figure blocked her view.

Adair looked up into a pair of sharp green eyes beneath a cascade of tawny hair, set in a face framed by a neat beard and a disarmingly warm smile. He was an undeniably beautiful man, and a rich Irish baritone flowed effortlessly when he spoke.

"That lad over there, Nash?" the Irishman said, subtly nodding his head in the direction of the stranger from before. "He's nothing but bad news. You don't want anything to do with him."

Adair could only stare, utterly dumbfounded, as the man's lips curled into a smirk.

Nadia typically attracted all the attention, but two exceedingly handsome men seemed to be vying for hers at the moment. It felt as though she had been thrown feet-first into a different dimension, and she felt very unprepared to handle this new reality.

"Huh?" she managed.

The newcomer tilted his head toward the man in the suit. "Pretty boy, over there? Not as pretty on the inside, I promise you. Bad. News."

She leaned slightly to look past him, catching sight of 'Nash' now in a heated exchange with a pale, sharply-dressed woman. The moment the woman's attention locked onto Adair, the conversation ended, and the two began striding toward her and the Irishman at an alarming speed.

A low growl from her unexpected companion sent a shiver down her spine. "Shit."

Adair's pulse spiked as he leaned closer. "Time to go," he commanded, extending a calloused hand in her direction.

His intense emerald eyes searched her own, and for a moment, she hesitated, her breath caught in her throat. She may not have known who he was, but something in his gaze spoke to her on a level she couldn't quite understand.

Making a swift decision, Adair placed her hand in his. The moment their palms met, the burly man pulled her up, snatched her bag and blanket, and swept her into the bustling crowd without a second thought.

"Nash and Éala are not people you want to get involved with," the stranger warned, glancing back over his shoulder.

Adair's eyes widened as she followed his gaze to the couple, who were hastening their pace in pursuit.

He paused briefly, his grip on her hand firm yet painless. Returning Adair's bag, he adjusted the blanket under his arm. "I know you're confused, and I understand that you have no reason to trust me." His tone was devoid of its earlier mirth. "But if you want to survive this, you're gonna have to do exactly as I say."

A brief nod from Adair had the Celt springing into action. Warm fingers tightened around hers as he pulled her up the road, quickening their already brisk pace.

"Wait!" she choked out over the noise of the bustling crowd. "Where are you taking me? Who are those people?"

Adair's skin tingled where their fingers had collided, and for a moment, all that existed was the electric connection of holding hands with a breathtakingly attractive stranger.

Nadia's voice echoed in her mind, snapping her back to reality. *Reign it in, Hanlon.*

"I'll explain everything as soon as possible, but for the moment, I need you to trust me."

The urgency in the man's voice sent a ripple of fear through Adair. Against her better judgment, she found herself nodding in agreement, fully aware of the absurdity of the situation.

"Wh-what's your name?" Adair stuttered.

"Ossian MacCumhaill, and you are Adair Hanlon. Now that introductions are out of the way, I need you to focus." He yanked her sharply to the right, the sudden movement nearly giving her whiplash.

It was the way he confidently stated her name, however, that truly sent Adair reeling.

"How do you know my—" she began, but Ossian cut her off.

"No time for questions, Hanlon. We need to lose them," he insisted.

Adair could feel her pulse pounding in her ears, but she nodded in response, forcing her legs to keep up with the tall Irishman presently leading her into the unknown.

Breaking free from the open grassy area, the pair burst into the busy streets of Seattle, weaving around corners and darting past pedestrians in a desperate attempt to shake off their pursuers. Adair's lungs burned as she clung tightly to Ossian's hand, the anchor that prevented her from stumbling as they made their speedy escape.

She dared another glance back in hopes that they had lost the couple, but instead she was dealt another surge of panic at the sight of their pursuers cutting through the crowds like wolves on the hunt, closing in on them quickly.

Ossian pulled Adair back to attention as he yanked her across the road, dodging honking cars as they weaved their way through the busy traffic towards freedom.

Even with the daring maneuver, Nash and Éala refused to relent, vaulting over the hoods of vehicles with unyielding determination as they continued their chase.

Spotting a drugstore in the distance, Ossian pushed on at what felt like an otherworldly pace, dragging Adair alongside him as he moved. "Pick it up. We're almost there!"

They burst through the drugstore's automatic doors, attracting judgmental looks from customers and sales associates alike. The quiet atmosphere was shattered by the sound of their pounding footsteps as Ossian and Adair hurried in the direction of the restrooms located in the back corner of the store.

Adair furrowed her brow in confusion, questioning whether her rescuer realized they were heading toward a dead end. She attempted to warn him, but her lungs seized from lack of breath.

Reaching their destination, Ossian flung open the doors to the women's restroom. He hauled Adair through the doorway just as the villainous couple closed in behind them.

The moment she crossed the threshold, the ground at her feet vanished as if it had never existed. Time seemed to stretch, and Adair's stomach flipped as she realized she was falling.

Eyes wide, she silently begged Ossian to catch her.

Various shades of blue and white streaked past them, the clouds swirling in a dizzying dance, kissing Adair's skin as she passed through. High above, the doorway they had escaped through was suspended in the sky like a picture frame.

As the portal began to shrink into nothingness, she spotted the man in black scowling at them from its fading edges.

The woman's panic surged as she twisted in midair, desperately trying to make sense of the impossible situation. She looked over to Ossian for guidance, who, to her astonishment, was grinning like a madman as he fell, his long hair whipping wildly in the wind.

He reached out and grabbed her arm, pulling her into an upright position mid-air. Adair's eyes watered from the sting of the icy wind against her contacts, but when she wiped away her tears, the view had her breath catching for an entirely different reason.

Below them lay a vast, shimmering sea, the likes of which she had never seen. At its center, a lush island loomed closer with every heartbeat. Jagged cliffs lined the shore, and vivid green forests stretched across the mysterious island's surface.

Adair wasn't quite sure how fast they were falling, but if the landscape rushing to greet them was any indication, they were in for one hell of a bumpy landing. That thought was the last thing to cross her mind before the world around her fell into complete darkness.

Chapter Four

Sunlight filtered through the trees, casting a warm glow on Adair's face. Soft black lashes fluttering open, she was momentarily entranced by dust motes floating lazily in the sunbeam, dancing over a thick carpet of ferns and underbrush. She felt disoriented, taking a moment to gather herself in an attempt to piece together the events that led her to this strange place.

The park. Poetry reading. Ossian. Being chased. Then... Falling.

Adair's heart raced as she bolted upright, her eyes scanning the unfamiliar surroundings. To her surprise, she found Ossian seated calmly at the base of a large tree, methodically working a whetstone in a slow, steady rhythm with a wicked-looking blade clutched in his opposite hand.

"Glad to see you're finally awake," he said, studying the knife carefully. With an approving nod, he slid the blade back into its sheath, tucking the whetstone in his back pocket before standing.

"H-how... Where... W-we were falling and..." Adair scrambled to her feet. Her panicked gaze darted around the dense jungle, where towering trees and lush greenery only served to deepen her confusion. The last place she had recognized was the women's restroom. Waking up in a forest did *not* seem like a logical conclusion to the order of events.

"Aye, we were." Ossian quirked an eyebrow at her, a hint of amusement playing on the corner of his lips. "And now we're not." He turned away from her with a shrug.

Adair blinked. She struggled to make sense of his indifference, throwing her head back as frustration bloomed beneath her skin.

"That is *not* an explanation!" she yelled, her voice trembling. "One second, we're running through a drugstore. The next thing I know, we're falling. And now what? We're just... *here*?" She waved her hands helplessly at their surroundings.

Her rant was cut short by a piercing screech.

Whipping her head around, Adair spotted a monkey perched on a branch overhead. The creature was glaring down at them, chittering angrily, as if her outburst had somehow offended its delicate sensibilities.

Without warning, the primate hurled a piece of fruit at them, and the woman's eyes went wide as she followed its arc through the air.

"Making new friends already?" Ossian asked, casually dusting off his worn and tattered jeans.

Bending down to pick up the strange fruit, he tossed it Adair's way, and she caught it reflexively.

Adair examined the curious piece of produce, but its fuchsia skin and bumpy texture only confused her further. She had never seen anything like it. Her eyes darted between the mysterious fruit and Ossian, her face littered with unspoken questions.

"It's complicated." The man shrugged, his confident smirk sending a wave of flutters through his companion's stomach.

As his gaze lingered on the woman, warmth spread across her

cheeks, daring to venture deeper despite the absurdity of their situation. Confused and embarrassed, her words slipped away, and she found herself nodding dumbly in response to the vague statement.

The smirk fell from Ossian's face. "That's it? No more questions? You're just gonna accept 'complicated' as a fecking answer?"

Adair's eyes dropped to the ground as she absentmindedly released the unusual fruit, crossing her arms across her chest protectively. She struggled to find her voice amidst the onslaught of emotions plaguing her mind. It wasn't simply the bizarre situation that had her flustered. She felt completely out of her depth in every way.

Ossian observed the reaction intensely, his keen perception catching the subtle shake of her head that others would have missed.

A sigh escaped his lips, stemming more from resignation than frustration. "There's a war on, Hanlon," he began, his tone softening. "A war that's been waging for thousands of years between two factions."

Ossian paused to tie back his long hair, the movement of his hands drawing Adair's gaze once more. "The Order consists of those who want to see our kind eliminated or bound in chains. And then there's us." His hands fell to his side as he stalked towards her. "*We* are the ones fighting to keep our freedom, the ones fighting just to stay alive."

Adair felt rooted to the spot as he advanced. "Our kind?" Ossian's strides were confident and powerful, and her heart raced wildly as he quickly closed the distance between them.

The Irishman's hand lifted toward her, his fingers grazing through the strands of her hair until they found a tiny piece of moss. He plucked it free without speaking, but the fleeting drag of his knuckles across her cheek ignited a slow, dizzying warmth beneath her skin.

The man's gaze lingered on her for a heartbeat longer than necessary before he flicked the unwelcome traveler aside, an amused curve tugging at the corner of his mouth.

"Focus, Hanlon. This is important." Ossian placed a firm hand on Adair's shoulder, his green eyes boring intensely into her own. "You? Me? We're Creators." He released her, throwing up a mock salute. "Congrats, you've been officially drafted to The Divide."

The man abruptly turned and walked deeper into the forest, leaving Adair in stunned silence. As the weight of his words sank in, she scrambled after him, nearly tripping over a tree root in her haste.

"Wait a second... *drafted*? What do you mean by drafted? That's not an explanation at all!" She ducked under low-hanging branches and pushed aside the vines in her path, determined to keep up with his brisk pace.

"Creators have abilities, Hanlon. The Order considers these abilities to be unnatural. As for the Fall..." Ossian stopped suddenly, causing Adair to careen forward and crash against his hard, muscular back. He didn't react to the collision, his body tense as he listened to something she could not hear.

Adair furrowed her brow. "What kind of abilities?" she pressed, her voice barely above a whisper.

Before she get a response, Ossian lunged, rapidly shoving her to the forest floor. The breath was knocked from her lungs as she hit the damp, moss-covered earth, her vision blurring. The Irishman landed on top of her a second later, his face mere inches away from her own.

Her amber eyes flickered towards his lips, the warmth of his breath brushing tantalizingly across her skin. A rush of unbidden thoughts swirled through her mind as the world around them faded into a distant whisper. Ossian's eyes followed the movement, his mouth pulling up in a cheeky half-smirk.

"Now's probably not the best time for that, Hanlon." His tone was teasingly dry, yet the intensity of his gaze held dark promise.

The sharp *thunk* of an arrow embedding itself in the tree above shattered the moment, pulling the pair back into the reality of their perilous situation. Ossian rolled to the side, and both lay still and silent.

Before them stood a ragged band of boys, the sun glinting off their menacing array of arrows and blades, each weapon aimed with unerring precision.

The eldest child, dark hair partially obscured by a feathered cap, stepped forward, his sharp eyes scanning them meticulously. "Pirates, I reckon. Should we kill 'em and be done with it, Tootles?" he asked, glancing at the stout boy on his right for confirmation.

Tootles, tightly gripping a crude blade in his fist, shook his head thoughtfully. "Not yet, Slightly. Let's see what they're about first."

Adair silently wondered if she was losing her mind. Everything about this situation felt strangely familiar, yet also completely foreign, as if she were trapped in a dream that she could not wake from.

"We should wait for Peter," Tootles said, wiping his nose with the back of his hand. He glared down at the couple. "Hmm, they don't look like pirates."

A sudden realization hit Adair as the name ignited a long-buried memory from her childhood.

An island, Slightly, Tootles, Peter... Could it be? Are these the Lost Boys?

She hadn't read the book since she was a young girl, but every detail of the scenery around her fit the description of *Neverland*. Her head whipped toward Ossian, disbelief etched across her face.

Ossian smoothly interjected before she could voice her question. "We've heard you were in need of storytellers. We're here to fill the position."

After a moment of exchanged glances, Slightly stepped forward. "You'll be taken to Pan," he announced, gesturing for them to stand. The other boys nodded, keeping their weapons poised and ready for any sign of resistance.

An unexpected shove to her back sent Adair stumbling forward, her mind still swimming with unanswered questions. *Creators, Neverland, The Order, Lost Boys, The Divide.* She attempted in vain to process it all as they were ushered into a hidden space nestled within the roots of a towering tree.

Adair crouched down, glancing behind her to find Ossian similarly hunched, as they struggled to make their way through the narrow tunnel. Eventually, the cramped passage opened up into a spacious underground chamber. Lanterns strategically positioned along the inner walls illuminated the space with mesmerizing shades of blue, purple, and green.

Straightening, they found themselves face-to-face with another young boy sitting proudly atop a homemade throne crafted from sticks and leaves, his sandy hair a messy halo around his wild grin.

Pan's eyes widened, his expression turning serious as he leapt from his seat. "Slightly says you're storytellers!" he declared, pointing an accusatory finger. He crossed his arms over his chest, puffing it out as if to intimidate the newcomers, and raised a single eyebrow, challenging them to explain.

Adair looked to Ossian, who stepped forward with a cocky grin. "We hail from the far-off kingdom of Seattle," he boasted, throwing a wink to Adair. "We bring tales of trains that drive themselves, and pictures that can speak!"

The boys' eyes sparkled with excitement at his words, murmurs of awe spreading through the underground base like a wildfire.

"My tales are true, and as you can see," Ossian continued, gesturing to their attire. "We're dressed far too strangely to be pirates." He finished his statement with a flourish and a grin aimed directly at the king of the Lost Boys.

Peter tapped his chin and paced the floor. "Hmm, it could be a *nasty* trick."

Swords and arrows were swiftly drawn, prompting Ossian to raise his hands in peace. Meanwhile, the boys' whispers escalated to roars as they debated the level of threat posed by the strangers who had invaded their land.

"Silence!" Peter demanded, the kids falling quiet at once. "I wish for the strange man to defend himself further. Go on, *strange man*. Plead your case." With that, he plopped back down on the makeshift throne, stretching his body as he laced his fingers behind his head.

"I know Wendy!"

Ossian's eyes widened in surprise at the outburst, and everyone's gaze shifted immediately to one individual.

Adair looked around, bewildered by the stares, until she realized that *she* was the one who had spoken.

Peter zipped across the room, his face just inches from the woman's as he searched her eyes with growing suspicion. "How do *you* know Wendy?"

Adair's mouth went dry. "We're friends?" she said, her voice cracking momentarily. Clearing her throat, she pressed on with increased confidence. "She told me stories of a boy who rides the wind, dances with faeries, and, most importantly..." She took a tentative step towards Peter, curling her finger into a hook for further impact. "Who strikes fear in the heart of the dreaded Captain Hook!"

A chorus of boos erupted in the air at the mention of the villainous pirate, but Peter silenced them all with a single glare.

"Go on," he commanded, head swiveling back to Adair.

"I have always wanted to meet the renowned Peter Pan," she continued. "After making your acquaintance, I can confidently say that you are *everything* she described and more."

Adair performed an awkward curtsy and took a step back, anxiously awaiting his judgment. The story she had woven was not entirely a lie. As a young girl, she had spent countless hours dreaming of flying to Neverland—fighting dastardly pirates, swimming with beautiful mermaids, and embarking on daring adventures with Peter Pan and the Lost Boys. What child hadn't?

Peter shrugged his shoulders, seemingly satisfied that he had found his answer. He soared back across the room, reclaiming his place on the throne.

"I believe you. You may live," he declared with a casual flick of his hand.

Cheers erupted throughout the cavern, but Peter's voice sliced through the chaos. "On *one* condition," he exclaimed, raising a single finger. An immediate hush settled over the crowd, all eyes now riveted on their leader. "You must..." He paused dramatically, reveling in the captivated expressions of his audience. "*Give us a story!*"

All heads turned to look expectantly at Adair, and the young woman felt her panic rise as she rifled through her memory to find an appropriate tale.

Sensing her struggle, Ossian took a step forward. "Have you ever heard the tale of the Ogre Overlord?"

The boys leaned in closer, their curiosity piqued.

"I demand you tell us of this Ogre," Peter urged, his hand now placed firmly under his chin, elbow resting against his thigh as his gaze bore into the Irishman.

The boys sheathed their weapons and hurried to find comfortable spots on the dirt floor, eager to listen as Ossian began to weave his tale. He spoke of a creature who ruled the land in terror, feeding on nothing else but greed and hatred. As Adair settled into her own seat, she gradually came to the realization that the narrative was more fact than fiction, revealing that humans could indeed be scarier than the monsters from our fairy tales.

The longer he spoke, the more Adair felt herself become engrossed in the narrative. It was evident that this wasn't Ossian's first experience telling tales. His captivating storytelling skillfully drew in all who listened.

Hours slipped away unnoticed, and before they knew it, it was time to eat. The boys began to yawn, the enchantment of the evening slowly giving way to weariness and hunger.

As the legend came to a conclusion, applause and whistles filled the small space. Peter, standing from his throne, raised a hand to silence the commotion. "You," he stated, pointing directly at Ossian, "are a *great* storyteller."

The room erupted in cheers once more as Adair was swept to her feet by a pair of twin boys. The group broke into a lively dance, enthusiastically pulling the newcomers along. Surrendering to the exuberance of the moment, they danced with joyful abandon until everyone was breathless.

Collapsing to the floor in a heap of laughter and exhaustion, Adair sent a grateful smile toward the Irishman who had drawn her into this grand adventure. Ossian returned the smile and offered his hand, guiding her to her feet so they could prepare for the evening meal together.

Chapter Five

Lethargy settled in after the carcass of the wild pig had been picked clean, the lively banter gradually fading into quiet as the boys departed from the table one by one. Some meandered off to tend to their weapons, while a few gestured for the couple to join them outside.

With considerable effort, they navigated through the cramped tunnel until breaking free into the silvery moonlight. Ossian reached out, his hand warm and steady as he guided Adair into the enchanting grove. Above them, the night sky unfolded like a dark canvas painted by millions of shimmering stars.

It was the bioluminescent plant life surrounding them, however, that was truly captivating. Thousands of vibrant blooms pulsed with a soft, ethereal light, illuminating the area with a magical glow that rivaled the stars above. Adair gasped as the floral scents of the forest enveloped her like a lover's embrace, each delicate note weaving a spell that threatened to overwhelm her senses. A cool breeze ruffled her shoulder-length hair, carrying with it the gentle whispers of the trees. Ossian's eyes met hers, a knowing smile dancing on his lips as he savored her reaction to the beauty surrounding them.

Amidst the gentle glow of the plants, small lights flitted from one spot to another, drawing Adair's attention. As a soft melody from a pan flute drifted over the darkness, she noticed Peter resting lazily on a branch, one foot dangling off the limb as the faint tune danced through the air.

Ossian turned to Adair, bowing slightly as he extended his palm for the woman to take. She tentatively placed her hand in his, a smile blossoming on her lips as he guided her to a secluded corner of the clearing.

Once they had settled in, the Celt released her hand and crossed his arms. The shift created an unexpected distance that caught Adair off guard, embarrassment washing over her as she realized she had misinterpreted the moment's intimacy.

"What are you..."

"Show me your best battle stance."

Her face paled at his command. "My what?"

"Your defense," he replied patiently. "Just imagine I'm about to attack you."

With a hesitant breath, Adair raised her fists, skepticism etched across her features.

"Keep your hands up like that and you'll break your thumb," he murmured, his voice smooth as silk as he gently repositioned her fingers. The warmth of his touch sent an unexpected jolt, making it difficult to concentrate on his words.

"I don't understand the point of this," Adair confessed, heart racing from his close proximity.

"Do you want to stay alive?"

"Alive?" The woman's hands fell to her sides, her fingertips tingling as she furrowed her brow.

"Yes, alive. The very thing you're doing right now, with the breathing and all."

Adair, who found his quip far from amusing, threw her hands up in exasperation. "Why me? I'm not even supposed to be here!"

With a sigh, Ossian stepped closer, rummaging through his pocket to produce a smooth stone. Etchings carved into its surface instantly caught Adair's eye, and her fingers instinctively moved to the chain hanging around her neck.

"An ogham?" she breathed.

A smile spread across Ossian's lips, delighted by her recognition. "You know a bit of your history," he said, turning the stone over before offering it to her.

Adair hesitated, struggling to reach out and touch the ogham, even as an unseen force urged her to do so. "I know it is the oldest written Celtic alphabet, but that's all."

"There's more to it than that," Ossian said, a playful smile spreading across his face as the lines etched into the rock began to illuminate, glowing a brilliant blue. He extended the stone toward Adair, encouraging her to take it, but she shook her head vigorously.

"Have I steered you wrong yet?"

Adair stretched out her fingers reluctantly. She allowed them to brush against the smooth surface, admiring the way the ridges dipped beneath her touch.

"It's vibrating!" she exclaimed, her astonished gaze locking with Ossian's.

He nodded, flipping the item over once more. "The text isn't just for communication. When wielded properly, it carries a touch of magic." He took Adair's wrist, gently turning her hand. "We can use these stones to sense if someone is manifesting," he explained, placing the stone into her palm. To her astonishment, the light flared brighter. "And you are *certainly* manifesting."

Adair's eyes widened in shock, a knot twisting in her stomach. She didn't *feel* special, yet the stone's reaction to her touch was undeniable. Taking a step back, her fingers began to tremble, causing the ogham to slip and tumble to the ground.

"This battle has been going on for centuries," Ossian continued to explain, his voice steady despite the flicker of uncertainty in his eyes. "And we are here to protect ones such as you." He held her gaze, waiting for a reaction.

Adair erupted in a fit of manic laughter, and the Irishman loosened his grip in shock. "Why are you laughing? This is nothing to laugh about." He stared at her, bewildered, as she doubled over, tears threatening to spill down her cheeks between cackles.

"Be-Because," she began, struggling to find her breath. "There is *no* way that any of this is real!" She waved her hand at their bizarre surroundings. "Creators, magic stones, Neverland... I either hit my head too damn hard or I need to be *institutionalized*!"

As panic began to bleed through her words, Ossian grabbed her by the shoulders. He inhaled deeply, coaxing her to match his rhythm.

"Breathe, Hanlon," he murmured, his voice low and soothing. "I swear to you, this isn't a delusion. *This* is your reality now. But you're not navigating it alone."

The sincerity in his eyes offered a flicker of reassurance that Adair drank up greedily.

"That's sweet of you to think I would have powers, but you're wrong," she whispered.

Ossian sighed, his composed facade cracking as annoyance took hold. He clamped a hand around her wrist and drew his dagger from its sheath, causing a wave of panic to surge through the writhing woman.

"What are you doing?!" she howled, desperately attempting to break free from his grasp.

He pressed the tip of the blade against her skin, a cry escaping her lips as he ran the cold steel against her palm. She stood in shock as a thin red line appeared where he sliced.

"What the fuck?!" Adair glared at him.

Ossian wiped his blade clean and sheathed it. "Heal it," he demanded, arms crossed tightly against his chest.

"I... I don't know how to do that," she whined, tears gathering on her lashes.

"Just take your shoes off, Hanlon."

Adair froze, incredulous at the bizarre request. Before she could form a response, Ossian rolled his eyes and took a step toward her. She recoiled instinctively, drawing a low growl from the Irishman as he closed the distance, capturing her arm in a firm grip.

"Do you want me to teach you or not?" Irritation peppered his tone, and Adair found herself nodding, albeit hesitantly. He pointed to her shoes, and she kicked them off, her misty eyes never leaving his.

"Socks as well?" she inquired softly, receiving a gruff nod in response. The woman peeled them off, her bare toes flinching as they met the cool, dewy moss below.

Ossian took hold of her other wrist, his touch becoming gentler as he pressed her palms together. Adair felt the warmth of blood, sticky and unsettling, staining her opposite hand as he finally released her.

Eyes remaining fixed to her palms, she felt Ossian shift so that he stood behind her.

"Close your eyes," he instructed softly.

She complied as he stretched around her, fully encompassing her hands with his own. Though pain throbbed from the injury, it barely registered in her mind as she focused on the warmth radiating from his body. His breath caressed her neck, sending goosebumps racing across her skin.

"Concentrate on the pain," he murmured, his voice a mesmerizing lullaby that blended seamlessly with his intoxicating scent of pine and wood smoke.

She closed her eyes, resolute in her determination to channel her thoughts as his grip on her wrists and forearms tightened.

"Listen to the sounds of the island. Take in the smells. Feel the cool air as it caresses your skin."

Adair leaned into his words, gasping softly as she felt Ossian's fingers begin to explore, tracing lazy, intricate patterns on her skin. Each touch sent a rush of heat coursing through her veins, leaving her struggling to stand upright. A smoldering fire ignited within, and her thighs tightened in response as she fought to follow his instructions.

Focus. Adair inhaled slowly, savoring the cold air as it filled her lungs. The scent of the ocean mingled with the sweet aroma of Neverflowers, all wrapped in the distinct fragrance of the man whose fingers roamed across her arms. Her eyes remained closed as she concentrated on the sound of Peter's flute. The melody echoed in the distance, accompanied by the laughter of the Lost Boys filtering through the trees. She could hear the gentle chimes of faeries at play as a neverbird called out, joyously greeted by a symphony of its brethren. The soft tickle of moss beneath her feet made her toes curl, and she felt her skin pebble beneath the man's touch, the throbbing in her hand in perfect sync with the rhythm of her heart.

"An bhfeiceann tú é?" Ossian's smooth lilt washed over her as tendrils of light danced behind her eyelids. "Open your eyes."

Adair looked down to discover a brilliant lilac glimmer coiled tightly around her hands, the pain from before gradually fading into nothing. Astonished, she turned her attention back to Ossian, who had stepped further into the clearing.

She pulled her hands apart, watching as the magic dissipated in an instant. She gazed back at her palm in awe, her fingers gliding through the stickiness until they came upon a faint pink line etched across her porcelain skin.

"Holy shit," she breathed.

"I wouldn't call shit holy, unless it was a Deity that did the deed." Ossian chuckled to himself.

Adair's eyes flicked to him in question. "Deity?"

"You know, like Zeus, Jesus, and Odin... All were Creators, but their powers manifested a bit more strongly. They're the exception, not the rule." The Irishman strode back over to her, pulling a handkerchief from his pocket to gently wipe the blood from her hands. His eyes met hers, searching for the unspoken permission to voice the truth.

"*You* are a Creator, Hanlon."

She recoiled as if he had burned her, her mind swirling with disbelief. A Creator? It couldn't be true. All her life, she had seen herself as ordinary, a quiet shadow roaming through a world of brilliance. What he was suggesting felt utterly impossible. He *had* to have mistaken her for someone else. That seemed like the only explanation for the situation unfolding before her. Nausea surged in her throat, but she forced it down.

"I don't understand... It isn't possible," she protested, her voice cracking.

"There are innate abilities you're born with, Hanlon. Whether you understand it or not, *you* have them."

Ossian moved with a slow deliberation, as if approaching a frightened animal.

Adair's chest tightened as the forest around her blurred and twisted, transforming her surroundings into an abstract nightmare. Leaning against a tree for support, she struggled to draw in breath, each inhale a battle against the weight of her alarm. Ossian's hand settled on her back in an attempt to calm her, but the unexpected touch only served to overstimulate her further. She yearned to pull away, but the strength drained from her limbs, leaving her feeling vulnerable and unsteady.

"Hanlon, look at me," Ossian urged, his voice muted through her fog of panic. She felt like she was submerged in icy water, her thoughts frantic bubbles rising to the surface. Her eyes were fixed to the forest floor, her breathing growing more labored with each passing moment.

Ossian's calloused fingers gently cupped her chin and tilted her face upward, his brow furrowed in determination. Though his lips moved, his words were muddled amid the swirl of her chaotic thoughts. Gradually, the distorted noise shifted into perceptible speech as his steadfast gaze anchored her back to reality.

"...tú fíneáil. Éist le mo ghuth, Hanlon. Anáil," Ossian spoke, the odd yet soothing cadence of his language gracefully rolling off his tongue. Adair found her breathing slowing, syncing with the rhythm of his words as the iron grip of her panic attack began to loosen. A wave of shame washed over her as she gradually became aware of her surroundings.

"I'm so sorry. I can't... I am... sorry," Adair stammered, her voice quivering as tears spilled down her cheeks. The feeling of losing control clawed at her insides like a wild beast.

"It's fine. There's nothing to apologize for," Ossian said, still cradling her chin with his hand. He used his thumb to gently wipe away the stray tears escaping her eyes. "You have to stop that now. I can't teach you anything if you're spouting off like a fecking waterfall."

Despite his efforts, Adair remained distant, the shadows of her distress still clinging tightly.

Ossian sighed, his shoulders dropping in disappointment. With a resigned huff, he released her chin and shoved her backwards.

Adair tumbled on her backside, eyes wide as she landed in a startled heap on the forest floor. She wiped the remnants of her tears away with the sleeve of her sweater, her hand trembling as a leather flask came into view, waved enticingly by the Celt. With a reluctant sigh, she accepted it, feeling the tanned leather scrape against her palm as she removed the cap, taking a moment to inhale the strong aroma of the brew. After a reassuring nod from Ossian, she shakily raised it to her lips and took a hearty swig.

Liquid fire coursed down her throat, prompting an uncontrolled sputter and cough as the warmth quickly transformed into a fiery blush that rushed across her skin. She chucked the flask to its owner, desperately trying to gain her composure.

Ossian's laughter boomed across the clearing as he caught it, earning him a retaliatory punch on the arm from his companion after he dropped down beside her.

"Well, at least the crying stopped," he teased, taking a swig for himself.

Adair shot him a withering glare, but the corners of her mouth betrayed her, twitching into a reluctant smile. Together, they settled into a comfortable silence, enfolded in the soft whispers of the surrounding forest.

"So, Creators, huh?" Adair asked after a while. She glanced at Ossian, who let out a long sigh, his gaze lost in the expanse of the sky above.

"Aye," he replied, taking another swig of his drink. He offered it to her, but she shook her head vigorously, the vehement rejection prompting a chuckle from the man.

"So what can Creators actually *do*? Is it like being a superhero?" Adair asked, looking down at the pink line etched across her palm.

"No, not like fecking superheroes, Hanlon." Ossian rolled his eyes. "You possess a gift for healing, that much is clear, but there may be more that lies dormant within you."

Shock flickered in Adair's eyes as he continued.

"Some are Travelers, Mentalists, Naturalists, or even Shifters."

"Wait, you weren't even sure if I was a Healer when you cut my hand?" Adair asked incredulously.

A roguish smirk tugged at the corner of the Irishman's mouth. "I had every faith in you."

A torrent of questions swirled through Adair's mind, but every time she opened her mouth to speak, the words eluded her.

Sensing her struggle, he added, "Most Creators only manifest one or two abilities, some three, and in rare cases, four. When you're young, it may be more, but it is what you decide to *hone* that becomes strong." He took one final swig from the flask before recapping it and storing it away.

Adair nodded slowly. "So what abilities do *you* have?" Her tentative gaze shifted to one of curiosity, and a half-smile reappeared at the corner of Ossian's mouth.

"I'm a Shifter, a Traveler, and a Naturalist. I can also do a few minor Mentalist tricks, but nothing special," he added modestly, shrugging as if it were a casual detail.

"But there are even more abilities than the ones you just mentioned, I take it."

Ossian responded with a thoughtful hum of agreement. "Think of it like a tree," he continued, his hands gesturing fluidly to illustrate his point. "Every ability is interconnected, like branches reaching out from a sturdy trunk. Beneath the surface, there are smaller twigs that have the ability to combine various skills."

Adair's brow furrowed momentarily. "So how did we end up in Neverland?"

"I'm a Traveler. As long as I have a doorway without an aegis, I can open a passage to another world."

"So, you can travel into *any* fictional world" Her eyes lit up as she envisioned the sprawling landscapes of her favorite novels.

"Not all of them," he corrected. "If a Scribe created the story, only *then* can you travel there."

Adair stared at him, perplexed.

"A writer or storyteller may not be a Scribe, meaning their world is just words or a movie. But if they *are* one, then it allows travelers the ability to step into their story. Some Creators aren't even aware they have abilities. Just like you weren't."

"Wow, that... is *a lot* to digest." Adair exhaled deeply, leaning back on her elbows to gaze up at the starry sky peeking through the leaves above. Her brow furrowed suddenly, turning back to Ossian in question. "So, why does this other organization despise the one *you* work for?"

A deep inhale followed by a harsh exhale was Ossian's only response as a shadow crossed his features. The Celt reached into the inner pocket of his weathered jacket and produced a long wooden pipe, its surface polished to a warm sheen from years of handling. He packed the bowl with a heady mixture of herbs before striking a match and lighting it. As he took his first draw, long tendrils of sweet-smelling smoke spiraled into the air, creating a hazy veil.

"Ossian?" Adair asked softly. Her eyes searched his face for answers, yet his gaze stayed fixed on the dark horizon above them.

"That's a story for another time," he said at last. The corners of his mouth drew tight before he finally looked at her with a grave expression. "But know this... the Order wouldn't hesitate to kill anyone who stands against them."

A chill rippled through Adair. "So, the Divide protects Creators from the Order?" she asked, her voice quieter now.

Ossian tilted his head, smoke curling around him as he took a long, thoughtful draw from the pipe. "The goal is to destroy the Order completely," he said, each word steady but carrying an undercurrent of urgency. "Until then, we protect those like us. We keep the fire of creativity alive, no matter the cost."

Adair studied the dancing cloud as it drifted into the sky. "You do realize that smoking is bad for you, don't you?"

Ossian barked out a hearty laugh, the deep timbre sending nearby fairies scattering in all directions. "That's the response you give?" He shook his head in disbelief. "Society is so desensitized these days." A smile danced on his lips around the stem of his pipe as he took a moment to consider her. "Care to try?"

He extended the pipe, it's wooden surface gleaming in the muted light as Adair plucked it from his fingers.

"Did you steal this from a hobbit?" she quipped. She took one puff before burning coughs erupted from her chest, forcing her to pass the smoking device back to its owner.

Ossian cradled the wooden piece, turning it over as he regarded it with a sense of nostalgia. "I didn't steal it. A dear halfling friend gifted this to me," he replied, his voice rich with fondness. He tapped out the remaining contents of the bowl before carefully stowing the entirety away.

Adair's eyebrows shot up in surprise, a myriad of questions on her lips, but before she could speak, Ossian cut her off with a wink. "Well, now you know the truth of it all." The Celt offered his hand, helping her to her feet.

Clearing her throat, she blinked back at the tears caused by smoke irritation. Her vision blurred, making the forest's lights merge into a vibrant tapestry. Just that morning, she had been sharing a coffee with Nadia, laughing at her best friend's antics and worrying needlessly when she felt pushed to do things out of her comfort zone. Now, she found herself in the *actual* Neverland, mingling with the Lost Boys and conversing with Peter Pan himself.

To top it all off, a gorgeous Irishman now stood before her, claiming she possessed special abilities. Excitement surged as she recalled the countless books and movies she had indulged in over the years.

This was her moment.

It felt like a call to something grand, and she was determined not to let it slip away.

Ossian stretched and rolled his shoulders, his muscular frame reflecting the dappled moonlight filtering through the leaves as Peter's enchanting song faded into the night. "I'd say it's about time to head to the Keep to see what abilities you're hiding."

The pair's fingers remained securely intertwined as he led her back to the grand tree, where several stray Lost Boys lay sprawled in the mossy earth, gazing up at the night sky.

With a determined expression, Ossian released Adair and pressed his palm firmly against the gnarled entrance of the ancient tree.

Nothing stirred.

His jaw tightened as he tried again, this time letting his fingers follow the winding path of the carvings etched deep into the wood.

Still, the doorway remained silent.

Brow furrowed, he stepped into the shadowed tunnel beyond, resolve carrying him forward into the dark.

Adair hesitated for a moment before trailing him through the pathway into the main living space, the air thick with the scent of earth and moss. The Irishman continued to glide his hands along the archways, as if searching for some hidden mechanism, until his frustration boiled over.

"Feck," he muttered, turning to face Adair, annoyance evident in the tightness of his jaw. "We have a problem."

Hooting and hollering echoed as the children streamed in, their cheers and laughter bouncing off the earthy walls of their hideout. Leading them with a confident stride was none other than Peter Pan, his mischievous grin illuminating the shadows around him.

Just as the last of the boys stumbled over a misplaced rock, Ossian spun to face Peter. "Have you had anyone put an aegis on this place?"

Peter's caramel-colored eyes narrowed with a spark of defiance. "Why?"

"Because we can't leave," Ossian replied, frustration boiling beneath the surface. He locked eyes with Peter, who met his glare with equal intensity.

"Wendy put the protections in place," Peter stated matter-of-factly as he casually trotted over to his hammock, allowing himself to drop into its embrace with an ease that contrasted sharply with the tension in the room.

Ossian ran a hand through his long, tousled hair, exasperation spilling forth in a string of muttered profanities that sent the younger boys into a fit of hysterics. Peter couldn't help but grin in response, feeding off the chaos he had unwittingly incited.

Amidst the raucous laughter, a small voice broke through.

"Can't we just make a door?" Adair asked softly, unsure whether or not anyone would hear her over the noise.

Ossian turned to her, his expression softening slightly. "When traveling worlds, we need something that's already in existence. Only the book's Scribe can create something from nothing," he explained. "It must have the intended purpose of being used as a doorway in the story. Otherwise, it won't work."

"So we can't go home?" Adair asked.

"We'll get you home, Hanlon," Ossian assured her as he fixed a piercing gaze on Peter.

The atmosphere shifted as the group fell silent, their playful banter giving way to a sense of anticipation. One by one, the younger boys began to unstrap their gear, the clinking of metal and the rustling of fabric breaking the silence as they settled in for the night.

Peter let out a long yawn as he stretched his arms above his head, tucking a single hand casually behind his neck. "We'll find you a fecking door tomorrow," he promised in a bad Irish accent before rolling over to sleep.

Ossian shot the boy a death glare in response, leading Adair to erupt into a fit of inopportune giggles. The Irishman trained his fierce gaze on her in response, forcing her to scurry away to the safety of a nearby cot.

Adair watched as the Celt muttered under his breath in that same unfamiliar language, the cadence of rolling consonants and softened vowels eventually slipping away into silence. He gathered a pile of furs and set about building himself a makeshift bed on the floor, while she snuggled deeper into the warmth of her surprisingly comfortable cot.

The weight of exhaustion suddenly felt too much to bear as the young woman allowed her eyes to flutter shut, the world around her gradually fading into a comforting oblivion.

Sweat trickled down Adair's back, soaking her t-shirt. Her sweater was tied securely around her waist, but its removal wasn't enough to combat the intense heat as they pressed onward through the dense underbrush of the jungle.

Out of nowhere, a sharp crack echoed through the air, and the woman let out a startled yelp as a low-hanging branch swung back, striking her squarely in the face. Adair shot a fiery glare at Nibbs, who stood a little way ahead, his mischievous smile betraying his amusement. Ignoring him, she resumed her place in the thrumming line of bodies pushing through the greenery.

Peter spearheaded the group, with Ossian directly behind him, his brow furrowed in concentration as he navigated the uneven terrain. Adair followed them in the midst of the Lost Boys, her gaze often drifting towards the Irishman whenever he came into view. Having long since abandoned her efforts to suppress her daydreams, she allowed her imagination to roam. Yet, every tree branch swung into her face jolted her right back to reality.

After what felt like an eternity, the group burst forth onto the soft sands of the lagoon's beach, the sight before them stealing the breath from Adair's lungs. Sunlight danced on the water's surface, and mermaids frolicked among the waves, their musical laughter carried on the sea breeze. She turned eagerly to share the moment with Ossian, but noticed he was already lost in his own thoughts, scanning the jagged cliffside for a potential entrance to a hidden cave.

She watched from afar as Peter soared gracefully through the air, his silhouette framed against the shimmering waters below as he approached a gorgeous mermaid perched on a rock. Settling down beside her cross-legged, they exchanged words, and a rare seriousness crossed Pan's features during the conversation.

After a moment, Peter offered a subtle nod before gliding back to the coterie, a grim look on his face.

A low growl rumbled behind Adair, pulling her attention to Ossian as he approached with a taut, frustrated expression, clearly having come up empty in his search.

"What's the verdict?" he asked, crossing his arms over his broad chest.

Despite the weight of the moment, Adair couldn't help but admire how his shirt strained against his biceps, as if it might rip with the slightest movement. She quickly forced her gaze back to Pan, reminding herself that this was not the time to entertain such distractions.

"We will have to use the Captain's door," Peter declared, his voice even but carrying a note of determination as his gaze swept over each of his companions. The boys were solemn at first, but several puffed out their chests or shifted their grips to their weapons.

"When will the guards be at their lowest?" Ossian asked, his eyes on Pan.

The boy's brow furrowed in thought before he gave a slow nod.

"At first light," he said at last. "Most of them will be too hungover to function."

At that moment, Tinkerbell descended in a shimmer of golden light, landing gracefully on the boy's shoulder. She crossed her legs elegantly, her bright eyes scanning the humans as though weighing their chances.

"We wait till morning," Slightly said softly, his voice echoing the resolve that settled over them all. The others nodded in agreement, and, with that, the group set out toward the glen, each quietly steeling themselves for the attack that would clear the path for Adair and Ossian's escape from Neverland.

Nadia sighed heavily as she glanced at her phone, which had once again gone to voicemail for what felt like the thousandth time.

Frustration pinched her brow, causing her to worry about premature wrinkles as she tossed the device onto her bed.

What on earth could be keeping Adair busy for this long?

She mentally chided her friend for not sharing any plans that might explain her silence. The thought of Adair being tied up in something for over a day without even a quick text gnawed at the woman, her unease overshadowing her irritation.

Nadia turned to face her reflection in the mirror, the soft light of the room casting gentle shadows across her features. Her earth-brown eyes, usually bright and warm, now flashed with annoyance.

"That bitch has another day before she catches hands," she muttered under her breath, half-exasperated and half-amused at her own melodrama.

The corners of her mouth twitched in a fleeting smile before the weight of her frustration returned.

With another audible sigh, she shuffled back to her bed, gripping her phone with renewed determination.

She hovered over Adair's contact, thumb poised over the call button once more as she tried to ignore the nagging feeling that something was very, *very* wrong.

Chapter Six

An eerie silence hung in the air, broken only by the gentle crunch of leaves beneath their feet as Peter and the Lost Boys trekked through the dense foliage, closely trailed by Adair and Ossian. The bioluminescence of the forest flickered softly in their wake, its glow muted by the thick fog that had settled in earlier that morning.

After an hour of careful navigation, the group arrived at a rocky outcrop where a pair of rowboats were skillfully concealed among the stones. Peter urged his crew forward, their approach marked by cautious determination.

Ossian leaned in to Adair, his eyebrows knitted together as he observed the boys solemnly packing their gear into the boats.

"Why's everyone so morbid?" he whispered.

Adair spun to the Celt in disbelief. "You can't be serious?" A chorus of shushes erupted from nearby, and she grimaced in response. "Sorry," she mumbled, a flush of embarrassment coloring her cheeks. Grabbing Ossian's arm, she pulled him to the side, lowering her voice. "They're going into battle…"

The man simply shrugged in response.

Adair glowered at her companion. "It's likely that some of them will die, Ossian. They're just children," she said, her voice tight. She swept her arm toward the cluster of kids, their innocent faces set in concentration as they worked diligently on their tasks.

The Celt remained unimpressed, and Adair felt the sudden urge to punch him.

"You know, these lads have a choice." He finally responded, nodding toward Peter, who was walking among his comrades. "But look..."

The sandy-haired boy placed a reassuring hand on one child's shoulder, offering encouraging words that sparked confidence before moving on to the next.

"Do you see how he inspires courage and uplifts them?" Ossian remarked. "Bravery isn't the absence of fear, Hanlon. It's about how you *respond* when fear is present."

Adair wrestled with his words, a tide of guilt washing over her. How often had she turned tail and fled from a confrontation or purposefully chosen the path of least resistance? Had she ever genuinely exhibited bravery or achieved anything that could be considered courageous in her life?

Even though she was unsure of the answers, Adair knew without a doubt that sending innocent children into battle was a hard line that should *never* be crossed. Just as she was prepared to voice her protests, she was interrupted.

"Stop, Hanlon. Don't diminish their fortitude with morbidity." Ossian straightened his back, his attention fixed on the sight before them.

Perched upon a towering rock, Peter surveyed his assembled army, the weight of their mission reflected in his gaze. He offered a nod to his loyal crew, sparking a fervent response in return. One by one, they gathered their gear and made their way towards the waiting boats, a buzz of anticipation filling the air as they readied themselves for the coming battle.

Adair took a step forward, eager to follow, but Ossian blocked her path. "I need to speak to Pan for a moment."

Doubts swirled in her mind as fears of being lost in this strange land crept under her skin. Yet, deep down, she believed that the Irishman wouldn't abandon her after all they had endured together. She stood there, nervously twiddling her thumbs, as Ossian approached the young leader busy assisting his crew.

The pair spoke in hushed tones, Peter's eyes widening in surprise at the revelations the man had shared. After a moment, he nodded and grasped Ossian's hand in a firm handshake before the Celt turned and strode back to Adair, a cheeky grin plastered on his face.

"Well?" she asked, her curiosity piqued as she glanced at the vessels currently being pushed out to sea.

"We're taking a different route. One a bit more... *fun*," he replied.

The glint of mischief in his eyes did little to calm the anxious knots tying up Adair's stomach.

"I doubt our current life-or-death situation could be remotely classified as *fun*," she murmured, placing air quotes around the word she vehemently disagreed with.

"Hold this," Ossian commanded.

He tossed Adair his sheathed blade, which she caught, albeit clumsily, as he began to meticulously remove his shirt.

"Wait, what are you doing?!" Adair's cheeks flushed a deep crimson, embarrassment mingling with disbelief as she fixated on the muscle definition of his newly bared torso. The tendons coiled and flexed beneath his skin, an intricate dance of sinew as he stretched, seemingly unfazed by the gravity of their predicament.

"Didn't you wonder how we plummeted from the sky and lived to tell the tale?" Ossian replied.

Before Adair could contemplate the implications of his query, the man's body began to twist and contort before her eyes, causing her jaw to drop in disbelief.

Ossian's joy at the sight of Adair's dumbfounded expression was palpable, a deep, almost primal satisfaction that rumbled in his chest. A low chuckle escaped his lips as his bones continued to crack and shift beneath his skin, sprouting outward as if in direct rebellion against the human form he had worn moments before.

It was a transformation he had performed countless times, but tonight was different. He wasn't just changing. He was putting on a show, savoring each moment so that the memory would forever be etched in Adair's mind.

Ossian arched his back, and with a shuddering exhale, leathery wings unfurled from his shoulders, stretching wide against the twilight sky. The air simmered with the rich scent of smoke and earth, and scaly skin enveloped him like ancient armor, glistening in multiple hues of gold as the sun's rays slowly began to peek over the waves.

Adair stepped back, breath catching as she absorbed the spectacle before her. The Celt had vanished, replaced by a magnificent creature that made the very air tremble with its presence.

A Dragon.

She found herself mesmerized, her heart racing in a wild rhythm.

The beast's forest green eyes caught the beginning vestiges of sunlight, sparkling with trouble and intelligence, and she could almost sense the snide remark bubbling just beneath the surface of his Draconian form.

Reminding herself of Ossian's earlier words, Adair stepped closer, each movement filled with a mix of trepidation and fascination. The gilded dragon regarded her with an expression of playful delight, a toothy grin spreading across his fearsome visage. She extended her fingers toward his great maw, drawn in by an unexplainable urge.

In a flash of mischief, Ossian playfully nipped at her hand, his sharp teeth barely grazing her skin, eliciting a startled shriek from his companion.

A shiver coursed down Adair's spine as she felt a strange tickle on the back of her neck. Whipping around, she scanned her environment, only to discover the space was empty.

Am I losing my mind?

A low, rumbling sound rolled through the dragon's chest at her movements, and Adair was *certain* he was laughing at her, prompting a swift smack directly to his oversized nose.

The surprise in Ossian's glowing eyes was fleeting, quickly replaced by a wicked curl of his lip that revealed rows of razor-sharp teeth. The air crackled with tension as the magnificent dragon began to lower his hulking form, each movement of his scaled body deliberate, powerful, and mesmerizing.

That all-too-familiar tickling sensation pricked at Adair's senses once more, just as Ossian's deep voice unfurled within her mind, resonating like thunder.

Are you ready?

The words reverberated through her skull, sending an unexpected jolt of electricity coursing through her body. Adair stumbled slightly, nearly losing her balance at the unexpected intrusion.

"What the fuck was that?!" she exclaimed, her pulse quickening with both confusion and intrigue.

Many Shifters are also Mentalists. It allows us to communicate while in non-human form.

Ossian turned his massive head toward her, his eyes reflecting the dim light as he held her gaze.

"You could have at least warned me," Adair muttered under her breath.

Didn't want to ruin the surprise.

A teasing grin broke through the dragon's fierce demeanor.

Adair rolled her eyes, yet a slight smirk betrayed her true feelings. "Of course not," she said, crossing her arms in a show of feigned annoyance. Deep down, however, she was captivated by the depths of his abilities.

"So, what's next?"

You must mount me if we're to begin our journey.

Adair's cheeks flushed as her mind spiraled into a whirlwind of vivid imagery. The notion of the command took on a life of its own, but within the daydreams, she was not the one doing the *mounting*.

Ossian chuffed a playful puff of smoke from his nostrils, a deep, rumbling laugh emanating from his chest. It was clear to her that he was not oblivious to the direction of her thoughts, and his amusement only served to intensify the heat in her features.

"Can you read my mind?" Adair asked sharply, her anger flaring at the perceived invasion of her privacy.

One need not read your mind when the hue of your cheeks tells such a pretty story.

The dragon's grin reappeared, igniting yet another urge within Adair to commit violence. This time, however, she stifled the impulse, choosing instead to observe the imposing figure before her as he lowered himself further, unfolding his wings with an elegance that belied his gargantuan size.

Riding on the back of a dragon had long been Adair's dream, but now, confronted with the living embodiment of that wish, a wave of apprehension washed over her. Her courage may have faltered if it were any other dragon, but Ossian was no ordinary beast. He had proven himself trustworthy through every trial they had faced thus far.

Taking a deep breath to steady her nerves, Adair carefully placed a foot onto the broad wing he offered. She climbed up and settled onto his back, her apprehension melting away, replaced by a thrilling spark of adventure coursing through her veins like wildfire.

Ossian's muscles tensed beneath her, and with a powerful beat of his wings, they soared into the sky. The crisp morning air danced against her skin, and she gripped his neck tighter, captivated by the solid strength beneath her hands as the ground vanished below them at a dizzying speed.

Her contacts began to water, but she blinked back the tears. The experience was well worth the temporary discomfort. The dragon straightened out after a few tumultuous seconds, gliding swiftly through the clouds while the wind roared around them.

"Why don't you just use your dragon form to scare the pirates into using the damn door?" Adair shouted, her voice barely audible given the circumstances.

Ossian's rich laughter cut through the tumult of the gale.

Pan mentioned they've been preparing for this raid for months! What's the thrill in jumping straight to the easy part?

His amusement rang out, unfazed by the surrounding chaos, and Adair felt a shiver run down her spine. She was unsure if it was from the icy gusts whipping around them or the casual arrogance woven into Ossian's words.

She hadn't noticed before, but he and Peter were unsettlingly alike. Both exuded a fearlessness that bordered on recklessness. For a fleeting moment, she wondered if that same pride would one day be Ossian's undoing.

As the clouds began to dissipate, Adair caught sight of the vast expanse of the sea stretching out beneath them. The rising sunlight sparkled on the water's surface, casting shimmering reflections as two rowboats skillfully navigated the gentle swells, gradually making their way towards a formidable ship anchored in the heart of the ocean.

Adair's eyes widened in disbelief as she recognized the unmistakable silhouette of the Jolly Roger, the legendary vessel belonging to Captain Hook.

The ship was large and imposing, its white sails billowing gracefully in the breeze. Perched high above, the crow's nest was crowned with a stark black flag, emblazoned with the fearsome skull and crossed swords she had read about countless times before. Adair squinted, eager to catch a glimpse of the infamous captain himself.

Just as she thought she might have spotted the pirate, Ossian dropped suddenly, veering downwards and carrying her away from the safety of the skies directly towards the chaos that awaited below.

A bone-chilling shout erupted from the deck as Ossian's enormous shadow loomed over the ship, eclipsing the sun and casting the crew into an ominous twilight. The dragon banked hard to the right, his scaled wings stretching wide to slice through the air with a powerful whoosh. With a thunderous flap, he circled back, his gleaming sea green eyes surveying the deck below.

As he landed, the impact resonated through the ship, sending vibrations that rattled the crew to their core. His colossal claws, each tipped with razor-sharp talons, sank deep into the sturdy wood, causing it to splinter with a gut-wrenching groan that echoed across the waters.

The pirates stood spellbound, their eyes fixed on the golden, scaly beast looming before them. In their awe, they failed to notice the crew of young boys stealthily creeping onto the ship's deck. The gleaming scales of the dragon caught the sunlight, casting a mesmerizing glow across the ship that seemed to enchant the pirate crew. Meanwhile, the Lost Boys spread out, with their young leader making his way directly to the captain's chambers. He knocked three times, a wicked grin spreading across his face.

From the shadowy depths of his cabin, Captain Hook emerged, irritation simmering in his piercing gaze as he came face to face with his archnemesis. "Pan! What in blazes do you think you're doing?! Kill the..."

His voice trailed off as he caught sight of the monstrous beast, its colossal form taking up half the ship's deck.

Seizing the moment, Peter let out a triumphant crow that sliced through the air, igniting the spirit of the boys around him. They fervently echoed his call, their voices merging into a powerful chorus of exhilaration as they charged forward in unison.

Ossian launched himself off the front of the deck, his powerful wings unfurling as bullets whizzed past him, harmlessly bouncing off his leathery hide. A cry escaped Adair as the projectiles flew toward them, strengthening her grip on the dragon's neck as they ascended.

Stop worrying. I won't let any harm come to you.

"Tell that to the pirates currently *shooting* at us!"

The sounds of battle faded into a hush as they escaped the pirates' line of sight, the chaos of clashing steel and cries of defiance replaced by the rhythmic roar of the wind. As the sun lifted higher in the sky, it wove through the fluffy billows of gray and white, casting vibrant pinks and fiery oranges that splashed across the heavens.

The view would have been breathtakingly beautiful had the stakes not been so high.

You aren't going to love this next part.

The dragon's voice rumbled, deep and gravelly, a knowing edge laced within its tone. Pulled abruptly from her thoughts, Adair opened her mouth to respond, but before she could utter a word, Ossian dove, plunging through the cloud cover. Her voice was snatched away, lost to the roaring winds as they descended.

Adair's eyes stung as they broke through the dense blanket of mist, the brisk air biting sharply at her cheeks as the vast expanse of the ocean unfurled beneath them. The dragon banked hard to the left, veering sharply as the horizon rushed to meet them, and Adair instinctively tightened her grip on the scales along his sides with her thighs, anchoring herself in place.

She silently thanked her aunt for every moment spent in the saddle during her horseback riding lessons as she leaned into the dragon's powerful movements.

The Jolly Rodger returned to view, and she felt the intimidating beast shift and flow beneath her. Fear coursed through her body, and she held her breath as the creature beneath her began to shrink and lose its form.

Get ready to roll.

Chapter Seven

Adair felt the rough leather beneath her transform into warm flesh as she was sent tumbling headlong onto the helm of the infamous Jolly Roger. Ossian sprang into a fighting stance with the grace of a seasoned warrior, ready to defend against any foe. Adair, however, was not so fortunate, her clumsy descent culminating in a hard impact against a pile of cargo.

Dazed and disoriented, the young woman brushed herself off and rose to her feet, only to be greeted by the sight of a very naked Ossian, his well-endowed form standing proudly amidst the chaos. He scanned the deck below, where a fierce battle raged on, his confidence unshaken.

Adair's shriek echoed across the ship, her cheeks flushing with shock and embarrassment. She instinctively shielded her eyes, tumbling backward onto the weathered deck.

"Why are you *naked?!*"

The unexpected outburst caught the attention of a pockmarked pirate engaged in a duel on the main deck below, who set his sights on the unlikely pair.

Sensing the villain's intent, Ossian spun toward Adair, his long, tawny hair tousled by the wind. "No time," he responded, raising his hand to her, palm out and expectant.

The woman's eyes darted around in a panic, searching for anything that could assist him. Her gaze landed on a tattered piece of canvas at her feet, a remnant of the ship's sails battered by countless storms. She lunged for it with renewed determination, thrusting the cloth toward Ossian.

Confusion peppered his features as he regarded the material now draped in his hands. "What the hell do you suppose I do with this?"

"Cover yourself!" she retorted, just as the determined pirate began to climb the stairway to their right.

Ossian huffed, hastily wrapping the rough fabric around his waist and securing it like a makeshift towel.

"A canvas has no strength when faced with a blade," he replied, dismissing the effort. "Tell me, do *you* intend to use that, or shall I?"

The Irishman gestured towards the sheathed knife that Adair had been keeping safe since his transformation. She followed his line of sight and hastily tore the blade from its confinement. With a toss, she sent it sailing through the air clumsily, and a tad too low, narrowly missing the man's waist.

Ossian arched an eyebrow, a playful smile tugging at his lips as he plucked the blade deftly out of the air. "A bit close to the goods there, eh, Hanlon?"

In one motion, he plunged the knife into the chest of the lean man who had finally dared to reach them. The marauder fell immediately, gasping and clutching his chest as red bloomed across his poet top.

Stumbling forward, Adair pointed frantically to the now lifeless man sprawled on the uneven ground. "Grab his clothes!"

It was apparent now that the threadbare fabric hanging precariously from the man's hips was a whisper away from losing its usefulness entirely.

Ossian barked out a brash laugh. "They're covered in stains that could rival the worst of our adventures. Besides," he paused and indicated to his body using the now bloodied blade, "Do you really think that it would fit?" His eyebrows hit his hairline, and Adair's mouth went dry, her face turning a lovely shade of crimson.

"Fine," he sighed dramatically.

A rather large pirate crept up behind them, his beady eyes glinting with ill intent. Reflexively, Ossian threw his elbow back, connecting solidly with the intruder's nose. A gratifying crack rang out like thunder before the raider crumpled to the ground.

Spinning, Ossian's movements were fluid as he seized the side of the fallen man's lapel. He pulled the heavy jacket free and draped it over his own broad shoulders, the remnants of the canvas dropping to the earth in defeat. A triumphant grin tugged at the corners of his mouth as he adjusted the pirate's frock hanging loosely on his torso.

"Better?"

Assured by his statement, Adair turned to him directly, her jaw dropping as she beheld the hulking man standing before her. Ossian's arms were crossed confidently as he donned the dark, billowing coat...

And *nothing* else.

The woman's mind went haywire as her eyes were pulled to the magnificent monster hanging proudly between thick thighs. If there had ever been a flicker of doubt about the Irishman's humanity, that had now been dispelled.

There was *nothing* human about his size. Either all her past lovers had been minuscule, or Ossian was truly a god.

Adair's intrusive thoughts were interrupted by a fake cough.

"My eyes are up here, Hanlon," Ossian declared, his smug grin telling Adair just how much he was enjoying this.

The woman's cheeks flamed with embarrassment, hands flying to shield her eyes once more.

"Pants," she whimpered.

"Fine." Ossian rolled his eyes, leaning down to grab the waistband of the fallen pirate's slacks. A playful glint sparked in his eyes as he shot a glance over his shoulder.

"You might want to avert your eyes, Hanlon. Pirates aren't known to wear undergarments," he ground out with a teasing lilt, punctuating his words with grunts as he grappled with the burly man's trousers.

He chuckled, adding, "...although, you've already viewed perfection. So, the sight might be a letdown." His amusement rang out amongst the sounds of battle.

Adair blindly felt the ground, her fingers sifting through the debris and dirt. Her eyes remained tightly shut, driven by a mix of determination and indignation at the antics unfolding before her. After a moment of searching, her fingers curled around a glass bottle, its slender neck cool to the touch. She hurled it in the direction of Ossian's laughter, the satisfying thud echoing her triumph as it struck him.

"Feck, what was that for?"

"You know what," she mumbled under her breath as she continued to listen to the chorus of heavy grumbles and fabric rustling beside her.

After a bit of struggling, Ossian announced, "Finished!"

Adair hesitantly opened her eyes to find an image that could have easily graced the canvases of forgotten artists.

He was clad in baggy trousers that hung rakishly from his hips, the sheen of sweat on his sculpted abdomen shimmering in the daylight, while the frock coat he had donned earlier billowed gently around him like a shadowy embrace.

Relief surged within her at the sight of his modesty restored, enough for her to function without the distraction of his unabashed charm. The feeling was short-lived, however, as the escalating sounds of battle forced her back to their current reality.

Ossian's focus locked onto Adair, brows knitted together in concern. "Stay close and keep your eyes on me," he instructed, the baritone of his voice cutting through the surrounding havoc. After a brief pause, the man began to move forward.

The woman trailed closely in his wake as he carved a path through the throng of pirates. The Celt moved with swift decisiveness, cutting down any villains they encountered, while never failing to assist the Lost Boys amidst the turmoil. Adair focused intently on the Irishman as they moved, utilizing his body as a shield to block out the carnage unfolding around them.

The harsh clang of metal reverberated in the air, mingling with cries of anguish and shouts of defiance as the battle raged on. Bodies, both children and men, lay scattered across the ship's deck, remnants of a relentless struggle. In the center of the fight, Pan faced his nemesis with unwavering determination, each movement a dance of adrenaline and skill. The air crackled as their swords met, sending sparks flying.

Just beyond the confrontation, the door to the captain's quarters stood ajar, the warm glow from its interior like a beacon in the storm. They were merely a few yards away from their escape.

"Come on," Ossian urged.

He clutched Adair's arm with one hand, whilst deftly fending off an assailant with the other. A gnarled pirate, his face a patchwork of scars and fury, charged at the Celt with a feral snarl, but Ossian was quicker. He dispatched the brute in one strike, sending him sprawling as the couple maneuvered across the bustling deck of the ship.

In the center of the chaos, James Hook's sword clashed fiercely against Peter's. With a wild grin, the boy continued to engage in the duel, exhilaration sparkling in his bright eyes. They were locked in a struggle, their blades glinting in the early light, when an ominous ticking sound echoed across the waters.

Hook's confident demeanor faltered, a shadow of dread crossing his face at the interruption. In contrast, Peter, ever the mischievous spirit, couldn't contain his laughter. With a swift shove, he sent the Captain stumbling back. Hook didn't seem to notice. His frantic gaze was locked onto the waves, searching desperately for the source of that relentless *tick, tick, tick*.

As the eerie echo intensified, a thick cloud moved to block the sunlight, casting a shroud of mystery over the duel. The morning air grew thick, and the whimsical world of Neverland seemed to hold its breath, awaiting the inescapable fate of its daring hero and the fearsome Captain.

Another bout of raucous laughter erupted from Pan, and Hook spun to confront him. Before the Captain could utter a word, the boy simply lifted a finger and pointed skyward. Hook's gaze slowly followed the direction, and there, suspended high above, hung the ticking crocodile, sparkling with fairy dust and poised to join the fray.

The captain let out a startled cry as the fairies cut off the flow of their magic, sending the great beast tumbling down to the deck with a thunderous crash. Adair spun around at the sound of splintering crates, her eyes widening in fear as she found herself face to face with the scaly creature, its eyes gleaming in the dappled sunlight.

Ossian's firm grip pulled Adair behind him, shielding her as he prepared to confront the monstrous crocodile, the wood beneath them creaking from the reptile's immense size. The beast flashed a wicked, toothy grin, revealing rows of teeth like ancient daggers, and a matching smile spread across Ossian's rugged features in response.

With a thunderous roar, the croc charged forward, its massive frame destroying all obstacles in its path. Just as Ossian readied himself to engage in a test of strength and wits, the reptilian beast veered sharply, bypassing him entirely and heading straight for Hook, who stood behind the Celt, his hat fluttering precariously atop his head as he fumbled to train his cutlass on the beast.

"Of course," Ossian scoffed, disappointment gnawing at him.

Adair looked up at the Celt, her eyes wide with confusion and concern.

Before he could explain, a menacing shadow loomed overhead, and Ossian instinctively pivoted. "Time to go, Hanlon," he shouted as he parried a vicious blow aimed directly at Adair's back.

The woman cast a furtive glance at the cabin door. Their escape was now tantalizingly close, yet it felt miles away thanks to the fierce battle that raged between them. Before her, a pirate with an evil glint in his eye clashed steel with the formidable Irishman. Ossian reveled in the duel, a devilish grin spreading across his face as he admired his worthy opponent.

"Hanlon!" he called, pivoting on his heel to intercept a deadly strike now aimed at her head. "Go!" His voice thundered, cutting through the dread that clutched at her heart.

With a rush of adrenaline, she surged forward, her legs unsteady as she propelled herself toward the doorway.

Blow after blow rained down upon Ossian as he skillfully maneuvered himself back toward their exit, each swing of his sword a desperate guardian for Adair's retreat. The battle raged around him, but he remained resolute, determined to protect the young woman as she fled toward freedom.

Adair reached the door, pausing to glance back at her savior, who remained locked in an aggressive struggle with the skilled pirate. As she spun back, a blade abruptly clattered to her feet, followed by a Lost Boy, blood swiftly pooling around his small, tattered body.

The pirate who had taken the child's life now turned his gaze to her, a menacing leer spreading across his face. Adair felt her heart race as she quickly scrambled toward the blade that lay abandoned on the ground, its handle still warm from the earlier struggle.

"Ossian!" she called out, but her plea was interrupted by a sudden strike spiraling towards her. Swiftly, she raised the sword, managing to deflect the attack. The impact reverberated through her small form, a fierce jolt coursing down her arm as the metal slipped from her grasp, falling back to the ship's weathered deck.

Meanwhile, her fearless companion was intercepting a new foe with a deft flick of his wrist, sliding his weapon through the marauder's defenses. "Behind you!" Ossian shouted, turning just in time to parry another blow.

Adair's focus shifted, her heart racing as she caught sight of Peter soaring over the fight, while Hook valiantly battled the snapping jaws of the fearsome crocodile below.

A bloody hand struck the door frame above her, and Adair's gaze met that of the agitated Irishman.

"Go," he commanded, his voice a low rumble before he whirled back to the skirmish raging around them. The once-mighty pirate he had been dueling now lay slumped over a weathered barrel.

Adair hesitated, scanning the war still waging around them. "What about the boys? The battle isn't over yet!" she shouted, her heart pounding as she watched Slightly, a valiant soul, wrestle against an opponent whose size dwarfed him by a staggering measure.

Ossian growled, wiping his blade on a nearby ruffian before sheathing it, his gaze narrowing as he turned toward her. Adair, singularly focused on the innocent children, was taken entirely by surprise as he yanked her to her feet, dragging her unwillingly through the doorway.

"Wh—let me go!" she protested, her eyes wide, but Ossian remained unfazed, continuing his determined march down the shimmering bridge of stars.

For a fleeting moment, Adair remained stunned, absorbing the surreal splendor around her. The moment's magic faded as she renewed her struggle against the Celt's firm grip, trying in vain to return to the fight. The distant sounds of conflict faded into the abyss, replaced by an eerie stillness as the celestial gate closed behind them, leaving the pair bathed in the low light of the magical hallway, utterly alone.

Chapter Eight

Adair spun around, her fury barely contained as she glared at Ossian. "Open the portal! We have to go back and help them!"

Her voice echoed through the vast expanse of the celestial hallway, the ethereal lights shimmering above reflecting off her determined stare.

"Hanlon, they're characters in a book. They'll be sound." The Celt marched onward, seemingly undisturbed by the chaos they had just escaped.

Adair shook her head. "It doesn't matter! We shouldn't have abandoned..." Her voice faltered as her gaze flicked to his side, where blood had thoroughly soaked through his coat, the dark stain barely visible against the inky fabric. "You're bleeding!" Her heart rate quickened as panic began to claw its way through her chest.

Ossian ignored her, stubbornly pushing forward as he approached the archway at the end of the path. He stepped through into a sunlit glade, Adair trailing close behind. The ground was a brilliant tapestry of verdant ferns and wildflowers, and the air was rich with the scents of damp earth and blooming life. Yet, Adair couldn't tear her worried gaze away from the injured man.

Ossian caught her watching him out of the corner of his eye, a smirk tugging at his lips despite her concern.

"No need to trouble yourself, Hanlon. It's just a cut. I've had worse."

"That's a lot of blood. I think it's more than just a cut," Adair responded, stumbling to keep up with him.

With a reluctant sigh, Ossian halted his stride and peeled open the frock, a flicker of pain crossing his features as the fabric tore away from the jagged wound marring his side.

"Well, would you look at that?" he replied, his tone disarmingly calm. The Celt's eyes were fixed on the gash that ran deep through muscle and sinew, crimson rivulets trailing down his skin. Adair's expression shifted at the sight, her typically pale pallor now an unsettling shade of green.

"It's nothing to worry about. Let's go," he insisted, allowing the tattered coat to fall back into place as if it could shield her from the gravity of the wound hidden beneath. He began to move again, striding further through the foliage.

"I'm sorry, but I really think you need a doctor." Adair jogged to catch up, carefully navigating the treacherous ground. She avoided the protruding roots that seemed to have conspired against her, each movement underfoot whispering warnings as they fled deeper into the embrace of the misty forest.

"That's where we are going." Ossian's words were clipped and resolute as he forged ahead, purposefully ignoring the glances she cast back at him.

Had he turned to meet her eyes, the skepticism etched upon her features would speak volumes. Each furrow of her brow pleaded with him to acknowledge the severity of his condition. Instead, Ossian bore the pain stoically, focusing on each breath, each step, willing himself not to succumb to the darkness that threatened to close in.

Minutes stretched for an eternity as the pair navigated the labyrinth of trees, their branches twisting like the fingers of an ancient creature reaching out to grasp them. A symphony of crickets played a haunting score beneath the gentle rustling of leaves. As they rounded a sharp bend, the silhouette of a small cottage emerged from the woods, materializing like a dream from the fog.

The building looked as though it had been hewn from the mountain itself, the stone walls, rugged yet resilient, nestled snugly among the venerable trees. Warm light spilled from the windows, flickering like fireflies, while soft grey smoke curled languidly upward from an unseen chimney, merging with the mist in a dance of warmth and shadows. It would have been enchanting, had it not been for the imposing raven perched atop the dormer, its dark, beady eyes staring down at them with an air of disdain, as if judging their very worthiness to approach.

A labored breath pulled Adair from her reverie, shattering the daydreams of fairy tales and mythical creatures that had momentarily gripped her imagination. She turned back to her companion, and her heart sank.

Ossian leaned heavily against a sturdy tree, the color drained from his face, a sheen of sweat making his skin glisten in the fading light. She moved closer, her own pallor mirroring his as the reality of their situation sapped the color from her cheeks.

"I'm sure I'm a hell of a sight," Ossian chuckled weakly, but the grin quickly faded as he grimaced, fingers pressing against the wound at his side. "You're gonna have to help me, Hanlon."

Adair swallowed hard, a knot forming in her throat as panic threatened to engulf her. Gathering her courage, she nodded resolutely and stepped to his uninjured side. She wrapped her arm around his broad shoulders, struggling as the weight of his body leaned into her.

They began to move forward in tandem, the door ahead seemingly drifting further away with every step. The rugged path to the mountain home was fraught with shadows and echoes, as the rasp of crows reverberated off the rocky walls. Adair glanced up, uncertain if their calls signaled a warning or an odd form of encouragement.

Finally, they reached the door, and to her relief, it swung inward with a creak, revealing a dimly lit entryway that felt both welcoming and foreboding.

"I only have so much blood, Hanlon," Ossian murmured, propelling her into motion. With a tremor in her hands, she gripped him tighter, fear surging as she half-dragged, half-carried him across the threshold.

The door slammed shut behind them with a deafening thud, plunging them into an oppressive darkness. Adair's heart raced wildly, each beat echoing in the stillness as she held her breath, her instincts heightened. She squinted into the gloom, willing her eyes to adjust.

Just as the shadows began to close in, a sudden flicker brought a multitude of candles to life. Their flames danced, casting a wavering glow that illuminated the walls with a warm, golden light.

Adair's breath caught as she took in her surroundings. Shelves filled with vials of swirling liquids lined the walls, each one glistening in the candlelight. Scrolls and tomes lay scattered across every surface, their spines cracked and worn, as if they held secrets long forgotten. Aromatic herbs hung from the rafters, their fragrances mingling in the air, and among them perched a single crow, black as night, observing them with an intensity that sent a shiver down Adair's spine.

Ossian sagged against her, nearly pulling the woman down with him as he struggled to remain upright. "Ossian," she murmured, her heart aching. She could see the muscles in his jaw working tirelessly as he fought against the waves of agony roiling beneath his hand.

A muttering voice pulled Adair's focus away from her injured companion. She looked towards the sound, discovering a mysterious old man with unkempt grey hair and a scraggly beard seated at a cluttered workbench in the back of the room, his gnarled hands working deftly amidst a chaotic array of glassware.

A bubbling chemistry set sat sprawled before him, vibrant liquids swirling and frothing in shades she struggled to name. The air was thick with the acrid scent of healing balms, mixing oddly with the aroma of aged wood. The faint glow from the candles cast shifting shadows over his furrowed brow, giving him an otherworldly appearance as he hunched over, lost in his arcane creations.

"Hanlon, meet the Woodwose." The Celt threw his hand out, gesturing to the stranger. As Ossian lifted his arm, blood from his injury welled and spilled over, spattering to the soft animal hide covering the ground like a makeshift rug.

"Don't bleed on my floor, boy," the man admonished in a thick Irish brogue, his gaze never leaving the intricate work before him.

Ossian let out a strained chuckle, his voice a low rasp laced with fatigue.

"Wouldn't be the first time," he replied, a hint of defiance lighting up his weary eyes.

The weather-worn man turned to face the pair, his frame imposing in the dim light of the cramped workshop. "Keep being a smartass, and it'll be your last." His words were a gruff rumble as he moved to Ossian's side with surprising swiftness, causing Adair to stumble as she scrambled to get out of his formidable path. The rug beneath her feet seemed to conspire against her, catching at her heels and almost sending her tumbling.

The gnarled man was more nimble than his appearance suggested, his hands deft as they worked. Each of his motions was deliberate, but the roughness of his demeanor mirrored the jagged lines etched into his weathered visage.

He applied an earthy-smelling poultice to the gaping wound. The Irishman winced, a sharp breath escaping his lips as the Woodwose's hands pressed the mixture deep into the flesh. Once finished, he shoved a small vial of viscous black liquid in Ossian's direction before turning away, intent on returning to his cluttered workbench.

Adair's gaze fixed on the swirling liquid trapped within the bottle, ethereal glimmers dancing across its surface, where veins of silvery steel shimmered ominously against the inky darkness. An unshakeable fear churned in her gut as Ossian uncorked it easily with his teeth, a habit borne from countless perilous encounters. Instinctively, she reached out, grasping his wrist with a trembling hand.

He offered her a pained smirk, his expression a mix of bravado and grim resignation. "I'll see you when I wake up, Hanlon." With a resolute nod, he dismissed her lingering hesitation and raised the vial to his lips, tilting it back in one swift motion. The contents vanished down his throat in an instant, swallowed without a second thought.

It took two heartbeats for his body to betray him. Ossian crumpled to the floor with a heavy thud. Adair flew to the man's side, her heart pounding in her chest as she shook him gently.

"Ossian? Ossian, can you hear me?" she pleaded. Adair lifted his arm, hoping for some sign of life, but it fell limply to his side. Panicked, she turned an accusatory glare toward the Woodwose standing a few steps away, his expression inscrutable. "What did you give him?!"

The elderly man raised a brow, his calm demeanor seemingly unfazed by her outburst. "What had to be done," he replied coolly. "Or was I mistaken in my assumption that you wanted him healed?"

Her gaze darted back to Ossian, taking in the sight of his injury. His coat had fallen open during his meeting with the ground, revealing the angry, red laceration at his side. Movement caught Adair's eye, and she watched in astonishment as the edges of the cut began to knit together, the flesh healing itself before her eyes. "Oh..." she whispered, her panic slowly giving way to embarrassment.

Hesitantly, the woman opened her mouth. "I am so s—"

"There is a kettle on the fire. Help yourself to some tea." The Woodwose spoke without turning, his voice gravelly yet brusque, an imperious command that brokered no argument. He gestured towards the hearth with a mortar that held the remnants of his earlier craft.

Golden eyes flickered to the crackling fire, the flames casting a warm glow, momentarily illuminating her features. She remained silent, lost in thought as she poured herself a steaming cup of the rich, aromatic liquid. Wings rustled softly in the rafters, the air brusquely filled with the heady scent of licorice, mingling with another elusive fragrance. There was something natural and wild within it, stirring a sense of nostalgia Adair couldn't quite place.

She approached an armchair near her unconscious companion, tucking a richly woven throw over Ossian's still form with careful consideration. She settled into the seat's plush embrace, feeling the tension of recent days begin to dissipate as she sipped from her cup. The warmth of the liquid coursed through her, enveloping her in a soothing calmness that eased the burdens that they had carried through the treacherous paths of the Neverwood.

"So, uh…" She hesitated, attempting to fill the awkward silence that had fallen. "How do you know Ossian?"

The Woodwose paused his work, moving to stoke the fire that crackled in front of the figure sprawled on the ground. Glancing down at the man's still form, he let out a low, gravelly sigh. "He needs frequent mending," he remarked. His gaze lingered for a heartbeat before delivering a sudden kick to Ossian's side.

The impact wrenched a groggy grunt from the Celt. "What was that for?" the man croaked, the words scraping against the dry confines of his throat as he struggled to push himself upright. Wincing, he rubbed the spot where the boot had struck.

"Ossian!" Adair squealed, rapidly placing her cup on a rough-hewn stool. She dashed to his side and threw her arms around his neck in a fit of relief. "You're awake!"

"Feck, Hanlon!" Ossian exclaimed, flinching from the unexpected embrace. The young woman quickly recoiled, stumbling back as she realized the poor timing of her enthusiastic advance. She rambled out a flurry of apologies, her face flushing in embarrassment.

A raspy chuckle from Ossian cut her off. "I'm just giving you shite. I'm grand," he said with a grin.

Reaching out, he offered her a hand, but Adair huffed in response, pushing away the offer. "That wasn't very nice," she asserted softly as she stood, deftly brushing the dirt from her pants.

The Woodwose observed the entire exchange before him, a flicker of amusement sparkling in his eyes that hinted at the smirk cleverly concealed behind his tangled beard.

"Took you long enough, Sleeping Beauty," he remarked at last, raising a single brow at the troublemaker. "Or were you just dragging it out for attention sake?"

"You know I love a dramatic entrance," Ossian declared with an exaggerated flourish. "But all this *healing* has left me famished. What do you have to eat in this feckin' hovel?"

He darted toward the kitchen area, disregarding the curious stares from both the Woodwose and Adair. He began to ransack the cabinets, flinging doors open in a frantic search for food. As he rifled through jars and containers, the clattering of utensils infused the once quiet space with a chaotic energy.

Adair opened her mouth, prepared to apologize for her companion's lack of gratitude, but the piercing eyes of the Woodwose halted her. She held his gaze, its depths revealing a wisdom both unfathomable and haunting. The frantic symphony of sounds gradually faded around her, leaving only the rhythm of her own breath in the stillness.

Time stood still as the man began to speak, his voice a low and serious melody that resonated through the small space. Otherworldly whispers caressed her skin, swirling in her ears, translating the words as if they were alive, each syllable imbued with a power of its own making.

Adair could not explain how the translation was unfurling in her mind with such clarity. All she was sure of was that this moment was pivotal, a turning point she could neither ignore nor forget.

"Bhí mé ina Trodaire armtha."

I was an armed fighter.

"Phóg mé fear agus cuireann mé naimhde ag rith agus cuirfear laochra i gcath."

I kissed a man. I send enemies running, and warriors will be put into battle.

"Tá mé ag crochadh anois, le ornáidí bródúil, ar an mballa nuair a fhaigheann fir freagraí."

I am hanging on the wall now, with proud ornaments, when men get answers.

"Ainm dom."

Name me.

The command hung in the air, charged with an urgency that sent a cascade of goosebumps up Adair's arms. Breaking eye contact at last, a sense of purpose propelled her across the room towards a wooden desk, its surface cluttered with scrolls and tomes.

With trembling fingers, she grasped a long, feathered pen and bit her lip in concentration as she jotted down the intricate riddle in her native tongue. Adair understood the immense power of words. Each was like a key, capable of unraveling the secrets hidden beneath the surface of reality. These, however, felt as if they held the ability to unlock something much larger.

The young woman carefully rolled up the parchment, her fingers lightly grazing its textured surface as she tried to steady her racing pulse. Taking a deep breath, she shifted her gaze to the center of the room, where Ossian sat comfortably entrenched at a sturdy wooden table, entirely content and blissfully oblivious to the event that had occurred mere feet away.

The Irishman devoured large chunks of soda bread as she approached, its golden crust cracking with each hearty bite. He tilted back a bottle of dark red wine, taking generous swigs of the deep burgundy liquid. Crumbs of bread sprinkled his beard, and a glint of mischief danced in his eyes.

"Did you hear *any* of that?" Adair asked, her fingers twitching at her sides.

"Aye," he replied nonchalantly, his mouth stuffed to the brim.

He didn't even bother to look up.

Just took another colossal bite as if to dismiss her concern entirely.

"*That's it?*" Adair exclaimed, gesturing broadly with her arms. "You aren't even the *least* bit curious how I know what those words mean?"

Her breath turned ragged as she recalled the strange incantations that had seeped into her mind.

With a heavy sigh, Ossian placed the loaf on the table with a thud. He stood up and stretched, the muscles of his arms flexing prominently.

"When you've known this old gadfly as long as I have, you learn to tune out the ramblings," he remarked dismissively. The Woodwose let out a gravelly chuckle at the comparison.

"But what if it's really important?" Adair whined, her eyes darting between the two men. She turned to the Woodwose. "Wait... it *is* important, isn't it?"

The elderly man met her with a knowing smile. "You are a key to ending the war, lass," he said. "The words exchanged here tonight will guide you on your journey to find what you seek."

Adair's heart soared, eyes widening with fierce determination. "See, Ossian! That sounds pretty *freaking* important to me!"

Ossian rolled his eyes dramatically as he turned to the Woodwose, stubbornly dismissing the woman's enthusiasm. "Why do you do this every time?" he sighed. "I was having a perfectly nice meal, and you just *had* to stir things up."

The Celt began to pace, his hands flying up in exasperation. "Do you see that look in her eyes? That's the 'I will not let this go, Ossian' look." His voice went up a couple of octaves in a horrible attempt to mimic her. "I'm not going to hear the end of this, and it's all *your* fault!"

The Woodwose huffed. "If you weren't such a masochist, maybe you would learn a thing or two from her thirst for knowledge. This war belongs to *all* of us. It might be time you took that a bit more seriously."

The challenge in the statement lingered in the air as the two men stood glaring at each other, the tension crackling like a fire. Finally, Ossian broke the stare, letting out a grunt of resignation. He ran a hand through his hair before gathering it into a messy bun atop his head. "Time to go, Hanlon," he said, his voice matter-of-fact.

"Go? Go *where*?" Adair questioned.

She stumbled after the Irishman as he strode toward the front door, the fabric of his coat fluttering slightly with each step. He stopped to snatch what remained of the loaf of bread from the table as he walked, giving it an approving nod before stuffing it into his pocket.

"We came here to heal, and look..." Ossian said.

He opened the side of his coat, revealing the taut, uninjured skin of his chiseled abdomen. The sight was breathtaking, and Adair felt her cheeks flush as heat rushed through her. His body was a sculptor's dream, all sharp angles and sinewy strength.

"Oh..." she breathed, her gaze lingering a moment longer than intended before collecting herself. Turning to the man who had been so kind during their ordeal, she added, "Thank you so much, sir. It was a pleasure to meet you, and I genuinely apologize if we were a nuisance at all." She cast a pointed glance at Ossian.

"The pleasure was all mine, lass," the Woodwose said with a grin. He extended a surprisingly large hand, and Adair grasped it, feeling a subtle shift as a smooth, flat object was passed to her through the contact. She pulled back, staring in astonishment at the stone now resting in her palm. It was breathtaking, adorned with intricate designs and patterns that mirrored the one back in Neverland.

Before she had a chance to examine it further, Ossian's grip on her arm tightened, tugging her toward the exit with a grunt that broke the moment's enchantment. Flustered, she turned back to the Woodwose. "Bye! Thank you for everything!" Her wave was awkward, but genuine, as the pair made their way to the door.

Ossian leaned his head back in for one last quip, the playful glint in his eyes never fading. "See you next time I'm bleedin' out!" he joked.

This elicited a hearty laugh from the Woodwose. "Easier to just say 'see you soon,' lad."

With a final chuckle, Ossian grabbed a bottle of port from a small table near the entrance before slamming the door shut behind them.

Adair groaned as they began their journey, carefully placing the stone in her side pocket. "I carried you halfway here. Couldn't you just turn into a dragon again and fly us wherever we're going?"

Ossian scoffed. "Sure, I would just *love* to be on the front page of every newspaper tomorrow morning."

"Okay, point taken," she said, letting out a resigned sigh. The Celt began to descend down a path through the woods, and the young woman stumbled, attempting to keep up with the brisk pace.

"Where exactly are we?" Adair inquired, her breath coming in quick bursts. "Are we trapped in another book or something?"

Ossian halted to look back at her, his expression suddenly earnest. "What fantasy world could compare to the magic of Ireland?" A proud smile lit up his face as he gestured to the enchanting landscape surrounding them.

"Ireland? Wait...we're on Earth? Like my planet?" Alarm flashed across Adair's face as she quickly drew her phone from her back pocket.

"You mean, I could have called for help this entire time?" She raised the device, and the home screen lit up, eliciting a gasp from the young woman. "Four bars! Oh my god, I have to contact my best friend. I have to tell her *everything*! She's never going to believe this!"

Before she could dial, Ossian deftly snatched the phone from her hand, flinging the lifeline into a nearby pond with a flick of his wrist.

Adair's eyes widened in horror. She lunged toward the shimmering body of water, but Ossian caught her in a firm embrace, holding her back with one arm.

"*Why would you do that?!*"

"Think, Hanlon! I can't protect you if you don't exercise even a modicum of common sense," he admonished, his gaze steady yet fierce as the small woman struggled against him. "There are forces at play here you do not understand. Trust me. We're not safe yet."

Ossian's hold softened momentarily, a flicker of concern crossing his rugged features. "That hunk of metal can track your location from anywhere in the world. Had it connected, we would have every member of the Order and their kin on their way to grab us."

Adair's fight faltered as the wave of realization crashed over her. She could have thrown both herself and Ossian into harm's way just as easily as he had thrown her phone in the lake.

What's more, she had nearly endangered Nadia, the person she cherished above all else. A deep pang of longing for her best friend tightened around her heart, but she knew that reaching out now could only lead to trouble.

Her body went limp in defeat, and Ossian slowly released her from his hold.

"I'm sorry. I wasn't thinking," she murmured softly.

Ossian sighed. "I understand the need to connect with the ones you love..." he said earnestly. "But safety has to come first."

Adair nodded in silent agreement. Ossian mirrored her, dipping his head before continuing along the winding trail.

After walking for a few minutes, Adair cleared her throat. "Um... Ossian?" He paused and glanced back at her, an inquisitive brow arched in question. "Would it be possible for us to stop by my place for a moment? I just need to grab a few things." Adair fidgeted with her fingers, her gaze dropping nervously.

"We have everything you need at the Keep," Ossian said simply, turning back to the path ahead in a clear dismissal.

"That...may be true, but there's something I *really* need to get," she insisted, her voice rising slightly.

Ossian let out a sigh resembling a low growl before turning back to her. "Gods dammit, Hanlon. Fine, we'll take you home first." With that, he spun back to the trail, picking up his pace in frustration. "But you'd better be quick about it."

Adair's head shot up. "Really? Are you sure?"

A smile illuminated her face as she hurried after him, only to stumble over a loose branch a moment later. She managed to right herself just in time, her heart pounding not only from the minor mishap, but from the exhilarating closeness of the extraordinary man leading her.

As they rounded the next bend, their destination came into view, a ruined doorway standing sentinel amidst vibrant ivy and wildflowers. Ossian approached, his large hand resting against the weathered frame as the celestial hallway beyond shimmered into existence.

"Seriously, Ossian. This means so much to me. Thank you!" Adair beamed.

Mirth twinkled in the Irishman's eyes. "It's the little things for you, isn't it, Hanlon?" A smile unfurled across his lips, transforming his rugged face into something undeniably beautiful, and Adair felt her breath catch at the sight. "Hanlon?" His mouth moved, soundlessly, as if drawing her from a spell. He snapped his fingers, jolting her back to the moment.

"Oh, I'm sorry! Uh... yes," she stammered despite not hearing a word he had spoken, a flush creeping up her cheeks.

Ossian barked out a laugh. "Good to know," he replied with a smirk. "Well, here we are. After you?"

He extended his hand toward the flickering portal, its colors swirling and shifting in a mesmerizing display.

With a tentative smile, Adair stepped forward, the portal's radiant glow enveloping her as she made her way through the decaying doorway. Ossian, shaking his head in amusement, followed closely behind.

Chapter Nine

As the pair stepped over the threshold, a whirlwind of motion erupted before Ossian could fully comprehend his surroundings. His hand reached for his blade instinctively, readying himself for whatever situation they had stumbled into.

Nothing could have prepared him, however, for the sight of a peculiar stranger lounging uncomfortably on an overstuffed couch. The 'intruder' had quickly clutched a pillow to his lap, his cheeks flushing a shade that nearly matched the upholstery.

"What the *hell* is a naked man doing in your living room?"

Adair dismissed him with a scoff. "Oh, that's just Carl. Don't mind him." She cast an expectant glance around, her eyes searching. "Laura? Are you home?"

A brunette woman peeked through the doorway. "Just a second, Addie!"

A cacophony of clattering dishes and an impressive crash echoed from the kitchen, shortly followed by the thunderous approach of Laura as she rushed into the living room, swathed in a striking dark green silk robe adorned with vibrant birds of varying shapes and sizes.

The middle-aged woman enveloped Adair in an exuberant hug,

eliciting a sheepish struggle from her niece. "What are you doing at home? I thought you were headed to the *grand exhibition*," Adair asked, her voice muffled by the embrace.

"My horoscope declared it an ill-starred day for travel. Oh, also the hostess discovered her husband was cheating on her, so she stabbed him and now she's on the lam!"

Adair's eyebrows shot up in disbelief, but her aunt was already sweeping past her, unfazed.

"And who might your very muscular companion be?" Laura asked, her gaze assessing Ossian with a mix of curiosity and bemusement.

Before Adair could respond, Ossian strode across the room, extending a large, calloused hand in greeting. "I'm Ossian. It's a pleasure to make your acquaintance, Miss Porter."

Laura met his hand with her own, donning a knowing grin. Drawing back, she leaned conspiratorially toward her niece and loudly whispered, "He looks like he jumped straight off the cover of a romance novel. Yummy!"

Adair let out a dramatic groan. Before she could retort, Laura turned her focus back to the impressive Irishman. "Please call me Laura. It's a pleasure to meet you. Come, sit!" She guided him toward the couch still occupied by a very naked Carl.

"Clearly, my niece has told you about me, but she has told me *absolutely nothing* about you," Laura stated, her eyes sparkling as they flicked towards Adair, who sat across the room, wishing desperately that she could morph into a cloud of smoke and vanish. "Would you like a cup of tea?"

The woman glided to the kitchen, short hair bobbing animatedly as she rummaged through cabinets with uncontainable enthusiasm. Adair followed closely in her wake.

"That would be grand," Ossian called out, glancing at the man beside him, who sat still like an overgrown garden gnome. "You might want to take care of that." The Irishman gestured discreetly at Carl's exposed body with a nod, who flushed crimson before bolting from the room.

"He isn't a male escort, is he?" Laura asked, grabbing a marble tray with gold handles.

Adair spun to face her aunt. "Laura!"

"If he is, can I borrow him when you're done?" Laura whispered loudly, her eyebrows wagging in exaggerated delight as she continued to set out four ornate cups onto the serving platter.

"Oh, my god." Adair pinched the bridge of her nose, a futile attempt to ward off the headache that was steadily building. Two men in various states of undress and her aunt discovering a hundred new ways to embarrass the hell out of her was *not* the way she had envisioned her afternoon going.

As the tea brewed, filling the air with its fragrant hum, Laura turned her attention back to Ossian. The burly man was now leaning casually against the counter, arms crossed, clearly relishing the playful banter with the older woman. With a brow raised in mock-seriousness, Laura asked him, "So, what are your intentions with my niece?"

A smirk tugged at Ossian's lips. "I plan on whisking her away to my manor in Scotland in an effort to avoid her being captured by an organization that wishes to exploit her magical abilities."

Adair whirled on him, taken aback by his honesty. Nervously, she glanced back at her aunt to gauge her reaction.

Laura tapped her chin thoughtfully, considering his words before nodding her approval. "Alright. Just make sure she dresses warmly," she said, her voice steady, as if discussing the weather was a far more pressing issue than the complexities of magical organizations and enigmatic men.

Adair shook her head in disbelief. Her aunt had always been lenient, but this? Ossian might very well be a ruthless murderer. He practically was, if you count ridding the sea of a few villainous pirates. A soft chuckle escaped her lips.

With practiced grace, her aunt poured the steaming tea into porcelain mugs. Carefully, she passed out the drinks before taking her own and settling comfortably into a plush, worn armchair across from Ossian.

"Are you a good person?" she asked him, sipping from her cup.

Ossian shrugged casually. "Well, that really depends on who you ask," he replied with a wink.

"Oh... Good answer," her aunt mused, her brows raised as she turned to Adair. The young woman wished for the earth to open up beneath her, swallowing her whole and sparing her from this overwhelming embarrassment.

Carl chose that moment to reappear in the doorway, hair tousled and fully dressed. He slunk back to the couch, silently nestling in next to his lover.

Laura ignored him, choosing instead to question the pair further. "So, did you two meet at the poetry exhibition?" she asked, blowing softly on her tea. Her eyes darted between Adair and Ossian.

Adair nodded. "Oh, that... yes...." She fumbled her words, heart racing from the turn in their conversation.

"I once met a man at a poetry slam," Laura interrupted, her gaze locking onto Ossian. "I have never orgasmed so many times in my life."

Adair sputtered into her drink, her face heating as she struggled to keep her composure.

Laura's free hand twisted a lock of her short mousey hair. "He was hung like a horse and *really* knew how to use his tongue," she continued, hand moving to her neck absentmindedly.

Carl cleared his throat, and Adair struggled to resist the overwhelming urge to splash her steaming cup across the woman's face to silence her.

Pulled abruptly from her reverie, Laura gently patted her man's hand. "You're good too, darling," she declared, though the sincerity of her words was questionable. It did little to soothe the man's horrified expression, but she continued on.

With a glint in her eye, the woman raised her teacup and waved it in Ossian's direction. "I bet he's packing too," she teased playfully. Adair's cheeks burned at the insinuation, and an uncomfortable heat began to envelop the room.

"It gets caught in doors quite frequently," Ossian replied dryly, taking a swig of his own cup.

"Okay!" Adair practically shouted, springing off the couch. "I'm going to pack now!"

Her voice was too loud, but the urgency of her escape from this mortifying exchange drove her forward. She hurriedly made her way toward the sunroom and threw open the trap door that led to her small apartment. She was in desperate need of her sanctuary of quilted comfort and blissful isolation from this chaos.

Laughter echoed from the corner of the room as Adair dashed down the spiral staircase, each step feeling like a small victory. With a final burst of energy, she slammed the trap door shut behind her.

The suitcase was packed to the brim when a creak of the hatchway signaled Laura's arrival. A soft knock on the wall caused Adair to let out a weary sigh. She lifted her head from a hastily scribbled list on a piece of paper.

As Laura entered the room, her soft gaze naturally settled on Adair, who met her with a challenging stare. It was a silent contest of wills set against a backdrop of open drawers and clothes scattered haphazardly around the small space. With a touch of theatrical elegance, Laura glided over to the bed and gracefully plopped down beside her, extending a small white paper bag like a peace offering.

Adair's eyebrows shot up, as if she'd just been handed a bomb instead of a gift. "Thanks," she muttered, skepticism evident in her voice. As she opened the bag, her eyes settled on the full pill bottle nestled inside.

"I know it gets worse around..." Laura hesitated, gauging the emotional meter of her niece before finishing with the delicate phrasing of *this time*. Adair flinched at the mention, gripping the medication tighter. Laura spoke slowly as if addressing a wild animal. "It's only been a couple of weeks, Addie."

The lean girl shot back, her tone razor-sharp and unnervingly calm, "You don't think I know that?"

"Is it because your father didn't text this year?" Laura probed gently.

With white knuckles, Adair stood, her voice unwavering. "I couldn't give two shits about what Michael does."

She spun on her heel and stormed into the small kitchen. She rummaged through the cabinets, searching for something to wash down the bitterness of the medication that now felt more like a curse than a cure. After downing the only semblance of calm she knew, Adair grabbed a snack bar and headed back to her task.

Laura's appraising eye tracked the girl as she darted around the room, tossing the last few essentials into her bag. The pill bottle that had been left on the kitchen counter was snatched up and tossed into the open suitcase with an exaggerated sigh.

"Do you need anything else, perhaps?" Laura asked casually, a teasing lilt to her voice.

"I swear to god, Laura. If you ask me if I need protection, I will end it all right here." Adair's amber eyes narrowed as they flicked to her aunt, who had stood to lean against the doorframe with a smirk.

"What would you like engraved on your epitaph?" Laura shot back. With a flourish, she reached into the pocket of her robe, producing a small box like a magician's prestige. "Ta-da!"

Adair rolled her eyes. "It isn't like that, Laura," she said, shaking her head as she attempted to shove her case closed. As she brought down the lid, Laura swiftly tossed the box into the suitcase, just in time.

Adair shot her aunt a glare, but Laura just winked back, the playful glint in her eyes unmistakable. "Just in case," she said, her tone dripping with mischief.

Laura held her arms out wide, beckoning her niece over with her fingertips like a diva welcoming an adoring fan. With a resigned huff,

Adair moved closer, closing the distance to accept her aunt's embrace.

"I already have the picnic planned and the bouquet ordered."

"Don't forget the..."

"Thistles, I know." Laura held Adair at arm's length, pausing to appraise her niece. "I know she is so proud of you."

A swell of emotion rose within Adair, her heart clenching tightly in her chest. The thought of her mother swirled in her mind, and tears threatened to spill over. "We had better head off," she managed, her voice cracking.

Pale fingers deftly pulled the suitcase onto the floor with a decisive thump. "Can you grab my backpack for me?" Adair asked, turning towards the door.

"Of course, wolfie." Slinging the precious cargo over her shoulder, she followed Adair as they exited.

Outside, Ossian leaned against the hood of the green SUV, arms crossed over his broad chest in a way that accentuated the sculpted muscles beneath his shirt. Adair swallowed hard at the sight of him, her eyes inadvertently drawn to the way the fabric strained against his biceps. She forced herself to meet his stormy gaze.

"You sound?"

Before Adair could muster a response, confused at the meaning of the Irish phrase, Laura interjected. "Make sure she eats. Sometimes she forgets, and when that happens, she needs to be hospitalized."

"Okay, stop. He doesn't need my entire medical history." Adair plopped the suitcase down next to the car, her cheeks burning as she willed her aunt to stop speaking.

"Well, lass, you better enjoy the craic!" Laura elbowed Adair affectionately in the ribs, laughter brightening her features. Her attempt at an Irish accent fell flat, sounding more like a delightful mish-mash of Russian and charm.

"And on that note..." Adair reached for her suitcase, but Ossian was faster. He swooped in with effortless grace.

"I'll handle that... *lass*."

He winked at her in a way that sent another wave of heat through her cheeks before opening the trunk of the vehicle.

She caught a glimpse of Laura dramatically mouthing, 'Oh my god!' in response to the exchange. A quick smack to the arm from her niece led to a chorus of laughter as the woman drew her into one last vigorous hug. "Be safe, little wolf," she whispered, the words infused with love and encouragement.

That damned lump formed in Adair's throat again, and she nodded against her aunt's shoulder as if grounding herself in reality before letting her go once more. A few more awkward waves were exchanged as the woman slid into the driver's side of the car, and the engine hummed to life beneath her as Ossian joined on the opposite side.

"Don't forget the thistles," she called to her aunt one final time, rolling down the window.

"I won't!" Laura called back, her hand waving fiercely as the SUV started up the steep driveway.

Adair turned for one last glance, her heart fluttering with a mix of excitement and trepidation, until, finally, the view of her aunt and the house vanished around the bend.

Chapter Ten

Twilight descended, bathing the ancient castle ruins in a mystical glow. The wind tousled Adair's hair, carrying the salty tang of the sea, while the grass on the moor swayed gently in the breeze.

The weathered parapets and crumbling walls loomed like sentinels guarding a forgotten past, clinging fiercely to the cliffs that overlooked the restless North Sea. She wondered how long it could endure the relentless assault of time and tide, or if the structure would one day succumb to the siren call of the waves below.

As she wove through the skeletal archways, the fading light cast a haunting aura over the roofless expanse. Centuries of unabating winds had eroded the stones and walls, yet Adair could still sense the grandeur that Old Slains Castle once possessed.

A nudge from her sturdy companion jolted her out of her daydream.

"This way," Ossian urged, guiding her away from the edge of the cliff and deeper into the ruins.

Adair picked her way carefully through the fallen tablets and tangled brambles. Her foot slipped off a mossy rock, but Ossian's hand shot out to catch her, steadying her before they resumed their journey towards a strategically placed pile of stones on the far end of the property.

Once they arrived, the Celt's palm rested against the ancient archway, causing the doorway to shimmer with a spark of ethereal light that unveiled the dimly lit corridor beyond. "After you," he suggested.

Using Ossian's hand to steady herself, Adair stepped across the threshold, anxiety creeping into her chest.

The portal closed behind the pair, leaving a corridor that seemed to breathe around them. Its rough-hewn stones exuded an age-old charm, and a musty scent tinged the air. Their footsteps echoed softly off the walls, creating a rhythmic soundtrack as the passage widened, unveiling a vast space that was teeming with activity.

At the heart of the room, desks were strategically arranged in pairs. Against the far wall, screens stretched from floor to ceiling, their flickering images showcasing breaking news from local towns to cities around the globe. To the right, a command center buzzed with energy, as figures moved purposefully around a large table adorned with an expansive map.

On the opposite side, a grand iron staircase ascended upward, leading to a large glass enclosure where a man stood, hands clasped tightly behind his back. The stranger's sharp gaze fell upon them, a silent invitation beckoning the pair forward. Ossian nodded and began his climb, leaving Adair momentarily stunned.

"Hanlon." The Irishman's voice cut through her reverie, and Adair shook her head, clearing the daze. She offered him a sheepish smile before following up the stairs.

As they stepped into the office, the two men clasped each other's forearms, engaging in a silent exchange. The stranger locked eyes with the Celt for a moment, before shifting his scrutiny onto her.

"Hanlon, this is Edmund Trevellan; Commander of the Scottish Division," Ossian introduced.

Adair extended her hand, but her heart skipped a beat as the light caught three jagged scars tracing down the left side of his face. An involuntary gasp escaped her lips, and she felt a rush of crimson flood her cheeks.

"I'm so sorry," she blurted out, her hands flying to cover her mouth in embarrassment.

The Commander offered her a soothing smile, his rich Scottish accent wrapping around his words.

"I get it all the time," he said, settling back in his leather chair. His hazel eyes flitted between the pair before landing back on her. "Oisín informed me that you nearly had an encounter with Nash and Éala."

Adair nodded slightly, glancing over at the Irishman, who stood at a polished bar lining the back wall. Ossian was a silhouette of relaxed confidence as he poured himself a glass of dark liquid from an ornately designed decanter. He leaned against the cabinet, the corner of his mouth lifting in a teasing smile that Adair found annoyingly distracting.

"We gave them the slip, didn't we?" Ossian responded, swirling the liquid in his glass. The crystalline structure caught the light beautifully as he raised it in a mock toast, winking at her with a playful glimmer in his eyes.

"It's fortunate that you were intercepted before falling into The Order's hands," the Commander rebuked, his voice dropping to a low, serious tone.

Adair tried to pay attention, but found it nearly impossible to look away from Ossian. Her heart pounded wildly in her chest as she watched him take a leisurely sip from his glass. She analyzed the smooth movement of his throat as he swallowed deeply, the sharp angle of his jaw as he tilted his head just so, the way his tongue flicked out to catch a drop of liquor on the edge of his full, tempting lips.

The Commander cleared his throat, the deep rumble jolting Adair back to the present.

"What? You want some, Eddy?" Ossian quipped, offering his glass to the man opposite him with a cheeky grin.

Edmund blanched slightly, his brows furrowing as he swiftly rejected the offer. "No, I want you to focus and stop drinking all my alcohol," he replied sternly.

The larger of the two men raised his hands defensively, an expression of mock innocence crossing his face before he sauntered over to the empty chair beside Adair.

"Now," Edmund said, running a hand through his beard as he gathered his thoughts. "We have a room prepared for you in the east wing. I suggest we start your testing first thing in the mornin'."

Adair nodded, her breath catching as she concentrated on the Scotsman's commanding voice, trying in vain to ignore the allure of the man beside her.

"Oisín will give you a tour of the facility and help you get settled in," the Commander finished.

He cast a glance toward the Irishman, who drained the last of his drink, setting it down with a soft click on the desk as he stood.

"Will do, Eddy," Ossian replied, executing a gibe salute. The Commander couldn't hide his disdain for the nickname, but the Celt chose to ignore it, striding confidently toward the door. "Let's go,

Hanlon," he called back over his shoulder.

Adair followed Ossian out of Edmund's office and down the cool, metallic steps, multiple questions hovering on the tip of her tongue. As they approached the bottom, the woman realized that her bags were nowhere to be found.

"Um, where's my stuff?" Adair questioned, her gaze darting back and forth, wondering if her items had been pilfered so soon after arriving.

"You have real trust issues. Eh, Hanlon?" Ossian raised a brow, huffing out a laugh before starting down the hall.

Adair swiftly followed, her voice calling after him. "No, seriously."

The Irishman halted, turning to her with a roll of his eyes. "Your stuff's sound. No need to worry."

She trusted him against her better judgment as they continued their way down through the halls of the castle. Her mind wandered back to the things the Commander had said, specifically the strange way that he had pronounced Ossian's name.

"Uh-sheen?" she fumbled, the unfamiliar syllables dancing clumsily on her tongue.

She glanced at the Celt from the corner of her eye, half-expecting a patronizing smile, but instead found him focused ahead, a faint smirk pulling at the corner of his mouth. "My real name," he replied with a shrug. "But Ossian's easier for you Americans and Brits, so feel free to stick with that."

The Irishman continued to guide Adair through the sprawling maze of hallways, pointing out various rooms along the way and explaining their purposes briefly before moving on to the next.

"And this..." Ossian paused dramatically in front of a set of imposing twin steel doors, before flinging them open with a flourish. "...is the laboratory!"

The interior reminded Adair of a scene pulled straight from a spy movie. Gleaming white surfaces were spread throughout, contrasted sharply by various futuristic gadgets of all shapes and sizes.

A tall, lanky figure, donning a lab coat and wire-rimmed glasses, was seated at the heart of it all, his hand running through disheveled hair, eyes intently fixed to the multiple screens before him. If the man had noticed their entrance, he didn't show it.

Ossian leaned over to Adair. "Takashi is the biggest nerd we've got," he whispered, loudly enough to break the scientist out of his trance.

"I'm not a nerd," the man snapped back, his eyes glued to his devices as his fingers continued to fly across the keyboard.

Ossian continued as if he hadn't spoken, slinking to the back of the scientist's chair. "I had this beautiful nerd transferred here myself, you know. He caught my eye, and I just *knew* that I *had* to have him."

Takashi's long fingers still for a moment. "My *technology* caught your eye. I was creating things at *fourteen* you couldn't even dream of. A feat I could still achieve right now if you weren't sitting here provoking me." He spun to shoot an indignant glare at the Irishman.

"Regardless, he's here now, and we love him," Ossian declared, affectionately patting the man's head. Takashi let out a frustrated sigh and returned to his work. Straightening, Ossian turned to his female companion. "He's really into all that geeky stuff you like, Hanlon, so you're in great company."

Before Adair could conjure a witty comeback, a deafening explosion erupted from the left, causing her to jump in alarm. The two men beside her remained unflinching, as if accustomed to such chaos.

"What the hell was that?" she gasped.

Takashi continued typing furiously, muttering technical jargon under his breath. Ossian shot her a knowing grin as the metal door on the opposite side of the lab swung open with an exaggerated thunk. Smoke billowed into the room, obscuring the entrance and revealing a lithe figure.

"I swear I had it that time!" the feminine voice echoed, thick with disappointment, as a beautiful woman emerged from the haze, her richly tanned hands planted firmly on her voluptuous hips.

"You say that every time, Amelia," Takashi replied dryly.

A broad grin spread across the woman's face as she playfully leapt onto the empty side of Takashi's desk, sending a cascade of pencils tumbling to the floor and rattling the various computer screens. He shot her an annoyed glare, but she simply laughed in response.

"Shi-Chan," the woman teased, "I've told you a thousand times to call me Mia."

With a playful jab, she poked her finger into his cheek, but he simply swatted her hand away with a sigh.

"Why do you two always have to bother me when I'm working?" Takashi complained, glancing up from his cluttered desk.

Glowering between the pair before him, his frustrations faded into resignation, and Adair couldn't stifle her giggles at his exasperation.

In an instant, the scientist shifted his attention from his tormentors to the stranger in his lab. "Is this her?" Takashi's eyes widened in disbelief as he turned to Ossian, who nodded with a sly smile.

With a sudden burst of energy, the scientist leapt across the room, narrowly avoiding the pile of blueprints that threatened to avalanche from his desk.

"It's an absolute pleasure to meet you!" he exclaimed, his voice a blend of awe and enthusiastic admiration. "Never in my wildest dreams did I imagine I'd meet someone who could be a potential Deity!"

Adair beamed back at him, at a momentary loss for words. She caught a glimpse of Ossian shaking his head beside her, his finger slicing across his throat in a clear signal for the man to stop speaking.

"Here, I made this especially for you," Takashi pivoted and dashed across the room once more, returning with a small black box.

Adair raised an eyebrow, her curiosity piqued.

"Go on. Open it," he urged, pulling a pen from his lab coat, clicking it impatiently. Mia nodded in encouragement, popping a piece of gum in her mouth as she observed from atop Takashi's desk.

With a gentle hesitance, Adair lifted the lid, revealing what appeared to be a sleek, high-tech smartwatch nestled inside.

"It's a metamorphose. Mia and I created them to aid Creator's in their travels," Takashi declared excitedly. He whipped the wristband from the box and deftly fastened it to her wrist. "This one was made specifically for Deities, and you're the first we've ever met!"

"*Potential* Deity," Mia corrected, flashing a cheeky grin before blowing a bubble that burst with a loud snap, perfectly punctuating her point.

"Right!" Takashi agreed, nodding vigorously while Adair carefully examined the device on her wrist. "The metamorphose allows the wearer to alternate their appearance based on where they are traveling."

"Basically, it prevents you from sticking out like a sore thumb," Mia chimed in, hopping down from the cluttered workspace. "And this one was specifically designed to handle the higher levels of energy that Deities possess."

Adair stared at the wristband, her head spinning at the revelation that she might actually be a *Deity*... or a *potential* one at the very least. "A Deity? Like Thor and Zeus?" She glanced over to Ossian, who visibly winced at the names. Takashi, in contrast, answered her with an enthusiastic dip of his head.

"And on that note," Ossian interjected, standing up and stretching his arms upwards. "It's time to go." His large hand enveloped Adair's. Before she could protest, he was steering her rapidly towards the exit. "Always a pleasure, nerds."

"Th-thank you!" Adair called out, her voice trailing off as the heavy doors closed with a resounding thud, cutting her off mid-sentence.

Amber eyes flicked toward the burly man standing beside her, a ghost of a challenge in her raised eyebrow.

"What now?"

"Now, allow me to show you the dining hall, the training grounds, and, of course, your room."

With that, Ossian pivoted sharply on his heel, the sound of his heavy boots resonating against the stone floor as he walked away. Adair, however, remained rooted in place, a knot of uncertainty tangled in her chest.

The Irishman paused, sensing her hesitation. Letting out a deep sigh that reverberated through the hallway, the large man turned and strode back to her, arms crossed over his broad chest. He fixed his gaze on her, refusing to look away until she met his eyes.

"Say it."

Adair fidgeted with the intricately designed watch-like object on her wrist, her heart racing as she gathered her thoughts. "You told me I was a Creator, but you never mentioned I had the potential to be a Deity."

"Well, can you blame me?" Ossian laughed, throwing his hands in the air. "When I told you about the former, you nearly had a full blown panic attack."

His tone was teasing and devoid of judgment, yet Adair shifted away from him regardless. The man took note of the movement, his stance softening as he continued.

"Hanlon," he said gently, extending his hand toward her. "We can finish the tour later. Let's get you settled in your room."

Adair exhaled softly. Nodding in agreement, she intertwined her fingers with his, the warmth of his palm grounding her.

As the pair wound their way through the twisting corridors, flickering torches cast playful shadows that danced beside them, illuminating the intricate tapestries adorning the walls. The Celt paused at a heavy oak door, releasing her and leaning thoughtfully against its ornate frame.

"Cheer up. This is where things get fun," Ossian declared, nudging her gently. He was attempting to lighten the mood, but Adair remained rooted in place, her gaze downcast.

A wry smile crossed the Irishman's lips as an idea formed in his mind. "I guess you aren't ready to see how the *magical bedroom planning* works," he said, stroking his beard pensively. "I guess I can always find you a spare cot in the meantime." He stole a sidelong glance at her.

Lifting her gaze, she met Ossian's eyes. "Why do I feel like you're teasing me?" she asked, her brow furrowed.

The hulking man raised his hands in defense, a playful grin spreading across his striking face. "Me? I would *never*."

Adair rolled her eyes dramatically, but a reluctant smile tugged at her lips despite herself.

Ossian stepped away from the doorframe and moved purposefully closer to her, the air thickening between them. He gently rested his large hands on her shoulders, the simple touch igniting a fire in her veins. Her pulse raced, and she found herself swallowing instinctively.

"Seriously, though," he said, his voice low and inviting as he leaned in further. "Imagine a dream apartment for yourself. What would it look like if money were no object?" He straightened and stepped around her, his fingers brushing her skin with a warmth that sent shivers down her spine. "What would be housed within it?"

Adair's mind spiraled into a whirlpool of yearning and desire, each thought transforming into tantalizing fantasies about the many things she wanted him to *do* in said room. What she truly craved danced just behind her eyelids. Her mind came alive with sensuous images of Ossian, the silken sheet clinging to his muscular form, accentuating every curve and contour. The sight was pure temptation, causing another rush of heat to surge through her body. She bit her lip, and dug her nails into her palm, a desperate attempt to anchor herself.

"Think about what you *want*," Ossian's warm voice continued to envelop her, his hot breath brushing softly against the sensitive curve of her neck. Adair inhaled sharply as the rich scent of cedar and woodsmoke permeated her senses.

Chuckling softly, the bearded man stepped back to lean against the opposite wall, a wolfish grin on his lips as he narrowed his eyes. He was fully aware of his effect on her, sensing the way her breath hitched and her heart quickened.

Adair tried to steady herself, her nails digging deeper into her palm as she sought the clarity needed to complete her task. Her focus sharpened as the vision of her dream room began to solidify, transforming into a cozy sanctuary. She envisioned walls lined with overflowing bookcases, bathed in soft lighting, creating a calming escape from the chaos of the outside world. In that moment, she imagined a space that truly felt like *home*.

"Don't stress too much about the details; the castle will fill in the gaps," Ossian's smooth voice shattered her concentration, pulling her back from the depths of her fantasy as she reluctantly opened her eyes.

"After you." He gestured toward the entrance, and Adair took a deep breath, her heart thrumming with anticipation as she stepped forward. Tentatively, pale digits brushed against the cool, black iron of the handle, and the door creaked open, revealing a scene that rendered her utterly speechless.

It was as if her cherished dream board of interior design had been brought to life before her eyes. Rich jewel tones cascaded across the room, deep emeralds intertwined with royal purples and bold sapphires harmonized with rich mahogany accents. A forest green velvet duvet adorned the bed, its surface flecked with shimmering gold stars that twinkled playfully under the gentle glow of the lights suspended from the ceiling. The sleeping area, large enough to swallow her whole, was surrounded by copious pillows of all shapes and sizes.

To her left, the room unfolded into a cozy nook that was a reader's dream. Plush couches adorned with subtle patterns were arranged throughout the spacious area, while an oversized armchair commanded attention in the corner. Bookshelves lined the walls, filled to the brim with volumes bound in worn leather. Nestled between two tall shelves, a window seat draped in a cascade of cushions beckoned, providing the perfect sanctuary to immerse oneself in the pages of a good book.

Her lips parted in shock as she glanced around the room, taking in the flickering fire crackling in a stone hearth. She turned to speak to Ossian, but the hulking man had already blown past her, his curiosity propelling him down the hall.

"Nice work with the bathtub, Hanlon." The Celt's voice was teasing, but heat crept up Adair's neck just the same.

Behind the wall where the bed rested, she discovered a large walk-in closet, wherein her clothing and every item from her travels lay precisely as she had packed them.

Panic quickly surged through Adair's chest as she recalled what she had hidden away before they left Seattle. She rushed to the closet, terrified of the possibility that Ossian would uncover the orange bottle she was so desperate to keep concealed.

Would he look at her with judgment? Would the warmth that often sparkled in his eyes melt away, leaving nothing but pity?

Logic told her that seeking help for her inner demons was nothing to be ashamed of, yet the stigma surrounding mental health felt like an anchor, dragging her down.

Adair pressed her palms against the cool wood of the drawers, her mind racing as she frantically searched for her medication. Forcing herself to breathe, she dashed into the other room, only to roughly collide with Ossian's solid form.

"You sound, Hanlon?" The burly man reached out, steadying her with his surprisingly gentle grip. The warmth radiating from his body made the woman's pulse quicken further, skin flushing as she shifted uncomfortably in his grasp.

He released her, and she swiftly maneuvered around him, darting toward the side table where the orange bottle awaited her like a long-lost friend. Adair tucked the container into the pocket of her jeans, just in time for Ossian to turn the corner.

"Ah, I understand." His appraising gaze bore into her, a flicker of amusement dancing in his eyes. "You didn't want me snooping and finding your *toys*," the Celt teased, utilizing air quotes to punctuate the insinuation as a devious grin spread across his strikingly handsome face.

Adair realized what he thought she was doing, and her anxiety deepened for an entirely different reason. Was it worse for him to discover what she had stowed away or to assume she possessed an absurd collection of 'self-love' tools? She dug her right thumbnail into that familiar spot on her left hand, attempting to quell the rising tide of panic.

Ossian leaned against the door frame, quietly studying the young woman. "I'll let you get settled in," he said, his eyebrows wiggling playfully.

Despite the overwhelming embarrassment, a small smile tugged at the corner of her mouth.

"I'll meet you in the dining hall in a couple of hours," the Celt added with a wink.

"Thank you." The words escaped her lips in a soft whisper, but Adair hoped her companion felt the sincerity behind them.

The only sign that Ossian had heard her was the faint dip of his chin, before he gently eased the door shut behind him.

Adair sank into the plush comfort of the bed, feeling its softness wrap around her like a warm embrace. She reached into her pocket and pulled out the bottle, lifting it to catch the light streaming through the curtains. With a deep inhale and exhale, her hand fell to rest beside her, fingers grazing the soft fabric of the bedspread. As she lay there, her gaze wandered to the ceiling, where she noticed a breathtaking array of constellations painted high above.

Her golden eyes traced the stars as she willed her breathing to steady. Slowly, Adair propped herself up and glanced at the container resting in her palm. Reaching for the carafe perched on the bedside table, she filled a glass with water and popped a couple of pills into her mouth.

After a few torturous minutes, the anxious woman finally felt her heart begin to beat at an appropriate rhythm.

Okay, Hanlon, she thought, mentally trying to envision herself through the eyes of the Irishman who believed she was stronger than she felt. *We survived being chased by villains. We survived traveling through portals. We survived freaking Neverland. And we* will *survive this. But first?*

Her mind drifted toward her dream bathtub, patiently waiting for her in the next room, a slight smile lifting the corners of her mouth.

Time for a hot bath.

Chapter Eleven

A knock at the door shattered the tranquility of Adair's warm, bubble-laden bath. Steam curled around the naked woman as she leaped from the tub, the cool air sending goosebumps racing across her skin.

"Coming!" she called, running to her closet for something to wear.

Her fingers deftly glided over an array of tops and bottoms until they settled on the comforting familiarity of her black sweatshirt. She tugged it over her head before quickly moving to pull on the slim jeans she had laid out before her bath.

She misjudged the space in her haste, crashing her knee against the sharp corner of an end table, a sharp gasp escaping her lips as pain blossomed from the point of impact. Wincing, Adair clutched her injury with one hand while using the other to button her pants before finally opening the door.

Takashi stood at the threshold, eyes widening at the sight of the freshly cleaned woman rubbing her knee furiously. He was undeniably striking, with dark, glossy hair partially hidden under a maroon beanie. The onyx strands framed his perfectly proportioned features, currently etched with embarrassment.

"I...I'm so sorry, I didn't realize you were bathing," he stammered, shifting awkwardly on his feet.

"No worries at all." Adair shot the man a reassuring smile. "I was getting all pruny anyways. It was definitely time for me to get out." As she spoke, water dripped from her wet hair and seeped into the dark fabric of her sweatshirt, dampening it. She leaned her head out, peering down the long corridor. "Where is Ossian?"

"He got called away for some urgent business. He asked me to give you the rest of the tour," Takashi replied, removing his hands from his pockets.

Adair's expression faltered for a moment, a flicker of disappointment crossing her face as she realized she wouldn't be seeing the Celt who had been dominating her thoughts while she was bathing.

"If that's okay with you, I mean," Takashi continued nervously. "If you really want him to give you the tour, I'll be off first." The man threw a thumb over his shoulder.

A smile tugged at the corners of Adair's mouth, breaking through her initial apprehension.

"I'll be off first?" she echoed, standing straighter now that her pain had eased.

"It's a Japanese turn of phrase," the olive-skinned man chuckled softly.

Adair felt her grin widen, the magic of her pills calming the anxiety of being alone with a stranger. "Lead the way."

Takashi swiftly moved down the corridor, his long strides forcing Adair to hasten her pace, nearly requiring her to take two steps for every one of his. The stone walls seemed to hum with history as the lanky scientist pointed out various doors, each adorned with elaborate carvings that hinted at the stories of their occupants.

They took a hard right, and the narrow passageway opened into a much longer hallway. An ornate silver carpet, threaded with golden floral patterns, unfurled under their feet as they passed walls adorned with large portraits, each canvas capturing noble figures in exquisite detail.

Takashi slowed his pace, taking the time to explain the meaning behind each painting as they moved.

"You sure know a lot about this place," Adair remarked.

Rubbing the back of his neck sheepishly, Takashi halted before a stern portrait of a long-haired man. "Sorry, I tend to get a bit carried away. Are you sure I'm not boring you with all of this?"

Adair began to reassure him, but her stomach had other plans. A loud growl reverberated off the ancient stone walls, and heat rushed to the woman's cheeks as she clutched her offending abdomen.

"Well, that answers *that*," Takashi chuckled. "Let's head to the dining hall, shall we? I'd hate to lose a hand." The scientist shot her a playful wink before starting down the path once more.

They continued to wind through the labyrinth of halls. Some corridors were constructed from ancient stone, their rough surfaces cool to the touch and marked with the history of time. Others featured more contemporary wood paneling, polished to a sheen that reflected the soft, ambient light from sconces lining the walls.

Finally, their journey brought them to a set of imposing mahogany doors, intricately carved with swirling patterns. The man paused for a moment before reaching out and shoving one open with surprising ease, the heavy wood gliding smoothly on its hinges.

The pair entered an expansive and well-lit dining room with a line of windows adorning its far right side. Long wooden tables and chairs were positioned around the hall, and raucous laughter bounced through from a group of men at two different tables toward the back. On the far side of the space, toward the ceiling, a large stained-glass window towered over the room, scattering fragments of multicolored light onto the slate floor.

The scene depicted a colossal wolf locked in a fierce battle with a boar of equal size. The boar's long, white tusk was viciously piercing the lupine's side, a red glint depicting the blood drawn.

In turn, the ferocious beast had its strong jaw clamped on the pig's neck, gleaming teeth and matching crimson glass highlighting the wolf's retribution. Adair's eyes roved over the image, absorbing every intricate detail.

"It's captivating, isn't it?" Takashi's voice sliced through her haze. "It was commissioned by Ossian when they first renovated this hall. The wolf clearly represents Ossian, but the boar... Well, that symbolizes his father, Fionn."

Adair studied the scene again, her brow furrowing slightly. "Doesn't seem like he has a great relationship with his da'," she replied, playfully twisting her words into a rough Irish accent, the attempt eliciting a chuckle from her guide.

"You would be right," he replied, his tone thoughtful as he slid his hands into the pockets of his trousers. Takashi turned slightly, nodding toward a nearby table. "Ossian's father created The Order," he added, his expression grave.

"And they don't like Creators," Adair remarked as they sat.

Takashi nodded slowly. "Fionn believed Creators were an affront against the very structure he sought to uphold. He didn't just dislike

Creators. He *hated* them. He demanded that they fall in line, but in the end, he truly wished to rid the world of Creators altogether." Shadows shifted across his face as he spoke. "That's why we do what we do, Adair. We fight to protect those who can't protect themselves."

The intensity of the moment was suddenly interrupted by the appearance of a portly woman with kind eyes. Her ample frame was draped in a crisp chef's apron, and her gorgeous auburn hair, flecked with spirited strands of red, spilled out of a loose bun, perfectly framing her round face.

Takashi shot a radiant smile at the newcomer. "What do we have today, Eta?"

With a melodramatic sigh, the woman lifted her gaze to the vaulted ceiling. "Today's specials," she announced, "are pan-fried seabass with root succotash drizzled in a rich cherry glaze. We also have succulent roasted chicken paired with a medley of root vegetables, all slathered in a velvety demi-glaze..."

As the list went on, Adair found her thoughts drifting away. She glanced around the area, taking in the camaraderie radiating from each corner. There was a sense of structure here, with every person engaged in their tasks, united by a common goal. Yet, despite the kindness she had been shown, the young woman couldn't quite determine where she fit into it all.

"Um, Adair..." Takashi's gentle voice drew her from her musing. "Do you know what you want to eat?"

"I'll have whatever he is having," she replied, casting a shy smile in response. "Thank you."

Without another word, the curvy woman turned on her heel and strode gracefully from the hall. Moments later, she returned, gliding softly over the slate floor. In one hand, she held two metal chalices filled with a honeyed amber liquid, while the other balanced a carafe of crystal-clear water. With a flourish, she set them down before disappearing back into the kitchen.

Takashi lifted his cup and extended it toward Adair. "Welcome to The Divide."

Adair smiled and raised hers in return, their glasses clinking gently. "Thanks, Takashi."

When Eta made her third appearance, she brought with her an exquisite array of dishes that could easily belong in a Michelin-star restaurant. The heavenly aroma wafting through the air made Adair's mouth water in anticipation, but just as she was about to take her first bite, a loud bang caused the double doors of the dining hall to swing open. The grand hall fell into a hush as every gaze turned toward the figure framed in the doorway.

Ossian.

As he surveyed the room, the Celt's striking green eyes locked onto the woman, igniting a spark of recognition in his expression as he tossed her a subtle nod. With an easy stride, he moved from table to table, greeting his comrades before finally settling in across from Adair.

"Hey, K-pop." The Irishman's tone was playful as he smacked Takashi on the back, eliciting an eye roll from the scientist. "Hanlon." Ossian turned to the woman, his voice dropping to a lower, more intimate register that forced a warm blush up her neck.

Moments later, another plate of food was placed on their table, and Ossian wasted no time, plunging his fork into the feast as if he had been starved for days. "Is Seo boring you with all of the science mumbo-jumbo about this place?" he quipped, waving his fork playfully in the air.

Adair chuckled, her smile apologetic as she glanced at Takashi. "It wasn't boring, just a lot of information," she replied.

"There will be a test later, too." Takashi chimed in, raising his own glass to her with a wink before taking a contemplative sip.

"Well, I guess your interest isn't in artificing then," Ossian chuckled through a mouthful of roast chicken.

Adair poured herself another serving of liquid courage from the bottle that had seemingly appeared alongside the Celt. "I'm curious," she began, gazing into her glass. "How are those abilities determined? Are they tied to what you're interested in?"

The men exchanged amused glances before sharing a laugh at her expense. Takashi was the first to speak. "You're born with your abilities, but they don't fully manifest until you grow older," he explained, taking a hearty swig of water.

Adair raised an eyebrow at him.

"Staying hydrated between drinks helps keep the hangover at bay," Takashi laughed, his gaze drifting towards Ossian. "Now that he's here," he said, jabbing a thumb in the Irishman's direction, "I can only imagine where this night is headed."

The man in question winked at Adair, a charming grin spreading across his face as he downed the last of his drink in one gulp. "And despite looking like he stepped straight out of a K-drama, he just can't keep up with me."

Leaning closer to Takashi, a tipsy Adair studied the man's features with an intensity that made the scientist visibly uncomfortable. "Hm," she mused, a devious smile creeping onto her lips as she reached out and snatched the beanie off his head. His onyx hair tumbled down, framing his face, and she couldn't resist the urge to tousle it affectionately.

"There. That's better," she declared, feeling a rush of warmth at the sight of his cheeks flushing.

The lanky man cleared his throat, picking up where they had left off. "Anyway, as a child, you may manifest anywhere between three and four abilities. Some are stronger than others. A Deity manifests every ability."

Adair clumsily tossed her umber hair over her shoulder, glancing up at the men with half-lidded eyes. "But I still haven't manifested any abilities," she declared, crossing her arms with a childish pout.

"You manifested healing in Neverland, Hanlon," Ossian reminded her.

"Oh, yeah!" Adair exclaimed, her pursed lips quickly transforming into a broad, drunken grin.

"And so it begins," Takashi said, raising his glass with a nod of his head. The coterie exchanged glances, a moment of silence hanging in the air, before all three erupted into a fit of laughter.

Before they knew it, the glow of the full moon began streaming through the tall windows of the dining hall. The trio had transformed their small corner into a lively gathering spot, pushing together more of the sturdy wooden tables until there was hardly room to breathe.

At the far end, a few canny souls engaged in a spirited games of cards, the sharp clap of their hands resonating with joy every time fortunes shifted. As Adair glanced around, the names of her new acquaintances danced in her mind, each one threatening to slip away as quickly as it had come.

Perhaps it was the intoxicating blend of honeyed alcohol coursing through her veins, mingling with her strong medication, or maybe it was the warm, inviting atmosphere. Whatever the case, she found herself finally embracing the moment.

"But what would happen if you jumped through one of the windows?" Adair slurred her words, her voice rising above the lively chatter of the crowd.

"You'd just pop back through a window on the opposite side of the hall," Takashi responded, his eyes lighting up with excitement as he eagerly shared his knowledge.

"And what if you step off the path in the celestial hallway?" she pressed, her hand instinctively reaching for her drink. It was a simple gesture of comfort that turned to confusion when she found nothing but the cool surface of the table. Frowning slightly, she turned to scan the area, catching Ossian's eye. He shook his head, a soft chuckle escaping his lips.

"I think that's more than enough for you, Hanlon," he remarked in his Irish lilt, a single eyebrow raised in mock seriousness.

"Hey! Do you mean to tell me that *ye think I can't hold my liquor?*" Adair shot back, an impish grin forming on her lips as she mocked his brogue, drawing laughter from Takashi and others scattered throughout the hall.

Ossian smirked, glancing around at the vibrant gathering of their squad. "Double time in the sparring ring tomorrow for that one," he declared.

Groans erupted from the group as many retreated, likely dreading the extra work and raging hangovers that awaited them in the morning.

"And on that note, I will also bid you goodnight," Takashi interjected, rising gracefully from the table. He looked at Adair, his dark eyes sparkling with warmth. "Adair, would you like an escort to your room?"

The woman shook her head, dopey grin spreading wider due to her inebriated state. "I need tacos. Not sleep," she insisted, her features set in determination.

The corners of Takashi's mouth turned upward. "Who could argue with that?" he replied, casting a glance at Ossian for confirmation, who nodded in understanding.

"Just... Take care of her, please," Takashi said to the Celt, a hint of caution lacing his voice, before stepping away.

"Wait! You forgot to give me a hug!" Adair exclaimed suddenly, springing up onto the bench. She flung her arms around the scientist, who was now at an equal height, catching him off guard with the spontaneous embrace.

The man's eyes widened in surprise, looking toward Ossian for assistance. The Celt barely hid a grin behind another sip of his drink, clearly relishing his comrade's discomfort. Slowly, Takashi softened, and, with a gentle exhale, he fully embraced the young woman, enjoying the comfort of her small body wrapped in his.

"See you in the morning!" Adair chirped cheerfully as the pair released one another.

The lithe man offered a small wave, though if she had been sober enough to notice, she would have caught the telltale flush creeping up from his neck to the tips of his ears.

As she plopped back down onto the bench with a satisfied sigh, Ossian chuckled into his drink.

"So, about those tacos?"

After Adair had indulged her cravings, the pair took to the stone corridor, the echoes of their footsteps mingling with the distant sounds of laughter and camaraderie fading behind them.

As they drew nearer to the bedroom, the woman's muddled thoughts flared to life, unleashing a cascade of vivid images from the scene she had replayed countless times in her mind—she and Ossian together, free from any dangers that might hold them back.

With a surge of newfound confidence coursing through her veins, she lifted her head to study the man's face. His square jaw, exuding rugged strength and framed by a prickly beard, drew her in, but it was his lush lips, parted ever so slightly in contemplation, that tempted her the most. As her gaze traveled upward, it collided with his striking emerald eyes, which locked onto hers with an intensity that sent a shiver down her spine.

Just as she opened her mouth to speak, a thunderous argument erupted from the bend ahead.

"Where is she? Tell me where she is *right the fuck now*!" a female voice boomed.

"I am so sorry. I had orders..." a softer, feminine voice replied.

"Orders? Fuck your orders!" the first voice snapped, each word laced with fury.

Adair's mind, still sluggish from the effects of the alcohol, struggled to place the voices, though she instinctively felt that she recognized one in particular. She took hesitant steps toward the argument, her heart thrumming in her chest, but was abruptly halted by Ossian's firm grip on her shoulder. Concern twisted his features into a mask of urgency.

"This isn't a problem to handle in your current state, Hanlon," he implored.

With a swift duck beneath Ossian's hold, Adair broke free of his grip, propelled by an unexplainable need to confront the faceless voice. She dashed around the corner, a blend of anxiety and dread churning in her stomach.

What she discovered shattered her reality into a million tiny pieces.

Mia stood facing the one person who held her heart in the palm of her hand. The person she had trusted above all else. Someone who, before this very moment, she would have jumped in front of a bullet to save without hesitation.

Nadia?

The sight struck her like a dagger thrust directly into her heart, leaving nothing but carnage behind.

Her best friend's eyes locked onto hers, shifting from angry to apologetic in an instant. "It's not what it looks like, Addie." She brushed past Mia and cautiously approached Adair, as if nearing an injured animal. "Okay, it might be a *bit* what it looks like," she admitted with a forced chuckle, desperately trying to lighten the heavy tension.

The room around Adair began to spin, and a dizzying whirlwind of emotions cascaded through her as her thoughts raced to keep up. How could Nadia be *here*? How much did she know, and for how long had she kept this secret?

Adair felt a panic tightening in her chest, her mouth opening and closing in silent protest. She stepped back instinctively as her best friend reached for her hand. The gesture was meant to comfort her, but it only served to ignite her fury.

"How long, Nadia? How long have you known?"

The woman's head hung low, her newly silvered hair cascading like a shroud. "The entire time. I am so sorry, Addie," she murmured.

"Sorry?" Adair's voice escalated. "How can you say that? You've kept an entire *world* from me!" She shook her head in disbelief, inhaling sharply. "Wait... Are you a Creator too?"

Nadia's silence was heavy, the slight nod of her head a confirmation that felt like an avalanche crashing down on Adair. Her mind whirled as she processed the implications.

"And you just happened to befriend a girl who turns out to *also* be a Creator? Or a potential Deity..." The color drained from her face as the gut-wrenching realization settled in. "It wasn't a coincidence at all, was it? Wait... Were you *spying* on me?" she asked, tears spilling down her cheeks as raw emotion clawed at her chest.

"Yes, I was sent to watch you, Addie," Nadia confessed. "But you never manifested! And I couldn't tell you anything. I swear, I wanted to. You started as a job, but you became so much more to me." Her voice cracked as she rambled on, reaching out in a desperate attempt to bridge the chasm that had opened between the pair.

Adair, feeling cornered and betrayed, stumbled, taking another step back, each movement a burning rejection. "Couldn't tell me? Or wouldn't?" Her eyes narrowed, glaring up at her 'friend' through tear-stained lashes.

"Both! Do you have any idea how dangerous this world is?" Nadia's voice grew louder, edged with desperation. "The horrific things I've seen? The experiences that haunt me every time I close my fucking eyes? You expect me to introduce a powerless girl to *this life*?" Her desperation began to give way to anger. Adair hadn't the slightest idea how much she had sacrificed to keep her safe. Even now, the voice of her mother echoed in Nadia's mind, reminding her of her worthlessness. "I am done defending myself. I did my best."

"You should have told me the truth," Adair shot back, her voice trembling. "You could have trusted me! For years, you *watched* me, and I am supposed to believe you truly cared about me? Turns out *your best* wasn't good enough."

A huff escaped Nadia's lips, a mix of resignation and exasperation. "It never is, is it? Think what you want, Addie."

With that, she turned sharply on her heel, storming away. Mia offered Adair an apologetic smile before following the silver-haired woman toward the exit.

As the door at the end of the hall slammed shut, Adair felt the weight of her emotions crash down on her, leaving her breathless. Never in her life had she felt so utterly betrayed. Not by her mother, nor her worthless father. The sting sank deep into her heart, each memory of laughter and friendship twisting into something painful. Overcome, she crumpled to the floor, the tears flowing freely as her sobs echoed off the stone walls.

Through her blurry vision, she noticed a shadow fall over her. A palm was outstretched, and she looked up to see Ossian's face peering down, his forehead creased with concern.

"I'm sorry, Hanlon," he said softly. Wiping her eyes, she gripped his hand, allowing him to pull her up from the floor.

"It's fine," she whispered, her voice hoarse. Ossian lifted an eyebrow, searching her tear-streaked face. Adair sniffled, wiping her nose on the back of her hand as she let out a half-hearted laugh.

Ossian opened his mouth to speak, but the moment quickly shattered. He turned his head, his expression instantly shifting from concerned to alert as he scanned the corridor.

Without warning, the Irishman thrust Adair against the wall, his hand roughly clamping over her mouth. He leaned in close, the warmth of his breath brushing against her face as he whispered.

"No matter what you do... *Don't make a sound.*"

Chapter Twelve

Adair flinched as a loud bang echoed through the corridor, and Ossian's breath against her neck ceased abruptly. Silently, they waited for the unseen enemy to reveal itself or retreat back into the shadows.

After a moment, a deep, resigned growl rumbled down the hall, followed by ominous footsteps fading into a nearby chamber. Adair let out a long, trembling sigh, but Ossian remained frozen in place. As she glanced up at the Irishman, she was startled by the sheer terror in his eyes.

Before she could utter a word, a sharp *Feck* escaped Ossian's lips. The man sprang away from the wall, effortlessly hoisting the young woman over his shoulder as he charged down the corridor.

Adair opened her mouth to protest, but the view from her current position silenced her immediately. Despite the gravity of the situation, her alcohol-muddled mind couldn't help but fixate on how Ossian's chiseled ass flexed in those perfectly fitting jeans as he pushed forward. Thunderous footsteps echoed behind them, accompanied by a monstrous roar that forced Adair's gaze upwards.

"Is that a fucking *manticore*?!"

"Jephte likes his rest!" Ossian bellowed in response.

He harnessed Adair's forward momentum, propelling the pair toward a nearby opening. The Celt slammed his hand against the stone wall, activating a portal before hurling both himself and Adair through the entrance. She heard the creature let out a long, frustrated yowl, just as the celestial doorway slammed shut behind them.

The sudden burst into Adair's bedroom knocked her off balance, sending her tumbling onto the arm of a loveseat with a loud grunt. Ossian absorbed most of the fall, causing a wooden coffee table to skid across the floor, breaking two of its legs in the process.

Adair inhaled sharply, the remnants of adrenaline still coursing through her veins as she pulled a pillow into her lap and sank deep into the embrace of the large, cushioned chair. The blow had knocked the wind out of her lungs, leaving her gasping for breath.

"Godsdammit, Jephte," Ossian groaned, pushing himself off the floor and brushing away the shards of splintered furniture that clung to his jeans.

Concern etched across his features as he glanced at Adair, his eyes roving over her body for any signs of injury. Once he was confident she was unharmed, he moved closer to his companion, silently settling in beside her on the seat.

Adair leaned forward to rest her forehead hard against Ossian's shoulder, a frustrated growl escaping her lips in the process. "What the fuck, McCumhaill?"

"Beastmasters can be a cranky bunch," he murmured in response, the corner of his mouth quirking up slightly.

Adair pulled back just enough to shoot him a withering glare.

"I meant all of it, eejit," she responded, playfully slipping in a bit of brogue, which elicited a chuckle from the Irishman.

Adair's eyes traced the curve of his smile as he laughed, taking in the way it crinkled the corners of his eyes. She noticed how the unique strands of his beard seemed to hold a different hue in each light. She suddenly found herself captivated by every minute detail, eventually settling on the rise and fall of the man's stubbled throat as he swallowed.

Slowly, she lifted her head from Ossian's shoulder, meeting his gaze. Her heart raced as she caught the shift in his expression. His eyebrow was arched in both surprise and intrigue, as if he could read her every intimate thought. The atmosphere in the room was instantly charged, forcing Adair to clench her thighs in a desperate search for relief.

Perhaps it was the warmth of the alcohol coursing through her veins, or the overwhelming heat radiating from Ossian's body where her hand rested against his leg. Maybe it was the fact that her entire world had been turned upside down, shattered by the betrayal of her best friend. Perhaps she had courage hidden within her that she never knew existed before now. Whatever compelled her to make the first move would remain a mystery, but no matter the reason, Adair was grateful.

Softly, she pressed her lips to his, her eyes fluttering closed as a wave of warmth surged from where their mouths met. Ossian's mouth began to move against hers, slowly exploring as his hand moved from the siderest to her chin. The rich, earthy scent of pine and woodsmoke enveloped Adair as he leaned in, heightening her senses until all she could smell, feel, and taste was *him*.

After a few heated moments, the Irishman's hand moved further up, firmly grasping the back of her neck. The movement caused the woman to gasp, her lips parting slightly in surprise at the sudden aggression.

Ossian seized the opportunity, sliding his tongue into her mouth to explore her sweetness, entwining the pair in a sensual dance that tasted like smoke and whiskey. The man's burly hand inched up to her long, umber hair, tangling his fingers in the dark strands. A gentle tug sent an electric spark through Adair, eliciting a soft whimper as powerful sensations coursed through her body.

The Celt pulled back just slightly.

"Hanlon," he murmured, his voice a low rumble as if he was straining to retain control. "As much as I..." He faltered. "Enjoy this..."

His grip softened for a moment, giving Adair the space to lean forward. She mashed her lips against his in a desperate effort to silence any arguments over the direction they were heading.

When he didn't argue, she settled herself onto his lap, her fingers weaving through his tawny locks. She knotted her fingers in his hair, giving the strands a tug that drew a hungry growl from the depths of Ossian's throat.

"Feck, Hanlon," he growled.

With a firm grip on her ass, he lifted her off the chair before tossing her to the bed as if she weighed nothing at all. Stormy eyes locked onto hers as he joined her on the soft mattress, the weight of his body pressing her down in a way that felt more exhilarating than stifling. His unwavering gaze held a request that Adair found herself more than eager to fulfill.

A slight nod was all it took to break the tension as their lips met once again in a desperate kiss, a fervent dance of intertwined tongues and teeth grazing on soft skin. As the heat of his breath moved down to her neck, she nipped at his earlobe, a gesture that extracted a low, shuddering moan from the Irishman.

"The ears..." he whispered, breathing heavily. "are very sensitive."

"Is that so?" Adair teased, her finger slowly tracing the nerve-filled area with a playful smirk on her lips. "I'll keep that in mind."

She bit her lip, reaching for the hem of his shirt. With Ossian's assistance, the fabric slipped away, unveiling sculpted pectorals and a perfectly toned six-pack.

Her breath hitched as her gaze caught on the sharp V of his hips, before moving lower and lingering. Ossian's form-fitting jeans clung tightly to his silhouette, accentuating his perfectly sculpted bulge, eliciting a soft, breathy *fuck* from Adair.

A chuckle escaped the Irishman's lips as he watched her eyes trace the inhuman length. He placed one finger under her chin and delicately directed her gaze back to his own.

"My eyes are up here, Hanlon," he growled with a smirk, before leaning in for another taste.

He gently removed her top before gliding his calloused fingers across the skin on her back, each touch igniting trails of fire that burned as much as they soothed. In one fluid motion, he unclasped her lace bra, letting it fall carelessly to the floor.

"Beautiful," he whispered against her flesh. He pressed his lips to one breast while softly kneading the other, savoring the softness of each curve.

Adair's moans filled the room, a symphony of pleasure as he lavished his attention on her body. The heat of his mouth enveloped the soft peak of her nipple, gently sucking and teasing to coax more of the guttural sounds from her throat.

She was lost to a pleasure-filled haze as Ossian's hand inched down her body, eventually reaching the bundle of nerves between her thighs that was begging for attention. Her moans grew thunderous, each sound escaping her lips unfiltered as his fingers began to move in slow, torturous circles.

After one particularly loud scream, embarrassment flickered through her, causing the woman to press her fist to her mouth to stifle her volume.

Ossian immediately halted his movements at her reaction.

"Stop," he commanded, grasping the hand that she placed on her lips. "Every utterance you make belongs to *me*, and I damn well want to hear them."

His voice was a feral growl, each word laced with a possessiveness that sent shivers down her spine.

Adair's breath hitched as he carefully brought her fingers to his mouth. Another rush of heat pooled at her core as he began to kiss each digit softly, the rough stubble of his beard teasing the delicate skin on her fingertips. He placed her index in his mouth and sucked gently, drawing additional moans from the young woman.

"What..." she murmured breathlessly, struggling to maintain a semblance of control. "What about the neighbors?"

Ossian released her digit from his mouth, his lips grazing against her fingertips as he pulled back. He absently laid the ring she had been wearing aside, the delicate piece of jewelry making a soft clink as it landed on the bedside table. Adair wondered when he had removed it, but the sight of his lips curled into a knowing smile made her shudder in anticipation.

"You really think we wouldn't take precautions in soundproofing all the rooms?"

Adair caught the deeper meaning of his words despite the inebriation that continued to blur her senses, the room spinning slightly.

As if sensing her struggle, Ossian produced a small vial from his back pocket, holding it out to her with a slight tilt of his head. The faint glimmer of the plum-hued liquid inside caught her eye, and she hesitated for just a moment, her brow furrowing in uncertainty.

"What's this?" she asked, her voice barely above a whisper, but Ossian remained silent.

Locking her eyes to his, she uncorked the vial with her teeth, spitting out the stopper and knocking it back in one go. The liquid rushed down her throat, and instantly, the fog clouding her mind lifted, leaving behind a startling clarity.

"What did that do?" Adair breathed in awe of the sudden shift rippling through her body.

The world around her sharpened. Colors deepened. Every sound, every movement felt brighter, crisper, more alive. The warmth of the alcohol that had been thrumming through her veins just moments ago vanished as though it had never existed.

Her eyes darted back to Ossian, who was studying her intently.

The Irishman reached up slowly, tucking a rebellious strand of her dark hair behind her ear. His fingers grazed the side of her neck on the way down, and the faint brush of skin against skin lit a trail of goosebumps across her arm.

"If I am to have you," he murmured, his voice a primal rumble. "I want *all* of you."

The vial slipped from her trembling fingers.

"Not a drink making you bold."

His hand slid up to cradle her face, his thumb tracing the shape of her bottom lip with slow, deliberate pressure, as though he *needed* her to feel each word.

"Not false confidence that can be taken back."

Adair leaned into him, the vibrations stoking the fire in her belly. She fully surrendered to his presence, her eyes fluttering shut as she felt the weight of his hand now resting on her hip with a possessiveness that both excited and terrified her.

"Not a moment for you to regret come morning."

The Irishman's voice was a promise, roughened at the edges, as his heated fingertip traced her curves. The touch was light, almost reverent, at odds with the feral hunger in his words. His hand lingered on her thigh, a slow claiming.

"*All. Of. You.*"

Ossian growled each word, the demand wrapped in finality, as though he could already sense her consent on the tip of her tongue.

When Adair's eyes flickered open, she found the man's pupils blown, his gaze dark as night while whispering promises of unmatched pleasure. He didn't move further. She could feel the tension radiating off of him, the force it was taking to hold himself back, and yet he stilled. He was waiting, she realized, for *her* permission.

Adair's mind had never felt so clear.

And she had *never* wanted anyone more.

Swallowing hard, she crawled to the edge of the bed.

"Yes. I consent. To all of it."

Adair reached for him without thinking, her fingers frantically hooking into the loops of his waistband. With a single pull, she yanked him closer, her mouth finding his in a kiss that was as hungry as it was desperate.

Ossian responded like a man starved, his hands sweeping down her body as his lips clashed against her own. His palm slid lower, gripping the curve of her ass roughly before delivering a sharp smack that sent a bolt of sensation straight through her core. Her startled yelp slipped against his mouth, and he caught the sound as though it belonged to him.

Adair's fingers shook as she fought with his belt buckle, the stubborn metal slipping under her grip until the button of his jeans gave way with a pop. Before she could catch her breath, Ossian's mouth claimed her breast again, hot and insistent, the scrape of his teeth followed by the slow, deliberate sweep of his tongue. He circled her nipple until it hardened to a stiff peak, then closed his mouth over his prize and sucked.

The sensation tore a gasp from Adair, her back arching helplessly as pleasure rippled through her in sharp, dizzying waves. Each pull sent another shudder racing through her until it felt like she might break apart from the intensity. Her body trembled with the wild, desperate need to feel more, take more, to lose herself entirely.

Without warning, the shrill ring of a phone shattered the moment.

Ossian growled against her skin in answer, the low sound vibrating through her chest and sending one last, devastating pulse of desire surging between her thighs. The device kept ringing, insistent and unrelenting, until, with a sharp motion, he reached into the back pocket of his undone jeans.

"What?" Ossian bit out, his voice feral. His eyes never left her as he listened, tracing over her body like he could commit this version of her to memory. Whatever the voice on the other end said made his expression harden, shadows cutting across his face. "I'll be there in five."

Reluctantly, he turned away, and Adair swiftly grabbed her sweatshirt from the bed, covering her bare top half. "Everything okay?" she asked, her brows furrowed as she tracked his movements. He pulled his shirt on and moved back to face her, an apology starkly written on every feature.

"Hanlon..." He hesitated, letting out a deep sigh.

Not sure of what to say, she pointed to his crotch, where his belt and fly had been left undone. The man scoffed and fixed himself before moving back towards the bed, placing his hands on either side of her body. She remained still, clutching her shirt as she felt the foolishness of the moment beginning to creep in.

"I'm sorry we have to cut this short," he said, his accent thick and his voice gravelly. "I wish I didn't have to go," He leaned into her, the stubble scratching as he placed his lips to her neck and sighed. "But duty calls..."

Adair swallowed hard as he pulled away and nodded distantly, avoiding his gaze.

Ossian gently cupped her chin, tilting her face towards him. When she still refused to meet his eyes, he let his other hand trail down her body, hooking a finger into her soaked panties and pulling them aside. He dipped his fingers into her folds, a low growl of satisfaction escaping him as he felt her wetness. Her amber eyes finally met his, wide and desperate, as he explored her thoroughly.

"Adair," he murmured, his voice a low, dangerous rumble. "This..." He slowly, deliberately inserted another finger, "Unfortunately...." Carefully, he curved them to hit that sensitive spot inside of her. "...will have to wait."

Adair's whimper was a sound of pure frustration and need. He brought his thumb to her mouth, and she sucked on it eagerly, her tongue swirling as she tried to draw him back to what she wanted. He teased her entrance with a third finger, his eyes never leaving hers, a silent promise of what was to come.

He stopped as suddenly as he had started, leaving her bereft and aching as he moved away. The Irishman crossed the room in a few long strides, his back to her as he reached for the door.

"Ossian," she begged, her voice a hoarse whisper.

He paused at the door, turning just enough for her to watch as he inserted his wet fingers into his mouth, slowly closing his eyes as he savoured her taste.

"I left you a gift over there," he said, nodding towards the bed stand, his voice hoarse. "To make up for the one I destroyed in the woods. Send me a little recording when you finish taking care of what I started."

Before she could ask what he meant, he was gone.

"Fuck," she shouted to the emptiness of her room, smashing her head back onto the pile of pillows on her new bed.

She looked in the direction he had pointed, finding a small box she hadn't noticed previously. With shaky fingers, she opened it, revealing a slick gold smartphone bearing a symbol she recognized from her time in Takashi's lab.

Ossian's words came back to haunt her as the ache between her thighs became unbearable. With a deep breath, she reached for the device, her fingers trembling slightly as she opened the camera app.

She propped the phone against a pillow, the lens aimed directly at her nearly naked body. She hit record and let out a shaky breath, her eyes fluttering closed as she inched her fingers into the warm, damp lace of her panties.

Her touch was tentative initially, a soft exploration that quickly became a desperate need. She circled her clit, her breath coming in short gasps as she imagined Ossian's hands on her, his fingers replacing her own, his touch more commanding and sure. She recalled the weight of his body, the security of his presence, and the way his breath had sent shivers down her spine. Her nipples hardened at the memory, her body responding as if he were still there, his mouth hot and hungry on her skin.

Her hips began to move in rhythm with her touch, her body arching slightly as she chased the pleasure that Ossian had so cruelly left her wanting. The orgasm built quickly, a tidal wave of sensation that crested and broke, leaving her gasping and shaking. Her moans filled the room, raw and uninhibited, as the pleasure consumed her, blinding her to everything but the sensation of her own body.

The aftershocks were almost as intense, her internal muscles pulsing with a life of their own, reminding her of the emptiness that Ossian had left behind. She panted, her chest heaving as she came down from the high, her body slick with sweat.

She had never come so fully, so intensely, and the thought of what the real thing would be like sent a fresh wave of desire crashing through her. Would she survive it? Would she go *blind* from the sheer force of it?

The sight of her disheveled appearance reflected on the phone's screen snapped her out of her post-orgasmic haze, and she blinked, her cheeks flushing as she realized what she had done. Quickly grabbing the device, she stopped the recording and closed the app, her heart pounding wildly.

If Ossian wanted to see her like this, then he would just have to be the one to push her over the edge. It was *his* hands she wanted on her, *his* mouth on her, *his* body inside hers, making her come undone in a way that no amount of imagining could ever replicate.

Disappointment washed over her as she stared up at the golden constellations adorning the ceiling. The weight of the day caught up with her, and Adair bit her lip, struggling to hold back her tears.

Hopping off the bed, she crossed into the living room and snagged an unopened bottle of vodka from the bar cart. She opened it with a single twist of the cap, tipping it back for multiple long, burning swallows before heading to the shower. The sting did nothing to dull the ache clawing at her chest, but at least it gave her hands something to do besides tremble.

Feeling the warmth of the alcohol begin to course through her veins, she turned on the shower, hoping for an added chance to wash away the pain that was now pulling her down like a weighted blanket. She let her fingers slip through the droplets, testing the warmth.

"Of course, the showers are always the perfect temperature," she muttered under her breath, pulling off her panties before stepping into the soothing cascade.

She thought it would be Ossian's face she would see when she closed her eyes, but in the serenity of the shower, her mind drifted to Nadia, and the betrayal cut her once again, reopening that gaping wound in her soul.

She resolutely turned the dial towards the blue, allowing the icy droplets to mingle with the salty warmth streaming down her cheeks. A wave of nausea twisted in her gut, and she doubled over, a wail escaping her lips as she allowed herself to succumb to the pain.

Chapter Thirteen

Adair fought to open her eyes, a guttural groan escaping her lips. The room spun as she pushed herself upright, only to be rewarded with a relentless pounding in her skull.

She blinked against the harsh sunlight streaming through the window, the bright rays painful in her sensitive state. Her eyes scanned the room, landing on the shattered remnants of the table lying beside the window seat.

The sight triggered a flood of memories from last night, the most vivid being the sensation of Ossian's lips pressing against her own. A blush crept across her cheeks as she recalled how his body fit so perfectly atop hers, the recollection of his fingers trailing paths of fire across her skin soothing some of the pain of her hangover.

She put on her glasses and reached for her new phone, eager to see if Ossian had texted after his untimely exit. Perhaps he had sent an apology, a 'thinking of you,' or a playful nudge reminding her about the video he had asked her to send. Anything to fill the void he had left behind. Hitting the device's home button, the screen lit up, seemingly mocking her with its complete lack of notifications.

Defeated, Adair collapsed back onto the bed, a frustrated huff leaving her lips as she calculated her next steps. Should she wait for him to get in touch with her? Should she reach out and message him first? As she contemplated her options, Nadia's face flashed through her mind. If anyone knew how to handle this sort of situation, it would be her.

The hopeful consideration was fleeting, eclipsed by the dark shadows of betrayal. Adair pressed a trembling hand to her temples as the memory of the silver-haired woman's anguished face seared into her mind. Nadia had been more than just a friend. She had been Adair's closest confidante, the sister she had never had. Their bond, once unbreakable, now felt like a lie, a cruel trick played on her heart. The realization left a bitter taste in her mouth, amplifying the throbbing in her head.

As her thoughts began to spiral, her panic surged, tightening her chest and turning each breath into a battle. Her eyes darted around the room, desperately searching for her anxiety medication. Spotting the familiar orange container perched on her dresser, she hurried over, her heart pounding a relentless rhythm in her ears as she opened the bottle and downed two pills. The bitterness was a small price to pay for the relief that they promised.

Steeling herself, she met her reflection in the mirror. What stared back could only be described as a wild creature of lore, an untamed beast with tear-stained cheeks, unkempt hair, and tired, red eyes.

"What am I doing here?" she whispered, her voice a ragged breath against the glass.

This wasn't her place. This wasn't where she belonged. The thought jolted her, and she turned from the mirror, her resolve hardening.

Adair rushed to the closet, her fingers trembling as she rifled through her garments, clumsily throwing on a pair of fitted jeans, a heather grey long-sleeved shirt, and brown leather boots. She longed for home, for the safety of Seattle, but the path to get there was uncertain.

Ossian was gone, and Nadia's betrayal cast lingering doubts that Adair just could not shake. Thinking back on the people she had met throughout the Keep, she found herself reflecting on the kindness and patience that Takashi had shown her throughout this ordeal. If anyone could assist her in finding an exit, he would most likely be the best bet.

Plan in place, Adair surveyed the room, ready to gather the few belongings scattered about to prepare for her swift and secret departure. Her gaze fell to the pants that Ossian had removed from her the night before, the memory as thrilling as it was painful. As she bent to retrieve them, a piece of parchment slipped from the back pocket, fluttering gently before settling at her feet.

Picking it up, she traced the delicate surface, remembering the riddle she had translated back at the Woodwose's cottage.

I was an armed fighter.

I kissed a man. I send enemies running, and warriors will be put into battle.

I am hanging on the wall now, with proud ornaments, when men get answers.

Name me.

The Woodwose's words echoed in her mind: *You are a key to ending the war, lass.*

Adair realized she couldn't escape her duty. She never asked for any of this, but neither did the countless innocent Creators losing their lives in a conflict that *they* never chose. If she left now, what would happen to them?

No. She resolved to stay long enough to decipher the riddle, to play what she believed would be her small part in the fight. Once she fulfilled that responsibility, she would return home and never look back. With a resigned sigh, she examined the parchment one last time before tucking it away for safekeeping.

A loud grumble from her stomach reminded her of her own needs. Deciding to take a break, she made her way to the dining hall, ready to gather her strength for whatever challenges lay ahead.

Boisterous sounds of laughter filtered down the hallway, the joyous din spilling from the refectory where the doors had been left slightly ajar. Adair pressed a hand to her temple, already feeling the throb deepening. She hesitated for a moment, weighing whether or not she should wait for the crowd to thin. But the enticing aroma of spiced meats and warm, baked bread wafted through the air, pulling her forward against her better judgment.

Adair pushed the heavy wooden doors open further. As they creaked, a collection of eyes turned toward her, several faces lighting up with recognition. "Adair!" one of them bellowed playfully, the exclamation echoing off the vaulted ceilings.

She thought she recognized some of the faces from the gathering last night, but the alcohol-soaked memories lingered just out of reach while they beckoned her over with enthusiastic waves. As she considered how to politely decline their invitations, a reassuring hand gripped her shoulder.

Turning to see who had come to her rescue, she was met with Mia's apologetic smile, her caramel eyes shimmering with understanding.

"Sorry, boys," the scientist shouted to her coworkers with a light laugh, "I'm sure she wants none of what you're having this morning after the night *she* had." Her tone was mirthful yet protective, a lighthearted barrier between Adair and the unruly crowd.

Mia led her through the throng with ease, eventually finding refuge at an empty table towards the back of the hall. Sunlight streamed through the stained glass windows, casting the illusion of rainbows on the surface as they sat.

"How are you feeling?" Mia asked, propping her chin on her hand, keen eyes appraising the woman across from her.

Adair attempted to act aloof, but internally, all she desired was to lay her cheek on the wooden table and fall asleep.

"Not too bad," she managed. The words felt flimsy even as they left her lips.

Mia remained silent, eyebrows dancing upward, clearly sensing the thinly veiled lie. Before she could formulate a response, Eta approached with two heaping plates laden with food.

"Perfect timing, Eta! Thank you!" Mia exclaimed, her dark curls bouncing as she unabashedly dove into her meal.

Adair's plate overflowed with savory sausages, perfectly scrambled eggs, spiced beans, and golden toast, further adorned with splashes of color from the blistered cherry tomatoes. Atop the mounds of food rested two disks, one white and one black. She didn't question the peculiar add-ons, focusing instead on the slice of buttered toast.

She all but moaned as she savored the crunch of her first bite. It tasted like magic, the food working wonders in her stomach, drawing out the remnants of last night's alcohol.

"So," Mia said, around a mouthful of food, "busy day today?"

Adair shrugged, "Not sure, honestly. Just along for the ride."

Mia nodded thoughtfully, pushing her beans onto a piece of toast, stuffing a hefty bite into her mouth. "About last night..."

Adair was unsure what Ossian had said to the others, but she wasn't prepared to discuss any of it with a practical stranger.

"What about last night?" Adair asked. Her voice trembled despite her best efforts to stay calm. She quickly stuffed an entire sausage into her mouth in a desperate attempt to regain her composure.

Mia set her fork down, suddenly serious as she fixed the pale woman with a knowing look. "I'm sorry about the whole Nadia thing."

Adair nearly choked, a strangled gasp escaping her lips. It was the last thing she expected to hear from the scientist.

"W...what do you mean?" she stammered.

Mia sighed, her expression softening. "I know it must be a shock... Nadia being sent to watch you and all."

With every word, Adair's agitation mounted, her leg bouncing rapidly beneath the table.

"But..." There was a pause as the woman leaned in. "Nadia truly does consider you a friend."

Adair was confused by this turn of conversation. She didn't know the scientist personally, yet she was intervening so assertively.

Memories of last night's altercation rushed back to her. At the time, she hadn't taken notice. Now, thinking back, she remembered Mia *was* there, holding hands with her so-called 'best friend.'

Suddenly, the pieces of the puzzle began to click into place.

"Mia…." The word came out as a whisper. "You're…"

She began to piece together all the past conversations with Nadia, recalling how fondly she had spoken of her mysterious, long-distance relationship with a captivating female scientist. Reflecting on the descriptions, it became clear that the enigmatic *mystery woman* was the beauty sitting in front of her.

"Of course. You're *her* Amelia."

"Nadia didn't ask me to speak to you about this," Mia said, voice rising as her words tumbled out in a rush. "In fact, she would be *so* angry at me if she knew I was having breakfast with you right now." Her tone grew more desperate as she continued. "But I *needed* to talk to you. I know you're upset, but Nadia promised me you're a good person. And I am hoping that means we can trust you to keep the… *situation*… between me and her a secret."

Adair's heart raced in her chest, a storm of emotions becoming more volatile by the second. The revelation had left her reeling, but the motive behind Mia's 'concern' had her gripping her plate so tightly that her knuckles turned white.

"Why even ask how I am doing? You don't care about me. You're just hoping I won't spill the beans about your little *relationship*." Adair spit the words out, each laced with as much venom as she could manage. "Well, you can stop worrying. Unlike your *girlfriend*… I'm not a *bitch*." She quickly lifted her plate, eager to escape the conversation.

In her haste, she collided with a tall figure nearby, sending her food crashing to the slate floor below.

"Oh no, I'm so sorry!" Adair exclaimed, her cheeks flaming as the remnants of what had once been a perfect Irish breakfast splattered over her, the floor, and the gentleman.

Takashi, donning a crisp white shirt that now bore the brunt of her mishap, stood frozen in surprise. He had made no attempt to shield himself from the carnage as greasy sausages, vibrant egg yolks, and runny baked beans transformed his attire into an unintended abstract painting.

Adair's heart sank at the sight of her ruined meal, but she quickly composed herself. Her hands trembled as she reached out to brush the mess off his shirt, only to create an even more chaotic tapestry of spilled food and frantic apologies. Glancing towards Mia, she found a half-eaten plate accompanied by an empty seat.

Of course.

Gentle fingers wrapped around her wrists, anchoring her in place. She bravely met Takashi's gaze, the understanding in his eyes causing her own to well up, blurring her vision.

"It's no worries. I was about to sit down for a plate myself," he reassured her. His smile radiated like the sun, breaking through the darkness she had been battling just moments before.

"I'm so so sorry," she stammered, pulling her hands from his grasp. She turned to flee, but Takashi gently grasped her arm, stopping her in her tracks.

"It's only a shirt. It's okay, Adair." His voice was soothing as he attempted to catch her gaze. She refused to look at him, but he maneuvered around her. Bending at the waist, he tilted his head up in another attempt to meet her eyes. "Oh dear."

"What?" She sniffled, the remnants of her mortification reflecting in her red-rimmed eyes.

"It appears that we are both quite the mess now." He tenderly wiped a small smear of bean sauce from her cheek. He then brought the finger to his mouth, deftly sucking the sauce from his digit as if he were tasting a rare delicacy. "At least we know breakfast tastes good this morning."

Adair felt her breath catch in her throat, but the moment was shattered when her stomach emitted an ungodly growl. The sound reverberated through the dining hall, causing her and Takashi's eyes to widen in unison.

After a moment of stunned silence, the scientist burst into a genuine laugh, and an unexpected warmth crept up the back of Adair's neck, turning the tips of her ears a fiery red.

"My room is closest to the dining hall," Takashi offered, his tone gentle yet playful. "We can get cleaned up there."

He beckoned her to follow, but she hesitated, glancing back at the remnants of her breakfast sprawled across the dining hall floor. Others passed by, stepping over the shattered pieces of her meal as if the mess were merely a mundane part of the day.

Takashi picked up on her unease instantly. "Magic castle, remember?"

Adair opened her mouth to speak, but quickly thought better of it, taking one last look at the array of food and plate pieces littering the floor. After a deep breath to ground herself, she mustered the courage to leave it behind, following Takashi out of the bustling dining hall and toward his private quarters.

Chapter Fourteen

Stepping into the scientist's bedroom, Adair braced herself for a sterile, metallic environment that screamed 'villain's lair.' Instead, she was pleasantly surprised by the cozy living area she found herself standing in. It was a harmonious blend of Japanese and Korean culture with Scandinavian furniture, creating a warm and inviting atmosphere that was far from what she had initially imagined.

To the right, a kotatsu graced a tatami floor, smartly positioned in front of a large television and an impressive array of gaming consoles. The blinds were flung wide open, allowing warm sunlight to flood the vibrant room that perfectly reflected the man's personality.

A sophisticated computer rig with three monitors and a sleek gaming chair occupied the corner on the left. Over the desk, a red neon sign written in Korean added a modern cultural twist, while a glass case to the left showcased an impressive collection of anime character statues. Separating the rest of the space was a paper screen door, and dark wood floors lined the hallway directly ahead.

Following Takashi's lead, Adair clumsily unlaced her boots before slipping them off and placing them at the front door.

A smile tugged at the corner of Takashi's mouth as he watched her, though he quickly turned away, sliding his feet into a pair of slippers before stepping onto the polished wood floor.

Before Adair could voice the question reflected in her eyes, he answered without hesitation. "The design is a mixture of the house I grew up in and my dream apartment," he explained, glancing around the entryway with a fond smile. "I go back to visit my family quite frequently. But it's always comforting to feel surrounded by them when I return home from work."

Adair slid her feet into a pair of oversized sandals before noisily clopping down the hallway, taking a moment to admire the photographs of Takashi and his family that lined the corridor. She paused, captivated by a vibrant image of the family at the beach.

A young Takashi stood with a shovel raised high above his head, resembling a warrior brandishing a sword. Beside him, another boy struck a playful victory pose, hands on his hips, chest puffed out, and a mischievous spark glinting in his eyes. The siblings beamed with pride as they stood tall above their creation: an intricate sandcastle featuring multiple towers, a makeshift bridge, and a shimmering moat filled with water from the sea.

"That was a great day," Takashi said, his warm baritone startling her momentarily. "I remember how we spent the entire day building that castle, even though all I really wanted to do was search for creatures in the tide pools."

Adair turned to face him. "You're a great big brother."

"Thanks," he replied with a light chuckle. "I like to think so, but I suspect Joichi might disagree."

Clearing her throat, Adair shifted her gaze to the next photograph, where four family members dressed in traditional kimonos were captured in a moment of solemnity. "Is that your mom? She's beautiful!"

A stunning woman with perfectly done makeup gazed back at her, a hint of a smile dancing on her painted lips.

Takashi's grin faded, a flicker of sorrow crossing his face. "Yes, she was."

Adair understood his choice of words immediately. "I'm so sorry," she whispered, instinctively placing her hand on his arm in a comforting gesture. "My mom passed too."

Dark eyes met hers, revealing a depth of emotions that made her heart ache.

Takashi turned back to the photo, his lips turning up in a bittersweet smile that failed to reach his eyes. "Yeah," the man nodded. "Our whole family dynamic changed after that."

"I know what you mean," Adair huffed softly, trying and failing to shove down the memories of her mother's passing.

She would never forget how her father's gaze had turned cold after the accident, as if she were merely a reflection of what he had lost. Rather than grappling with his own pain, he had sent her away, leaving nothing but the sorrowful realization that she had lost not simply one parent that day, but two.

"Anyway." The lanky man said loudly, his voice breaking the tension and drawing her gaze to the warm smile that lit up his face once more. "Let's get out of these clothes."

A flush crept up Adair's cheeks at his insinuation, the heat both thrilling and mortifying in light of last night's 'activities' with Ossian. Despite her better judgment, a flicker of excitement surged through her at the thought of Takashi shedding his garments. She followed the scientist down the corridor, her heart racing to a curious rhythm.

As they stepped into the room, the sight of a small kitchenette, complete with a modest fridge and stove, made her stomach growl in protest from neglect. She regretted not equipping her own quarters with similar amenities. Although she didn't consider herself much of a cook, she had many late-night cravings for snacks while indulging in her favorite novels or games.

Takashi moved with a fluid grace, his deft fingers working the buttons of his shirt. As the fabric slipped away, it revealed the chiseled planes of his torso.

Adair's mouth fell open, a gasp catching in her throat as she observed him. Compared to Ossian, Takashi stood the same height but appeared leaner, almost willowy, until he stripped away his clothing. As he turned to face away from her, the muscles of his back rippled beneath his skin, each flex sending heat rushing to her cheeks.

Steeling herself, Adair swallowed hard, licking her lips in an effort to regain her composure. "So…" The word slipped from her mouth just as he turned around, her gaze instinctively locking onto his bare abs.

"I am so sorry! I totally forgot." Takashi hurried over to a clothes horse stationed in the corner, an air of innocence surrounding him despite his half-clad state. He grabbed a deep maroon sweater. "You may want to wash up before you get changed. The bathroom is right across the hall."

The woman reluctantly tore her gaze from his sculpted chest, quickly wiping her food-stained hands on her pants. With a softly murmured thank-you, she accepted the cozy sweater he offered and hurried to the safety of the restroom.

As the door clicked shut behind her, Adair turned to face her reflection in the mirror, attempting to calm her racing heart. What on earth were they feeding men at the Keep to make them all look like *that*?

Carefully slipping her soiled shirt over her head, Adair worked to wash the remnants of food from her face, careful not to disturb her makeup. As she slid into the oversized sweater, the warm scents of cinnamon and sandalwood enveloped her, filling her senses with the rich, sultry aroma. She inhaled deeply, taking a moment to savor the comforting fragrance.

The sweater was larger than she had expected, nearly swallowing her lithe frame, but she adored the warmth it provided. Examining herself in the mirror, Adair felt it suited her perfectly.

After a hurried touch-up of her tousled hair, she made her way back to the kitchen, only to find that, much to her disappointment, Takashi had already dressed himself. He stood tall in a fitted shirt that highlighted his toned shoulders.

The scientist extended a hand toward her, ready to take the stained laundry she still held.

"Oh, that's alright!" Adair protested, her sleeve-covered hands waving dismissively, warding off his kindness. "You really don't have to clean my things."

"I insist." Takashi's fingers lightly brushed against hers as he took the top and placed it on the washer alongside his own dirty clothes. He began treating the stains on her shirt with the same meticulous care he dedicated to his own garments. "So, do you have anything on your schedule today?"

Adair shifted awkwardly from one foot to the other, her gaze flickering over the kitchen's rustic decor rather than lingering on the enticing curve of his back.

"Aside from dealing with this hangover? Not much else."

"I can help take care of that," he offered, turning his head slightly to give her a sidelong look that sent her pulse racing once again. "After all, I did ruin your breakfast."

"If anything, I'm the one who ruined *your* breakfast," she replied, her voice faltering as she took a small step back, nearly colliding with the clothes horse.

Ignoring her protests, Takashi tossed her shirt into the wash, skillfully added detergent, and set the machine humming before making a beeline for the fridge.

"I insist," he reiterated.

Adair watched as he began pulling out various containers, each one filled with leftovers that smelled tantalizingly delicious. "No, really. I think Ossian mentioned something about some kind of training today anyway," she interjected, taking another tentative step back.

Takashi halted, eyebrows rising in genuine surprise. "Training? On your first day here? I mean, I get you potentially being a Deity and all. And yeah, I'm excited to see what you can do, but shouldn't you settle in first? Get your bearings?"

Adair shifted uncomfortably under his gaze. "Um... I guess he wants to get a jump on things?" she ventured.

"Well, you can't do that on an empty stomach," Takashi said with a playful wink.

As he approached, Adair couldn't help but notice the way he expertly balanced two plates filled with steaming delicacies. She followed him as he set the dishes down on the low table in the front room.

"Would you like some coffee?" he asked while laying out the silverware. "I can't function in the morning without mine."

She nearly declined the offer, but the memory of the espresso machine sitting on the kitchen counter tugged at her resolve. Trying not to overthink it, Adair blurted out, "Can you make a latte?"

A laugh, mimicking the sound of air escaping a balloon, bubbled from Takashi's lips. "Can I make you a latte? Get ready to have your mind blown." With an extra bounce in his step, he vanished down the hall. "Do you have a preferred way to enjoy it?" he called back.

"Nope, just a regular latte." Adair struggled to conceal her excitement as she settled into the warm embrace of the futon quilt. It felt like a dream come true, cocooned in the cozy warmth of a kotatsu against the biting chill of the Scottish air that lingered in the castle. A soft sigh of contentment escaped her lips as she glanced down at the plate resting before her.

The dish was a mix of colors and textures: tender meat swimming in a rich, savory sauce, fluffy bread, and pale, glistening fruit artistically arranged alongside. As long as the food could fix her dizzying head and grumbling stomach, Adair truly didn't care what they ate or how it tasted, but the smell was *very* promising.

After a few minutes, Takashi returned, setting a large latte mug and a tray of small banchan plates down in front of her. The foam on the cup was adorned with an exquisite thistle, each detail painstakingly crafted to make it seem as if it were jumping right out of the cup.

"You do latte art too?" Adair exclaimed, awe evident in her voice. Quickly, she whipped out her phone, angling both the plates and mug to capture the perfect aesthetic shot, before glancing up to meet the man's beaming smile.

"Well, I'm glad to see *someone* appreciates it," he said, taking a sip from his mug, the corners of his eyes crinkling with joy. "Most people around here aren't coffee drinkers, so I have to order it specifically for myself." Glancing down, he noticed Adair hadn't touched her food. With a light chuckle and a wave of his hand, he added, "You didn't have to wait for me. Feel free to dive in!"

Adair ducked her head sheepishly, taking a tentative sip of her drink. A soft groan of satisfaction escaped her lips as the warm, creamy flavors enveloped her tongue. "Oh my god, this might be one of the best lattes I've ever had, and I work at a bookstore that *sells* coffee!"

She set her mug down and reached for a bite of one of the mystery foods, her eyes suddenly wide as a symphony of tastes captivated her. "What the hell? Takashi, did you make this, too? This is unreal!"

Each morsel was an experience in itself, every flavor a celebration that far surpassed anything she had tried at the Keep, or anywhere for that matter. How was she supposed to enjoy normal cuisine after this masterpiece?

Takashi's face lit up at her enthusiasm. "Most of it. There's a new chef at the Keep, and he's been giving me private lessons." He took a bite of his meal, clearly pleased with her reaction.

"Let me make sure I've got this right," Adair said, eyes wide and mouth filled with food. "You cook, you make a killer cup of coffee, you game," she continued, counting the points off on her fingers for emphasis, "...and you're the lead Artificer for The Divide. What *can't* you do?"

Takashi's cheeks flushed a light shade of pink, which he quickly tried to mask with a large sip from his cup. Clearing his throat, he remarked,

"Gods, you sound just like my dad. Aside from asking when I'm going to get a girlfriend, that is."

Adair jolted, her spoon scraping loudly against her plate.

Rubbing the back of his neck sheepishly, Takashi attempted to alleviate the sudden awkwardness. "Anyway... the answer is cinnamon."

"Cinnamon?" Adair echoed, her brows knitting together in confusion.

He nodded, continuing with a thoughtful chew. "It's the secret ingredient to a great latte, or really any cup of coffee for that matter."

"I've never considered adding that." Adair took another grateful sip of her drink, relishing the comforting warmth spreading through her. "But now that I know, it will be a permanent fixture in my morning mug!"

Takashi chuckled brightly. "Glad to hear it."

The remainder of the hour passed in a delightful blend of food, stories, and laughter, with conversation flowing effortlessly between the pair. Just as they were settling into their rhythm, Takashi's phone erupted with unmistakable, deep, resounding french horns playing a popular villainous theme.

"Shit," he muttered, quickly silencing the phone as he checked the time displayed on the screen. "That's Mia. I *might* be running a little late to the lab." He offered Adair an apologetic glance just as the phone rang a second time. "If I don't pick up, she'll just keep calling. I am so sorry about this."

Takashi rose from the table and made his way down the hall. Before he disappeared from view, she heard him respond, "What do you want, you treasure-hoarding tiefling?" A few minutes of hushed arguing followed, and soon the frustrated man strode back into the room, his expression one of genuine apology as he approached Adair.

"I'm so sorry," he said again, dipping his head slightly but never breaking eye contact. "I really need to head over, or Mia will never let me hear the end of it."

"Oh, that's okay! You've already done so much for me this morning, so no worries!" She flashed him a bright smile before moving to the front to wrestle her boots back on, an arduous task in itself.

To her surprise, Takashi settled next to her on the wooden floor, effortlessly slipping on a pair of white sneakers. "Before you head out, I'd like to give you a map of the castle. It'll help you avoid getting lost."

"Yeah, I definitely want to avoid any more angry manticores in the middle of the night," she teased, winking at him playfully. As she finished tying her laces, he did the same, and they found themselves standing side by side in the entryway.

"Oh shit, I take it you've met Jephte? That guy is *really* grouchy about his sleep. Sorry about that," Takashi said, crinkling his nose.

"*You* have nothing to apologize for. You weren't the one dumb enough to wake him," Adair laughed, pulling her phone from her back pocket.

As Takashi pressed his device to hers, a familiar *Zelda* tune chimed, instantly bringing a grin to the lips of the game-loving woman.

"All set! It's a special app I've installed on your phone. I'm sure you'll figure it out. You seem pretty tech-savvy," he said, gesturing with a relaxed wave of his hand before opening the front door.

Adair followed the man down the stone-lined hallway. "I really appreciate the breakfast, and I'm sorry for the mess," she said, her voice cheerful. "And thank you for this too!" she added, waving her phone enthusiastically in the air.

"No problem at all. I'll make sure to return your shirt once it's clean, and you can keep the sweater as long as you need," Takashi replied, his voice warm. The nefarious march echoed through the corridor once again, causing the man to growl in annoyance. "Well, it seems I'll be heading off first. Cheers, Addie."

The use of her nickname caught Adair off guard as he jogged away, but she couldn't help but smile. If anyone deserved to call her that, it was the kind scientist who had brightened her morning on a day that felt doomed to darkness.

She hoped she could find a way to repay his kindness someday, no matter what the future held.

Chapter Fifteen

Adair was able to meander through the ancient castle without getting lost thanks to the map Takashi had provided her. She navigated the winding corridors, carefully checking around each corner to avoid crossing paths with her ex-best friend. She had enough to think about without adding a confrontation with Nadia to that list.

The Keep was a labyrinth, and though she occasionally ventured into forbidden areas, she relished every moment spent uncovering its many mysteries. After hours of exploration, her phone buzzed, revealing a message from Ossian:

Meet me at the indoor training ground.

Checking the diagram, she was able to pinpoint the location with ease. The woman bit her lip, her gaze drifting down to her casual outfit. It was clear that a quick pit stop was in order.

Back in her quarters, Adair slipped into some sleek black leggings, paired with sturdy runners and a white sports bra, and quickly switched out her glasses for contacts. Remembering the chill of the Keep's passageways, she finished the ensemble with a grey zip-up hoodie.

With newfound determination, she set out for the training grounds, her heart fluttering with nervous anticipation. The intimate moment she and the Irishman had shared the night before weighed heavily on her mind, as did the biting silence that had followed. She wasn't sure whether to confront him or pretend nothing had happened. In the end, she decided it was just best to focus on her training. Everything else would have to wait.

As Adair approached the open doors to the grounds, an unsettling realization halted the woman in her tracks. *My medication.* In her rush, she had completely forgotten to take her pills. She froze at the threshold, torn between the urge to turn back and the pressure to move forward.

Ossian noticed her lingering, raising a brow at her indecision. "What are you standing around for? Get your arse in here."

Reluctantly conceding that she had missed her opportunity, Adair forced a smile, refusing to meet the man's eyes.

Entering the training area, she took a moment to survey the grand space. Adair marveled at its impressive scale, despite it being the smaller of the two spaces indicated on the map.

To her right, the walls were lined with an array of high-tech equipment: free weights, cardio machines, and benches, all ready for action. On her left, the smooth wooden floor transitioned into packed dirt, creating a purposeful contrast that defined the dedicated sparring area, a section clearly designed for grappling or combat training. Functional mats lined the edges of the dirt patch, their frayed borders telling stories of countless rigorous sessions.

Beyond the sparring zone, her gaze was drawn to several multifaceted practice stations catering to a variety of regimens. Heavy bags swung freely overhead, and agility ladders rested neatly on the ground, poised for use. In a nearby corner, brightly colored yoga mats were meticulously arranged, adding a splash of vibrancy to the space. If this was the smaller of the two workout areas, Adair could hardly imagine what she would discover in the larger.

A forced cough took her out of her musings, bringing her gaze to the man staring at her from the center of the room.

"How are you feeling this morning, Hanlon?" Ossian asked with a cheeky grin. He sat upon a weathered stool, focused intently on sharpening his dagger.

In close proximity to the inhumanly attractive male, Adair's mind was flooded with memories of the previous night. She couldn't escape the vivid flashes of their electric moments, his warmth enveloping her, and the promise that had hung tantalizingly in the air.

She swallowed hard, struggling to push those unwelcome thoughts aside. "A bit hungover, but Takashi cooked me breakfast, so I'm starting to feel a little better."

Ossian's gaze flicked to her, sharp as the blade he honed. "Takashi made you breakfast?"

His motions stilled.

"Yeah, I kind of smashed into him this morning with my plate of food," Adair laughed nervously. "It ended up all over the floor, and on us, and it was so loud in the dining hall, which obviously didn't mix well with my pounding headache..."

Ossian's warm chuckle caught her off guard, halting her mid-sentence. "Maybe I should give you one more day to settle in before we train. Last night's festivities seemed a bit much for you," he teased, his brow arched in amusement as he resumed grating the steel against the whetstone.

The implication of his words sent her cheeks flushing. "Oh, pshhh,"

Adair waved a dismissive hand, trying to counter his teasing. "I can totally handle a Scottish drinking party," she bluffed, awkwardly tugging the oversized sleeves of her sweater over her hands.

The steady, rhythmic sound of stone against blade ceased abruptly as ocean-green eyes locked onto the woman. "That was a typical Tuesday, Hanlon." A slow, enigmatic smile spread across Ossian's face as he stowed the blade. "Well, if you say you can handle it, then gas."

He stood, dusting himself off before gesturing for Adair to follow. The pair moved across the weathered wooden floor to an open area where a mat lay spread out, reminiscent of a dojo.

"We practiced a bit of self-defense on the island," Ossian began, his voice taking on an instructional tone, "and learned you have healing abilities. But we need to test for the others."

Reaching into his pocket, he produced a small pebble, its surface worn smooth by time. He held it out to her, his gaze steady and unwavering.

"Take this."

Adair hesitated before reaching out, pinching the stone between her fingers. Her amber eyes, filled with a mix of trepidation and curiosity, met his gaze.

"Move it," he instructed, crossing his arms across his broad chest. His half-lidded gaze appraised her, drinking in every flicker of emotion that crossed her face.

The woman *wished* to follow his instructions, but her eyes were drawn to the bulge of his biceps, tight against the fabric of his shirt. Swallowing hard, she forced her gaze back to the pebble.

Anxiety bubbled up within Adair, spilling out in a rush of words. "Move it like how? Like, up or down? Away or towards me? How do

I even draw *on* the power? Is it like the last time I had to heal my cut in Neverland? And what ability does this even test for anyway?"

Ossian's voice, firm and gruff, cut through her ramble. "Hanlon." He huffed and took a step back, running a hand through his tousled hair. "You need to calm yourself. Don't overthink it. This is to test for the Traveler ability. It doesn't matter what direction you move the rock. Just *move it*."

Adair nodded softly, her eyes fixed to the pebble. She drew in a deep breath, attempting to clear her mind, to reach deep within herself for that dormant power she had harnessed before, but his touch had been a catalyst back then. What was it about that hulking man that made her feel so *alive*? Images from the night before flashed through her head, and she felt the heat rise in her chest.

Stop it, Adair, she chided herself. *I am a Creator. It's time to act like one.*

Her brows furrowed as she glared at the still stagnant rock before her. A frustrated growl, low and primal, escaped her lips, causing the Celt's eyebrows to shoot up in surprise.

"Hanlon," Ossian said, moving towards her. "I know it *seems* difficult, but the pebble is an extension of you. Should be as easy as moving a finger." He closed her hand around the stone, his calloused fist wrapping around hers.

An unwilling gasp left Adair as electricity flooded her body at his touch.

The Irishman let out a huff, a smile tugging at the corner of his mouth. "What do they teach you in those American schools?" he teased.

"How to take tests and hide," she replied, a strangled laugh escaping her at the strange question.

Her confusion only grew when he released her hand and crossed the room, touching his palm to the wall. A bright portal abruptly opened up before them, shimmering with an otherworldly light.

"You coming?" Ossian asked.

Adair followed him into the celestial hallway, her breath stolen away as stars and galaxies swam before her eyes. A brilliant comet or meteor streaked by, leaving a trail of stardust in its wake. She couldn't be sure which, her senses overwhelmed by the breathtaking display.

The man turned his scrutinizing gaze on her. "What are we made of?"

Reluctantly, she turned towards him, shifting from one foot to another.

"Atoms?" she ventured.

Ossian sighed, a sound that was more growl than breath. He ran a hand through his hair, frustration etched on his face.

"Should've had Takashi doing this shite," he muttered.

Adair's heart pounded as he moved behind her, placing his hands on her shoulders. Gently, he turned her back to face the view before them, heat pooling in her middle from the feel of his rough hands on her body.

"Every Unremarkable creature, plant, stone, animal, *Deity*... We are *all* made up of the same thing," he said, his voice a low rumble in her ear. "We are all made up of galaxies. Stardust flows within your veins, as it does mine."

She fought to tear her gaze from the floor, reveling in the feel of his touch, and back to the beauty of the universe before them. The sight was almost too much to bear. "*How rare and beautiful it is to even exist,*" she whispered, the lyrics a soft sigh on her lips.

A warm chuckle sent a rush of air over her hair, leaving a shiver down her spine. "Couldn't have said it better myself," Ossian replied, giving her a reassuring pat on the shoulder before heading back toward the entryway.

"Oh, uh, it's from a song," Adair called after him, unsure if her words reached their target.

Stealing one last glance at the dazzling display, the woman slipped back through the doorway. By the time she crossed the threshold, Ossian's long strides had him nearing the exit of the gym.

"Best of luck, Hanlon," he called, waving a hand in farewell before answering his phone.

Suddenly, she was left alone once again, with nothing but her thoughts...

...and her goddamn rock.

Cheers echoed through the Keep, the sound reverberating off the walls and filtering down the stone hallway. Adair, feeling the weight of the pebble pressing heavily in her pocket, reluctantly set aside the book she had been absorbed in. The story had provided a wonderful escape from her training, but the enticing sounds of commotion proved too strong to ignore.

With a soft sigh, she pushed away from the comfort of her solitude and made her way toward the bustling command post.

As she approached, the light pouring from the room assaulted her vision, forcing her to squint. She quickly wiped at the corner of her eye beneath her glasses. The area had transformed into a lively gathering spot for members of the Divide. They huddled around the flat-screen televisions lining the walls, their faces a mix of concern and excitement.

The flickering monitors displayed live footage from international news networks, but only one broadcast had the volume cranked high enough to capture the room's attention.

A grim headline split across the screen:

Gas Main Explodes in New York, Destroys Half a Neighborhood Block: 78 Injured, 12 Dead, and More Missing.

With tentative steps, Adair moved closer to the clusters of people, befuddled by their varied reactions. She leaned toward a tall man shaking his head, her voice barely above a whisper. "Excuse me, sir. Why is everyone so invested in this?"

The man turned to face Adair, the solemnity etched into his features making her blood run cold.

"This has been in the works for months," he replied, his tone grave. "It was only supposed to take out the target building. Not half the block." He shook his head slowly. "Those poor Unremarkables."

Shock intermingled with horror as Adair's gaze snapped back to the screen, where the numbers of the injured and deceased continued to climb steadily.

Reactions in the room varied. Some of the members wore grim faces, while others clapped and exchanged smiles, as if reveling in the unfolding chaos. Hadn't Ossian just told her that every person was crafted from the same material? With a furrowed brow, she scanned the room for the

Irishman, her gaze eventually landing on him in the glass office above.

The Commander paced impatiently behind his desk, his face a deep shade of crimson that betrayed his mounting frustration. In stark contrast, Ossian lounged effortlessly in one of the plush leather chairs, one leg draped over the other as he languidly swirled a glass of amber whiskey in his hand. Though Adair felt a strong urge to speak with him, the gravity of Edmund's demeanor made it clear that now was *not* the time to interrupt.

Stealing one last, lingering glance at the row of televisions, she slipped out of the open space and sought refuge in the cool, stone-walled hallways. With her book securely tucked under one arm, she meandered back to her room, each step feeling as if her feet were dragging through thick, wet cement.

The weight of Ossian's indifference settled heavily on her shoulders, prompting Adair to tighten her grip on her novel, as if it could anchor the woman against the tumult of emotions swirling within. Her heart thudded against the pages, a rapid rhythm that mirrored the uneven beat of her footsteps on the cobbled stone.

As Adair curled her fingers around the cold iron handle, a familiar voice echoed down the hall, halting her in her tracks. She hesitated, torn between the urge to flee and the pressing need to confront the questions swirling in her mind. Turning to face the Irishman, she swallowed hard, her fingers turning white as her grip tightened.

Ossian approached her with a relaxed gait, his hands buried deep in his pockets. "Wanna hit the pub?"

Adair stepped back, but curiosity compelled her to meet his gaze. "What's wrong with the drinks in the dining hall?" she asked, making an effort to sound casual.

The Celt's nostrils flared slightly. "Just a chance to get out and see some *real* sunlight, Hanlon," he replied, his grin widening.

"Let me just put my book away."

Forcing a smile, she stepped into her room, feeling instant relief when Ossian didn't follow. His presence, a heavy weight, confused her emotions, and she needed a moment to gather her thoughts.

Adair snatched her purse from the small table by the entrance. She paused to catch her breath before stepping outside, closing the door firmly behind her. As the door latched, the echo of footsteps reverberated down the hall. A commanding voice called out unexpectedly, making her jump.

"MacCumhaill! We aren't finished!" The Commander advanced towards them quickly.

"Fecking shite," Ossian muttered, frustration boiling over as he slapped his hand against the wall.

Without a second thought, he yanked the woman through the doorway and slammed the portal shut behind them, effectively silencing Edmund's relentless cursing. Letting out a relieved sigh, Ossian sagged against the wall.

"So," Adair began, quietly trying to ease the tension. "About that drink…"

Chapter Sixteen

The pub was dimly lit, yet the two windows in the front allowed light from the setting sun to cast a warm glow on its rustic interior. Ossian strode confidently to the bar, claiming a stool with the casual authority of someone who felt entirely at home in this vibrant yet unpretentious space. With a broad grin, he greeted the bartender, a small man sporting stark, white hair, and a voice beaming with a rich familiarity.

Adair lingered a few paces behind, her posture tense and uncertain. She was enveloped by lively chatter and the clinking of glasses, but in her current mental state, the sounds barely registered. It felt as though she were trapped in a bubble, the noise muffled and distant. Finally, she settled onto a stool beside the Celt, retreating into her thoughts as Ossian continued the conversation with his old friend.

With a lilting laugh and a shake of his head, the bartender skillfully poured two frothy pints of Guinness from the tap, the dark liquid swirling gracefully in the glasses. Just as Adair reached for her drink, Ossian's hand intercepted hers.

"You have to let it rest," he advised.

Adair watched in fascination as the malty elixir transformed, a dance of toffee hues melding seamlessly into the raven-black depths of the brew. With an approving nod, Ossian seized his drink, prompting her to follow as they skillfully navigated through the crowd toward a cozy snug tucked away in the corner.

"Is the bartender Irish?" Adair asked as they sat, confusion knitting her brow at the rich timbre of the man's accent.

Ossian arched an amused eyebrow. "Sláinte! Here's to your second trip to Ireland!" he exclaimed, lifting his glass in a ceremonial toast.

Adair's eyes widened as a wave of shock washed over her. "Ireland?" The word escaped her lips, substantially louder than she intended, drawing curious stares from other patrons.

Heat flooded her cheeks, intensified by the attention. She redirected her focus to the beer in front of her, taking a tentative sip. The hoppy concoction swirled on her tongue, and her face lit up with delight.

"Oh my god, this is the best Guinness I've ever had!"

"Different than that shite in the States, aye?" Ossian quipped, his eyes sparkling as he took another hearty swig.

Adair nodded vigorously, savoring the rich symphony of flavors that danced across her palate. She placed her glass down, feeling its icy chill seep into her fingertips as she struggled to avoid the intensity of Ossian's scrutiny.

Instead, her attention wandered past the burly man to the flag that hung proudly above a black pipe stove. Its vibrant greens and oranges stood out in striking contrast to the dark wooden floors and matching furniture that surrounded the room.

She could vividly envision a night filled with smiles, drinks, and dancing, all set to the backdrop of traditional Irish tunes. Nadia would be by her side, her laughter ringing out, as a mischievous spark danced in her eyes.

A sharp ache twisted in Adair's heart at the thought, tightening like a vice around her chest. She took two large gulps of her drink, feeling the bite of the alcohol slide down her throat. She desperately hoped it would wash away the haunting memories of a former friendship that still felt all too raw.

"Why didn't we go to a pub in Scotland?" she asked, attempting to shake Nadia from her thoughts. Adair took another swig of her drink, craving the warmth it provided.

"Figured you would want to see where some of your family lived," Ossian said with a casual shrug.

Adair's eyes widened in surprise, sputtering into her drink. "Wh-what?"

The Irishman raised his glass, downed the remaining liquid, and leaned out of the nook to signal the bartender.

"This pub is connected to your family by marriage," he revealed, nudging her drink closer. "Started coming here about six months ago, but none of your kin are here today."

Adair could hardly believe it. The Divide seemed to know more about her family history than she ever had. If they possessed this information, then surely they were aware of the circumstances that had led her to live with her aunt. The thought made her stomach churn. It was unsettling to realize that strangers could access such intimate details of her life. The last thing she wanted was for others to look at her with pity, especially after all the effort she had put into rising above her past.

Even worse, *Nadia* was a part of all of this. The idea that her closest friend might have offered her comfort while intentionally keeping her in the dark about her own identity felt like a violation she simply wasn't ready to confront.

She needed another drink.

As Adair finished the last half of her beer, the bartender slid a fresh one in front of her, his weathered hands deftly lifting away the empty glasses.

"Sláinte, Cyril," Ossian said, raising his glass with a grin aimed at his friend. The man nodded in acknowledgment before returning to his duties behind the bar.

The Celt leaned in. "Aren't you going to ask?" He took a hearty swig of his Guinness, his seafoam eyes carefully appraising her.

"Ask about what?" Adair replied, her brow furrowing in confusion. She instinctively clasped her hands beneath the table, feeling a sharp sting radiate from the flesh of her left purlicue.

"We're just after that explosion, Hanlon." He crossed his arms over his chest, tilting his head as he waited for her response.

Typically, Adair would have meticulously tracked every movement the man made, but the casual way he mentioned the disaster sparked grotesque imagery in her mind. The very hands that had explored her body only the night before were now stained with blood, marked by violence and destruction. A wave of nausea washed over her, bile rising in her throat as she dug her nails deeper into her skin.

Ossian remained silent. She sensed the pressure of his gaze without lifting her eyes, feeling her skin crawl under the force of his attention.

"Must be hard not knowing what it's like to be discriminated against," he finally mused, voice laced with an unsettling mix of condescension and empathy. Adair shifted away from him nervously as he leaned over, forearms braced against the table. "I bet *Nadia* knows what it feels like."

His words sliced like a blade, clean and deliberate.

"Shut up," Adair whispered, her voice small yet laced with defiance. When her amber eyes met his, the fire within them blazed fiercely.

Ossian let out a laugh that cut through the tension, causing her to look away. She mumbled an apology as she focused intently on the intricate wood grain of the table.

The Celt's laughter faded abruptly, replaced by a heavy silence as his demeanor shifted to one of deadly seriousness.

"*Never* apologize for standing up for something or someone you care about," he said firmly.

Adair avoided his gaze, her fingertip meticulously tracing the condensation that had formed on the glass before her. After a tense moment of silence, she finally decided to confront the swirling unease that had been steadily building since she first saw the news report.

"Why," she began slowly, "were *some people* happy about the gas main explosion?"

She hadn't intended for her question to come across so pointedly, but the query had been gnawing at her. After hearing the news, Ossian had shown no signs of mourning or regret. Instead, she'd noticed an unsettling glimmer of *pride* in his eyes. So many lives had been lost, and the very thought of anyone celebrating that reality made her flesh crawl.

With a subtle nod, the Irishman pushed a half-empty glass toward her, an unspoken invitation to drink. She took a hesitant sip, the taste barely registering as she felt the knot of anxiety tighten in her stomach, sensing the storm brewing in his response.

Adair finally lifted her gaze to meet his, but quickly wished that she hadn't. She shifted uncomfortably in her seat, studying the rigid set of Ossian's jaw and the fierce intensity in his eyes. Silence hung thick between them, stretching on for what felt like an eternity.

Eventually, his lips parted, and his voice emerged, deadpan and unyielding. "Spoiler alert, Hanlon. Everyone dies."

Adair's mouth fell open in disbelief, struggling to comprehend how someone could react with such coldness. She felt the urge to speak, but a heavy lump rose in her throat, and hot tears quickly accumulated, threatening to spill over.

She had thought they were discussing a tragedy, yet here sat Ossian, utterly devoid of sympathy, as if the loss of life were nothing more than an inevitable fact. How could she have believed that a man like him could have *ever* cared for her? In her mind, she was just as *'unremarkable'* as those whose futures had been torn from them just hours earlier.

A frustrated sigh, more akin to a growl, erupted from across the table as Ossian chugged down his beer. He rose abruptly, wordlessly grabbing his empty glass before padding off to the bar.

It could have been a small kindness that he had left her alone, as it granted the woman a moment to dab at her eyes before her carefully applied makeup betrayed the true extent of her emotions. Adair downed the rest of her Guinness, willing the dark brew to take its hold and dull the sharp edges of dread tightening her chest.

After a few minutes, Ossian returned carrying a newly filled brew, a glass of whiskey, and a shot filled to the brim with a golden spirit. He placed the smallest of the three in front of Adair, who clasped her hands tightly beneath the table. Fingers trembling, she silently cursed herself for remembering to bring her purse but neglecting to grab her prescription in the rush.

The silence was deafening as Ossian took a measured sip of his whiskey, the amber liquid swirling gracefully in the glass. Finally, his gaze drifted away, and Adair seized the moment. Taking a deep breath, she grabbed the shot and downed its contents in one swift motion.

A shudder coursed through her as the warm alcohol filled her belly, momentarily clouding her thoughts. Ossian, seemingly unfazed, took another swig from his drink, the glass lingering at his lips as he considered something in the distance. A brief shadow flickered across his face, only to vanish as quickly as it had appeared.

"There will always be casualties in war," he uttered, his voice flat.

"But couldn't you have done more to make sure innocent people weren't involved?" Adair's voice was strained, her attention once again diverted to the grain patterns embossed in the wood of the table. She couldn't bear to meet his eyes, fearing what emotions, or lack thereof, she might find reflected in them.

Ossian shrugged casually, his whiskey still firmly clutched in his calloused hand. "Our cause is more important than a few Unremarkables," he replied dismissively.

The lump in Adair's throat resurfaced, prompting her to take two deep draughts of her stout. "It was more than just a few," she finally managed to reply, her frustration simmering just beneath the surface.

"Semantics." The Celt waved his hand as if he found the entire conversation tiresome.

His response only served to fuel Adair's anger. She understood that war came with casualties, but it wasn't the body count that troubled her the most. It was the complete lack of empathy in the man who had dragged her into this conflict.

"When we first discussed it, you made it sound like your goal was *freedom*... not anarchy," Adair challenged, her voice gaining steadiness as she confronted the doubts that had plagued her since their conversation began.

The Irishman swirled the dark liquid in his glass, as if judging its depth and complexity. "It *is* about freedom, Hanlon, but who doesn't love a bit of anarchy along the way?"

He took a deep swig from his drink, the corners of his mouth twisting into a faint, sardonic smile.

"So, you would be fine with the so-called 'Unremarkables' dying, as long as your precious *Creators* are spared? Do I have that right?" Adair's incredulity spilled over, frantically searching his eyes for some sign of empathy.

Ossian slammed his glass down on the table without warning, making Adair jump. Leaning forward, his substantial figure loomed in the dim light, nearly overwhelming the small space.

"Do you know what an anam cara is?" he asked, his voice low and deadly.

Adair shook her head, struggling to grasp the abrupt shift in conversation. She couldn't fathom where he was going with this, yet something in his gaze compelled her to listen.

"Anam cara roughly translates to 'soul friend.' It's a bond that transcends anything you could ever envision." Ossian bowed his head, voice now thick with emotion. "Losing one... It's like losing an arm or a leg. In truth, it is more akin to losing a piece of your very soul. Do you think me soulless, Hanlon?"

Adair shook her head, unable to speak.

"I've been at this a *long* time," he continued.

The Celt lifted his head, locking his stormy gaze onto hers with an unsettling intensity.

"Do not speak to me of death as if you know Her as intimately as I."

A shudder ran through Adair's small frame as the oppressive darkness that had enveloped the booth dissipated as quickly as it had arrived.

Ossian sighed and ran a large hand across his beard before standing abruptly.

"Cyril can get you back to the Keep," he said, his voice soft.

The man turned to leave but hesitated, as if weighing his next words.

"Patrick," he muttered, glancing back to lock eyes with Adair. "My anam cara's name was Patrick. And *he* was an Unremarkable."

With that, he strode toward the exit, leaving Adair alone to grapple with the emotional aftermath. With Ossian's imposing form now a memory, the tears flowed freely down her cheeks, leaving dark trails of mascara in their wake. She pulled off her glasses and shoved them into her purse, finding it easier to wipe away her tear-stained eyes without the added obstacle. Muffled sobs escaped her lips as she pressed her sleeve against her mouth, suddenly thankful for the Irishman's decision to choose the bar's secluded snug for their conversation.

As the sun dipped lower in the sky, more patrons began to filter into the pub, quickly filling the space with bodies. Seizing the opportunity, Adair slipped out the front door unnoticed. With a heavy heart, she crossed the narrow road, pausing to take one last look at the bar through her blurry vision.

Flahives.

Though she doubted she would ever be able to pronounce its name correctly, she still made a note of it on her phone. Ossian had mentioned that the owner was connected to her family by marriage, but her understanding of her extended family was limited. Aside from her aunt, who served as a vague reference point, much of her family history remained a mystery.

With a deep breath, Adair shoved her device into the pocket of her sweater and began to wander down the peaceful Irish street, aimlessly lost in her thoughts. As the sidewalk gradually disappeared, it gave way to rugged stone walls that lined the road. To her right, the ocean roared, while warmly lit houses dotted the landscape on her left. Adair made her choice instinctively, drawn to the rhythmic crash of the waves against the rocks.

Navigating a few more meters, she discovered a set of worn steps leading down to the bay, where the water surged far from the edge of the sand, indicating that the tide was out. The last remnants of sunlight spilled over the horizon, bathing the shoreline in the gentle grey hue of twilight.

As darkness began to veil the landscape, Adair's feet sank into the sand, and she found herself toeing at rocks scattered across the beach. Absentmindedly, she picked up a few and tucked them into her pockets, feeling the damp seep through her sweater. She didn't mind. Her distractions lay elsewhere, and she shifted her phone to her back pocket, making room for more of nature's treasures.

The relentless crash of the waves against the shore created a soothing rhythm, gradually easing the overwhelming weight of the past three days that had threatened to pull her under.

Adair walked along the shoreline, her hair whipping in the sea breeze as she pushed forward. A dark shape jutted up in the distance, like a lighthouse guiding the lost. As the woman numbly focused on the silhouette, her foot struck a stone that skittered across the packed sand, causing her to stumble in her drunken state.

"Stupid fucking rock," she muttered under her breath.

She prepared to kick it closer to the surging tide, eager to clear her path of the annoyance. However, as she bent down to act on her impulse, something unusual caught her eye.

Unlike the smooth stones filling her pockets, this one was perfectly round and rough to the touch, featuring a peculiar hole carved straight through its center. Delicately, Adair sank to her knees and began to dig into the cool, damp sand. As she retrieved her find from the gritty embrace of the shore, tears began to trickle down her cheeks once more.

Holding the rock up to the remaining light, she carefully turned it over in her fingers, tracing the edges where the sand clung stubbornly. A manic laugh escaped her lips, surprising even herself.

Clutching the stone tightly against her chest, she felt the moisture of the sea spray mingle with her tears, soaking through her shirt and creating a cool sensation against her skin. Memories of her mother flooded her mind with piercing clarity, and she cradled the stone as if it were the most precious treasure in the world.

Life had once been vibrant, alive with color and light. Adair still remembered the sun-drenched days in the garden, where petals danced gently in the breeze and laughter echoed endlessly among the blooms. The day her mother was taken from her, it felt as though a filter had been cast over her world, draining all the vivid hues and leaving everything cloaked in shades of grey.

In response to the tragedy, her father, Michael, had become a ghost within their home. He seemed to avoid her gaze, as if it were a mirror reflecting his own pain. The day he signed away his parental rights was etched into Adair's memory, the pen gliding across the paper with a finality that burned. It shattered any remaining sense of stability she had, propelling her across the country to live with her mother's sister, Laura. In her new surroundings, she desperately sought to rediscover those fleeting glimmers of joy, but they felt increasingly rare, slipping further and further from her grasp.

Fortunately for Adair, her aunt was perceptive and had swiftly noticed the heavy cloud of depression and anxiety that had wrapped itself around her. This realization led to a seemingly endless cycle of therapy and psychiatrist visits, each appointment feeling more invasive than the last.

She often felt like a lab rat, dissected and scrutinized under the harsh light of their questioning. Laura's gentle insistence pushed her toward finding the right doctors and medications, and after much trial and error, she finally began to see the light at the end of the tunnel.

Adair had met Nadia shortly after, a kindred spirit who had entered her life like a warm breeze. Though the surrounding nightmare still has its claws embedded, she found that she could move more freely, as though the weight of the world lifted, ever so slightly, from her tired shoulders.

"The grief of losing someone never truly lightens," Laura often reminded her. *"Instead, you grow stronger from carrying the weight."*

Adair frequently felt bogged down by the heaviness, but her aunt and Nadia remained by her side, always ready to help share the burden.

Small things still brought her some measure of comfort: landing a job at her local bookstore, the soothing sounds of rain tapping against glass windows, the brisk chill of cold weather, and an escape into a good book. Yet, even these joys felt tainted, underscored by a dark mass that lurked just beyond her line of sight.

Every day was a fight against an invisible enemy, an unseen assailant that wore her down, waiting patiently for her to fail. Her mother had been her armor, but with that vital piece of her essence stripped away, all that remained was a constant state of hypervigilance.

Beth, Adair's mom, had shared countless stories and fairy tales with her over the years, but one story always lingered in her mind.

The tale of the hag stone.

According to legend, if you found one and looked through it, you could catch a glimpse of Tír na nÓg, the land of the fairies. While plenty of hag stones were available online, Adair always yearned to travel to Ireland in search of her very own.

Looking down at the treasure in her hand, it felt as though Beth had guided her to this moment. Adair's breath hitched in shallow, uneven gasps as another sob tore through her, folding her in on herself. She didn't pay mind to the waves that were now lapping at her jeans. The water was rising steadily, bringing with it the numbing relief she was desperately seeking.

A shudder coursed through her small frame, likely a reaction to the cold that had begun to soak through her clothing. In her chest, a small flicker of something began to bloom. Adair gripped the stone tightly in one palm and clutched her necklace in the other.

Another wave crashed, the frigid water now lapping at her chest. A warm sensation brushed against her shoulder, and for a moment, she feared it was something from the sea, ready to take her to the Otherworld.

The flicker in her chest burned a little brighter as she tried to shrink away from the touch. Strong hands pulled her to her feet, but her knees buckled beneath her. Despite the struggle, her fists remained tightly clenched around her precious items. Panic surged as the world around her began to spin.

"Hey, hey."

A smooth voice wrapped around her like a heated blanket, steady hands preventing her from succumbing to the waves.

"I've got you."

She felt herself being lifted under her knees, and the scent of cinnamon and sandalwood flooded her senses.

"I've got you," he repeated softly, his voice a lifeline amidst her fading consciousness.

He cradled her shivering form against his chest as the world around her began to drift away.

In that moment, she surrendered to his warmth, seeking comfort in his presence while the darkness closed in around her.

Chapter Seventeen

Hours Earlier

The warmly lit corridors stretched ahead of Takashi, casting elongated shadows across his face as he moved steadily toward the war room. Tablet cradled in one hand, he immersed himself in the diagnostics from the last raid. His thoughts were trapped in a loop, replaying footage of his latest prototype with relentless clarity. Data flickered across the screen, but it was the burden of failure that pressed most heavily against his skull.

The sound of cheers echoed down the hallway, pulling Takashi from his musings. Filled with curiosity and caution, he crept closer, sensing the air shift as he approached his destination. The energy of the room ahead buzzed like the restless heartbeat of an unseen beast. He slowed to a stop just short of the doorway, one shoulder brushing against the edge of the frame.

Members of The Divide were gathered around television screens, their faces illuminated by the sharp glow of the monitors. A headline scrolled across one display in stark red letters:

Gas Main Explodes in New York, Destroys Half a Neighborhood Block.

Takashi's heart dropped at the sight. He didn't need to ask. He already knew.

It was one of ours.

He scanned the room, unease twisting in his stomach as he took in the wide range of expressions. Some faces glowed with pride, while others remained calm and unreadable, as if they were simply witnessing another routine event.

High above, through the glass-walled office that overlooked the command floor, he could see Ossian lounging in a chair, a drink in hand, as though it were any other night. In contrast, Edmund looked ready to shatter the entire room in his rage.

Nothing new there.

He continued his survey, noticing a woman near the back of the room, her small frame standing rigidly as her glasses caught the pale glow of the screen. A furrow of confusion creased her brow, and nervous energy seemed to radiate from her in waves.

He hadn't seen Adair since that morning, and now she stood alone, her earlier jovial expression vanished. In its place was a look of vulnerability that hinted she might break at any moment. He longed to speak with her, but just as he gathered his courage, she unexpectedly turned and started making her way toward the exit.

Takashi weaved through the crowd, slipping between bodies that pressed too close together. His eyes remained fixed on Adair's retreating form, a quiet figure disappearing through the far doorway like a shadow sliding from view. She moved like someone unraveling stitch by stitch, and he knew instinctively that she needed air.

By the time he made it into the corridor, she was already a few paces ahead. He followed at a respectful distance, not wanting to startle her, but also unwilling to let her vanish entirely. The lights flickered faintly as she moved, and he caught a glimpse of the worn leather book clutched tightly to her chest. Her fingers were white at the knuckles, locked around its spine as though it were the only thing keeping her grounded. There was something achingly vulnerable in the way she held it, like the words inside might hold her together when everything else threatened to fall apart.

Takashi slowed his steps, wrestling with the urge to call out. She was clearly struggling. Her shoulders were tense and pulled in, the lines of her back rigid with unspoken distress. But was this the right time to intervene? Would his presence be a comfort, or just another weight she didn't ask to carry?

He had struggled with his emotions since his mother's passing, but something about Adair had carved out space in him he hadn't expected. She wasn't like the others in the Divide. This person hadn't yet been worn down by the endless cycle of violence or detached from the consequences of their missions. She still felt everything, openly and without apology. Where others hid behind masks or silence, she wore her heart just beneath the surface of her skin. And tonight, in that room full of cold celebration and callous indifference, her pain had shone through like a signal fire.

He admired that about her, more than he could ever say. Her grief wasn't weakness. It was a strength that none of them seemed to remember how to carry. If she was trying to make sense of that pain alone, perhaps he could be the person who helped her hold it, even if only for a short while.

Takashi exhaled slowly and steadily, then resumed his pace with quiet determination. He didn't know precisely what he would say when he reached her, but he knew one thing with certainty...

He would not let her disappear into the dark without knowing that someone *saw* her.

Final in his decision, the scientist rounded the corner only to stop cold at what he witnessed.

Ossian stood outside the entrance to Adair's quarters, half-consumed by the corridor's shadows. His head was bowed, a deep frown carved into his rugged features. Whatever thoughts moved behind his eyes were unreadable, but the tension in his posture spoke volumes.

Takashi didn't have time to weigh his options before everything erupted into motion. Adair stepped out of her room, clutching her purse with both hands, just as Edmund's voice cracked through the corridor like a whip.

"MacCumhail! We're not finished!"

The scientist froze, his mind racing to catch up as Ossian's jaw clenched and his palm slapped hard against the stone wall. A shimmering portal erupted beside him, light spilling into the hallway like a flood. In one swift movement, the Irishman grabbed Adair's hand, and the pair vanished through the doorway.

The Commander skidded to a stop, rage burning behind his eyes. His gaze landed on Takashi, who now realized with cold certainty that he was standing in full view.

"Track them," Edmund ordered, voice sharp with fury.

A moment later, the Commander was gone, his footsteps receding into the distance.

Left alone in the silence, Takashi's thoughts spiraled. The portraits lining the hallway seemed to glare down at him with ancient judgment as he turned and headed back toward the lab, unease coiled tightly in his chest. He could still hear Edmund's command ringing in his ears, but it clashed violently with his conscience.

After everything Adair had endured, how could he justify *more* surveillance? She deserved space and peace, but Ossian had a history of going rogue. Tonight felt like one of those nights.

The man could charm and fight his way out of almost anything, but Adair wasn't built that way. She was strong, yes, but her strength was quiet and still healing. There were fractures within her that she hadn't even admitted to yet.

Takashi reached his desk and hovered over the keyboard, hesitation written in the set of his shoulders. His instincts screamed that this was a betrayal. Still, Edmund rarely gave an order twice.

With a reluctant sigh, he tapped the keys, and the screen flickered to life, cold, sterile, and impersonal. He navigated through encrypted firewalls, working until the hidden dashboard materialized, revealing the familiar interface of the metamorphose tracking system.

For a moment, Takashi simply stared, his fingers hovering above the keyboard, unmoving. Finally, he typed in their names, and two faint signals emerged on the map, glowing softly like distant beacons.

Leaning back in his chair, his jaw clenched. *Sorry, Addie.*

Remembering his orders, he typed out a concise message to the Commander, relaying the coordinates of Ossian and Adair's location. His fingers moved on autopilot as he set a passive alert within the tracking system, designed to notify him the moment their signals returned to the

Keep. It was not the most thorough solution, but it provided him with a measure of oversight without being invasive. A compromise, however imperfect.

Nearly thirty minutes later, the chime of a system notification sliced through the quiet hum of the lab. Takashi swiped to the map, hope briefly flaring in his chest, but it faltered the instant he laid eyes on the screen.

Only one signal had returned.

Why would she be alone? There were only two options. Adair had either miraculously developed the traveler ability in an impossibly short amount of time, or Ossian had left her behind, isolated and vulnerable.

The man didn't wait for his brain to catch up. His body moved first, already thumbing out a message to Rowan, the Keep's primary Traveler, as his feet hit the floor in a dead sprint. His heart pounded a frenzied rhythm against his ribs, dread knotting tighter with every step. Whatever Ossian's reasons, whatever game the man thought he was playing, Takashi refused to stand by and let someone be abandoned.

Not her. Not this time.

The night staff barely lifted their heads as he burst into the command center. A few glanced up, only to return to their monitors, unfazed by the intrusion. Rowan, already waiting near the portal archway, met his gaze.

The man was half-dressed, hoodie thrown over a wrinkled T-shirt, jeans tugged on in a rush, his brown hair tousled and damp with sleep. The glittering threshold beside him pulsed with celestial energy, the soft cosmic shimmer casting streaks of amethyst across the floor. Without exchanging a word, the two men stepped through the portal and emerged at the last known location Adair's metamorphose had pinged.

Flahives Pub was alive with late-night warmth and noise. The air was heavy with the scent of spilled beer, woodsmoke, and something earthy, like peat and old stone. In one of the cozy front nooks, a trio of Irish Trad players filled the air with their welcoming and lively tunes.

Takashi pushed through the doorway first, his sharp eyes scanning the crowd as he threaded through the tables. His presence earned a few curious glances, but no one interfered. He searched for her dark hair, her lithe frame, but the crowd was full of strangers.

No Adair.

Rowan stepped in behind Takashi, his gaze sweeping across the space with the quiet precision of someone long accustomed to fieldwork. His movements were unhurried but deliberate. He caught the eye of the bartender, stepping forward without hesitation.

"Seen a dark-haired girl?" Rowan asked as he reached the bar. He lifted one hand to indicate a modest height. "About yea tall. American. Accompanied by a man. Broad. Tall. Shoulder-length hair."

The bartender studied them with wary interest, his gaze lingering on Takashi with a flicker of unspoken judgment before settling on Rowan. He scratched his neatly cropped white hair before leaning a little closer, his accent thick but not unkind.

"Lass left not long after Oísin stepped out the front," he said, nodding toward the door with a tilt of his chin.

Takashi's muscles tensed. His jaw flexed tightly as he stepped forward. "Any idea where she went?"

Cyril gave a slow shake of his head, his expression unreadable.

"Headed right. That's the last I saw of her."

Rowan silently slid a folded bill across the counter in gratitude before turning and striding toward the exit. Takashi followed, phone in hand, his eyes scanning the faintly glowing signal trails on the screen.

"Why would she be there? The only thing in that direction is the beach," he muttered, worry etching his brow as he walked.

They stepped out into the quiet embrace of the Irish night. Moisture gathered low over the landscape, wrapping the road in a silvery veil. Moonlight filtered through the thick clouds, casting everything in a ghostly, dreamlike glow. Rain fell in a fine, steady mist that clung to their jackets and turned their hair damp within seconds. The old two-lane road stretched into the darkness ahead of them, flanked by low stone walls worn smooth by centuries of sea air.

Takashi barely noticed the cold. His attention remained glued to the screen in his palm, the soft glow reflecting in his eyes as he murmured under his breath, "Where the hell did you go, Addie?"

The crash of waves reached them moments before the sand did. Descending the wide stone steps carved into the hillside, they reached the shoreline, the surf roaring beneath a sky that felt far too vast and uncaring.

Takashi flicked on a new piece of equipment calibrated to track residual heat signatures through his metamorphose. He found nothing while scanning the sand, but as he angled his wrist toward the water, a shape blinked into view through the overlay, faint yet unmistakable. His breath hitched.

Addie.

He took off across the beach, his feet pounding against the wet-packed sand. Sea spray lashed against his cheeks as he raced forward, the wind ripping at his sweater. Stones slid underfoot as he surged ahead, not bothering to slow as the figure finally came into view.

She was waist-deep in the freezing ocean, facing the open water. Her silhouette was motionless against the horizon, and for one horrifying second, he feared he had found her too late. As the sea shifted around her, a tremor rolled through what little he could see of her body.

He plunged into the waves on instinct.

The cold hit him like a blow, numbing and merciless. His body screamed in protest, but he dove forward, pushing through the surf with single-minded focus. Water surged around his knees, then his thighs, every movement a battle against the elements. When he reached her, the sight stole the breath from his lungs again.

Adair trembled so violently that her entire body seemed to vibrate, her skin pale and lips tinged an alarming shade of blue. Her hands clutched something tight against her chest, her grip rigid and unyielding. She didn't turn. Didn't speak. Didn't even seem to know he was there.

"Addie," Takashi said gently, his voice low and calm, despite the frantic pounding of his heart. Panic would do them no favors.

He stepped closer and reached out slowly, carefully brushing his hand against her soaked shoulder. Her skin was icy, nearly unresponsive. She slightly flinched at the contact, but didn't pull away. His voice softened further.

"I've got you."

He slipped his arms around her frail frame, one beneath her knees, the other behind her back. Lifting her from the water, he cradled her tightly against his chest, holding her as if she might slip through his arms. Her head fell against his jacket, her body limp and shivering with relentless force.

"I've got you," he whispered again, this time to himself, like a promise he wasn't willing to break.

Her breathing was uneven, hitching in tiny gasps against his chest, but she didn't resist.

Takashi trudged back through the icy surf, the water dragging at his legs with every step. The shore rose to meet him, but he didn't pause.

Not once.

The scent of the ocean was overwhelming, but beneath it lingered something faint and familiar: mint and vanilla, the essence of who she was. It stirred something deep within, a quiet reassurance that whatever remained of her had not yet disappeared. He drew her closer, as if holding her tightly might keep it from slipping away.

Rowan waited at the top of the path, his face unreadable as he watched them approach. Takashi climbed the stone steps without speaking, the weight of Adair in his arms anchoring him more deeply than exhaustion or the bite of the wind ever could. Rain slicked his clothes to his skin, and the chill had sunk into his bones, but none of it mattered.

He didn't stop pressing forward. He didn't ask why she had been left alone. He didn't need to know the details right now.

She was safe. She was with him.

And for now, that was enough.

Adair caught the familiar scent of Nadia's expensive perfume wafting through the air. Her friend had purchased it during one of her glamorous trips to fashion week, likely in Milan or Paris. Nadia had even gifted her a bottle of the same fragrance, but it never quite suited her. The scent felt out of place on her skin, prompting her to regift it to someone she felt it would fit better.

As she sank into the enchanting scent, Adair was transported to a ballroom reminiscent of Jane Austen novels. She gazed out at couples waltzing gracefully to the music of a live band, but no matter how much she tried to ignore it, an unsettling chill lingered in the air.

As the song grew in intensity, the once beautiful dancers became shadows, their masks falling to reveal faceless blurs lost in the ebbs and flows of the dance. Adair frowned at the back of a man she could barely make out, a figure with cropped grey hair who appeared to be slipping away. The stranger vanished quickly as she was whisked into the swirling crowd by a gentleman she fully recognized.

She turned to face her dance partner, who felt both familiar and distant amid the haunting visions surrounding her. Ossian moved with grace, his tawny hair pulled back into a neat ponytail, a furrow creasing his brow. His mouth was set firmly in a frown, framed by his neatly trimmed beard.

His eyes, however, conveyed a depth of emotion she struggled to decipher. The Irishman appeared to be saying something, lips moving rapidly, but the thunderous music drowned out his words.

The Celt halted abruptly, his eyes filling with a silent apology as his features began to distort before her. The man's nose elongated grotesquely as fur erupted across his body. Bones audibly cracked as his body twisted and contorted, a horrifying transformation that doubled his size in an instant. His clothing tore at the seams, while his once tranquil, sea-foam green eyes shifted to a piercing, blood-red.

Adair inhaled sharply and took a step back, stumbling over the hem of her dress. Panic froze the woman in place as the hulking, wolf-like creature loomed closer. A twisted smile stretched across its maw, glistening with salivation.

She opened her mouth to call for help, but no sound emerged. In a last-ditch effort, she threw up a hand in defense, the gold of her bracelet reflecting the light of the candles that adorned the room.

Adair let out a piercing scream as Ossian lunged forward, his once familiar form now a nightmare of flesh. The creature's jaws clamped around her throat with a sickening crunch, dragging her back into the suffocating darkness she knew all too well.

Chapter Eighteen

The room was too bright, and Adair's head throbbed as she raised a hand to shield her eyes, tugging at a cord in the process. The sound of hurried footsteps echoed in the room, followed by the soft click of a light switch. As she lowered her palm, the glow from the bedside table illuminated the lanky figure of a man at her side.

"Here." The voice, low and husky, felt like a soothing balm as she reached for the paper cup the man offered. Her fingers trembled as they brushed against his, and a fleeting warmth spread through her skin before she fully wrapped her hands around the small glass.

The first sip of water was like ice down her throat, jarring and wonderful all at once. She tried to drink more quickly, desperate to soothe the sandpaper dryness in her mouth, but the man tilted the cup back with a soft shake of his head.

"Not so fast," Takashi murmured.

Adair attempted to sit up in protest, but the room immediately pitched sideways. Her vision blurred, and a sharp wave of nausea pierced her stomach. A soft moan slipped from her lips as she pressed a hand to her temple, fingers splayed as if trying to physically hold her head together.

Takashi reacted instantly, one arm slipping behind the woman's back as the other guided her gently down to the pillow. Gradually, the spinning eased, the pain inside her skull quieting to a dull roar.

She blinked, letting her eyes adjust, and found the scientist sitting in the chair beside her. He was hunched forward slightly, watching her with a mix of worry and relief etched onto his face.

"This is going to sound like a stupid question, but how do you feel?" he asked, his British lilt comforting a part of her addled mind.

She smiled weakly. Her throat was raw, and her voice came out in a rasp.

"Like shit."

Embarrassed.

Something in her chest cracked at his expression, and he leaned back with a relieved exhale, one hand adjusting his glasses. "Well, that's an improvement. At least you're awake."

Adair chuckled, though it came out more as a grimace. The movement sent a fresh ripple of discomfort through her head.

"Yeah. I guess that's something." Her voice faltered when she spoke again. "Were you..."

She didn't finish.

The memory of the freezing water clawed back through her, dragging her breath with it.

Takashi nodded slowly. "Rowan brought us there," he said. "I'm not a Traveler, obviously, but we arrived quickly."

He hesitated, then added with a note of strain in his voice, "Finding you like that wasn't... ideal."

The understatement made her stomach twist. She remembered the cold, the numbness, and the weightlessness of the sea.

Then warmth. Arms around her. A voice saying her name.

"Thank you," she whispered. "For saving me."

Takashi's cheeks flushed as he looked away, coughing into his hand to mask the reaction. "It was nothing, really. The Commander asked me to track you, so I used your metamorphose. When Ossian returned and you didn't, I... I just had to make sure that you were okay."

Her heart stuttered as she experienced a multitude of emotions at once. If Takashi hadn't come, she might not have survived. That reality loomed heavy over her. But there was also Ossian and the unbearable silence he had left her with. She didn't understand his pain, but whatever it was, it hadn't given him the right to leave her like that.

It was all too much to process.

Adair cleared her throat. "So, I'm assuming Nadia was here?"

Takashi blinked, clearly thrown by the shift in topic.

Adair looked around the room for the first time, her tired eyes sweeping over the space. Bright white roses bloomed from nearly every surface. The arrangements were wild and uneven, spilling out of mismatched vases with a kind of chaotic vibrancy that could only belong to Nadia. Neon-colored 'Get Well Soon' signs jutted out like miniature flags, accompanied by handwritten notes that read things like *I Am Sorry* and *Please Don't Die* in bubble letters and crooked lines.

It was so unmistakably *her* that Adair couldn't help but let out a soft chuckle.

Even so, the warmth that flickered in her chest was tangled in a web of unresolved pain. The betrayal still sat heavy in her gut, but somehow, in the way Nadia always did, she had managed to wedge herself back in, not with words, but with flowers and frantic, heartfelt scribbles. It was *just* like her, and that hurt more than it should have.

In a moment of painfully perfect timing, a loud bang echoed from the hallway outside. The sharp sound of a door crashing open was followed by a familiar voice shouting with full-bodied indignation.

"I don't care about your dumb fucking visitor rules! Let me in!"

A screech of shoes across the tile rang out next, then a quick shuffle of feet, and finally, a knock at the infirmary door.

Takashi glanced toward the entrance with a sigh, his shoulders already tense in anticipation. He turned back to the incapacitated woman, his brow creased with concern.

"Do you want me to tell her to go away?" he asked gently.

Adair hesitated, torn. The last thing she wanted was to put Takashi in the middle of her mess. Not after everything he had already done for her.

But she wasn't ready for this. She was still raw, her mind spinning with everything that had happened, and the thought of facing Nadia in this moment just felt like too much.

Her gaze dropped to her lap as she gave the slightest shake of her head. "I'm sorry. I just can't..."

"It's okay, Addie," Takashi said before she could finish. He spoke in the same calm and sure tone he'd used in the freezing surf. "I understand."

Standing slowly, he brushed off his pants and paused at the door. For a moment, he breathed like he was bracing for impact.

Then he opened it.

The door didn't make it halfway before Nadia shoved her way through with all the force of a hurricane. It struck Takashi square in the face, the edge catching his nose and sending his head back with a sharp snap. He stumbled, hand flying up as blood began to seep between his fingertips.

Nadia didn't notice, or if she had, she paid him no mind. Her chest rose and fell in ragged breaths, hair wind-tossed and cheeks flushed, as her eyes locked onto Adair.

"You," she said, pointing a shaking finger across the room.

Takashi stood frozen beside them, clearly caught between pain and disbelief. His glasses were crooked, and he had one hand pinching the bridge of his leaking nose as he looked from one woman to the other.

"Okay," he said quietly. "I think I'm going to give you two some privacy."

"Some bouncer you are," Adair muttered.

The man sighed in defeat, shoulders sinking as he backed toward the exit. Without a word, he slipped through the doorway, pulling it gently shut behind him.

Nadia stood in the center of the room, the silence suffocating. The woman's eyes searched her face with desperate urgency, but Adair couldn't bring herself to meet her gaze. She looked anywhere else, hands fidgeting anxiously in her lap.

Nadia took a step closer, but still, Adair refused to look up.

"Adair," she said softly, then louder, "Addie, please. Look at me."

When that didn't work, Nadia reached out and took her face in both hands.

"*Look*, bitch," she said, her voice cracking in the middle, "I almost lost you."

Adair finally relented, and what she saw made her breath catch.

There was so much in Nadia's gaze. She could see grief, fury, guilt, but beneath it all, there was something even more difficult to bear...

Love.

Adair's resolve crumbled under the weight of it, and she looked away, eyes stinging.

With a heavy sigh, Nadia let go and dropped to the edge of the bed. She reached for the woman's hand, curling her fingers around it with surprising gentleness. Her voice softened.

"Please," she whispered, "Just talk to me."

Adair looked down, her thumb brushing absently across the back of Nadia's hand. That was when she noticed it.

Her brows pulled together. "Where's your bangle?"

Nadia's mouth pressed into a line, then relaxed.

"It's gone," she said quietly. "It fell off the night you saw me at the Keep. The bangle... it was an aegis. Part of the oath I swore when they assigned me to watch you. I couldn't break it, Addie. I wanted to tell you everything so many times, but the binding wouldn't let me." Her voice trembled at the end, desperately pleading for her friend to understand.

Adair blinked, trying to process the words, but Nadia didn't stop.

"When I was first sent, yeah, it was a job. Surveillance. Just watch the girl, keep her close. But it didn't stay that way. You became my best friend. My family. I didn't just *care*. I loved you." Her shoulders dropped as she let out a breath. "Hell, I *love* you, Addie. You're my *sister*. The oath wouldn't let me tell you about this world. Not until the binding was broken. When you saw me at the Keep, that was it. The magic let go. The bangle just... fell off."

Adair sat with that for a long beat, her heart thudding unevenly. Then she tilted her head and narrowed her eyes. "Why didn't you just say so in the first place?"

Nadia raised an eyebrow. "Uh, someone was drunk off their ass and screamed at me in front of an entire hallway. Ring any bells?"

Adair tried to hold back a smile but failed. A laugh burst from her chest, sharp and wet at the edges, and Nadia joined in, loud and snorting. Both girls were crying and laughing at the same time, the tension airing out of the room like a soft breeze.

Nadia leaned in for a hug, but Adair pressed a hand against her shoulder, holding her back. Her expression turned serious. "Don't you *ever* lie to me again."

Nadia held her gaze and nodded solemnly. "I won't. I swear it."

This time, when the hug came, Adair let it happen. She leaned in and closed her eyes, breathing in the familiar, grounding scent of her best friend, and for the first time in what felt like ages, something inside her settled.

It took a little over a week, but Adair finally managed to escape the infirmary. She was supposed to be released days earlier, but a sudden fever followed quickly by a persistent cough had set her back. Knowing that cursing her unreliable immune system would do nothing to speed her recovery, she chose instead to focus on how thankful she was for her many visitors. While confined, Takashi, Nadia, and Mia had been working endlessly to keep her spirits afloat.

Nadia appeared the first afternoon with a fresh bouquet of white flowers and Adair's favorite candy. The sweet scent of roses and eucalyptus was lovely, and the chocolate and peanut butter should have felt like comfort, but the air between them was heavy with unspoken words. Despite the warmth of their long friendship, the betrayal still lingered, leaving cracks neither of them knew how to bridge. Still, it wouldn't stop the pair from trying.

The next day, Nadia returned, this time with Mia in tow. They came armed with more treats and battery-powered candles, but the true highlight was the book Nadia had hidden under her arm. The wrapping of the next installment to Adair's current favorite series was so elegant that she hesitated to tear into it. Sensing her reluctance, Nadia stepped in to help, all while scolding the healers for not doing their jobs properly.

Mia rolled her eyes and mouthed *bossy* at Adair, earning a soft giggle from the bedridden woman.

Takashi brought his own brand of comfort—an armful of video games, movies, and a warm container of rice porridge made using his mother's own recipe. He had an uncanny way of knowing what Adair needed before she could even ask.

His quiet attentiveness touched her deeply, and she had to turn her head more than once to wipe away tears that had snuck up on her uninvited. They settled into a gentle rhythm, talking when they wanted, sharing easy silences when they didn't. On the rare days he was unable to visit, it was either because Nadia was already there or he had been called back to the lab. Still, throughout it all, Takashi remained a comforting constant she was grateful to have.

On the day of her release, Nadia made an event of it, as she did with everything. It was one of many things Adair had always loved about her. Nadia never needed a reason to celebrate, treating even the most minor victories as sacred. Adair suspected this was more than just a welcome-home gesture. It was Nadia's way of trying to stitch things back together, to return to the rhythm they once shared.

The trio greeted her with balloons and confetti poppers, cheering as she emerged from the hospital ward. Hand-painted signs lined the walls and hung from the ceiling, some wishing her a swift recovery, others offering congratulations. One particularly large banner read, in bold, uneven letters, "*Welcome Home, Andy.*"

Nadia stopped in her tracks and turned to Takashi, hands planted firmly on her hips, her perfectly manicured nails digging into the fabric of her jeans. "Who the fuck is Andy?"

Looking affronted, Takashi turned to Mia, seeking backup. "Andy Dufresne. Seriously? Don't tell me your girlfriend hasn't seen *Shawshank Redemption.*"

Adair chuckled as the three of them bickered, but beneath her laughter was an ache she couldn't quite swallow. Ossian hadn't spoken to her once since the night he had left her at the pub. Not a single visit, nor a word about continuing her training or testing her abilities as a potential Deity.

The uncertainty gnawed at her, relentless and sharp, and the smile she wore didn't quite reach her eyes. She cleared her throat and gently interrupted them. "I'm kinda tired. I think I'm going to head to my room."

Nadia's brow furrowed, the shift in mood not lost on her, but before she could speak, Takashi jumped in.

"We were going to take you to a sorcery sphere match tonight."

Adair blinked. "A what?"

Nadia cut in with a grin. "Don't even ask if we use lances, bitch. It isn't like jousting."

Adair let out a soft laugh despite herself. As much as she wanted to curl up in solitude, she didn't have the heart to say no. Instead, she agreed, asking only for time to take a proper shower before heading out to the game. She had no idea what to expect. The only instruction she received was a text from Nadia that read:

Don't forget your boots. Trust me.

The hot shower was a gift. She let the water pour over her, soothing the lingering aches in her body. After weeks of enforced stillness, it felt good to move again, even if her muscles protested with every stretch.

As she dried off, her thoughts drifted back to Ossian. The emptiness his silence left in her chest felt vast and stubborn. She tried to push the feeling away. Tonight wasn't about him.

Adair pulled on soft, fleece-lined black leggings, a long-sleeved shirt, and her warmest jacket. A knitted beanie, freshly blow-dried hair tucked underneath, completed the look. Whatever this sorcery sphere was, she was ready. Or, at least, she hoped she was.

Takashi, Nadia, and Mia stood just outside the towering entrance of the main portal, their breath curling in the frosty evening air as they waited for Adair to arrive. The moment she stepped through, Nadia flung her arms around her in a dramatic flourish, pulling her into a tight embrace that was equal parts affectionate and theatrical.

"Look at you, all cozy. Ready to freeze your ass off?" Nadia grinned, her large silver eyes sparkling with mischief as she took in Adair's bundled-up form.

Adair arched an eyebrow, a smirk tugging at her lips. "You make this sound so appealing," she replied, catching the quiet scrutiny in Nadia's gaze but choosing to ignore it for now.

Takashi stepped forward with his usual charm and a gleam in his eye. "You'll love it. Think soccer, but more violent and a whole lot more magical." His enthusiasm radiated off him, infectious and warm despite the frigid cold, and Adair felt the second flicker of genuine curiosity stir within her chest.

The walk to the sorcery sphere stadium was brief, but the temperature dropped sharply, biting at Adair's cheeks and nose. As they reached the grounds, the field came into view, glowing beneath the surreal shimmer of magical lights. A kaleidoscope of color rippled across the arena, as if responding to the mounting excitement of the crowd. Cheers rang out, a chorus of voices rising and falling, and Adair's eyes widened as she took in the vast arena.

It was less a field and more a battlefield, massive and pulsing with enchantment. Glowing sectors were marked off by flickering magical barriers that crackled with latent energy. Hovering just above the ground were translucent orbs of swirling light, each one vibrant and mesmerizing in a different hue.

Players moved through the space with a breathtaking mixture of grace and aggression. Some wore sleek leather armor traced with glowing runes, magic woven visibly into their gear. A few soared effortlessly overhead, their powers propelling them through the air, while others vanished and reappeared in rapid bursts of light, leaving shimmering trails behind them like shooting stars.

"Welcome to Sorcery Sphere," Mia said, leaning closer with a mischievous smile. "It's kind of a big deal around here."

Adair stared, jaw-dropping in disbelief. "This is insane. How does anyone survive this madness?"

"They don't always," Takashi replied with a grin.

Nadia jabbed an elbow into his ribs, but there was a glimmer in her eyes that mirrored Adair's growing excitement.

As they found their seats, Adair felt her thoughts begin to shift, drawn away from her lingering uncertainties. She sank into the rhythm of the spectacle, absorbing every detail.

On the field below, a lone figure emerged from one of the arched entryways. He carried a long bronze pole topped with the sculpted head of a boar, its maw agape, a wooden tongue lolling with every movement. She tilted her head, intrigued as he raised the pole to his lips.

A low, resonant note echoed across the stadium, deep and haunting like a typical war horn. The sound swelled into something melodic, then shifted again into a piercing, ethereal call. It was strange, beautiful, and eerie, like a symphony meant to awaken something ancient. The man moved slowly across the field as he played, his steps deliberate. As he neared the far side, he released one final note, high and trembling, a call that reminded Adair of a distant elk's cry.

The crowd held its breath as silence descended, and then, without warning, the match began.

Both teams surged into action, casting spells at blinding speeds and darting across the battlefield with stunning agility. Orbs of energy were hurled toward glowing rings at either end of the field. Players moved like comets, dodging, weaving, leaping, and colliding in an elegant chaos that left Adair breathless. The game was wild and beautiful, its violence tempered by artistry, and she felt herself completely swept up in it.

Partway through the match, a chill ran down her spine, sharp and sudden. Her instincts flared as her pulse quickened. She scanned the crowd, a strange awareness prickling at the back of her neck as her eyes locked onto a figure standing in the shadows near the far edge of the stadium.

Ossian.

He was still and unreadable, his gaze focused solely on her. The world around them faded into nothing, the vibrant lights and thunderous cheers reduced to background noise. Adair couldn't move. Her breath caught in her throat, her heart thudding in her chest. There was something in his expression, something unreadable but intense. Then, as quickly as he had appeared, he turned and melted into the crowd, vanishing from sight.

Adair remained frozen, the echo of his presence lingering like a poison mist. The rest of the match passed in a blur. She faintly registered Takashi's shouts of celebration and Mia's laughter beside her as questions flooded her mind with relentless urgency. Why had he come? Why hadn't he approached her? When the final horn sounded, Adair barely reacted.

Nadia's voice broke through the fog. "Hey. You okay?"

Adair blinked, forcing a smile as she nodded. "Yeah. Just, a lot on my mind."

As they began their walk back, Adair lagged behind the others, her hands shoved deep into her coat pockets, eyes fixed on the ground. Ossian's presence haunted her, his silence even louder than words might have been.

Something was coming. She could feel it in her bones, an undercurrent of change stirring just beneath the surface.

Whatever it was, she knew it would change *everything*.

Chapter Nineteen

The training grounds lay still, save for the occasional crackle of magic in the air. Adair stood alone, her breath rising in misty clouds in the biting cold, hands clenched tightly at her sides. Her fingers trembled, not from the chill, but from a weight far greater and more defeating.

She had been coming here every day for weeks, and all she had to show for it were burns, bruises, and a patience that was worn thin from constant failure. If life possessed even a hint of mercy, she mused, there would be a cinematic montage whisking her past this grueling chapter. A fast-forward through the struggle. Some triumphant sequence of breakthroughs and epiphanies where everything finally clicked.

But there was no montage.

Just more cold mornings and the slow grind of inadequacy.

Omar stood facing Adair, his arms folded and gaze fixed on her with cool detachment. The master of elemental magic, particularly fire, watched as she struggled with even the simplest of tasks. No matter how hard she tried, the power seemed to elude her grasp, seemingly mocking her relentless efforts.

"Again."

Adair exhaled slowly and lifted her hand, palm facing upwards, her fingers shaking from the effort. She closed her eyes and reached for that small core of heat buried inside, an elusive flicker she could sense hidden beneath the surface. With every ounce of strength that remained, she willed it to respond.

A spark flared to life in her hand. The woman eagerly adjusted her fingers, curling them slightly to cradle the flame. She hoped to coax it into something more stable, but as quickly as it had appeared, the fire sputtered and died, leaving only a faint puff of smoke rising from her palm before fading into nothing.

Dammit.

Adair's jaw clenched as she shook out her hand, heat flushing up her neck in humiliation. She didn't need to look at her instructor to know that his expression hadn't changed.

Omar stepped forward, his boots crunching softly in the frosted dirt. "You're overthinking it again. Fire isn't math. It's not a problem to be solved. It's instinct. You need to let go and guide it with direction, not logic."

Adair blinked up at him, incredulous. "Let go, but with direction?" she echoed. "That's not helpful. That's a riddle."

Omar only lifted a brow. "And *yet*, it's true."

She wanted to scream. Or cry. Or both.

Letting go had never come naturally to Adair. Instead, she found her safety in control. When her world spun too quickly, she could ground herself by counting her breaths, swallowing her pills, and adhering to her carefully crafted routines. But that wouldn't help her here. The answer lingered outside of her comfort zone, and she was determined to find it.

Adair summoned heat to her fingertips. She concentrated harder this time, intent on holding it steady. The flame sparked to life with surprising ease, quicker than before, and its glow flared just a touch brighter. It still danced with that same delicate uncertainty, but now there was a hint of steadiness in its sway, as if something inside her had finally aligned. A small, breathless smile tugged at her lips.

For a fleeting heartbeat, pride rose in her chest.

I'm doing it!

Without warning, the fire surged. The heat turned wild, licking violently across her palm. Adair cried out, stumbling backwards as the fire snapped out of control. Her hand jerked away on instinct, and she slapped frantically at the hem of her coat where the flames had kissed the fabric.

"Fuck," she hissed, the curse barely audible over the angry crackle of extinguishing embers.

Omar didn't flinch. "You're gripping too tightly," he said, his tone level. "The more you try to strangle it into obedience, the more it resists. You need to trust the element to meet you halfway."

"I'm trying," Adair snapped back, though her voice cracked with exhaustion.

Her hands were shaking again, not just from the magic but from sheer mental fatigue. How many hours had passed? She had lost count. Each failed attempt felt like a reminder that she wasn't good enough. Not for this, not for Ossian, and not for whatever the gods had planned for her.

"Take a break," Omar said, softer this time. "You're wearing yourself thin. Pushing harder isn't always the solution."

Adair's thoughts drifted to the Irishman. Ossian hadn't come back to observe her training in months. What if he had already decided she wasn't worth it? What if every day she had spent floundering like this was just proving him right?

"No," she said, straightening with shaky resolve. "I can do it."

Omar studied her intently, his eyes searching. Finally, with a reluctant nod, he gestured to the space around her. "Okay, let's try something different. A flame shield. Nothing aggressive. Just enough to wrap around your body."

Adair nodded, though the knot coiled in her stomach only pulled tighter. She lifted both hands in front of her, fingers spread, eyes narrowing with determination. Magic sparked at her fingertips, eager and impatient, but still formless. She reached inwardly, grasping for control, willing the energy to bend, to shape itself into the familiar curve of a shield, but it wouldn't listen. The fire bucked against her hold, and with a sudden burst of resistance, it lashed out.

Flames shot in sharp, uneven jets, streaking away from her palms with no clear guidance. One seared across the dirt at her feet, leaving behind a trail of scorched earth. Another snapped sideways, curling with reckless heat, and came far too close to her leg. She flinched, heart leaping, and scrambled back a step before the fire could find skin.

Adair bit her lip and lowered her hands, chest heaving. "I can't..."

"Stop," Omar said, stepping in with a raised hand. "You're thinking about controlling the flame. I need you to connect with it."

She stared at him, hollowed out and weary. She didn't feel connected to the fire. She didn't feel connected to *herself* half the time. Was it possible for Deities to make mistakes? It felt like a mistake to bestow magic to someone who struggled so greatly with control.

The thought spiraled, looping tighter and tighter until it choked her. Frustration cracked open beneath her skin, sharp and sudden, and the magic responded before she could stop it. Heat surged up her arms and burst outward with a violent force, flames leaping from her in every direction.

It was an eruption, pure and raw.

Omar didn't recoil. He lifted one hand, expression unreadable, and with a breath so calm it almost felt cruel, he absorbed the fire into his palm. The flames vanished in an instant, snuffed out by a soft word of elemental command.

"Adair," he said, shaking his head. "You're not the first to struggle with this, but you need to stop fighting yourself. You're not trying to *tame* the fire. You're trying to *work* with it, and that takes time."

The woman said nothing. Her throat was tight with unshed emotion, her muscles aching with every heartbeat.

She had no fire left in her, not the magical kind, nor the metaphorical one...

Just the smoldering remains of disappointment.

Omar stepped closer and placed a hand gently on her shoulder. "Enough for today. You're doing more harm than good at this point. Go rest. Give yourself the space to come back stronger."

Adair nodded slowly, though every step she took away from the center of the training field felt like something valuable was being stripped from her. Each stride carried the quiet ache of disappointment, not just in how the session had gone, but in herself.

She had come here hoping to leave stronger. Instead, she walked away with the bitter sting of defeat, along with the old, familiar dread that maybe she hadn't changed at all. Maybe she was still the weak girl she had always been, pretending to belong in a world that kept proving that she didn't.

It was during this reluctant march across the grass that she noticed Nadia perched on a bench near the edge of the field beside Adair's abandoned bag. Somehow, she hadn't seen the silver-haired woman sitting there the entire time.

Nadia looked up from her phone, her fingers flying furiously across the screen, full lips pressed into a thin, displeased line. Her perfectly shaped brows were pinched in frustration, but her features softened the moment she saw Adair approach.

"Hey," Nadia said, her voice laced with concern. "How are we feeling...?"

Adair didn't answer the question. She didn't have the energy to admit the truth, not out loud. Instead, she asked her own. "Nasreen?"

Nadia rolled her eyes, flipping her long hair over one shoulder with practiced ease. "She told Omar I would train with him today, but I made plans with Amelia to go to Bali."

Most of the Keep operated with a 'don't ask, don't tell' approach when it came to personal lives. Still, Adair had noticed over the past month that Mia and Nadia were always careful about where and how they showed affection. It was subtle, but it was there.

Adair slung her bag over one shoulder and adjusted the strap before glancing back at her friend. "Any idea how you're going to get out of it?"

Nadia's phone buzzed again. She looked down, a flash of irritation crossing her face. White, stiletto nails tapped on the glass in rapid succession as she shot off another text before shoving the device into

Adair's hand to read.

The thread between Nadia and Nasreen was lengthy and full of tension, but Adair stood still, reading every line. Nasreen had been badgering her daughter about neglecting her elemental training and accusing her of prioritizing social media metrics over her role in the Divide. There were a few less-than-subtle jabs about vanity, responsibility, and how Nadia was losing sight of her duty to her family and their cause.

Nadia, to her credit, had defended herself, pointing out that her content actually *did* generate income, supplementing what she received from the Divide. Still, her mother had swept the argument aside. The last few messages were all in bold, pushing the same tired agenda that Nadia's responsibilities were bigger than herself, and that the Divide's mission aligned with everything she was *supposed* to stand for.

"Fuck, that's rough," Adair breathed, handing the phone back with a grimace.

"That's the godsdammned understatement of the century." Nadia snatched her phone and shoved it into a gym bag that perfectly matched her lilac-colored workout attire. "The last thing I need is a surprise visit from her, so I'll appease the woman while I still have the choice.

"I'm sorry, Nadi." Adair offered the words with as much sincerity as she could manage through the fog in her head. Her medication had worn off hours ago, and everything felt like it required more effort.

"Not as sorry as I am." Nadia tossed the words over her shoulder as she strode toward the training grounds, already steeling herself for another performance.

Leaving her friend to her reluctant training, Adair headed into the

Keep. She kept her head low, eyes darting from face to face, avoiding recognition wherever possible. Her morning had been hell, and she couldn't bear the thought of conversation, not even the casual kind. As she neared the exit of the war room, she scanned the path ahead, pausing only once she was sure that no one was watching.

With one last glance at her surroundings, Adair slipped her fingers into the secret pocket of her bag, retrieving a small bottle of water and her pill organizer. She hesitated for only a moment before taking two bars from the pack and swallowing them down with a quick sip of water. Everything went back into her bag in a flurry, hidden from view before guilt could take hold.

She already felt drained, her body and mind worn thin, and it wasn't even lunchtime.

Thankfully, there was one place within the Keep that offered something akin to peace. It had taken her weeks to find it, and when she did, it had felt like stumbling upon something sacred. She wished someone had pointed her towards it sooner, but nevertheless, she was grateful for her quiet discovery. Without a second thought, her feet began to move in the direction of her newfound sanctuary.

Adair pushed open the heavy oak doors of the library, the soft creak of the hinges breaking through the stillness.

The shift in atmosphere was immediate.

Inside, the world slowed. The relentless grind of elemental training, the pressure of eyes watching her every move, and the endless cycle of proving and failing were nonexistent here. The air was cool, a balm against her flushed skin, and the dim lighting made the towering shelves feel almost protective.

Books lined every inch of the space, their spines faded and frayed, while dust motes floated in the beams of light spilling through the arched windows. The scent of aged parchment and leather filled her lungs with each breath, and with it came a strange calm. This was a place of knowledge, but more importantly, it was a place untouched by judgment.

Here, she could just *exist*.

She walked slowly, her fingers trailing along the edges of worn bindings, grounding herself with the rough texture beneath her skin. Stories of faraway kingdoms, long-dead heroes, and ancient wisdom lived here, breathing between pages. Among it all, Adair still held hope that she would someday find the key to the riddle the Woodwose had given her.

She found her usual chair in the far corner of the room. The high back curved around her, offering privacy without the need for walls. She sank into it with a slow breath, allowing her muscles to release one by one. As she settled in, her gaze drifted to the courtyard below, where Omar and Nadia had already begun sparring, sparks of electric energy flashing and fizzling in the air. Omar deflected Nadia's strikes with ease, while her friend's frustration mounted with every failed attempt.

With an amused chuckle, Adair turned away from the scene to open the book resting in her lap. Though she had chosen the tome carefully, her eyes barely skimmed the words. Her thoughts were elsewhere, still tangled in the lines of the riddle that had haunted her for weeks.

I was an armed fighter.

I kissed a man. I send enemies running, and warriors will be put into battle.

I'm hanging on the wall now, with proud ornaments, when men get answers.

Name me.

She had read it a hundred times, maybe more. The phrases echoed in her mind at all hours, taunting her with their meaning just out of reach. She had chased them through ancient texts and scrolls, flipped through old maps, and asked the most learned Creators in the Keep for clues. Still, none of the lines made any sense.

Her thoughts drifted to an entirely different part of the Keep. The Sorcery Sphere arena. She had only been there once, yet the memory lingered vividly in her mind. The match had unfolded like a fierce battle of magical forces. A battle?

I was an armed fighter.

Adair sat up slowly, pulse quickening. It had never quite fit... until now.

I send enemies running, and warriors will be put into battle.

Sorcery Sphere wasn't just a game. It was a stage for combatants who wielded their energy like weapons, who stepped onto the field with fierce intent. Pride. Fearlessness. And just before all that power was unleashed, the entire arena had gone silent.

Adair recalled the lone figure who carried a bronze pole, its top adorned with the sculpted head of a boar, a wooden tongue dangling from its open mouth. When he raised the horn to his lips, the notes had surged through the stadium, reverberating like a slow earthquake. This sound didn't merely signal the start of the match; it had left the crowd breathless in its wake.

And now, sitting in the quiet safety of the library, it hit her.

Kissed.

The line in the riddle had never made sense to her.

I kissed a man, and I send enemies running.

But what if it wasn't romantic at all? What if it was about breath? About ritual? The man who played the horn had pressed his lips to the mouth of that strange instrument, had breathed life into it, and in doing so, had stirred something in everyone who heard it. That kiss had been an offering, a call to arms.

Her eyes widened as the pieces began falling into place. It most likely wasn't *that* horn. Not the one from the arena. But it was a starting point. A reference. The horn in the riddle had to be something similar. Something once used by warriors. A horn blown before battle.

A horn *kissed* in ritual.

The chair scraped softly against the carpet as she stood, her movements sudden and sure. Adair's mind was already moving faster than her body, leaping through corridors of memory and possibility. The Woodwose's riddle had always seemed like some cryptic game, but maybe it was simpler than that. She didn't know where the *actual* horn was yet, but at least she knew what she was looking for.

Adair pulled her notebook out of her bag, quickly scrawling her thoughts as she rushed towards the exit. She was nearly to the library doors when a familiar voice stopped her cold.

"Hanlon?"

A familiar man stood in the doorway, his expression unreadable. He hadn't spoken to her since that night at the pub. In the days that followed, his silence carved out a hollow ache in her chest. Now, as she stood before him, the tension that had been building surged to the surface.

"Ossian," she said, her breath catching. She tried to sound steady, but the tremor in her voice betrayed her. "I think I found something... about the riddle."

His brow lifted with careful interest. "You've been busy."

The weight behind the statement lingered longer than the words themselves. It wasn't just about her research, and they both knew it. She felt a flicker of heat crawl up her spine, tempered not by shame, but by the quiet defiance she'd begun to lean into. With her medication bolstering her confidence, she straightened her back and held Ossian's gaze, unwavering.

"I'm trying to prevent more *casualties*," she said plainly.

Ossian inclined his head slowly and looked down at her, his jaw feathering.

She continued, words spilling out like a blade finally drawn. "I can't just sit around training, waiting to fully manifest. If this is my chance to end the war, I have to do something. I have to try."

A faint smile touched the corner of his mouth, subtle and quickly gone. "That's not what I meant..." It seemed like he might say more, but he reined it in, letting the silence hang before nodding once. "I'm impressed. Tell me what you've found."

Adair hesitated for a moment, but then nodded, stepping closer to show him what she had written in her notebook. As they pored over the details, the tension seemed to ease, replaced by a sense of shared purpose.

"The horn," Ossian murmured, tracing his finger across the scrawled ink. "I remember the stories from when I was a lad. Borabu."

Adair's brow furrowed. Her lips parted, dry, and she ran her tongue along them, eyes catching briefly on the movement of his hand. She forced herself to refocus.

"Bora-boo?" she asked, unsure if she was pronouncing it correctly.

He nodded. "The battle cry of the Fianna."

The Irishman let out a breath and rubbed a hand down his face, glancing toward the ceiling. The tendons in his neck flexed with the motion, and Adair looked away before he caught her watching.

"You were right about it not being the carnyx from the field," he said. "It's the Dord Fian, a *specific* horn. It belonged to the Fianna, an ancient order of warriors."

Her heart skipped. "Shit," she whispered. "But... there has to be a way to find it."

The Celt didn't answer right away. His eyes searched hers, holding her gaze with quiet intensity before giving a slight nod and turning back toward the library.

Adair followed Ossian without hesitation, head spinning with the revelation. This wasn't just any horn, nor was it the same one featured in the Sorcery Sphere games. This was something far older and more significant. A wave of excitement coursed through her, mingled with a tinge of frustration. She was closer to unraveling the riddle, but now another layer had been added to the intricate puzzle.

Ossian led her into a section that had gone unnoticed, a quiet, forgotten corner cloaked in dust. The shelves here groaned under the weight of old tomes, their leather bindings cracked and brittle, gold lettering faded by time.

"We need the histories," he said, his voice low but focused. "The Fianna's horn was said to be used in times of great need, to rally warriors and summon aid. If the Dord Fian still exists, there might be some record of where it was last seen."

Adair nodded, though she couldn't shake the sense of urgency pressing against her chest. She could feel time slipping through her fingers, the weight of the war and the responsibility on her shoulders growing heavier by the moment. She reached for a thick volume, brushing the dust from its cover before cracking it open.

They read in silence, time slipping by unnoticed as page after page turned beneath their fingertips. Ossian moved with ease, eyes darting across lines of old script like he'd done this hundreds of times. Adair occasionally stumbled over the archaic phrasing, but her mind stayed sharp, her focus unrelenting.

It wasn't until she turned a particularly brittle page that her breath caught. She leaned in, squinting at the script. The translation came to her slowly, but the words struck deep.

"And when the flames of war threatened to engulf all, the Fianna sounded their Dord, and the mighty horn's call summoned warriors from realms both near and far. The horn was last heard at the Stone of Destiny, where the King of the Old World stood."

Her heart leapt in her chest. "Ossian, look at this," she said, pushing the book toward him.

He leaned over, reading in silence, and the crease in his brow deepened.

"The seat of Fionn," he murmured. "That's in Alúine. But the Dord Fian... If that's where it was last heard..."

"Do you think it's still there?" she asked, her tone hopeful.

He shook his head slowly. "It's possible. But Alúine's been raided over the centuries. Artifacts scattered, stolen, destroyed. Still... it's a start. If it was ever at the seat of Fionn, there could be more clues there."

Her stomach dipped slightly. "Alúine's in Ireland, isn't it?"

The last time she was there, Ossian had abandoned her. She didn't speak that truth out loud, but it hung between them all the same.

Adair drew in a breath, trying to push aside the fear. If the Dord Fian could rally the kind of power that the legends described, if it could shift the tide of war, then she couldn't afford to hesitate.

"When do we leave?"

Ossian watched her for a moment, eyes narrowing with quiet consideration before nodding. "We'll need to prepare supplies, and I'll need to get you a permission slip from Eddy."

She blew out a breath, the resolve settling in her chest like stone. Whatever lay ahead, they were finally moving in the right direction. The scattered pieces of the puzzle were beginning to form an outline, and even if the shape was blurred and incomplete, it was something.

As they gathered their things, she glanced at Ossian, catching the profile of his face as he moved through the soft light of the library. The distance between them hadn't vanished, not entirely. But for the first time in a while, it felt bridgeable, as if they might find their way back to one another through the shared weight they carried.

"We'll get through this," she said, more to herself than him.

He glanced her way, and something warm sparked behind his gaze.

"Aye."

They stepped into the quiet hallway together, leaving the dust and dim light of the library behind. Outside, the world waited, feeling uncertain, dangerous, and impossibly vast.

This time, however, they walked into it side by side, carrying the first thread of an answer that might just save them all.

Chapter Twenty

Adair's fingers tightened around the leather-bound journal as she walked beside Ossian in silence. The weight of it felt different now, as if the riddle contained was beginning to take shape beneath her touch. While she kept her eyes fixed ahead, her mind lingered behind, still struggling to process what they had discovered back in the library.

"Are you ready?" Ossian spoke beside her, pulling her back into the present.

She turned slightly, studying him out of the corner of her eye. The Irishman's expression held that familiar confidence, but it was softer now, shaded with something else. That fleeting emotion danced across his features before disappearing, but not without reminding her that this was no simulation or theoretical exercise.

What they were trying to accomplish was *real*. Tangible. If the Dord Fian truly existed, then *everything* was about to change.

Adair swallowed, then gave a slight nod. "As ready as I'll ever be," she replied, her voice steadier than she felt. "How long do we have?"

The muscles in Ossian's jaw shifted as his gaze slid down the long stretch of corridor ahead. "We need Eddy's approval first. That'll take a few hours. Long enough to get what we need. If all goes smoothly, we can leave by dawn."

Adair nodded again, slower this time, the thought of Ireland stirring a fresh twist of nerves in her stomach. Her last visit had not been a pleasant memory, and the feeling of being abandoned in that place still lingered just beneath her skin. There was no turning back now. If the horn was out there and had the power to turn the tide of the war, she had to see it through.

Too many lives hung in the balance to justify any vacillation.

She watched as Ossian veered away, his long strides carrying him down the corridor until the shadows swallowed him whole. A long breath escaped her as her shoulders eased.

It was happening. There was no longer any room for doubt, no remaining time to question whether she was ready. She *had* to be.

Adair pivoted on her heel, swiftly retracing her steps to her quarters, keeping her footsteps silent to avoid any unwanted attention. There were too many eyes in the Keep, and while some might not give her a cursory glance, others had a keen sense for the difference between duty and something unsanctioned.

A dry smile crossed her lips. Was she on a rogue mission?

The thought transported her back to that fateful day. She remembered the Commander's voice raised in fury after the gas main explosion, recalled Ossian sitting there with maddening calm as he absorbed the verbal blows without flinching. Had that mission been approved, or had he gone off-script then, too? The idea made her stomach drop.

Inside her room, Adair moved quickly, grabbing the worn travel bag from beneath the plush bed to pack the items she needed: a change of clothes, daggers, and her journal filled with notes about the Dorn Fiann.

Adair hesitated before kneeling to reach beneath the mattress. Her fingers rapidly found the wooden box, its surface decorated with intricate carvings she had traced a thousand times. With a quiet snap, it clicked open, revealing the familiar bottle of colorful pills staring back at her.

For a moment, she sat there, crouched beside the bed, staring at the multitude of tiny capsules with a complicated sort of resentment blooming in her chest. She hated needing them. Hated what they meant. But the alternative—the suffocating terror, the spiral of anxiety that turned her mind to static, the depression that dragged her under, drowning her on dry land—was worse. She didn't have the luxury of unraveling now. Not when so much was at stake.

Adair popped open the bottle and slipped a few pills into her back pocket, keeping them close yet concealed. As her reflection in the floor-length mirror caught her eye, she couldn't help notice that she didn't look brave. Her face was pale, her eyes weary, and her hair disheveled from the day's training. Despite that, there was something new that had emerged in the curve of her jaw and the set of her shoulders. A steadiness that hadn't been there before.

As she closed the box and slid it back beneath the bed, a knock startled her. She froze mid-motion, looking towards the source of the sound.

"Addie? It's Nadia."

The woman's voice was muffled, but there was an edge to it. Adair's fingers fumbled to adjust the bedsheet, hiding the disrupted space before crossing the room to open the door.

Nadia stood in the hallway, freshly showered in a black off-shoulder blouse, silver hoops catching the light, a layer of dark lipstick punctuating her incredulous expression.

"Hey," Nadia said, sweeping her eyes over her friend's face. "You look like you're about to do something really fucking stupid."

Adair exhaled slowly through her nose. "Yeah, you could say that." She hesitated, then added, "Ossian—"

Nadia cut her off. "I already got the skinny from Amelia. What the fuck, Addie?"

She pushed past her, stepping into the room, and zeroed in on the half-packed travel bag resting on the velvet duvet.

Adair shut the door with a quiet click and turned to face the woman. "We're going to Ireland," she said softly. "We found something in the library. We think it might be connected to a riddle I've been trying to solve. To the war. Maybe even a way to stop it. We just need to find this horn, and Ossian—"

Nadia's brows shot up. "You can't *seriously* be thinking about trusting him again."

Adair shifted her weight, avoiding her friend's gaze. Her hands clasped awkwardly in front of her, nails itching to dig into skin. "I know what happened last time. But I'm fine."

"Liar," Nadia said, the word striking like a slap to the face.

Adair's head snapped up. "What did you just call me?"

"I said you're a *fucking liar*, Adair Hanlon."

Nadia was moving before the sentence had settled, furiously crossing the space between them. "You are anything but fine. And don't you dare pretend otherwise. You haven't been okay since he *left* you in Ireland. And now what? You're just... following him back?" She hurled the travel bag to the floor with one hand, its contents scattering in every direction.

Adair's chest ached, but she lifted her chin, stubborn even in the face of truth. "You don't understand, Nadi. You didn't hear the things he told me. The things he's been through. What he's sacrificed. He didn't *mean* to hurt me."

Nadia's voice rose, her hands clenching at her sides. "And what about what *you've* been through? What about *you*, Addie? He *abandoned* you. You almost *died*. There is no story you can tell me that makes that okay."

The heat of it stung. And maybe it was the pressure of the day, or the gnawing self-doubt she'd been trying to ignore, but something in Adair snapped. Her voice came out too loud, the words brittle and raw.

"Maybe you're just *jealous*."

Nadia blinked. "What?"

Adair pushed on, even as regret began to curl in her stomach. "You're jealous that he was the one who told me the truth. You had years to say something, *anything*, and you didn't. But *he did*."

Nadia huffed out a humorless laugh. "Jealous?" Her tone cracked. "You think *I'm* jealous because he decided to give you the crash course, *before* dragging you halfway across the world to ditch you?" Her voice rose again, sharp as glass. "You *know* why I didn't tell you. *I couldn't*. I was bound by that oath. But I've *always* been honest when it mattered. That's why I'm here now, trying to stop you from walking off a fucking cliff."

Adair stepped back, hands raised in a clear dismissal. "I can't do this with you right now. I don't have the energy."

Nadia raked her fingers through her silver hair, visibly shaking. "Believe what you want," she said bitterly. "Go find your magical horn with your 'charming' Irish heartbreaker." She used her lilac stiletto nails to use air quotes, punctuating her point. "But listen to me, Adair. He is *not* who you think he is. He's not a hero. He doesn't help people. He just fucks them and leaves a trail of broken hearts behind. Every. Time. If you want to cling to a sinking ship, go ahead."

Without waiting for a response, Nadia spun on her heel, storming out with a slam of the door.

Adair stood, unmoving, her arms wrapped around her middle. Her pulse pounded in her ears, and her throat felt dry. They had just begun to rebuild what was once broken between them, but now it all felt like kindling again, ignited by the same fury that had previously torn them apart.

Maybe Nadia *was* jealous. Or perhaps she was trying to protect her. Adair didn't know what hurt more: not knowing which to believe, or the realization that she no longer had anyone in her life whom she could trust without question.

The woman's gaze drifted to the papers on the ground. Her notes on the Dord Fian had been scattered during the argument, and she moved toward them thoughtlessly. She began to collect the fragments with slow, mechanical movements, her mind spinning out of control.

Nadia was often right about many things, but Ossian's dedication to Creators and his commitment to ensuring everyone's freedom set him apart. He *was* a good man. That meant her friend had to be wrong about him, right? The silence only fueled her overthinking, but at least sorting through the papers gave her something to do. Something to control.

Adair moved through the space with quiet purpose, folding and unfolding the same few shirts over and over again, the repetition steadying her.

Lunch came and went.

Then dinner.

She ignored the dull pang of hunger, too tangled up in everything else to care. Her phone buzzed twice beneath the blanket on the bed, but she didn't reach for it, unready to hear anyone's voice.

By the time night settled fully outside her window, Adair hadn't changed her clothes or showered. The energy required to do either felt unattainable. Her skin itched beneath the fabric of her workout clothes, hair clinging to the back of her neck, but she didn't move. Her pills had worn off long ago, and without their dulling effect, every small thought echoed louder than it should have.

She dragged the thick fur blanket from the back of the couch and pulled it around herself as she climbed onto the bed. Her limbs felt heavy, her body sluggish from the emotional weight of the day. She curled inward, pressing her cheek to the pillow, and stared at the wall until her vision blurred, the tears coming without warning. Chest aching with every breath, eventually exhaustion swept her under, dragging her into a restless, broken sleep.

The first morning light had only just begun to trickle in as Adair made her way to the meeting point. She was standing at the edge of the main portal chamber, bag slung over her shoulder, when she spotted Ossian emerging from the armory. He moved with calm precision, his gear strapped across his body. His expression was unreadable, but there was a spark in his eye, something quiet and determined that didn't quite reach his mouth.

"Got everything?" he asked.

Adair nodded, gripping the strap of her bag tightly. "Yeah."

Her response felt strained, yet it was the best she could manage in the moment.

"Eddy granted us permission to leave. Two days. That's all we've got."

She blinked. "Two days," she echoed, trying to keep her voice even. "No pressure, right?"

A flicker of amusement crossed Ossian's face, a wry smile curling the corner of his lip. "Wouldn't be fun without a little pressure."

Adair managed a faint smile in return, but her thoughts were still spiraling from the night before. Nadia's voice, raw and accusing, had rooted itself deep inside her mind. Even as Ossian stepped forward and pressed his palm to the wall, she couldn't stop the feeling that part of her had been left behind in that room, hidden beneath scattered pages and shattered remnants of trust.

The portal opened in a rush of light, revealing the shimmering celestial hallway. The pair walked without speaking, their steps echoing along the polished path as the destination steadily came into view. When they stepped through to the other side, they emerged onto a narrow road just outside a quaint Irish village. The crisp morning air nipped at Adair's skin, prompting her to pull the leather jacket tighter around her body.

They walked for a while, Ossian concentrating on their mission, while Adair was lost in her thoughts. Stealing a glance at the Celt, she couldn't help but notice the massive broadsword strapped to his back. He moved as if it were an extension of him, every step seemingly more assured than the last. It was that unshakeable confidence that both drew her in and made her question everything. Could she really trust him?

Her thoughts kept circling back to Nadia's words.

He just fucks them and leaves a trail of broken hearts behind.

A lump formed in her throat. Ossian had always been enigmatic, but she thought she had glimpsed something deeper in him. Was it real? Or was she just another pawn in whatever game he was playing?

"Something on your mind?" Ossian's voice broke through the quiet.

Startled, Adair blinked, shaking her head. "Not really. Just thinking about what comes next. If the Dord Fian is really where the texts say... I don't know. It's a lot to process."

Ossian nodded once, his gaze still fixed ahead. "'Tis, but we've done impossible things before. Just need to take it one step at a time."

The words were intended to calm her, to anchor her in the present, but they rang hollow. Adair understood that this wasn't just another step. Human lives were at stake, and failure was not an option.

The pair continued on the path, the narrow wall-lined road winding gently through the countryside. The cold morning mist hadn't lifted. If anything, it had thickened around them, pressing in at the edges, muting the world into a strange, suspended quiet.

Adair's thoughts drifted once again to her argument with Nadia, the sharp words echoing in her mind. They intertwined with her growing doubts about Ossian, swirling together like a storm she couldn't escape.

The Irishman remained silent beside her, cutting through the mist with unwavering purpose, unfazed by their surroundings. Adair felt the urge to ask him about Nadia's warning, to gauge whether he was aware of the mistrust that seemed to cling to him like a shadow. However, the gravity of their mission weighed heavily on her heart, prompting her to question whether those concerns truly mattered in this moment.

"We should be near the ruins," Ossian said. "If the texts are accurate, Rath Lugh is just beyond that ridge. The horn should be buried beneath it."

She nodded. "And if we're wrong?"

His stride didn't falter. "I'm not wrong."

The response made Adair uneasy. That level of confidence could be comforting, but, from him, it felt as if it concealed something darker. She had always admired the man's decisiveness, but now, in the midst of their mission, that same certainty only heightened her defenses.

Maybe Nadia was right. Perhaps Ossian *was* playing a game that she couldn't see, one whose rules she might not even desire to understand.

The road curved sharply and dropped into a wooded path. Ossian stopped at the edge, scanning the thick line of trees ahead.

"We'll cut through here," he said, gesturing to a barely visible trail that snaked through the underbrush.

The moment they stepped into the woods, the air seemed to shift, the fog growing heavier and the shadows longer. Adair could feel the magic here. It was ancient, pulsating beneath the earth like a sleeping giant. Never before had she experienced a force this strong.

Her breath caught as she looked around, wide-eyed. "Do you feel that?" she whispered excitedly.

Ossian nodded, his hand rising to the hilt of his sword. "Aye. We're close. Stay sharp."

Adair mirrored his movement, her fingers brushing the leather of her belt, hovering just above the handle of one of her daggers. They ventured deeper into the brush, their footsteps softened by the damp forest floor. The further they went, the more the trees closed in around them, their branches weaving together tightly, causing the light to grow steadily dimmer, and the air colder.

It was hard to tell how much time had passed before the pair stumbled into a clearing. Minutes? Hours? Finally, standing before a wide mound covered in grass and small trees, Adair felt it.

The power here was unmistakable. It felt like it was both ancient and alive, as if it had been waiting millennia for this very moment.

Ossian stopped beside her, his voice low and reverent. "This is it."

Adair swallowed against the dryness in her throat, her eyes tracing the lines of the mound. "Do you think it's here? The Dord Fian?"

"We're about to find out." The man's words were clipped, but there was something caught behind them.

She looked at him sidelong and noticed a strange flicker in his features. Ossian's eyes were glassy, his jaw tight. His throat bobbed once, but when he blinked, it was gone.

They approached the slice in the ridge, a line of trees running down the back of it like gems in a crown. Ossian took the lead, his steps careful but confident. Adair remained close behind, her pulse quickening. Despite her best efforts, she couldn't shake the unsettling feeling that something was watching them, waiting.

At the top, the trees parted to reveal a thin forest, where a magnificent beech stood at the center, resting in eerie stillness. Ossian walked directly towards it, his movements careful but deliberate. He placed a hand on the bark and knelt, speaking in tones too low to make out.

Adair stayed back, something about the moment holding her in place.

She could sense that there was a reverence in the meeting that didn't belong to her. She watched as the man pulled a thistle from his bag, setting it gently at the roots of the tree. The wind picked up, soft and strange, and his voice drifted closer. She realized he was speaking in his native tongue, the Irish lilt flowing through the breeze like a melodic song.

After a few moments, Ossian rose from his position. His fingers fumbled through his pocket, pulling free a stone etched with ancient script. He paused in front of her and ran a hand through his hair. Adair couldn't be sure, but for a fleeting moment, she thought she detected redness in the man's eyes.

Ossian held the stone in his palm and spoke again in Gaeilge, the words thick with meaning.

"Taispeáin dom cad atá caillte. Tabhair chugam an rud atá uaim."

The ogham carved into the long stone flared a soft blue, just for a second, before blinking out. Ossian's shoulders tensed. Adjusting his stance, he repeated the phrase, this time in Gaelic.

"Seall dhomh na chaidh a chall. Thoir dhomh na tha mi a' sireadh."

His voice was darker now, almost growling, a thread of threat in his tone.

Again, the lines sparked, pulsed, and died. Ossian cursed under his breath, then roared it louder in English. "Show me what has been lost. Bring me what I seek."

This time, there was no response.

"Feck!" The stone flew from his hand and crashed through the trees, vanishing into the underbrush.

Adair jumped at his response, her body curling in, heart thudding hard behind her ribs. Ossian stood there, fists clenched at his sides, his back rigid. The silence stretched, too tight, and for a heart-stopping moment, Adair feared he might storm away, leaving her behind once more.

Instead, the man took a deep breath, then another, as he tried to wrestle himself back into a state of calm.

Adair took a hesitant step forward, just close enough to make her presence known. "It's okay. We'll figure it out."

Ossian's voice came out raw. "It's not okay." He turned, eyes hard, mouth tight with frustration. "We don't have time for this. The Dord Fian could be *anywhere* in the world. If the stone doesn't work, then we're guessing. And if we're guessing, then we're *fucked*."

Adair's breath caught. The certainty she had leaned on was cracking. "Maybe we're missing something. Another clue. Another path."

"I thought I'd figured it all out." He sounded exhausted. Not just from the journey, but from the weight of his own expectations. "I was so sure..."

Adair closed the gap between them. "Hey," she said softly, "We've faced worse odds before, right? We can do this."

Ossian's anger didn't vanish, but it softened at the edges.

"You're too kind, Hanlon," he said, and the weariness in his smile broke something in her. "Even when I don't deserve it."

Adair hesitated, unsure of how to respond, so she gave a slight shrug. "We're in this together. You don't have to do it alone."

Ossian's eyes met hers, and for a brief second, something unspoken passed between them. Before either could say more, a rustling in the bushes to their left shattered the fragile moment.

Adair instinctively reached for her daggers, her senses on high alert.

Beside her, Ossian swiftly drew his sword. They stood frozen, straining to listen as the rustling grew louder.

A figure emerged from the underbrush. A young girl who couldn't be more than twelve stumbled into the clearing, a silver collar attached to her neck like a shackle, eyes wide with fear.

"Please," she gasped, breathless and shaking. "Don't hurt me. I-I was just trying to get away. I was hiding."

Ossian didn't lower his weapon, but he didn't advance either. "Hiding from who?"

The girl flinched, looking over her shoulder as if expecting someone to appear from the shadows. "There are others," she said, keeping her voice low. "Men... searching for something. They've been tearing across these lands for days. I just barely got away, but... they're close."

Adair's heart skipped a beat. "Others? What are they looking for?"

The girl's eyes darted between the pair. "A horn," she whispered. "They're using people like me to find it. They think it's here."

Ossian swore under his breath, the line of his jaw tightening. "How many?"

The child swallowed. "A dozen that I saw. Maybe more. They've been hurting people. Forcing them to help."

Adair felt cold all over. The Order. It had to be. They would do whatever it took to get their hands on the instrument. She and Ossian were no longer alone in this race.

The Irishman looked at her, his expression grim. "We need to move. Now."

Adair nodded, already shifting her bag on her shoulder. The new development had thrown everything into chaos, but they couldn't afford to let it slow them down. Time was running out, and the enemy was closing in.

"We can't leave her here," Adair said, glancing at the girl. "They'll find her."

There was a beat of silence as Ossian hesitated, his eyes narrowing as he considered the situation. Then, with a sharp nod, he gestured for the child to follow. "Stay close, and keep quiet."

Before they could move further, he grabbed the girl by the shoulder. "One thing first."

He grabbed the dagger from Adair's main hand, exchanging it with his broadsword, and the child immediately panicked, squirming under his grip.

"Stay still," Ossian commanded. "Or this *will* hurt."

The girl stilled, her frightened eyes locked on the sharp blade. Ossian leaned in closer, the tip of the dagger gliding over the silver collar. He began etching a mark into the band, the soft scratches filling the silence.

Adair cleared her throat. "What's your name?" she asked softly.

"Kay." Dark eyes shifted toward the woman, the child's attention fixed on remaining perfectly still while the Irishman finished.

Ossian stepped back, examining his work before trading weapons once more. "I'm no Artificer, but that ogham should prevent anything too nasty from happening before we get it removed." He glanced at Adair, tilting his head to gesture behind them. "Let's move."

Kay nodded, falling into step behind them without a word. The trio began to weave through the trees, the weight of their mission pressing down more heavily than before.

Adair's heart raced in her chest, the urgency of their task now amplified by the threat of others hunting for the same artifact. The forest loomed darker and more foreboding, its ancient magic now feeling less like a guiding presence and more like an ominous warning.

As they pushed onward, an unsettling sensation once again gripped Adair. Her breath quickened, and with it came a terrible clarity.

This wasn't paranoia. They were being watched.

Maybe it was the forest.

Maybe it was the Order's presence.

Or maybe... it was something else entirely.

Something far older and more dangerous than any of them realized.

Now that it *had* noticed them, Adair had a sinking feeling that it wasn't going to look away any time soon.

Chapter Twenty-One

The morning light strained to pierce the dense canopy above, its pale glow filtering into ghostly beams that danced across the forest floor as the trio pressed deeper into the woods.

Ossian led with one hand resting on the hilt of his dagger, shoulders squared in grim anticipation. Behind him, Adair stepped quickly, her breath coming out in puffs of smoke in the frigid air. Kay trailed close by, her slight frame quaking with effort, chest rising in quick, fluttering gasps.

As they made their way through the underbrush, Adair became acutely aware of the forest's strange energy. The ground beneath her boots hummed with an ancient power unlike anything she had ever experienced.

This was no ordinary place.

The earth seemed alive, pulsing with the weight of something hidden, just waiting to be discovered.

Ossian lifted one hand and froze, and the others followed instantly. They remained alert as a chorus of voices began to filter through the trees. Adair dropped to a crouch beside the girl, who clung to her arm with trembling fingers. They held their breath, still as statues, watching the figures pass like shadows through the thickets.

Adair's pulse thundered in her ears as she leaned forward, trying desperately to make out the muddled speech. After a strained moment of observation, Ossian turned to her, jaw clenched, and mouthed two words.

The Order.

A shiver climbed Adair's spine. The Order was more than a faction. It was a religion dressed as a military. They obeyed without question and acted without hesitation. Their goal was simple and absolute: Enslave all Creators. Anyone with magic was a tool to be bled dry or a threat to be erased. Either fate was a victory in their eyes.

Adair knew the Order's agents were here for the same reason they were. Whispers of the Dord Fian would have called their soldiers like a moth to a flame. The power within that horn was legendary, a relic capable of turning the tide of war, and in their hands it would be *catastrophic.* The thought twisted something deep in her gut.

Adair pressed herself against an oak tree, her heart racing. They couldn't be caught. Not with so much at stake. Her mind was running a million outcomes when a sharp cry pierced the quiet.

Kay had tripped over a thick root, crashing to the ground with a loud thud that shattered the fragile silence. The voices fell still, and for a brief moment, the forest held its breath.

Then came the unsheathing of blades.

"Run," Ossian hissed, already springing to his feet.

Adair grabbed Kay's arm and fled into the underbrush, her body moving before her mind could catch up. Brambles clawed at her skin and tangled her hair, but she didn't stop.

Behind them, metal clashed as Ossian's sword flashed through the misty air with lethal precision. She could sense his strain, hear the fury in every strike, but she didn't look back. Not yet.

"Keep going," she gasped, tugging Kay forward.

A sharp whistle split the air.

Adair ducked instinctively as the arrow slammed into the trunk beside her. The wood splintered where her head had been, sending shards across her cheek. Her heart seized. That shot had been deliberate, precise. If she moved more slowly the next time...

She yanked Kay behind a massive tree, pressing her low into the damp earth. Her voice came out whispered, but steady, even as her lungs burned. "We have to fight."

The girl's eyes widened. "We can't. They'll kill us."

"We don't have a choice." Adair's voice trembled, but her hand didn't. She pulled her dagger free, the hilt cold and unfamiliar against her skin. "Stay here. Do not move."

She didn't wait for a reply. The woman slipped through the trees, letting the sounds of battle guide her. She spotted Ossian through the foliage, a blur of movement and steel as he fended off two attackers, but others were rapidly drawing near.

Adair's gaze shifted. She was scanning the edges of the fight, when she saw him.

A man stood just beyond the fray, unmoving, watching the battle with cold calculation. Shadows obscured his face, but there was something in the stillness of his posture that sent a chill up her spine. She had the feeling that stopping him might just be enough to tip the scales in their favor.

Adair's feet moved before her mind could conjure an excuse to hold back, her grip on the dagger tightening as she crept closer.

When the moment arrived, she lunged. The blade sliced through the air, aimed for the vulnerable skin of his throat.

She was fast.

But he was faster.

In a breath, the man turned and caught her wrist, twisting until the dagger slipped from her fingers and disappeared into the underbrush. Pain shot up Adair's arm as she stumbled back, landing hard against the rough bark of a tree. Her gaze flew upward, and everything inside her went cold.

Nash.

His icy blue eyes locked onto hers. "You've walked straight into a trap, abomination," he spat. "The Order has been waiting for you."

Adair's stomach twisted, and she struggled to maintain a neutral expression, determined not to give him the satisfaction of seeing the fear currently pressing down on her chest.

"You'll have to do better than this." She attempted to sound brave, but the tremor in her voice gave her away.

Nash stepped closer, savoring the moment. "We don't need to do better," he murmured. "You're already ours, *pet*."

Before she could react, the man lifted his hand. A flash of silver streaked toward her, and in a breath, the net struck. Enchanted cords wrapped around her frame, binding her arms to her sides and dragging her to the ground. The more she struggled, the tighter it pulled, crushing her ribs until every breath was painful.

Nash crouched beside the woman, his smile cutting deeper than any blade.

"You belong to the Order now, Deity."

Adair gasped, her vision blurring at the edges as panic surged. Her mind scrambled for a way out, but nothing came. She could still hear the melee through the trees, the sounds of Ossian fighting for all of their lives, unaware that she had fallen. The urge to call out burned in her throat, but she couldn't draw enough breath to attempt it.

She had never felt so helpless, ensnared in the very nightmare she had spent her life trying to avoid. For as long as she could remember, her existence had been about maintaining control, anticipating every situation, and preparing for the unexpected. It was how she had survived her day to day life.

But now, there was no strategy to cling to. No escape plan, no blade within reach, no clever lie to buy her time. Her thoughts spun in frantic circles, desperately searching for a way out.

Then, Omar's voice broke through the haze.

You need to learn how to release that need for control.

He had told her time and again.

There will come a moment when you won't have the luxury of planning. When you'll have to let go. Trust your power. Trust yourself.

Adair's heart pounded. She closed her eyes. She could still feel the weight of failure closing in, but beneath the fear, the shame, and the need to fight, there was a quieter current. A place untouched by panic.

It's now or never.

The runes began to pulse with energy, glowing faintly as they tightened their hold. Instead of fighting against them, Adair focused on the intricate patterns. Her vision blurred momentarily, then sharpened, and the lines of the ogham carved into the net became clear. She saw the delicate interweaving of magic, the ancient symbols the Order's artificers had painstakingly crafted.

One by one, she studied them, her mind honing in on each detail, every line, each stroke of alchemy. She felt the waves of thaumaturgy woven into the net, and something inside of her shifted.

Adair's power began to stir, surging forward in response to the net's energy. It pulsed, moving through her veins like liquid fire.

With each beat of her magic, she felt the threads of the net weakening. She no longer struggled physically. She didn't need to. All she had to do was focus. Her power rippled, and she mentally grasped the first rune, the ancient ogham glowing brightly.

With a single thought, she shattered it.

A slight tremor of relief bloomed in her chest, but she didn't let it break her focus. Her confidence curled inward, quiet, as she moved on to the next. Her power swelled again, more easily this time, answering her intent as if it had been waiting for permission. Another ideograph broke apart, and the cords around her relaxed just enough to shift.

Nash stepped closer, his expression darkening as he felt the change in the air.

The enchantment was faltering. His trap was unraveling.

But it no longer mattered.

Adair reached for the final aegis, gathering her magic in a single breath, and *destroyed* it. The net collapsed in a lifeless heap. She pushed it off with trembling hands, adrenaline roaring in her ears.

With a scream of defiance, Adair surged to her feet. She drew the second dagger from her belt, gripping it tightly in her bruised palm. Her chest rose and fell in sharp bursts, eyes burning with wild, unfiltered purpose. Control was irrelevant now. It had always been an illusion, a leash she had wrapped around her own throat.

What she had in this moment wasn't control.

It was fire.

Unshackled, merciless, and hers.

It shot up her spine, raw and untamed, and she let it take her as flames erupted from her fingertips.

Nash dodged, rolling sideways through the dirt, but not quickly enough. A streak of fire caught his coat, tearing a hole through the sleeve. He stood, scowling, and brushed at the charred edge with a look of disgust, his lips curling as he examined the damage.

"You will pay for that, you little bitch."

Adair smiled, high on a cocktail of pain, manifestation, and whatever pills were still dulling the edges of her restraint.

"Put it on my tab," she muttered.

Her feet shuffled sideways, subtly inching toward the open duffel that Ossian had left behind. The flap had fallen back in the scuffle, and she could see exactly what she needed lying safely inside.

Nash charged forward, his rapier slicing through the air in a deadly arc.

Adair dove to the side, her shoulder slamming hard against the ground, but she didn't hesitate. Her fingers plunged into the bag, quickly finding her companion's flask. In one fluid motion, she popped the cork and hurled the liquid. It splashed across Nash's coat, and before he could comprehend what was happening, she snapped her fingers.

The fire caught instantly.

It spread fast, climbing the man's clothes with greedy hands as his cry of pain pierced the air. He flailed and shrieked, desperately slapping at the flames that engulfed him. His once-pristine coat curled and blackened with smoke as he staggered, the sword slipping from his fingers. In an instant, his cold, cruel composure shattered. Fury contorted his face, and his wild, bloodshot eyes betrayed his panic as the fire gradually gave way to sputtering embers.

Adair didn't wait for him to get his revenge. Her dagger flashed in her grip as she lunged, the blade connecting and slicing across his cheek in a brutal, wet line.

Nash howled, staggering back with a hand pressed against the gash, his mouth twisted in agony.

"You little..." he started, voice shaking with fury, but Adair was already circling, the blood-slicked dagger gleaming like a ruby.

Nash slapped out the last of the embers, eyes narrowing as he ground his teeth.

"You think you can win this?" he snarled. "I'll make you regret every second of your miserable little life."

Adair just smiled, reckless, feral, and utterly fearless. "You're going to need more than words to stop me."

She spun the dagger in her hand, her muscles tense and ready.

Nash gave a guttural roar and charged, bare-handed. His refined demeanor was gone, replaced with something animalistic and unhinged, but Adair was already moving.

She sidestepped his attack with ease, her movements quicker, more fluid than they had ever been before. The fear that had once gripped her was gone, replaced with an intoxicating sense of invincibility.

The world narrowed down to just the two of them. Every second stretched out. Every motion clear and sharp in her mind.

Nash was off balance now, his rage blinding him, and Adair used it to her advantage. She kicked out, her boot connecting with his knee, and he bucked forward with a grunt. She struck again, her dagger rising toward his throat, but he dodged just in time. The blade grazed the side of his neck, drawing blood but missing anything vital.

"You'll regret this, cunt," he rasped.

"Maybe," Adair answered, her grin splitting wide as she stepped back, breathing hard. "But *you're* the one who's bleeding."

Before he could spit out another insult, a blur sliced through the clearing.

Ossian crashed into Nash with a force that knocked the air clean from his lungs, driving him to the ground in a violent, breathless heap. Before the man could so much as flinch, the Celt had him pinned, one knee pressing into his back, his broad hand locking him to the dirt with effortless strength.

"Stay down," Ossian growled, his voice low and lethal.

Adair stood frozen, captivated by the man's presence. Ossian radiated an undeniable aura of power and authority, a sensation that swept over Nash as well, quelling any lingering resistance within him.

The Irishman raised his blade, the impending killing blow a promise rather than a question.

Adair's voice cut through the moment. "Wait!"

Ossian's head turned sharply, their eyes locking in a tense moment. His shoulders remained braced, ready to finish what he had started, the edge of his jaw twitching with the effort of restraint.

After a heartbeat, he relented. With a low exhale, he sheathed his sword, forcefully shoving Nash's face into the dirt as he pushed himself upright. The Englishman groaned, choking on the turf as Ossian advanced toward Adair.

A soft ripple stirred the air, barely noticeable at first, until another figure materialized beside Nash. Where there had been nothing a moment before, a woman now stood. The newcomer was tall, composed, and seemingly indifferent to the chaos surrounding her.

Éala.

Adair had seen her only once before, but recognition hit her instantly. She was Nash's partner, the one who had chased Adair through the streets on that very first day.

The woman's silver eyes scanned the clearing with detached precision before she knelt beside Nash, the fold of her cloak brushing against the bloodied earth. She reached toward him calmly, her fingers glowing faintly with onyx light, the healing spell already gathered and ready to be released.

Nash jerked away from her touch with a snarl, the rejection as violent as it was instant. His hand lashed out, smacking hers aside.

"Don't you dare," he spat, fury crackling in his voice. "I don't need your filthy Creator magic. I'll go to a *real* doctor before I let you touch me." The insult rang louder than the shout itself, slamming into the stillness left in the wake of battle.

Éala didn't flinch. "As you wish," she replied, her tone calm and detached. With a graceful motion, she pulled her hand back and rose effortlessly to her feet.

Adair couldn't look away. The exchange had left her breathless in a different way than the fight had. This was the first she had heard that

Éala was a Creator. Not only that, but she'd used magic, her own, freely offered. If she was on the side of the Order, then why had Nash recoiled from her like she was diseased?

It didn't make sense.

The Order didn't *let* Creators keep that kind of power unless they were... What? Collared? Enslaved people wrapped in obedience spells? But Éala had moved on her own. No collar. No restraint. Just unflinching, invisible submission. Or was it loyalty? Adair couldn't tell. All she knew was that something was *very* wrong about the entire situation.

Nash, still seething, turned toward her. "You'll regret this," he hissed, his voice scraping through clenched teeth. "All of you."

The words hung in the air as he pushed to get up, his hand still pressed over the wound Éala had attempted to heal.

Adair saw the flicker in Ossian before he moved. Just a twitch in his hand toward the hilt of his blade, but it said enough. She reached for him without thinking, fingers catching the fabric of his shirt. There was no resistance in her hold, only a gentle presence reminding him that the fight was over. For now.

Éala stepped forward again, raising her hands in the same composed, unhurried motion as before. Her fingers traced patterns through the air, weaving through the remnants of magic that still lingered in the clearing, until a portal shimmered open beside her. Nash glared at them both one final time before finally stepping through the archway, leaving only the sharp scent of blood and charred skin behind. Éala followed, her movements as unreadable as the rest of her.

Before she stepped through the threshold, the woman glanced back.

Her silver gaze met Adair's, devoid of any emotion. In an instant, she was gone, the portal sealing shut with a low hum.

The silence left behind was more unsettling than the noise. Adair stood frozen, heart pounding, unsure if it was from fear or adrenaline or some strange mix of both. The fight was over, but her body hadn't caught up to the truth of that yet. Her palm remained on Ossian's shirt, fingers softly gripping the fabric. She didn't realize that he was watching her until he gently placed his hand over her own.

"You did well," he said, voice quiet.

Adair looked at the Celt, feeling the weight of his approval, and for the first time in a while, she allowed herself to believe it.

"But that was also really fecking reckless."

The words felt like a punch to her gut.

Ossian's hands came to her shoulders, his grip nearly painful as he spun her to face him fully. His green eyes searched hers, sharp with fury. "Don't *ever* engage Nash again. Do you hear me?"

Adair flinched at the force of his words. Her gaze fell to the ground between them, as if seeking balance in the earth itself. Silently, she nodded, her cheeks flushing with shame as he released her.

"Nash's hatred for Creators far outweighs the desires and missions of the Order," Ossian muttered, crossing the clearing to retrieve his duffel. He paused, eyes searching the clearing, and retrieved the flask that had been haphazardly discarded to the earth. He shook it once, frowned at the weightless sound, and then sighed, dropping it back into the bag. "He will not hesitate to kill you."

Any trace of pride she'd begun to let herself feel dissolved under those words. The adrenaline that had sharpened her senses moments ago now felt like a residue clinging to her skin, making her limbs heavy and her thoughts slow. This wasn't a storybook moment of triumph. It was a warning.

Without a word, Ossian bent down to gather their scattered equipment. The duffle landed on his shoulder with practiced ease, yet Adair could see the tension coiled through every line of his body. He wasn't just angry. He was also afraid, though he would never admit it. Still, his silence felt like a wall rising between them once again.

Adair despised how easily he could make her feel like a child who had reached too far, too fast. She wanted to snap back, to argue that she wasn't some reckless girl playing at war, but the image of Nash's sneer, the loathing in his eyes, silenced the urge.

Ossian wasn't wrong. She had been bold, and it had nearly gotten her killed.

"We should head back," he said, his voice distant, as though the fight and the tension between them had already been packed away with the rest of their gear.

Adair gave a tight nod, her eyes drifting to the now unconscious girl crumpled at the base of a tree. The child's chest rose and fell in shallow breaths, the cruel metal collar still fastened around her neck like a brand.

She hadn't forgotten about her, but Nash's arrival had stolen her focus. Now, looking at Kay, she felt the sting of guilt prickle behind her ribs. She hadn't been part of the plan, but plans didn't matter when people were suffering.

Ossian moved first. He dropped to one knee, pressing two fingers to the girl's neck. His brow furrowed as he checked the aegis that prevented the collar from constricting further. She was stable for now, but there was no mistaking the urgency in the Irishman's voice.

"We need to get this off her," he muttered, frustration seeping into his tone.

Adair crouched beside him, her fingers grazing the edge of the metal. It was beautifully crafted, and that only made it worse. Someone had poured time and power into building a device meant to crush whatever spark had once lived inside this child. The injustice of it made her blood boil.

"Will we be able to remove it at the Keep?" she asked.

Ossian didn't look at her as he answered. "Aye. Contreras' been working on a way to neutralize them. But we need to move. Now." He gathered the girl in his arms, Kay's limp form slumping easily against his broad frame.

Adair moved quickly, scooping up the last of their supplies, her hands steady even as her thoughts swirled. She couldn't stop replaying the confrontation in her head. Nash's words, Éala's empty gaze, the way her own magic had roared to life, running on an endless loop. She was just beginning to understand the weight of what she carried.

The descent down the hillside was quiet. Only the muffled sounds of their boots on the forest floor and the whisper of wind through the trees kept them company.

As they trudged down the road towards the farm gate, Adair finally voiced one of the questions that had been gnawing at her. "How did Éala open a portal at the hill?"

Ossian paused, shifting the girl's weight and pressing his hand to the iron gate. In an instant, the celestial hallway flared into existence before them, the shimmering threads of magic weaving a pathway back to the

Keep.

"The collars seem to intensify abilities," he grunted, before stepping through.

Adair had to mask her surprise as she followed.

Faye and Mia were waiting on the other side, their faces etched with concern as they reached for the unconscious girl. The healer's hands were gentle, her voice patient as she murmured a quick assessment.

Adair watched the child vanish into the care of the two women with a tightness in her chest. She didn't know much about Kay, but she knew with certainty that she deserved more than what the world had given her. She needed to learn to control her magic if it meant that she could prevent something like this from happening again.

If the collars can help intensify abilities...

Ossian's voice cut in. "I know what you're about to ask. And no, they're not helpful. The collars push abilities far beyond their limits. They force the magic to overexert itself. It can damage the body. *Kill you.*"

Adair sucked in a sharp breath as the realization hit. She hadn't understood the full extent of the danger until now. The collar wasn't just a shackle. It was a weapon.

She would have to train the old-fashioned way.

The flow of people thinned as they moved deeper into the Keep, and Adair found her eyes drawn to Ossian again. There was something quieter in him now, almost hesitant. He adjusted the strap of his duffel before glancing over his shoulder.

"Hanlon."

She slowed, waiting for him to speak.

He turned fully, and this time, his eyes didn't hold judgment. "I know you mean well. But this is more dangerous than you realize. The Order isn't playing games. Nash will stop at nothing, and you need to be ready for that."

Adair's pulse thudded in her ears, but she held his gaze. "I understand."

A long moment passed between them before Ossian gave a single nod and turned toward the staircase leading to the Commander's office. He climbed the first few steps before pausing again, glancing back at her with a look that was part warning, part invitation.

"He's going to want a report from you as well."

Adair's mouth parted slightly, a bubbling warmth spreading through her chest that threatened to become a smile. This was it. A real mission. A real report.

As they climbed the stairs, the weight of what had happened still clung to her, but beneath it, something new stirred. Something stronger.

This wasn't over.

Not by a long shot.

And now, more than ever, Adair knew she had to see it through to the end.

Chapter Twenty-Two

Adair felt a mix of excitement and apprehension as she followed Ossian up the steps. Being summoned to provide a report felt like a clear indication that she was evolving beyond the role of a mere fledgling Creator under Ossian's guidance. The importance of that recognition felt heavy on her shoulders.

Edmund raised a hand in greeting before gesturing for them to sit. With a soft click of a button, the glass behind them fogged until the world outside disappeared, cloaking the office in privacy.

Adair eased into one of the chairs, her back straight, fingers curled into tight fists to keep them from fidgeting. Ossian, true to form, ignored the Commander's invitation and instead wandered to the line of cabinets built seamlessly into the far wall.

The huff that escaped Edmund's throat sounded long-practiced, as though he had sighed over Ossian's antics a hundred times before.

It didn't faze the Irishman in the least. Ossian poured himself a generous measure of amber liquid from the decanter, then dropped into the chair beside Adair with a contented sigh, boots thunking unceremoniously on the Commander's desk. Edmund's face turned a deep shade of red as he smacked the man's feet off the polished wood, only for the Irishman to settle into a more modest ankle-over-knee pose, lifting his glass in a toast.

"Are you done fucking around?" Edmund asked through gritted teeth.

"What's life without a bit of craic?" Ossian replied with a wink. "You need to get out and relax a bit, Eddy."

Adair watched the interaction, caught between secondhand embarrassment and reluctant amusement. The tension was building quickly, but she could sense the rhythm underneath it, the way their barbs had a history. She let out a soft chuckle before she could stop herself, and both men turned their sharp gazes to her in perfect unison, surprise etched on their faces. Quickly, she bit down on the inside of her cheek to stifle a full-bodied laugh.

Edmund muttered something sharp in Gaelic as he reached for the remote on his desk, flipping the screen behind him to life.

Adair caught Ossian glancing at her from the corner of her eye, his face unreadable, though his earlier warning echoed in her head.

Do not engage Nash again.

She knew he was right, yet the fire in her veins still simmered from their encounter. For now, she would need to keep that part of herself in check, especially in front of the Commander.

"Report," Edmund said, his tone clipped, clearly eager to expedite Ossian's departure from his office.

Ossian took the lead, recounting the details of the encounter with Nash and Éala. He described their ambush, the girl they had rescued, the cursed collar, and how they had barely escaped just before Nash and his partner disappeared through the portal.

He left nothing out but also refrained from embellishing the situation, presenting the facts in an unusual, no-nonsense manner. It was rare to witness him be so precise, and that alone signified to Adair how seriously he regarded the confrontation.

When he finished, Edmund's gaze shifted to the woman.

"Adair?" The Commander's voice was steady yet probing. "I'd like to hear your perspective."

The woman's breath caught. This was the test. She straightened her spine and forced herself to meet his eyes, clearing her voice before she began.

She recounted how she had broken the magical restraints meant to hold her, how she had conjured fire in a panic and used it against Nash, and how she had used the flask to spread the flames. Her words were honest, but although she tried to sound measured, the weight of her recklessness still lingered in her tone.

Adair could feel Ossian shift beside her as she spoke. He didn't interrupt, but she noticed the way his jaw ticked with unease.

Edmund leaned back in his chair, hands steepled under his chin as he stared at her for what felt like an eternity. The stillness in the room was sharp, oppressive, and her skin itched under the scrutiny. She wondered if she had said too much. If, in trying to prove herself, she had only confirmed that she wasn't ready.

"You've taken bold actions, Adair," the Commander said at last. "Risky, but effective." His gaze flicked to Ossian, then back to her, sharpening. "You showed potential. But there's something you must understand."

Adair's pulse quickened, bracing herself for the reprimand she felt sure was coming.

"The Order," Edmund continued, his voice growing darker, "is no ordinary enemy. They've grown more dangerous with each passing day, and Nash is one of their most fanatical enforcers. His hatred for Creators runs deeper than we've seen in a long time. If you cross paths with him again, it won't be just *your* life on the line."

He leaned forward, eyes boring into hers. "It will be the lives of every person who is counting on you. One misstep could undo *everything* we've built."

The words hit harder than Adair expected. Not because they surprised her, but because they echoed something she'd already feared.

This wasn't just about proving herself anymore.

"I understand, Commander," Adair said softly.

Edmund gave a single nod, satisfied. "Good. Now, about the girl…" His focus shifted back to Ossian. "You said Contreras is working on neutralizing the collar?"

"Aye," Ossian confirmed. "She's running tests. The kid's stable for now, but until the enchantment's broken, we won't know the extent of the damage."

Edmund's brow furrowed, his mind moving ten steps ahead. "If she *can* break the aegis, it could give us a foothold against the Order."

Ossian gave a slow nod in agreement, and with that, Edmund stood, the meeting clearly drawing to a close.

"I want to be informed the moment Contreras has a breakthrough," Edward commanded before turning back to Adair. His gaze slightly softened. "Remember what we've discussed. You've earned your place here, but this war is bigger than any one of us."

Adair nodded solemnly, feeling the gravity of her place within the Divide for the first time.

Edmund's attention slid back to Ossian. "And you... I'll need a word with *you* later."

Ossian saluted with infuriating nonchalance, the corners of his mouth twitching into a smirk. "Looking forward to it, *Commander*."

As they left Edmund's office, the tension between the pair seemed to loosen.

The corridor beyond was quiet, dimly lit by lanterns in iron sconces, their flames swaying gently with the draft. The Keep always held a hush after nightfall, but tonight it felt heavier somehow, as though even the stone walls braced for what was coming.

"Now for drinks and avoiding that meeting at all costs."

Adair's brow lifted. She let out a soft chuckle, assuming it was sarcasm, until she glanced up and caught the look in his eyes. "Wait, you want to drink? Now?"

Ossian shrugged as he adjusted the strap of his sword across his back. "Why not? We just trudged through hell and lived to complain about it. That earns us somethin'."

The Irishman didn't wait for a response, just turned and started down the corridor with that unhurried swagger he wore like armor.

Adair hesitated for only a moment, then fell into step beside him, the weight of her gear feeling heavier with the exhaustion. They walked in companionable silence, echoes of distant voices from deeper inside the Keep floating around them. The usual stiffness that clung to her shoulders had loosened by the time they reached the dining hall doors.

As she stepped inside, laughter bubbled up around her, mingling with the clink of cutlery against stoneware and the inviting aroma of fresh bread and spirits wafting through the air. The hall was alive with the hum of people seeking normalcy in the lull between storms.

They found a table tucked near the far wall, half-shadowed by the curve of an old pillar. It was quieter there, a little removed from the crowd, just enough for the noise to blur into background texture.

Eta appeared moments later with two drinks, her grin quick and knowing as she set the mugs down. "Figured I'd find you here," she said. The woman winked at the pair, then vanished before Adair could ask what that meant.

The cup felt cool in her hands, but she didn't drink right away. She rolled it between her palms instead, watching the way Ossian leaned back in his chair like he'd done this a thousand times before.

The place was bustling with activity, yet they had managed to carve out a pocket of privacy in the shadows. Despite this, her thoughts *refused* to settle.

"Ossian," Adair began softly, eyes on the rim of her drink. "Why did you agree to save Kay?"

He didn't respond right away.

"You didn't seem to care about the casualties during the gas main explosion, but with her…" She paused, heart skittering, but the words pressed forward. "You didn't hesitate."

Ossian froze mid-swig, the mug pausing just short of his lips before he lowered it to the table with a quiet thud. For a long breath, he didn't speak or move. He just stared at the space between them like the weight of her question had knocked something loose in him.

Adair held still, watching the tension gather across his shoulders, the way the flickering light painted hard lines across his face.

Maybe she'd gone too far. Maybe this was the moment he closed off again. But she couldn't let it go.

During the Divide's sabotage, he had been shockingly pragmatic, showing a chilling level of calculation that bordered on cruelty. Civilians had perished, and he had allowed it to happen. Yet with Kay, he acted without hesitation, as if the girl had always been his to protect.

"I didn't expect you to ask that," Ossian said at last. "But I suppose you deserve an answer."

He leaned forward, resting his bulky forearms on the table. "The gas main explosion wasn't our fight. Civilians were collateral. Sad as it is, in war, there's always going to be acceptable losses. We couldn't save everyone."

Adair's hands curled tighter around her glass. "So those lives didn't matter? Just *acceptable losses*?"

"It's not about whether or not they mattered. It's about stopping the bleeding where you can. That day, the fight was already lost. But Kay..." Ossian released a heavy sigh. "Kay's a Creator. The collar's got the lass on lockdown, but if we save her, she can choose to join us or be free. That's something we *can* control."

Her stomach churned at the cold logic. "So you saved her because she's useful?"

"Aye," Ossian said bluntly, taking another drink. "That's part of it."

"But not *all* of it..." Adair pressed, eyes searching the man's face for any signs of humanity under his gruff exterior.

The Irishman shook his head with a sharp exhale. "You don't let up, do you, Hanlon?"

"Not when I know there's more to the story."

His expression softened, threaded with something unspoken. "The girl reminds me of someone I couldn't save a long time ago. That's the part you're looking for, right?" He scrubbed his face with a hand before continuing. "She's not just useful. She's a kid caught in the middle of something she never asked for." Ossian shook his head, his brows furrowing as his eyes wandered to something in the distance. "The gas explosion...those people weren't my responsibility. But Kay? She's one of us."

Adair blinked, caught off guard by the rare glimpse beneath the surface. Over the past month, she'd learned he rarely let anyone see past the bravado, but here it was... the unvarnished truth.

"So it wasn't just about the mission," she murmured.

Ossian huffed out a laugh, glancing at her with a mixture of exasperation and resignation. "You've got your answer now. Satisfied?"

She studied him for a moment before nodding. "I guess I am."

They sat in a comfortable silence for a while, the sounds of the surrounding camaraderie filling the space between them. Ossian leaned back, taking a slow breath as if the weight of the conversation still lingered. Then his mouth quirked, a glint of mischief returning. "You're a nosy one, Hanlon. But you've got guts."

She smiled. "Thanks... I think."

Before she could say more, a voice rang out above the din.

"Why the long faces?"

Adair startled, head snapping up to find a stranger approaching the table. His accent was American, warm and round in a way that caught her off guard. He was broad-shouldered with warm brown eyes and a neatly trimmed goatee. His dark hair was combed back with care, and the most striking detail of all was the black chef's coat he wore, a messy contrast to the rest of his clean-cut appearance.

Ossian lowered his glass and grinned. "McCloud. Join us!" He gestured to the empty seat with a flick of his wrist, and the man slid onto the bench beside Adair without hesitation.

He extended a calloused palm across the table. "Cale McCloud. Head Chef of the Scotland Keep. Nice to meet you."

Adair took his hand a bit awkwardly, her mouth already moving before her brain caught up. "You're a chef and your name is Kale?"

As soon as the words left her lips, she slapped both hands over her face, heat rushing to her cheeks.

Ossian choked on a laugh, and Cale let out a rich, amused sound that echoed around the table.

"I get that a lot with newbies," Cale said, grinning. "Spelled with a 'C,' though, not a 'K.'"

Across the room, Eta's sharp eyes caught the gesture when Cale raised two fingers, but her expression softened the moment that she recognized him, practically beaming as she made her way toward the back.

"She likes you," Ossian said under his breath, knocking back the last of his ale. "You'd be quite the ride for her, McCloud."

A flash of blue lightning shot across the table, striking Ossian square on the nose.

"Feck!" the Celt swore, rubbing at his face as his grin returned full force. "Just wait 'til I kick your arse again in Brandubh after you've had a few."

Cale rolled his eyes. "Of course you're going to kick my ass. Unlike you, I haven't been playing the damned game for literally *thousands* of years."

Adair stared at Cale, then slowly turned toward Ossian, who didn't so much as flinch.

Thousands of years?

The number echoed, absurd and impossible. But Ossian didn't deny it. Didn't laugh or brush it off like a joke. He just leaned back like the truth *wasn't* seismic. Like he hadn't just cracked the earth open beneath her feet.

Eta returned before Adair could say anything, quietly placing the next round on the table. Her hand lingered on Cale's shoulder just long enough to make the woman glance between the pair before turning and slipping back into the blur of movement behind them.

The question still burned in Adair's throat, but Cale had already launched back into his rant, utterly unaware of the shift in the air. "And making one mistake in this stupid game means it's all over for me. It's brutal."

He tipped back his drink and downed it in one practiced motion. Across the room, Eta was already pouring his next.

"I'm telling you," he muttered, running a hand through his hair, "Can't we just play chess?"

Adair opened her mouth again, the question forming, but it was too late.

Laughter rang from the entryway, followed by the unmistakable thud of boots and the clatter of something that might have once been orderly.

"Is this where the party's moved to?" Takashi appeared beside their table, grinning as he shrugged off his coat.

Nadia trailed behind him, arms crossed and eyes sharp. "Didn't realize we were all getting piss drunk tonight."

Between them came Mia, practically bouncing with excitement. Her wild curls bobbed with every step as she leaned across the bench and peered at the table. "Ooooh, is that whiskey? Can I smell it?"

Adair's chance to press Ossian vanished, swept away by the sudden warmth and motion that spilled into their quiet corner.

The Irishman sipped from his glass and said nothing.

But the smirk tugging at the corner of his mouth told her he knew exactly what he'd just gotten away with.

Chapter Twenty-Three

Adair groaned as she pushed herself upright, her head pounding in time with the faint throb behind her eyes. The dry, bitter taste of old ale still clung to her tongue, and her stomach swirled in quiet protest. Fragments of the previous evening drifted through her mind in no particular order: Takashi's sharp wit, Nadia's raucous laughter, and Mia's warmth spilling into every conversation.

Yet, amid the haze, something felt... off.

She recalled starting the night with Ossian, but when had the others arrived? The memories felt just out of reach, drifting together like random pieces to a puzzle she had yet to assemble. She remembered the main points. They had played games, swapped ridiculous theories, and poured drink after drink until the hours melted away. Still, beneath this messy collage of images, a sliver of unease gnawed at her.

She was forgetting something.

Something important.

Rubbing her temples, the woman reluctantly pulled herself out of bed, squinting against the morning light streaming through her window. Her muscles ached, but not from the conflict or battle with Nash. Something else had clearly transpired.

Glancing at her bedside table, she noticed an empty flask alongside a scattering of Taco Bell wrappers.

"What the hell happened last night?" she murmured.

A knock pulled her from her thoughts. She reached for a rumpled sweatshirt at the foot of her bed, tugging it over her head before calling out, "Come in."

The door opened to reveal Takashi leaning lazily against the frame, his usual calculating expression softened into mischief. "Good morning, Sunshine. Looks like someone had themselves quite the night."

She blinked at him, frowning. "You were there, weren't you?"

"Of course." He stepped inside, folding his arms. "You don't remember?"

"Bits and pieces," Adair admitted, the words cracking from her parched throat. "I'm surprised you guys found us."

Takashi smirked, moving further into the room. "Ossian brought you to the dining hall. Cale texted me, saying something about you needing more than just Ossian's *charming company*, so naturally, we all joined in."

Her brows knit together. "What did we talk about?"

The man's grin spread wider. "Oh, the usual...missions, conspiracy theories about the Order, a heated debate over why Ossian can't make it five minutes without saying something inappropriate."

Adair frowned.

Ossian.

A loose thread tugged in her mind until the memory of Cale's voice cut through the fog like a blade: *Unlike you, I haven't been playing the damned game for literally thousands of years.*

Her stomach dipped. She turned sharply to Takashi. "How old is Ossian?"

The scientist's brow arched at the question. "Old. Like... ancient-old. If I'm remembering correctly, he was born around 223 AD or so. Why?"

Her mouth went dry. "Two hundred...?" She pressed her palms against her eyes, grumbling. "Nope. No, you can't just say that like it's normal."

Takashi tilted his head, clearly entertained. "Are you okay? You look like you've just seen a ghost."

"I don't typically drink that much," she said slowly, "and I don't *typically* find out that the man I've been traveling with is an ancient, immortal fairy tale creature... or whatever..."

Takashi's lips twitched, and then he laughed so hard that he snorted, a genuine sound that seemed to surprise even him. "Oh, my sweet Addie. I would give my entire salary to watch you call him fae to his face."

Adair groaned, flopping back on the bed and dragging her blanket over herself as though she could hide from the information. "This is worse than the hangover. I trusted him without knowing *anything* about him. And now I find out he's... thousands of years old. What else is he hiding?"

Takashi leaned casually against her desk. "Well, according to the reports, you've seen him shift forms. He's older than dirt. He is insanely self-destructive for a man who is fairly indestructible. Oh, and he's in charge of everyone here at the Keep."

The blanket fell to Adair's waist as her head shot up, and she regretted it instantly, clutching her temples as the pain spiked. "He's *what*?"

"Oh, Commander Trevallan likes to *think* he's running the place," Takashi said, clearly enjoying himself. "If he *actually* was, he'd have shipped Ossian off ages ago. But, nope. Ossian's the one at the top. The boss. The big, very *old* boss."

Adair's mouth fell open. "That can't be true. He sure doesn't act like it."

"Right, because you were expecting a brooding, dignified commander who sits in a throne room and issues orders with perfect posture?" Takashi's grin was merciless. "Sorry to disappoint you. Instead, you've got a man who would happily drink you under the table, then set the table on fire just for the fun of it."

She threw a pillow at him. "That's not reassuring!"

"Welcome to the Divide," Takashi said lightly. "We've got eccentric immortals, questionable leadership, and apparently..." He picked up some of the trash littering her floor with a glint in his eye. "Taco Bell wrappers in your bedroom? You're fitting right in."

She muttered something unrepeatable under her breath. "This is too much for my poor hungover brain to process."

"Well, you've got a while to get used to it. Or at least the rest of the day. Now, unless you want me to tell Ossian that you compared him to a 'fairy tale creature', I suggest you—"

"Don't you dare." Her glare was sharp.

Before he could fire back, another knock sounded. Nadia poked her head in, looking disgustingly awake for someone who had been drinking just as much as the rest of them. Her hair was swept up into a loose knot, her eyes bright with mischief. "Gooood morning! How's everyone feeling on this beautiful day?"

"Terrible," Adair groaned. "Where's your girlfriend?"

"Feeling last night as strongly as *you* seem to be," Nadia said, stepping into the room with something in her hand. "Here." She tossed the small pouch towards Adair, and it landed on the bed with a soft thud. "Herbs for the headache. Brew some tea, and you'll feel better in no time at all. No thanks needed... I know I'm amazing." She smirked at her friend, clearly in a much better mood than the pale woman under the blanket.

Adair eyed the medicine like it might bite her. "Does it taste like boiled dirt?"

"Probably," Nadia chirped.

Takashi smirked. "That's true friendship, right there. Poisoning you for your own good."

Adair ignored him. "Did I make a fool of myself last night?"

Nadia's grin widened as she glanced at Takashi. "No more than usual."

"I didn't know Scotland even *had* a Taco Bell," Adair blurted, deciding that changing the subject was safer than letting Nadia sniff out her rattled state over Ossian.

The woman may be her best friend, but she was completely unbearable when she was proven right.

Takashi chuckled. "There's one in Glasgow. Apparently, you were *very* excited about it last night."

"It's tradition," Nadia said, already pulling her phone from her pocket. "Speaking of... Taka, you *have* to see this video from the last time we went there after drinking."

Takashi's interest sharpened instantly. "I would *love* to."

Adair's face flushed, and she lunged across the bed, grappling with Nadia for her phone. "There's nothing to see! It's just... no, seriously, Nadia, don't show him!"

Nadia, laughing wildly, held the phone just out of Adair's reach. "Oh, come on, Addie! You can't deprive him of this gold!"

Adair groaned, managing to knock the phone out of Nadia's hand and onto the floor. "That's it! I'm taking both of you down!" she declared, throwing herself over the bed and wrestling her friend into a playful headlock.

Takashi, now highly amused, bent down and swiped the phone from the floor. "Let's just see what we've got here..."

"No, no, no!"

The video started playing before Adair could even scramble upright. Her own voice filled the room, slurred and far too loud: "*No, your stance is all wrong! Like this... legs wider, or you'll get knocked on your...*"

"Oh my god, turn it off!" she groaned, burying her face in her hands.

Takashi was already doubled over, laughing so hard he had to brace himself against the desk. "You were giving a sword lesson... to a Taco Bell employee?"

"I'm a teacher at heart," Adair muttered, her cheeks burning.

Nadia struggled to speak, the words spilling out between fits of giggles. "You made him swear an oath before handing over our food. You called him '*Squire*'!" The last word came out as a squeak, sending her into another round of uncontrollable laughter.

Adair groaned into her hands. "I resign from this friendship."

Takashi, still grinning, flopped onto the edge of the bed. "Come on, this makes you *legendary*. Not many people can demand fealty over a quesadilla and pull it off."

Adair peeked up at him through her fingers. "I hate both of you."

"Love you too, sword-master," Nadia said, giving her hair a playful ruffle.

"Don't worry," Takashi added. "This will stay between us." He paused for dramatic effect, then grinned. "Unless, of course, you give me a reason to leak it."

Adair pointed a finger at him. "You wouldn't."

"Oh, I absolutely would."

Before she could retaliate, Nadia clapped her hands together. "Alright hangover crew, we're grabbing breakfast. Taka, tell her about the thing."

Takashi's grin turned conspiratorial. "Chef let me add some things to the menu here at the Keep. We collaborated on the perfect hangover fix. A tater tot casserole *covered* in cheese."

Adair's stomach growled loudly enough for them both to hear, and she whined. "Fine. But only because my body is about to mutiny."

Takashi stood and gestured toward the door. "That's the spirit. Let's go before this one tries to feed you *herbs* instead."

He jabbed his thumb towards Nadia, who responded with a middle finger in his face before shoving him playfully on their way out.

Adair didn't realize how wide her smile had grown until the sides of her face began to ache. Though a mountain of questions still weighed on her mind, the presence of her friends beside her and the promise of breakfast ahead made that heaviness feel a little lighter.

For now, she could simply be Adair, not the 'potential Deity.' Merely a young woman surrounded by people who made her laugh, even when she felt like throttling them.

The trio made their way to the Keep's dining hall, the smell of sizzling bacon and fresh coffee practically dragging them toward the long buffet table. Adair's gaze zeroed in on the far end of the line, where under the warm glow of the lamps sat *exactly* what the scientist had promised.

Takashi pointed at the dish with theatrical pride. "Behold, my masterpiece! Hangovers cured in one simple bite. Money back guarantee."

Adair eyed the greasy, cheese-slathered heap as if it might try to fight her. "If this doesn't work, I'm holding you personally accountable for whatever happens next."

Her stomach rolled at the smell, but she still scooped a generous portion, clinging to the hope that the shimmering pools of oil might coat whatever battlefield was happening in her gut. Nadia piled her plate high, muttering something about *fuel for survival*, while Takashi ladled a bowl filled to the brim with his proud creation.

They carried their spoils across the room, claiming a quiet table by the window where sunlight poured over the Keep's training grounds. Adair squinted against the brightness, silently vowing she would never again allow alcohol to make decisions for her body.

"So," Nadia took a slow, luxurious sip of coffee, her eyes glinting, "any plans to humiliate yourself again tonight, or are we attempting sobriety?"

Adair groaned, shoveling a mouthful of cheesy potatoes. "Sobriety gets my vote. At least for the next week...."

Takashi grinned. "See? She's already planning her next conquest."

"Conquest?" The woman scoffed. "You act like I stormed the place."

Nadia choked on her coffee. "You nearly had a repeat of that exact video last night in Glasgow. You quite literally said, '*This Taco Bell is now under my protection*' when we arrived."

Adair buried her face in her hands. "And this is why I don't go out."

"You were the life of the party, though!" Takashi grinned. Then his tone softened. "It's just... good to see you laugh. All that *Deity* business seems to be weighing on you lately."

The words landed heavier than he probably intended, and Adair felt the old tension creep back in, threading its way between her ribs. She'd been trying to avoid thinking about everything, but the doubts were never far away.

Nadia must have caught the subtle shift in her demeanor, because she set her mug down and rested a hand on Adair's arm. "We're not just here to wind you up. If you want to talk about it, we will. If you don't, we won't. Your call."

Adair toyed with her fork, staring at the mess of cheese. "Every time I think I've got a handle on things, something changes. Feels like I'm back at square one."

Takashi leaned back, serious now. "That's part of it, though. Nobody expects you to have all the answers, Addie. We just want you to be honest when you need help."

Gratitude and discomfort twisted together in the woman's chest. Asking for help wasn't in Adair's nature, but with them, it didn't feel like weakness. It felt like... trust.

"I'll try," she said quietly.

"That's all we ask," Nadia said with a small smile.

Takashi raised his fork in a mock salute. "To trying... and to tater tot casserole."

Adair's mouth tugged upward as she raised her own fork. "To tater tots and terrible drunk decisions."

The clink of metal against metal was absurdly small for how grounding it felt. For a little while, with friends beside her and warm food in front of her, the weight of their mission slipped to the edges of her mind. She knew it couldn't stay there forever, but she held onto the reprieve like something precious.

They lingered for over an hour, trading jabs about Takashi's so-called "culinary genius" and mocking Nadia's shoe collection, which Adair maintained was bordering on a criminal offense. By the time their plates were scraped clean, her headache had dulled to a faint echo, and the knot of tension in her chest had loosened with it.

As they stood, Takashi leaned in with a conspiratorial smirk. "Next time you decide to train fast-food workers in swordplay, I'm ready. We could make it a whole program. 'Drive-Thru Defense 101.'"

Adair snorted and gave him a shove. "Repeat it and I'll bury you under the tots."

"Honestly?" Takashi said as he led them out of the dining hall, "there are worse ways to go."

"What's on the agenda for today?" Nadia asked as they strolled down the corridor. "Once Amelia recovers, she's headed out to New York to visit her parents, so I'm free most of the day."

"Oh, Mia's leaving? What a *devastating* loss," Takashi said sarcastically, earning himself a sharp smack on the back of the head from Nadia.

"I want to dig into horn research again. Maybe track art dealer sales for anything similar," Adair said, chuckling at the pair's antics. "I'm heading to my bedroom to grab my stuff, and then it's off to the library."

"Still on that, huh?" Nadia arched a brow.

"Yeah. I'm not expecting a miracle, but it's worth a shot."

"I'm in," Takashi said. "Got my work done yesterday. And really, nothing gets the blood pumping like dusty auction records. Riveting stuff."

"I can help for a bit," Nadia added. "Got a promo to post later, but I'll stick around until then."

Adair had intended to continue the search by herself, but the thought of company eased a knot she hadn't realized she was carrying. Her frustration over their previous failure had been sitting heavily in her gut. She might turn up nothing today, just as she had before, but at least she wouldn't have to stare down that emptiness alone.

"Okay, crew. If we're going to do this, let's do it right," Adair said, letting a thread of hope wind through her words. "Takashi, grab your laptop. Nadi... pens, paper, whatever you can find. We're meeting in the library in fifteen."

Determined nods passed between them before the trio split off down the hall, their hangovers all but forgotten in lieu of their new mission.

The library greeted them with its familiar perfume of aged paper and polished wood as Adair led her companions to her favorite table in the back, far from distractions. They quickly spread out, Nadia placing the pens and paper next to Adair's laptop and notebook, and Takashi setting up his high-tech portable computer on the sturdy table between the shelves.

"Historical references first," Adair said, opening her laptop. "See if there's a pattern in who's interested in ancient instruments like the one we're looking for."

Nadia veered toward a wall of scrolls. "I'll check older texts."

Takashi nodded. "I'll dig through recent art sales. If the horn's got a reputation, someone's bragged about it somewhere."

Hours slid by as they scoured books, scrolls, and ledgers. Adair lost track of time, her focus honed in on every mention of the horn, but the more she read, the more questions piled up. Each mention sent chills down her spine, making her wonder what the Order would use it for.

Finally, she leaned back, rubbing her eyes. "Nothing solid here. Just stories."

Takashi didn't look up from his screen. "Found a few auction records for similar relics. Nothing exact, but..." He froze mid-sentence, then grinned. "Okay, this *is* something! There's a private collector, Roderick Wainwright. Big on ancient artifacts. Last seen in a town an hour from here."

Adair sat forward. "How secretive are we talking?"

"Think dragon hoard with better dinner parties," Takashi said. "Never shows his full collection. He may have the horn."

Nadia scribbled his name into her notes. "We'll need a careful approach. People like that aren't known to open up to strangers." Her brow furrowed mid-thought. "Wainwright... why does that sound so familiar?"

The woman pulled out her phone and began scrolling through her contacts, her fingers flying with the kind of efficiency that came from too much practice. Halfway down the list, she stopped, her expression shifting from confusion to horror.

A groan tore from her throat as she dramatically dropped her head back. "Oh, you have *got* to be kidding me."

Adair leaned forward, concern furrowing her brow. "What? What is it? What do you know?"

"It's not what I know," Nadia muttered, glaring at the screen as though it had personally betrayed her. "It's *who*."

She flopped into the nearest chair with a thud, shoulders slumping in defeat. "I can get us into the next event. We will go in as buyers. Maybe then we'll get him talking about the horn."

Adair's eyes lit up. "Can you really get us in?"

"Oh, I can." Nadia threw one arm over her face with an exaggerated sigh. "You two are so lucky that I love you, because this? This is going to be *torture*."

Chapter Twenty-Four

"Couldn't you two just go? Or even Ossian?" Takashi grumbled, tugging irritably at the collar of his tuxedo. "I don't do fieldwork."

"Technically, this isn't fieldwork, Taka." Nadia glided past him with a knowing smile, her peach dress clinging to every curve as if it had been sewn for the sole purpose of turning heads. She placed a gold-dipped fingernail beneath his chin, tilting his face toward hers. "We are just going for a *casual* night out."

"What in the absolute *hell* is casual about this, Nadia?" Takashi hissed, pulling away from her touch.

The woman's eye roll was nearly audible in its intensity. "Ugh. You and Amelia are cut from the same cloth." She rapped twice on the entrance to Adair's apartment.

Before Takashi could formulate a reply, the door swung open, presenting a sight that had every argument freezing on his tongue in an instant.

Adair stepped out in a sweep of red silk, her auburn hair gathered in a bun held together by a matching dagger. Loose strands framed her face, falling in a way that only deepened the darkness of her lashes and the lure of her lips, painted a striking shade of maroon. The long-sleeve dress clung to her body before dipping low across her back, revealing pale, luminous skin. She closed her clutch, blowing a strand from her cheek with a little huff. "Sorry. I couldn't find my phone."

"You look absolutely banging, babe." Nadia's tone brimmed with triumph as she circled her best friend, inspecting every angle before presenting her to Takashi like a prize. "Doesn't she look incredible?"

The man's composure cracked instantly. Heat surged across his throat and ears, his mouth suddenly dry. "Y-yeah. She does."

Adair's cheeks burned as she shook free of Nadia's hands. "We're going to be late if we don't head out soon."

Nadia flung her silver hair over one shoulder with an exaggerated sigh. "Fine. I was just trying to hype up my bestie." She spun away, peach fabric whispering at her heels as she strode toward the war room.

"Aw, you *do* love me!" Adair called after her, laughter tumbling from her lips as she adjusted her clutch and prepared to follow.

"Wait."

The word stopped her in her tracks as Takashi's hand closed firmly around her wrist. Adair turned toward him, and for an instant the world seemed to tilt, narrowing to the quiet pull of his presence. His onyx gaze held hers, dark and unreadable, and the weight of it sent her breath faltering.

"You look better with your hair down." His voice was husky, almost reluctant, as though he had not meant to give the thought shape.

With a flick of his fingers, the dagger that secured her bun slipped free. One additional twist and the pins loosened as well, sending her dark hair tumbling down in loose waves across her shoulders.

His hand lowered slowly, knuckles brushing her collarbone in a fleeting touch that unraveled her composure with humiliating ease. His eyes dropped briefly to her lips before rising back to meet her amber gaze, causing the space between them to feel impossibly small.

"Hello! Weren't you just bitching about time?" Nadia's sharp voice cut down the hall, shattering the moment. "All my hard work on her hair, gone just like that! Shame on you, Taka." She brandished her clutch like a weapon, waving it in the air with one hand while holding the hem of her dress firmly in the other.

Adair startled, tugging free of Takashi's hand.

"Coming!" Her reply was pitched too high, and she nearly tripped over her heels as she hurried toward Nadia, desperate to escape.

Takashi lingered in the spot where she had left him, his hand flexing slightly as if trying to shake off the memory of her skin. His jaw tightened, and for a heartbeat longer, he stared at the space she had inhabited.

Finally, he forced himself to move, following the women toward the portal and whatever trouble awaited on the other side.

The trio stepped through the ornate entrance of the gallery, greeted by the tinkling chime of crystal glassware and the low hum of refined conversation. Light from the chandeliers spilled across gilded frames and polished marble floors, highlighting the vivid colors of the canvases lining the walls. The air thrummed with cultivated energy as they stepped into a room alive with practiced smiles and watchful eyes.

Nadia was already gliding through the crowd with effortless grace, her presence folding seamlessly into the glamour around them.

"Remember, business first," she murmured over her shoulder, her lips curving in a mischievous smile. "No antics, no drama. We find the information on the horn, and then we disappear."

Adair arched her brow, unable to stop her own grin. "I feel like *you* need that reminder more than we do."

Takashi tugged at his collar, his broad shoulders making the tuxedo look restrictive. "Casual night out, right? Nothing says casual like an overpriced penguin suit." His eyes swept the glittering room, unimpressed. "This is *really* starting to feel like fieldwork."

Nadia's laugh rang bright as she twirled back to face him. "It must be painful to be *so* wrong, Taka. We are just *blending in*."

Adair nudged him lightly. "Just think of yourself as James Bond."

Takashi huffed out a laugh. "If anything, I am a Q, not a Bond."

Adair fell into step beside him. "Could have fooled me." Before she could think better of it, her fingers grazed his arm, the brief contact sending a spark of electricity buzzing between them.

The man cleared his throat sharply, covering the slip with a cough as he angled his face away, pretending to focus on anything else.

"Guys." Nadia rolled her eyes. "Can we please keep our focus on the mission?"

"Fine," Takashi muttered, though his lips twitched with the beginnings of a smile. "We should, at the very least, make sure Wainwright is here tonight."

"He is," Nadia replied breezily. When both of them turned toward her, she sighed dramatically. "Social media isn't just a side hustle for me. It just so happens that I know Wainwright's daughter. *That* is how we scored an invitation. *You're welcome*."

The woman swept into a theatrical curtsy that went entirely unacknowledged by her two companions, who were currently stunned into silence.

Before they could demand further explanation, Nadia's attention flicked across the gallery, her eyes narrowing on a striking woman with flaming scarlet hair. The corner of her mouth lifted as she raised her hand in an exaggerated wave. "Show time, my loves."

Takashi blinked, clearly caught off guard, but Nadia was already looping her arm through his and propelling him forward. Adair sighed and followed, heels clicking against the marble floors.

A passing waiter swept by with a tray of champagne, and Nadia plucked a glass. "I highly recommend you both do the same," she murmured to her companions, eyes wide with warning. "I have a feeling we're going to need it." She tipped the glass to her mouth, then plastered a flawless grin in the direction of their mark.

Exchanging a glance, Adair and Takashi each grabbed a flute as well, steeling themselves as they approached the redhead standing at the center of the crowd.

"Victoria," Nadia sang, her voice pitched higher, dripping with a false affection that Adair knew she only saved for those she truly despised. "It has been *far* too long."

Confusion flickered in the woman's eyes for only a heartbeat before a man at her side leaned in to whisper something. All at once, her expression warmed. "Nadia. You are right. It *has* been much too long."

They embraced with twin air kisses, both smiling in a way that looked more like an act of war than a greeting.

Watching the interaction made Adair's stomach clench.

"And these must be your companions," Victoria purred, tilting her head as she extended her hand with aristocratic grace.

"This is my best friend, Adair, and her boyfriend, Takashi," Nadia said without missing a beat.

Takashi choked on his champagne, coughing violently into his hand as he tried to regain composure. At the same time, Adair nearly tripped over her own feet, forcing her lips into something resembling a smile.

Boyfriend. Wonderful.

She would kill Nadia later.

"Takashi is a collector," Nadia continued in a stage whisper, her hand rising to shield her mouth. "And *filthy* rich."

Their laughter rang out, brittle and insincere, and Adair's skin prickled with secondhand embarrassment. Still, she reached for Takashi's arm, squeezing lightly as his eyes darted toward hers.

The message in her look was simple.

Play along.

Takashi gave her a quick nod, and something in him shifted. His shoulders squared as he leaned forward to take Victoria's hand. He brushed his lips across her knuckles with such smoothness that Adair almost forgot how much he had been grumbling moments before.

"The pleasure is all mine, Miss Wainwright. If the art tonight proves even half as beautiful as its hostess, I imagine I will leave with more than I bargained for." The words rolled off his tongue like silk, and Victoria's lascivious grin confirmed their effect.

Adair's stomach dropped. She had asked him to play along, but she hadn't expected *this*. The ease with which he charmed the woman unsettled her more than she cared to admit. She told herself it didn't matter, that this was part of the act, but the sharp twist of jealousy in her chest said otherwise.

A rapid, grating trill burst from Victoria's mouth, causing Adair to flinch. It took a moment for her to register that the sound was meant to be laughter. "*You* can call me Victoria," the woman said, her voice dripping with desire.

Her gaze lingered on Takashi with a heat that was *far* too hungry for someone wearing an engagement ring the size of a small asteroid on her left ring finger.

Takashi's Adam's apple bobbed violently as he swallowed hard, eyes flicking between the floor and Victoria like he was negotiating for his life.

Relief finally arrived in the form of a server drifting toward them with another tray of drinks. Takashi lunged for it, placing down his empty glass and tilting back a new one in a single, desperate gulp. He set the glass down with the faintest tremor in his hands before immediately reaching for a third. Adair could only stand there and watch, torn between horror and amusement.

Victoria ignored Takashi's theatrics, elegantly raising her flute before taking a sip of her own. "If you will excuse me, I must find my father before the event begins."

Without sparing them another glance, she drifted into the crowd, her diamond-studded black gown catching the light as it trailed behind her.

The moment she vanished, Nadia released a quiet breath and leaned in, her voice pitched low enough to be swallowed by the conversation around them. "That could have gone worse," she murmured, before her gaze flicked toward Takashi. "Please, for the love of all things sacred, can you try to keep it together a little better, Taka?"

"Of course. Should I simply throw a handful of hundreds in the air and be done with it?" He tipped back the remainder of his glass, but

Nadia rolled her eyes, hooking her hand firmly through his arm and tugging him into the dense current of bodies.

He allowed himself to be led, but with his free hand, he reached back for Adair. The unexpected touch startled her, but her fingers slipped into his as easily as breathing. Takashi's palm was warm and calloused, yet the fit felt so natural that it sent her pulse racing.

They weaved through the ever-shifting sea of silk and tuxedos until, at last, they arrived at their destination: a stunning painting illuminated by brilliant lights, its colors swirling together in bold, vibrant strokes. A small rectangle with cursive writing identified the piece as belonging to an anonymous collector.

"Anonymous collector? Looks like we are on the right track," Adair whispered, her finger hovering over the golden plaque.

"Stay close," Takashi murmured, scanning the room. "We don't want to draw too much attention."

Nadia leaned in. "I'll see what I can overhear. You two... just *try* to look like you belong here. Pretty please." She smoothed her dress, squared her shoulders, and melted into a group of critics, her laugh rising like a golden melody above their conversation.

Adair lingered by the painting, her eyes tracing the dizzying whorls of color. The longer she stared, the more familiar the brushstrokes felt, as if they were whispering to some hidden part of her she couldn't quite identify. The feeling only served to convince her further. This piece *had* to be connected to the horn.

"Stunning, isn't it?"

Adair turned to find an older man in a perfectly cut suit standing beside her.

"Absolutely," she said, forcing her voice to remain even. "I find the colors particularly... evocative."

"Ah, yes," he said, leaning in slightly, as if bestowing a secret. "Rumor has it this piece was once part of a collection tied to artifacts of remarkable power. 'Tis a shame that the original owner prefers to remain in the shadows."

Adair's breath hitched. "Do you know who the owner was?"

The man's eyes gleamed with amusement. "Only whispers. Someone who dealt in things *far* beyond art."

Adair looked away for a moment. She tried to calculate her next question, but when she turned back toward the stranger, the space where he had stood was empty.

Before her brain could make any sense of it, Takashi appeared at her side, his expression tight. "I parsed out some intel," he said quietly, his voice pitched for her alone. "There's an additional series of auctions. *Invite only.* Each piece appears to be tied to venerable antiquities. This could be bigger than just one painting."

Adair's stomach clenched. "The horn?"

"Possibly. Or something that can lead us closer to it." His gaze swept the crowd, restless and wary.

Nadia rejoined them, practically vibrating with triumph. "You will *not* believe this. Victoria all but admitted it. Wainwright himself donated the painting."

Adair's pulse jumped. "If he donated it, then he must have access to more like it. Maybe even the horn!"

Takashi's jaw tightened, but his eyes gleamed with excitement. "That makes *him* our strongest lead yet." He reached again for another glass, but Nadia smacked his hand before it could reach the tray.

"You are a renowned art collector tonight, not a lush," she hissed.

Takashi only grinned and plucked a drink anyway. "Every great character deserves an interesting backstory."

Adair smothered a laugh with her hand, but her amusement froze when a shimmer of red caught her eye. She nudged Nadia, whispering, "Incoming."

Victoria sauntered up to the trio and gestured gracefully toward the massive painting before them. "If you truly love this piece, you may want to wait until the end of the auction to speak with my father."

Her gaze lingered on Takashi, searching for any reaction. "He has other items that are more... *mystical*."

It was almost too perfect. Nadia had laid the groundwork with effortless precision, scattering just enough hints to make Victoria believe she was the one in control. The woman's smug confidence all but confirmed it. In truth, the Wainwright family had walked straight into their net, every event unfolding exactly as Nadia had intended.

Takashi stepped forward. "That would be lovely," he replied with a dazzling smile that could have charmed half the room.

It worked a bit too well.

Adair felt that unwelcome pang low in her chest as she watched Victoria's eyes linger on him, a flicker of satisfaction in her gaze.

The chime of a bell interrupted them, signaling the start of the evening's event. A subtle shift rippled through the crowd, the buzz of conversation quieting as anticipation took hold. Beneath the rising tension in the room, Adair felt a flicker of excitement. Wainwright was within reach.

They followed Victoria through the press of elegantly dressed guests to the front of the auction room, where a reserved row awaited them directly opposite the stage. Adair scanned the space as they took their seats, letting her gaze drift over the crowd.

Nearly every chair was filled. Faces of power and wealth surrounded them, each eyeing the pieces on display as though they might devour them whole.

Takashi leaned over to his companions, his voice a whisper. "We need to tread carefully. If Wainwright is as involved in this as we think, he won't be easy to reach. We might have to be the winning bid on something tonight just to get his attention and prove we belong here."

Nadia smoothed a strand of silver hair behind her ear, her expression cool and composed. "Do not worry, darling. I have a plan." Her eyes flicked to Victoria, who was speaking animatedly with one of the coordinators near the stage. "Victoria is already where we need her. Now we let her think she's leading the game."

The auctioneer took the stage to polite applause, introducing the evening's first piece. It was a marble sculpture, centuries old and beautifully carved, but nothing that hinted at deeper secrets. The bidding opened and rose quickly, yet Adair barely heard the numbers called. She was too busy keeping her attention fixed on the room, watching and waiting.

Item after item passed, each fetching impressive sums, until finally the piece they had been anticipating was unveiled. The painting's surface shimmered faintly beneath the lights, its swirling patterns alive in a way that defied explanation. A ripple of interest moved through the crowd, subtle but undeniable.

Takashi straightened. "This is it. We need to make sure we're the winning bid."

"Patience, love," Nadia murmured, her fingertips drumming lightly against her clutch. "Remember, *we* are in control. If we look too eager, Wainwright will get suspicious."

She tilted her head towards Victoria, who had turned her attention on them with a keen, measuring gaze.

The auctioneer began the bidding at a modest price, but the number climbed swiftly, spurred on by eager voices across the room, paddles lifting in a flurry.

As Adair scanned the congregation, she noticed something strange. Two rows behind the trio, a tall man in a perfectly tailored suit had raised his paddle. He had not bid on a single item all evening, and yet here he was, eyes locked on *their* prize.

She leaned toward Takashi, indicating subtly in the man's direction. "Do you recognize him?"

Takashi's eyes narrowed as he risked a glance. "No, but he seems serious about the painting."

As the numbers soared higher, Nadia joined in with an elegant lift of her paddle, but the man countered immediately. A prickle of awareness ran along Adair's skin. This wasn't a casual buyer testing the waters. Whoever he was, he knew what that painting was *truly* worth.

"Five hundred thousand," the auctioneer announced.

The man behind them didn't hesitate, his gaze locking on Nadia as his paddle rose.

Nadia's lips curved into a faint, almost amused smile, as though this were nothing more than a game between them. She raised her paddle once more.

"Seven hundred thousand," she announced.

The room fell still as all eyes shifted to the man in the back. His cold stare lingered on Nadia for one long, unblinking moment before he stood, adjusted his cufflinks, and strode from the room, leaving a stir of muted whispers in his wake.

"Sold," the auctioneer declared, bringing his gavel down with a decisive crack. "To the lady in the front."

Nadia's grin was victorious. "That was easier than expected."

Takashi turned to her, his brows furrowing. "*Too* easy. That man was *not* here for the art."

"Takashi's right," Adair's gaze lingered on the door where he had disappeared, her unease coiling tighter. "He knew something about that painting. We need to stay on our guard."

Victoria appeared at their side, smiling brightly. "You've done it! My father is thrilled."

She gestured toward the back of the room, and Adair's breath caught in her throat. The man Victoria had indicated was standing among a cluster of well-dressed patrons, his graying hair swept back neatly.

It wasn't his air of authority that sent a prickle down her spine. It was his face. She instantly recognized him as the strange man who had intercepted her in the gallery, causing any lingering doubt about his involvement in their world to dissolve in an instant. They had come to the right place.

Victoria spoke up, her eyes locking onto Takashi. "Would you like to meet him?"

Takashi's polite smile never faltered, though there was a flicker of calculation in his eyes. "We would love that."

Adair's pulse quickened as they followed Victoria across the polished floor, every step bringing them closer to the man she believed held the key to the horn's location.

Wainwright greeted them with a measured smile. "Congratulations on your purchase." He reached out to shake Nadia's hand. "That painting is one of my more... *unique* acquisitions."

Nadia inclined her head. "It's an honor, Mr. Wainwright. We've heard you have an eye for the mystical. We couldn't resist the chance to see it for ourselves."

Interest flickered on Wainwright's features, subtle but unmistakable. "Ah. Collectors with taste. Perhaps you'd enjoy seeing something more... *exclusive*?"

Adair felt a jolt of anticipation. This was the opening they had hoped for. She met Nadia's gaze briefly, the silent exchange speaking volumes.

"We'd be delighted," Nadia replied smoothly.

Wainwright gestured toward a private door at the far end of the gallery. "Follow me. I think you will find this particular piece *fascinating*."

He guided them through a pair of gilded double doors into a smaller, dimly lit room adjacent to the main gallery. Inside, the atmosphere transformed dramatically. The walls were adorned with pieces that were not only far older but also more esoteric than the modern art displayed in the bustling auction hall. Ancient artifacts, relics, and paintings filled the space, each one exuding an inexplicable sense of mystery.

"Here we are," Wainwright announced with a flourish, gesturing to a large, intricately carved sculpture that dominated the center of the room. "One of my more prized possessions. It's not for sale, of course, but I thought collectors of your taste might appreciate its beauty."

Nadia feigned awe, her eyes widening as if it were the most impressive art she had ever witnessed. Adair couldn't even pretend. Her mind remained focused on the true goal of the evening. Takashi was the single individual, however, whose eyes Wainright's eyes locked onto. The man stood back, his gaze drifting away from the piece as if it wasn't worth his precious time.

"I'll admit," Takashi began, his tone edging on boredom, "this isn't quite what I've been looking for."

Wainwright arched his brow, intrigued, almost offended. "Oh? And what could you be seeking, if not this?"

His tone was polite, but it exuded the confidence of someone accustomed to being admired, regardless of whether it was warranted.

Takashi met his eyes evenly, his voice dropping to a quieter, more serious register. "I've been hunting for a horn. A renowned heirloom, not unlike the ones in this room. *This*, however, is much older and more powerful. Far more than the pieces I have seen up for sale tonight."

Wainwright's smile faltered for the briefest moment, but then he recovered, eyes narrowing slightly as he studied Takashi.

"A horn, you say?" Wainwright folded his hands in front of him. "I'm familiar with many such items. And you thought you'd find this instrument here?"

Takashi drew a slow breath. "It is said to be linked to legends. I've heard whispers that it has been lost for centuries, passed quietly between private owners, hidden from the world. It is supposed to reside in one of the greatest collections known to man. I had *assumed* that meant I could find it here."

Adair's eyes followed Wainwright, noting the shift in his posture. The man's charm had faded, replaced by a careful calculation. He was no longer just playing host. He was being tested, baited, and the sharpness in his gaze confirmed that it was working.

Wainwright nodded slowly. "Ah, I see. You speak of something more... *mythical* than material." He chuckled lightly, but there was an edge to it. "A friend of mine once acquired such a horn long ago. A rare and valuable piece, steeped in legend, as you say."

Takashi's eyes sharpened. "And what happened to it?"

Wainwright's gaze drifted over the surrounding items, as though measuring how much to reveal. "He is a private man, much like myself, with an extensive collection that could rival the world's greatest museums. I will admit, I tried to acquire the horn myself, but he was not inclined to part with his treasures, least of all something as singular as that piece. As far as I know, it remains in his possession. The one that got away, as they say." His chuckle was dark, carrying a hint of regret beneath the amusement.

Adair's heart raced at the revelation. If the horn still existed, locked away, then this was precisely the lead they'd been hunting for.

"Who is this man?" Nadia asked. "Surely, someone of your standing could help us make contact."

Wainwright's smirk was cautious. "I wish it were that simple. My friend is... elusive. He does not welcome visitors, particularly those seeking to negotiate for his treasures. I have known him for years, and even I have not seen the inside of his vault in some time."

Adair exchanged a glance with Takashi. Unless they could discover a way to get closer to this elusive 'collector', they had reached a dead end.

Takashi leaned in slightly. "You have certainly piqued my interest, Mr. Wainwright. Perhaps if you could arrange an introduction, we might strike a deal. I am prepared to offer whatever it takes to acquire that horn. Your commission for the assistance would be... more than generous."

Wainwright huffed out a laugh. "That is a compelling offer, Mr. Takashi, but as I said, my friend is not easily persuaded. If, however, you are as serious as you claim, I can put in a word. But understand this. If he refuses, it is best not to push. Some things are better left *untouched*."

The warning hung heavy in the air, but Takashi did not flinch. "I understand. Let's hope it does not come to that."

Wainwright gave a slight nod, acknowledging the shared understanding, before adding, "Very well. I'll contact him, though I cannot make any promises. In the meantime, enjoy the painting you've won tonight. I sincerely hope I will have the pleasure of your company again in the near future."

As Wainwright slipped out of the room, Adair, Takashi, and Nadia huddled together, quickly lowering their voices.

"This is it," Adair whispered. "We're one step closer."

Takashi's gaze swept over the room before settling back on her, his expression tight. "If Wainwright's friend has the horn," he said slowly, "we will need a way to gain access. And something tells me it will not be as simple as making an offer."

At that, Nadia's face lit up in a knowing smirk. "Oh, Taka. Didn't you know? Simple is overrated. I think chaos suits us *much* better."

Chapter Twenty-Five

Nearly a month had passed since that night at the auction, and the silence from Wainwright was beginning to weigh on them all.

Takashi had worn his usual mask of indifference, but after the lengthy wait with no news, the cracks were starting to show. Adair had caught him pacing more than once in his lab, phone in hand, eyes flicking to the screen every time it buzzed, only to scowl when it was never the call he wanted.

Nadia, of course, seemed entirely unbothered. If anything, her amusement had only grown as the days dragged on, especially after the '*bill*' incident.

"*You should've seen his face,*" Nadia said, wiping a laughter-induced tear from her eye. "*The higher-ups were* livid. *Seven hundred grand for a painting we didn't even need!*"

Takashi shot her a glare from across the room, arms folded tightly against his chest. "*I cannot believe you bid that much and then threw me under the bus for it. Why couldn't you just get approval?*"

Nadia planted her hands on her hips. "*And how exactly was I supposed to ask for approval while in the middle of an unauthorized mission, locked in a bidding war with a tall, dark stranger? Besides, we both know they're good for it."*

Mia reached over and brushed a stray lock of hair from Nadia's face, her smile beaming. "Awe. I hate that I missed all the fun."

"Your idea of fun is about as thrilling as Adair's," Nadia replied with a scoff, spinning around to press a long, deliberate kiss to Mia's lips. "But yes, it would have been better with you there."

"Blowing through the boss's money isn't my idea of fun," Takashi muttered under his breath, shoving his glasses up the bridge of his nose and turning back to the data streaming across his computer screen.

Nadia waved him off. "Oh, spare me the moral outrage. Watching you get reamed out was worth every penny. Amelia and I even placed a bet on whether or not you'd have an aneurysm."

Takashi's gaze swept the room in search of something he could throw, while Nadia let out a squeal and darted behind her girlfriend, clutching her like a makeshift shield.

Adair smiled faintly at the memory, though her attention quickly returned to the task before her.

Training had felt all-consuming these past weeks, leaving her muscles aching and her knuckles raw. She had spent countless hours in the sparring hall, blade in hand, practicing until her body moved without thought. The thing that truly troubled her most, however, was more *compact.*

In front of her lay a single pebble. It was so small and ordinary, it seemed *absurd* that it was the source of so much grief. She stared at the stone, desperately willing it to move, her brow furrowing as she poured everything she had into that tiny, stubborn thing.

Nothing.

She lifted her hand to try again, summoning the energy the way that Ossian had taught her. She imagined it rising, light as air, answering her call. Her focus narrowed until the world shrank to this one simple act.

But still, it refused to budge.

"It's like it's glued to the damn floor," Adair muttered. With a groan of frustration, she allowed her hand to drop.

"Try again," came a familiar voice.

She turned to see Takashi leaning against the doorframe, his tuxedo from the auction long replaced by his usual fitted shirt and worn sweater. The man's expression was guarded, but concern shone clearly through his onyx eyes.

"I've tried a hundred times," Adair admitted, letting out a long breath. "It won't move."

The man stepped forward and crouched beside her, examining the tiny stone as though it might reveal some hidden truth.

"Looks like a normal rock to me," he teased gently.

She shot him a flat look. "Hilarious. It's not that simple."

"I know." He rose to his full height and crossed his arms. "But maybe you're overthinking it."

Adair frowned. "What's that supposed to mean?"

"You've been training to fight, right? And when you fight, you don't think through every motion. You react. It's instinct. Maybe this should be the same. Stop trying to force it. Just... *feel* it."

The woman hesitated, mulling over his words. He wasn't wrong. All this time, she had been trying to bend the pebble to her will. Maybe what she needed wasn't force, but surrender.

"I'm not a traveler," Takashi said quietly, stepping behind her, "but do you mind?"

Adair shook her head, though her pulse quickened when she felt the warmth of him close at her back. He placed one hand lightly at her elbow, the other settling at her hip. The contact was deceptively casual, yet her skin tingled where his fingers rested.

"Let everything else fall away," the man murmured, his breath ghosting against the curve of her ear.

Adair closed her eyes and drew a slow, deliberate breath, willing her thoughts to settle. The tension in her shoulders began to loosen as she focused on the quiet current humming through her veins. With Takashi's help, she could feel it.

She could sense his steadiness, the strength coiled beneath the calm he wore like armor. It grounded her as she reached beyond herself into that shared energy that bound all living things.

Adair reached for the pebble, not with force but with quiet intent. She did not command it to move. Instead, she invited it, and the air around her responded with a faint shiver.

Her eyes flew open just as the stone gave a subtle, undeniable tremor.

"I... I did it!" The words tumbled out in a breathless laugh, and before she could stop herself, she spun and threw her arms around Takashi's neck.

The man caught her effortlessly, hard muscle beneath her hands, waves of heat extending from every place their skin met. For a heartbeat, she simply reveled in it.

Then reality struck.

She shifted to retreat, but his arms tightened around her further.

"See?" Takashi's voice was low, intimate. "I knew you could do it."

He reached up slowly to push a strand of hair behind her ear, his gaze lingering on her mouth before meeting her eyes again. "I never doubted you for a moment. You are... amazing."

"Thank you," she whispered, unable to tear her eyes away. "You... uh... aren't so bad yourself."

A slow, deliberate clapping cut through the quiet, and Adair and Takashi jumped apart, startled by the interruption.

Ossian stood in the doorway, one shoulder propped casually against the frame, his gaze fixed on them with cool amusement. He let the sound of his applause die steadily before speaking.

"Well done, Hanlon," he drawled. His tone was light, but his eyes told a different story.

As Ossian sauntered into the room, Adair fought the urge to look back at Takashi, her focus fixed instead on the storm in the Celt's eyes. The burly man stood nearly the same height as the scientist, but his broader frame carried a weight of authority that made the space feel smaller the moment he had entered.

"Seo." Ossian acknowledged Takashi with a clipped nod, something passing between them before his tone sharpened. "You trying to bankrupt me?"

Takashi's typically easy manner hardened as his shoulders squared, dark eyes reflecting the challenge. "You can thank Nadia for that. But the purchase brought us the lead that we needed on the Dord Fian."

Ossian scoffed loudly. "Fecking Nadia."

The words felt laced with an amount of venom that Adair didn't understand. She wanted to ask for clarification, but instinct warned her that this was not the moment to do so.

The Irishman shook his head before redirecting his gaze to Takashi. "Did you, or did you not leave the Keep with Hanlon?"

Ossian's eyes were currently burning into the scientist, but Adair felt the weight of his anger all the same. Her stomach dropped as she realized that this was not about money at all.

This was about *her*.

Takashi narrowed his eyes. "I did."

Ossian stepped forward, his voice dropping to a deadly calm. "You removed a potential Deity from the Keep, without permission from me or the Commander. What in the ever-loving *fuck* were you thinking?"

Adair flinched at the word.

Commander.

He had said the word so seriously. In the past, she had only heard the term come out of the Irishman's mouth in a way that was meant to mock the position. It had always been Eddy, casual and familiar.

Hearing the title fall so formally from his lips was jarring, but it was not the formality that unsettled her most. It was the way he loomed over the dark-haired man, as though the scientist before him was not a friend at all but an enemy on the battlefield.

Takashi's jaw tightened. "We needed a contingency in case Adair doesn't manifest. Something to keep her safe and off *your* chessboard."

His words were directed at the Celt, but his eyes flicked toward Adair for just a heartbeat too long.

In a flash, Ossian had Takashi slammed against the wall. His fist was knotted in the man's shirt, face flushing with barely leashed fury. "The ogham don't lie, Seo."

Adair's gasp tore from her before she could stop it, fear surging sharp and hot through her chest. She attempted a step forward, but her feet refused to move, as though the floor had trapped her in place.

Takashi sneered in the man's face. "You have been fighting this war too long, Ossian. You will sacrifice *anyone* if it gives you an advantage. You don't care what pieces get lost in your little game."

He indicated to the woman at Ossian's back with his chin. "Even *her*."

The fist cracked across his jaw before Adair could draw a breath. Takashi staggered and fell to the floor, blood marking his lip.

"*You* put her at risk," Ossian snarled, towering above him.

He dragged Takashi back to his feet.

Another brutal strike split the silence, then another, until a final blow drove into his ribs with a crunch that echoed across the stone walls.

The scientist doubled over, spitting red onto the slate floor, but Ossian's rage wasn't spent.

"P-please, stop." Adair's voice trembled, barely audible over the harsh rasp of her ragged breaths. Her hands clawed at her throat as if trying to pry it open, struggling for air that refused to come.

At once, Ossian released Takashi, turning to her as if waking from a trance.

"Hanlon."

He was at her side in a heartbeat, his calloused hands hesitating, suddenly aware of the pain his actions had inflicted. With a slow breath, he gently cradled her face, his eyes shining with regret.

Takashi wiped the crimson streaks from his mouth, his gaze lingering on Adair, watching the way she responded to his touch.

With a bitter shake of his head, he slipped silently from the room, chest tight with the knowledge that he had lost the fight in every way that truly mattered.

"Anáil, Hanlon." Ossian's fingers traced Adair's jaw, tilting her chin until her golden eyes met his stormy green.

He pried one of her hands away from where she had begun to clutch her middle and guided it to his chest, pressing the other against her own ribcage. His body was solid beneath her palm, his heartbeat steady as a war drum, while her own raced like a frightened animal. He inhaled slowly, urging her to follow, and though at first her breaths came in jagged snatches, little by little they began to steady.

Tears sliding down her cheeks, Adair met his gaze with trembling resolve. "It was me," she whispered. Her throat felt raw. "*I* found the lead. *I'm* the one who pushed them to follow up on it. *I* made them go to the auction. You should be angry with *me*."

The blood drained from Ossian's face, his hands falling away from her. "Hanlon, I know Nadia, and I know you."

She grabbed his arm with surprising force, nails digging into his skin. "I swear it. They only followed because of me. It was my idea from the beginning. I knew how much the horn meant to the Divide. To *you*."

The Irishman's face tightened, torn between indignation and something more fragile. He raked a hand through his hair and stepped back, his chest rising hard and uneven.

"Hanlon," he said, shaking his head. "What if Order agents had been there?"

She swallowed, her voice small. "I... don't know what we would have done. I wasn't thinking."

"No, you weren't. None of you were. Aside from Collins, not one of you is a field agent, and she's only good for reconnaissance."

The weight of his words crushed down on her. She did not want to imagine what might have happened if the night had gone differently.

"You are far too important to this cause, Hanlon." Ossian closed the space between them, gently brushing away a tear that stubbornly clung to her cheek.

His fingers lingered, a fleeting balm against the heat of her skin, and Adair's breath hitched at the contact. After a moment, his hand drifted down, reaching for the small stone that lay in the center of the floor.

"You moved the pebble. That's the first manifestation of a Traveler." He weighed it in his palm, turning it over once before tossing it lightly into the air.

Adair stood frozen, her eyes locked on the small rock as if it carried the answer to every question that haunted her. A fleeting sense of pride swelled in her chest, but unease quickly followed. Progress brought with it a sense of expectation, and along with that expectation came a burden that she wasn't sure she was ready to bear.

"The first manifestation," Ossian repeated softly. He caught the pebble and gently pressed it into her palm, his touch sending a spark racing through her nerves. "The road ahead is long, Hanlon."

Adair swallowed hard and nodded. "I know."

Ossian searched her face briefly before turning away, tension lining his broad shoulders. "This isn't only about the horn. It is about keeping you alive."

Adair's stomach gave a sharp twist, but before she could voice a response, the doors swung open.

Laughter spilled into the room as Nadia and Mia entered the training hall, only to quickly falter when Nadia's eyes landed on the pair in the center of the room. Her smile slipped, replaced by a sharpened focus as her gaze flicked between Adair and Ossian.

"Interrupting something?" Nadia's tone was light, almost teasing, but there was a pointed edge beneath it. She leaned against the frame, arms crossed.

Mia, quieter but no less observant, tugged gently on her girlfriend's sleeve and stepped farther inside. "What happened?" she asked softly.

"Nothing you need to concern yourself with," Ossian snapped, his annoyance quick to rekindle under Nadia's scrutiny. He spared Adair a glance before turning back toward the couple. "Wainwright responded."

"How did you know that?" Nadia's eyes narrowed.

The Irishman let out a scoff. "When would you ever come to the training hall on your own, Collins?"

Mia clapped a hand to her mouth, struggling not to laugh, leading Nadia to turn her glare on her girlfriend. "Don't encourage him, traitor."

"The details, Collins. We don't have all day." Ossian folded his arms across his chest, one brow lifting as if daring her to keep stalling.

Nadia exhaled sharply and pulled out her phone.

"Wainwright sent an address. It's somewhere in the countryside, far away from any town or village. He says he couldn't get in contact with the collector, but he guarantees the location is legitimate."

Ossian leaned back against an elliptical, a smirk tugging at his mouth. "And you trust this?"

Mia peered at the screen over Nadia's shoulder. "That is far from any city. What kind of collector hides out in the middle of nowhere?"

"The eccentric kind," Ossian muttered. "And Wainwright gave no other details?"

Nadia shook her head. "That's his personality...theatrics, always, but I agree it seems off. We should be careful."

Adair sat in silence, her mind turning over the possibilities. The Dord Fian wasn't just an artifact to the Order. It was a source of power, a chance to unleash more harm on those they wished to control. The Divide *had* to reach it before the enemy did, and with each passing moment, the urgency of that mission grew stronger.

"We go," Adair said finally. "We can't afford to wait any longer."

Mia's lips curved into a faint smile, but her eyes were solemn as they met Adair's. "Then we need to prepare. We have no idea who this collector might be or whether the Order has already learned of the location."

Ossian stretched his arms up, resolute in their decision. "Gather what you need. We leave at dawn, Hanlon." He started toward the door.

Nadia took a step forward. "I am coming with you," she stated firmly.

Mia caught her arm, already sensing the argument, as Ossian spun on the woman, nostrils flaring.

"You are recon, Collins, not a warrior. Perhaps if you had spent more time in this room, things would be different." With that, he stormed out.

Nadia bristled, but Mia slipped a hand over her mouth and whispered against her ear. The tension drained from her shoulders, if only a fraction.

"Mia, I cannot just..." Nadia broke off, swallowing the rest as her girlfriend's hand cupped her cheek.

"I know," Mia said gently.

Adair cleared her throat, and Nadia rolled her eyes.

"I didn't forget you were here, bitch." Crossing the room, she caught the woman's pale hands in her own, her usual grin replaced by an uncharacteristic seriousness. "I'm going to say something you're not going to like," she began, squeezing tighter. "You're a grown woman, and I can't tell you what to do. And I know we've had this argument before. But please, Addie. Be careful trusting Ossian."

Adair opened her mouth, already ready to protest. "I really don't think—"

"No." Nadia cut her off, shaking her head. "I'm not arguing with you about this. I'm giving you my *blessing*..." She made a face, as if the word tasted sour, "...to make your own choices. But my gut won't shut up about this. Something is coming. Something bad. And I can't lose you again. I just can't."

Adair's first instinct was to argue, but the sincerity in her friend's gaze gave her pause. "You won't," she said quietly. "I know you don't like it, but I do trust Ossian. He has his demons... more than most, but he has *always* had my back."

Nadia arched a brow, and Adair winced as the memory of frigid waves came flooding back. "Well... except that one time. But honestly, I could have made better choices in Ireland, and I don't blame him for that."

"I fucking do," Nadia muttered darkly.

Mia bumped her shoulder with a playful nudge, and the woman's gaze softened.

The Brit exhaled, still reluctant. "Fine. But promise me, Addie. At the first sign of trouble, you run. You run faster than you ever have in your life. Got it?"

Adair's throat tightened. She held Nadia's gaze, taking note of the unshed tears her friend was struggling to hold back, before throwing her arms around the woman's neck in an impulsive embrace. "I promise."

A beat later, she stretched her free arm out and tugged Mia into the circle, trapping all three of them together in a tight hug. They stood like that for a while, leaning into one another, stealing what peace they could before the incoming storm.

Adair knew there was plenty to be afraid of. The war. The Order. The lives already lost, and the countless more they were fighting to save.

But in the middle of it all, she had *this*.

She had people who loved her enough to worry, enough to fight for her, enough to hold her steady when the ground was shifting beneath her feet.

And *that* was worth every risk she was about to take.

Chapter Twenty-Six

Adair moved quietly through the corridor of the Keep, her hands absentmindedly brushing the rough stone walls. She told herself she was only walking to clear her head, but deep down she knew better.

She needed to check on Takashi.

Since the fight with Ossian, guilt had been slithering beneath her skin, spiking every time she thought of the way the man had stood there, taking hit after hit for *her* decisions. The thought that she had allowed this to happen weighed heavily on her conscience.

More unsettling was the quiet fear that perhaps *he* blamed her too, that maybe he hated her now. Even if that were true, she would rather face his anger than sit with the hollow ache of not knowing whether or not he was okay.

Adair paused at the entrance to the lab, her hand hovering for a moment before she finally knocked. The sharp rap of knuckles against metal echoed down the hall, but no sound came from within. With a quiet sigh, she pushed the chrome door open and slipped inside.

Takashi sat hunched at his workstation, the sharp light of the screens reflecting in his glasses. He did not look up as she entered, his focus locked on the string of data in front of him.

"Takashi?"

The scientist's hands stilled above the keyboard. He turned, blinking in surprise, but his features softened the moment he caught sight of her. "Hey! You look worried. Is everything alright?"

Adair had rehearsed the words on the way here, but they slipped away the moment he met her eyes.

"I... just wanted to check on you," she said finally, stepping further inside. "How are you holding up?"

"Oh, you know. Never better."

Takashi tried for a smile, but it faltered as he pulled his glasses away, revealing the full extent of his injuries.

"Oh, gods. Taka." The words tumbled out before Adair could stop them.

She crossed the room quickly, fingers rising to carefully cradle his face. She tilted it multiple ways, attempting to assess the damage. Concern furrowed her brow, and a knot formed in her stomach as she took in the sight of his split lip and the dark bruise that had rapidly spread beneath one eye.

"No, really. I'm alright, Addie," Takashi said softly. He reached up and gently took her wrists, easing them away.

"Don't tell me you're fine when I can see that you aren't." Adair dropped her hands reluctantly, folding her arms across her chest as she moved away, leaning back against a nearby table. "What Ossian did was unacceptable. How am I supposed to focus on the mission when the people I care about are hurt?"

Adair's words and their underlying meaning seemed to catch the man off guard, his eyes flicking to her, unsure how to respond. A charged silence stretched between the pair, but the moment was broken when Takashi's attention seemed to snap to something she couldn't see.

He straightened slowly, his gaze narrowing on her face. "Hold still."

Adair blinked at him, her frown deepening. The way his eyes had locked on her made the hairs at the back of her neck prickle.

Did she have something *on* her?

"Wait, what? What is it?" Her voice climbed, tight with the kind of panic she hadn't felt since the time a hornet had gotten trapped in her hoodie as a kid.

Oh gods.

It had to be a spider.

Or worse.

She slapped a hand over her hair, twisting as though she might catch whatever monstrous thing he'd seen before it burrowed in.

"Is it a bug? Please tell me it's not a bug."

As she flailed, her weight shifted just enough against the table behind her that one leg screeched across the slate floor. She wobbled, arms flying out, the sudden movement of the desk inciting pure instinct as she let out a strangled yelp.

The table lurched as her balance vanished, and she stumbled forward in the least graceful way possible. Reaching for anything to stop herself, her hand smacked against the corner of his desk, and something metal and entirely too sharp bit into her palm.

She hissed, jerking back, and clutched her hand against her chest, heat flooding her cheeks as she caught sight of the angry line of red forming across her skin.

Of course.

"You really can't be left alone for a minute, can you?" Takashi's brows lifted, his mouth curving slightly.

The dryness of his tone was so unexpected that Adair let out a giggle despite the situation.

"Ignore the laugh. That was not funny," she muttered, pouting with mock seriousness.

"It is a *little* funny." Takashi's eyes lingered on her face, and before she could process what he was doing, his hand lifted, fingers brushing lightly against her cheek. "To answer your question... No, there is no *bug*. You just had a little dirt, silly girl. Nothing to break tables over."

The touch was so gentle that Adair froze, caught between the warmth of his hand and the sudden, disorienting rush in her veins.

Then, as if nothing had happened, Takashi stepped back and reached for a small device on his desk. The slender piece of metal gleamed with faintly glowing runes, and he turned it in his hand as though weighing whether or not to use it.

At last, he crossed the space between them.

"This time, *actually* hold still, please."

Adair frowned, bristling at the command, but before she could respond, he activated the tool. A soft yellow light spilled across her palm, and she blinked down in surprise. The sting faded almost instantly beneath the warm glow, leaving behind only the steady thrum of her pulse as she looked up at him.

"I've been working on this for quick healing in the field," he said, holding her hand gently as he checked the device's work. "It's designed for minor wounds, but it could buy someone enough time to reach a healer."

A small smile tugged at Adair's lips. "You and your inventions. Always finding ways to keep us safe."

Takashi shrugged with a grin, "All in a day's work, I guess." He looked up to meet her eyes, but the woman's attention was locked elsewhere.

Adair paused for a moment before reaching for the device, her fingers grazing his as she gently took the piece of metal from his hand. Slowly, deliberately, she guided the healing light across his face and ribs, each movement lingering as she worked to ensure every bit of damage was undone.

Takashi's eyes softened, gratitude flickering across his features. When she returned the tool to him, their digits met again, and a spark flared at the point of contact. She jerked back instinctively, a shiver tracing her spine as she dropped the device back into his palm.

Adair's gaze darted to a cluttered table farther away, a feeble attempt to distract herself.

"Oh, wow. That looks cool. What are you working on now?" she asked, her voice too light.

Takashi's expression brightened in an instant. He gestured toward the metallic sphere suspended in its containment field. "A prototype for a new energy source. If it works, the Keep could operate independently without requiring external supplies. Entirely self-sustaining."

Adair raised her brows, genuinely impressed by his ingenuity. "That's huge!"

"Assuming it doesn't explode before I can stabilize it, then yes. It's pretty *huge*." Takashi wiggled his eyebrows.

A bright laugh slipped from Adair, loosening some of the tension that had been knotting her chest. "Only you would invent something that might blow us all sky-high," she said, rolling her eyes.

The scientist leaned casually against the table beside her, shoulders easing as the moment lingered. She realized, with a quiet pang, how rare it was to see him like this. After everything that had happened, Takashi still seemed at peace in his little world, and for a few breaths, she was happy to share in that. Figuring he needed to get back to work, she started for the door.

"Stay for a while," Takashi said suddenly. "If you need to... We don't need to talk or anything. I... just don't mind if you want to be here."

Adair hesitated, then nodded, grateful for the offer. She sank into a nearby chair, her body relaxing as she let the hum of the lab envelop her.

The lanky man returned to his desk, but she noticed the way he kept glancing at her, making sure she was alright. It was a small thing, but it meant more to her than she could explain in words.

It wasn't long before she spoke again. "I really am sorry about earlier. With Ossian."

Takashi's tongue brushed the newly healed skin of his lip, his mouth turning up into a smirk. "Oh, right. I almost forgot *you* were the one throwing punches."

Adair rolled her eyes, relieved that he didn't harbor any resentment. "I'm serious. I never meant for you to get caught in the middle."

Takashi set his glasses aside and met her eyes. His voice was quieter now, though there was an edge beneath it. "He wasn't wrong, Adair. Leaving without telling anyone was reckless. You could have been killed."

Her chest tightened with guilt all over again. "I know, I'm so sorry. I put us *all* at risk."

Takashi exhaled slowly, weariness touching his features as he shook his head. "Addie, don't apologize. Please. Trust me when I say that I understand."

She leaned forward, elbows on her knees, as she searched his face. "I didn't think Ossian would react the way he did. If I had known…"

Takashi's gaze dropped to the desk, his fingers tracing its edge. "You and Ossian… there's always tension there. And now, with everything happening, it's only getting worse."

Her heart stumbled. "It's not like that," she said quickly, though even to her own ears it sounded thin. She pressed on. "I don't think he even cares if people get hurt. Collateral doesn't matter to him."

Takashi lifted his gaze to hers, his expression tightening. "Maybe his methods are flawed. But someone needs to remind us, especially Ossian, that innocents don't need to be involved."

Her eyes lifted sharply to his, catching the flicker of doubt there.

Takashi's voice softened. "Addie… you're one of those innocents, too. You shouldn't feel forced into all of this. Some things aren't worth the risk, *especially* if you're not ready."

She sat back, the words hitting like a stone in her gut.

Her reply came, quiet but firm. "No one is ever ready to fight a war, Takashi. And no one is *forcing* me. Ossian may have his flaws, but *he* trusts me to do this."

Takashi closed his eyes briefly, letting out a slow breath. When he looked at her again, there was something raw in his gaze.

"I *do* trust you. It's everything *else* I don't trust. My life has always been numbers and variables. There are too many unknowns here, and I just… don't know how to handle that. I will do my best, though."

The man pushed to his feet and crossed to one of the cabinets before she could respond. From it, he retrieved a small vial filled with shimmering liquid and pressed it into her hand.

"What is this?" Adair asked, lifting it toward the light.

"Something Mia and I have been testing. It might help with your anxiety. Still experimental, but it could ease some of the weight." His voice had returned to its careful, professional cadence, though she caught the flicker of nerves behind it.

Adair blinked, warmth flickering through her chest at the thought. "You two made this for me?"

He shrugged. "You're not the only one struggling. We thought it might help."

The woman opened the vial and swallowed the bitter liquid in one go. A slow calm spread through her chest, her racing thoughts quieting just enough to let her breathe.

Takashi watched her closely. "Better?"

She nodded, releasing a long, contented sigh. "Thank you, Takashi. This means the world to me." Reluctantly, she rose to her feet. "As much as I want to stay, I really need to get going. I still have to pack for tomorrow."

Takashi leaned back against the counter, folding his arms. His gaze lingered on her as though he wanted to say more, but the words never came.

"Tomorrow's going to be a lot," he said instead.

Adair moved toward the door, pausing at the frame. She glanced back, her words more vulnerable than she intended.

"You'll be here when I get back, right?"

"I'll always be here for you," Takashi replied without hesitation.

Then, almost too quickly, he corrected himself. "We, I mean. *We* are all rooting for you, Addie. You're not alone in this."

Adair caught the shift, but her shoulders eased anyway.

"Thank you," she whispered.

The woman slipped out into the corridor, the door sliding shut behind her with a soft hiss. Her footsteps echoed softly as she walked through the silent hallway, her thoughts racing about what lay ahead. She told herself to focus, but the calm Takashi's vial offered her had already thinned to nothing, leaving the familiar gnaw of anxiety in its wake.

Well, that didn't last long.

Back in her room, Adair moved on autopilot, folding clothes and gathering the necessary gear she would need the next day. Despite the grueling hours of training, she felt she was standing in front of a test she hadn't studied for, and Takashi's comment had only chipped further at her waning confidence. Between the rising stakes, her own doubts, and Ossian's temper flaring, it felt like everything was on the verge of breaking.

Her hand paused over one of her daggers, fingers tracing the hilt. The weapon felt heavier lately, not because of its physical weight but because of what it represented. She wasn't just carrying it for herself. She wielded it for the thousands of lives counting on her not to fall apart. With a weary sigh, she picked it up and added it to her gear.

She had barely settled at her desk, the half-finished packing list waiting beneath her pen, when a sharp rap split the quiet.

The sound cracked through the room with enough force to make her flinch.

"Come in."

The door creaked open to reveal an imposing frame.

Ossian.

The firelight struggled against the breadth of him, shadows curling greedily along the hard lines of his shoulders and the sharp cut of his jaw. He took a step further into the room, slamming the door shut behind him.

"We need to talk."

Adair braced herself. "What is it?"

The man crossed the room slowly, his jaw tight, a predator stalking his prey.

"Tomorrow. You and I... We're walking into something with a lot of unknowns." He stopped a few feet away. "I can't afford to have any distractions. And you? You've been one big *fecking* distraction."

Adair's stomach dipped.

"A distraction?"

The words came out too soft, betraying the rush of heat that crawled up her neck. For one irrational moment, she thought this was about what had nearly happened between them months ago, but then his following words landed like a slap to the face.

"You and Takashi. Whatever's going on between the two of you..."

The woman's eyebrows hit her forehead, but he plowed forward.

"It's affecting everything. The team, the mission. You're not focused,

Hanlon."

Adair felt her pulse hammer as anger coiled hot and sharp in her chest. "No. You don't get to do this."

Her chair scraped back hard as she stood, closing the distance between them until she was glaring up at the man who towered over her. "This isn't about Takashi or me. This is about *you* and the fact that you can't keep your own temper in check."

Ossian leaned in, close enough that she could feel the heat radiating off his body. His voice came deep, a rough growl that seemed to vibrate between them.

"You think this is about me?" His mouth curved, but there was nothing soft in it. Only the promise of something dangerous. "You and you're emotions are the liability here, Hanlon. I need you to get your head straight before tomorrow."

Adair's hands curled into fists. She was so damn tired of the constant pressure, the endless expectations, the weight of everyone's emotions crashing down on her. "Maybe if you stopped trying to control everyone around you, you'd see that I'm handling things just fine."

Ossian's eyes narrowed. "Are you? Because from where I'm standing, it doesn't look like it."

Adair's heart hammered, and for a fleeting moment, she wanted to throw all her doubts and frustrations at him, but fatigue weighed her down, pulling the fight from her bones. She drew a slow, shuddering breath and stepped back.

"Maybe you're the one who needs to sort out *your* feelings, Ossian," she said, her voice quieter now.

Ossian's nose flared. "What are you on about?"

"Nothing," she murmured, turning her gaze away.

"Nothing at all?" His voice slid lower, scraping against her nerves.

"I'm just tired, Ossian," she said softly, crossing her arms. "I need..."

"You need what?" The man pressed closer, each movement deliberate, until there was no space remaining between them. "You need to stop hiding behind those walls and tell me what's going on in that head of yours before it tears you apart. You can't run from this."

Adair's hands went to Ossian's chest, gripping the solid strength beneath her palms. She had meant to shove him away, to put distance between them, but her fingers betrayed her, curling into the thin fabric of his shirt. She felt his body stiffen under her touch, muscles coiling as if resisting her, and then, just as suddenly, he began to pull back.

Adair let out a sharp scoff.

"See? *I'm* not the one running from this."

Ossian moved before she could blink, his hand coming up to catch her chin and tilt her face, leaving her no choice but to look at him. The intensity in his green eyes set her pulse racing, heat coiling low in her belly.

"I never run, *little wolf*."

The words punched the air from Adair's lungs. Her mother's nickname for her.

How did he know?

Her mind scrambled, flashing to the last time she'd heard it spoken out loud. It had been months ago, as she was saying goodbye to her aunt Laura.

For him to use it in this way was nothing short of cruel.

Defiance flared, and Adair wrenched against his grip. His fingers only tightened, holding her fast, and the frustration that surged through her became uncontrollable. Her palm rose on its own, slapping across his cheek with a sharp crack.

He let her go immediately.

And then, infuriatingly, he smiled.

A slow, *dangerous* smile.

"I hope you bring that same fight with you tomorrow." Ossian's hand raked through his hair, exhaling hard, then his piercing gaze locked on hers again. "You can do this, I have no doubt, as long as you can keep your *emotions* out of it."

"That's the pot calling the kettle black."

His laugh was short, sharp, and humorless. "My duty to this community is *far* different than yours, Hanlon."

Adair took another step back until the backs of her knees hit the bed, and she sat down hard on the edge. "Don't you want more than just your duty?" The words escaped before she could stop them.

"That's the problem with wanting, Hanlon. It makes us weak."

She swallowed, feeling that tight pain in her chest.

"Is that how you really feel?" she asked, her voice steadier than she expected. "So we should just bury everything we want, pretend none of it matters, until there is nothing left but war?"

Something flitted across the Irishman's face, so quick she almost doubted she had seen it. A crack in the armor, there and gone, swallowed up as his jaw tightened.

"Desires cloud judgment," Ossian said at last. "Right now, judgment is all we have. This is about more than what any one of us wants."

He stepped closer.

"We can't let what we want control us."

His voice had changed, deeper now, a thread of gravel in it.

"Especially not now."

"Why not?" she breathed. "Maybe wanting isn't the weakness you think it is. Maybe it's the only thing that keeps us *alive*."

His gaze sharpened, searching her face.

"Hanlon," he murmured, his voice strained, "You don't understand what you're asking..."

Adair rose to her feet slowly, refusing to retreat. She had spent enough time cowering. She didn't know what was coming tomorrow, but she knew that she didn't want to waste tonight.

"Maybe I do. And I think *you* do too."

Ossian made a sharp sound as if her answer had stolen what breath had remained in his lungs.

When he finally spoke, her name left his mouth like a warning and a promise all at once, low and rough enough to make her stomach twist.

"Hanlon."

The way he said it made her hungry in ways she hadn't experienced. Not to this level.

Need.

Frustration.

It curled through her like smoke and made her knees threaten to give way.

She looked up at Ossian, expecting to see him moving towards her, but he didn't advance. Instead, he tore his gaze from hers and stepped back, severing the charge that had built between them.

"Focus on what lies ahead," he said finally, his voice cold where it had once been warm. "Tomorrow is all that matters."

Adair's heart sank at the withdrawal as Ossian turned his back and left her standing there...

Again.

She waited for the heartbreak to come, but instead, a strange calm fell over her. She knew the man well enough now to understand. He never pushed her away without reason.

His defences were high, as they always had been.

Fine.

She would train.

She would master every spark of magic until the day came when she was strong enough to burn down *every last wall*.

Chapter Twenty-Seven

Adair awoke to the gentle sounds of birds, their faint melodies filtering in from the false garden outside. She took a moment to appreciate the brief sense of tranquility, fully aware it would most likely be the last for a while.

As she dressed, her gaze fell on the carved wooden box resting on her nightstand. With a steadying breath, she pocketed a few of the remaining pills before tucking the box deep into her bag and heading out the door.

It didn't take long to find Ossian.

The Irishman moved with precision, his boots barely making a sound as he fell into step with her in the narrow hallway. Neither of them acknowledged the other, and Adair was glad for the silence. She needed her focus, not the chaos he so easily stirred in her chest.

The pair made their way to the war room, where they found Commander Trevellan standing in his office, hands clasped behind his back. His eyes tracked Ossian as they entered, sharp and calculating, but his expression gave nothing away as he watched the Celt step towards the stone archway on the far wall. With the wave of the man's hand, the portal opened, its swirling light flooding the chamber with a pale, celestial glow.

Ossian's eyes flicked back to Adair. "Time to go."

The woman couldn't tell if the edge in his voice stemmed from agitation or nerves, but she nodded, heart racing as she followed him into the light.

The familiar sounds of the portal seized her, colors blurring in a whirlwind before bursting into an endless galaxy. The passage seemed to stretch longer this time, and her stomach flipped with relief when their destination came into focus.

The cool, damp air of the Pacific Northwest met them like a wall.

Adair blinked, her vision adjusting as she took in the gray sky and the heavy clouds pressing low above the city. The smell of rain on pavement and freshly brewed coffee drifting from somewhere close by hit her all at once. Cars hissed through shallow puddles. A man with an umbrella over his head hurried past.

Adair felt disoriented after the journey, but two things were immediately clear.

First, this was *not* the secluded countryside they had expected to land in.

Second, they were currently standing in the middle of Seattle.

The brick facade of *Walmsley's Bookshop & Bindery* stood across the street, its small, weathered sign creaking faintly above the door. The humble, cozy storefront looked untouched, almost out of place in the ordinary world after everything Adair had been through.

"Um... Ossian? Why are we *here*?" she whispered.

"This is where the portal brought us," Ossian responded, his expression tight as he scanned the surroundings. "Something isn't right."

Adair's chest ached as she gazed at the bookshop, memories rushing back in waves.

It had been months since she last stepped through those doors. Back then, Walmsley's had been her refuge, a quiet sanctuary when the world felt overwhelmingly loud. But now, standing at the entrance of her second home, a new sensation enveloped her.

"Can you feel it?" Ossian asked, gaze still fixed on the building.

Adair nodded slowly.

Something about this place had shifted in the past few months. The pull to enter was no longer the natural longing of a lonely girl to escape into her favorite pages. Instead, there was an odd energy in the air, something both familiar and foreign, tugging at the edges of her awareness that just felt...

Wrong.

"Stay close," Ossian murmured, his hand settling lightly over the hilt at his hip, hidden beneath his metamorphose. His eyes flicked toward every shadow, tension lining his shoulders.

Adair nodded, clasping the ogham necklace around her throat for support as they crossed the final stretch of sidewalk.

The familiar jingle of the brass bell above the door welcomed them as they stepped inside, and at once the smell of vanilla and weathered parchment overwhelmed her. It was a scent that had always meant safety to her, a quiet promise that the chaos of the outside world would not follow her here. For the briefest moment, standing in the warmth of the shop, she let herself pretend this was still her life. That she had simply come in on her day off to browse the shelves before returning to her normal, untroubled routine.

The shop had not changed one bit. Light filtered through the tall front windows and fell across the narrow aisles lined with towering shelves, their rows packed with spines in every shade of fading cloth and cracked leather. The spiral staircase wound its way upward toward the loft, where more books waited in hushed, shadowed corners. To the right sat the wooden counter, familiar in its clutter of ledgers and dog-eared paperbacks. The air carried the same reverent stillness it always had, but something within it felt altered, like a melody played in a slightly different key.

The espresso machine expelled a sudden burst of steam, setting her nerves on edge. Ossian shifted almost imperceptibly beside her, his hand brushing the hilt of his dagger, though it remained hidden beneath the metamophose's magic.

Before either could speak, a voice rose from the back room, warm and familiar enough to nearly undo her composure.

"Adair?"

She turned sharply toward the sound. Her heart gave a painful leap as Ian Walmsley stepped into view, looking exactly as she remembered him. His gray hair was perfectly combed over, his moustache was as perky as always, and the small spectacles perched low on his nose caught the light when he tilted his head.

Surprise flashed across the man's face before it softened into relief, the lines at the corners of his eyes easing as he took in the sight of her.

"Mr. Walmsley," she breathed.

Ian crossed the room, wiping his hands on the apron tied over his shirt, his voice thick with disbelief. "Well, I'll be damned. It *is* you. I didn't think I would be seeing you back here so soon, my dear. Laura told me you'd gone off to Scotland."

The mention of her aunt pulled at something deep in her chest. She had missed Laura more than she cared to admit. Despite the occasional call or text, it was not the same as seeing her aunt in person, never enough to quiet the homesickness that crept in during long nights away from this life.

"She said you hadn't been well," Ian continued softly, his brow furrowed with concern. "Told me you went to stay with a friend. She thought it might help you feel like yourself again."

Hearing that Laura had created an alibi to explain her absence left Adair feeling both grateful and exposed. She had left so abruptly, swallowed whole by a world that demanded everything from her and had offered no time to explain. And through it all, Laura had shielded her, filling in the gaps with stories to keep questions at bay.

The thought of it left a dull ache beneath her ribs.

She would visit her aunt as soon as this was all over.

She owed her that much.

"Yeah," Adair said finally, the word rough as it left her mouth. "I... I needed some time."

Ian's eyes lingered on her face, full of the same warmth and steadiness she had known for years. "I'm glad you're back, even if it's just for a little while. You gave us all quite a scare."

Adair tried to smile, though it felt thin and fragile beneath the weight of everything unsaid.

Beside her, Ossian stood silent, his attention on the room itself. He had not spoken a word, yet his presence grounded her, a reminder of the true meaning behind this visit.

"We won't be staying long," Adair said softly, forcing her voice to stay even. "There's something we need to check."

Ian's gaze lingered on her for a moment, as though he could sense the current of unease running beneath her words.

"Well, you know this place is always here for you, Miss Hanlon." He offered a small, reassuring smile. "Whatever you need. These shelves have missed you."

Adair's heart broke a little at the sentiment.

She wanted to imagine the stacks waiting patiently for her return, their books humming quietly in her absence, but something had changed. What had once been an escape now felt watchful, different somehow, as though something unseen moved beneath the surface.

Her eyes drifted across the familiar aisles before coming to rest on the half-open door at the back of the shop. That was where the feeling was strongest, a subtle pull drawing her in like a moth to a flame.

"I figured since I was in the neighborhood," Adair said carefully, "I could show my friend Ossian your collection of old books. He's really into that sort of thing. Would that be alright, Mr. Walmsley?"

Ian adjusted his spectacles, tilting his head toward Ossian with a look of mild curiosity before his face broke into a wide grin. "Of course. You know I have quite the collection," he said, a note of pride in his voice. "I started it back when I lived in England, and brought the whole lot with me when I moved here. It's more than just books, too. There are antiques, rare manuscripts, and even a few oddities that I picked up along the way."

He waved toward the back room. "Most of it's back there. Not for sale, mind you, but I don't mind showing it off now and then. Not many come looking for things like that these days."

Adair stepped closer to the counter. "We were told by an old acquaintance of Ossian's that there was a private collector in the area who might have something we need. It reminded me of the things I've seen here over the years, so I thought maybe Mr. Wainwright was referring to you."

At the name, Ian paused, his brow knitting.

"Wainwright? I have not heard that name in a very long time." He rubbed his chin as though sifting through old memories. "If I recall correctly, he was a bit of an eccentric. Always rambling on about artifacts with strange properties. You do not mean that Wainwright, do you?"

"That's him, all right," Adair said, keeping her tone steady despite the growing anticipation curling in her chest. "He mentioned the collection might hold something specific. He spoke of a horn, or a fragment of one, maybe?"

Recognition sparked faintly across Ian's features.

"A horn," he repeated slowly, then gave a small chuckle. "Well, that *is* peculiar. Yes, as a matter of fact, I do have something like that. Acquired it a while back, though I never knew much about it beyond its age. It is old, certainly. Very old. I thought it was little more than a random artifact, but if *Wainwright* was the one pointing you here..." He trailed off, the humor in his tone fading into something more cautious.

Adair's pulse quickened. The lead hadn't been a dead end after all. Whatever lay in that back room might be the very thing they had been searching for.

The air itself seemed to grow thicker the longer she stared at the narrow door beyond the counter.

Ian set his pipe between his teeth, the stem resting there as he studied them both. "Why the interest in the horn?"

Ossian spoke for the first time since they had entered. "We believe it may be connected to something my company is investigating. It is important that we see it."

Ian regarded them for a long moment, his eyes shifting from Adair to Ossian and back again, before finally giving a slow nod.

"Very well," he said at last. "But I will warn you, it has been gathering dust in the corner for years."

Ian turned and started toward the back room, and Adair followed with Ossian at her back, each step carrying them closer to whatever waited beyond that threshold.

The familiarity of Ian's workspace wrapped around Adair, the air thick with dust and ink and the faint scent of tea leaves that had long ago settled into the walls. She could almost feel the weight of the novels she once shelved, the warmth of the shop's light pooling across the floor as she worked late into the evenings. There had been long afternoons of learning under Ian's steady guidance, his calm voice instructing her on how to mend a broken spine or stitch a torn page with the kind of patience only he possessed.

Here she had found peace, one volume at a time.

But now, everything felt different, the warmth of those memories clashing with the weight of their mission.

Adair wasn't the same person who once sought solace in the quiet rhythm of this place, and she couldn't help but feel the distance between her past and present. It felt as if this room, this life, no longer fit the person she had become.

A soft thud broke through her thoughts.

Ian, half-buried in the corner of the workshop, had shifted a precarious stack of books, sending a few volumes tumbling to the floor. He bent slowly, muttering under his breath as he unearthed a long, weathered instrument from the pile. Its polished metal glimmered faintly in the light, the intricate carvings along its length whispering of a history far older than the room that now held it.

Before Ian could struggle with its weight, Ossian stepped forward swiftly, his hands moving to help lay the horn gently on the table. The two men exchanged a brief nod, the Irishman's gaze focused as his fingers brushed over the complex ridges along the horn's surface.

Mr. Walmsley struck a match, lighting the pipe clamped between his teeth. A slow curl of smoke wound upward as he studied the horn, his expression one of somber respect.

"It's a carnyx," he said at last. "An ancient warhorn, used by the Celts to terrify their enemies. Its design was meant to strike fear into their combatants. They say that the sound alone was enough to unsettle even the most seasoned warrior." He drew on the pipe again, eyes never leaving the artifact. "Terrifying, in the right hands."

Ossian's digits danced across the bronze with a reverence that startled Adair. There was nothing hurried or careless in his movements. He touched it as though it were something sacred, his palm smoothing over the cool surface as though he could feel the echo of its power lingering beneath.

She saw the subtle shift in his expression, the flicker of emotion in the set of his jaw, the way he swallowed hard before his features settled back into neutrality. For a moment, the weight of his past hung so thick around him that she almost stepped forward, wanting to ask what this meant to him, but instead she held herself back.

Adair's gaze moved across the room toward Ian, who stood at the door with his phone in hand, the faint glow of the screen lighting the well-worn lines of his face. When he saw her approach, he slipped the device into his coat pocket.

"Mr. Walmsley," she said softly.

The smile he gave her was warm, yet it stopped just shy of his eyes. "Can I safely assume you've found what you were looking for?"

Guilt pressed down on her at once. Ian had been like a father to her, offering quiet guidance when she had needed it most. He had been a constant in a life that so often felt like shifting sand. And yet here she was, only returning to see his collection, and not him.

"Yes," she said, her voice quiet but earnest. "You have no idea how much this means to me. How much *you* mean to me. I am sorry I didn't visit."

His eyes softened, though the sorrow lingering there made her throat tighten. "Oh, my dear," he murmured. "You'll have this old man in tears if you go on like that. I'm only glad I could help. My collection's been unappreciated for far too long."

Ian glanced toward the shelves, his gaze drifting over relics that had been his companions for decades. "Strange, isn't it? That you crossed paths with Mr. Wainwright. A peculiar man, but brilliant in his way. Many of my finest pieces came from him. That vase in the corner is one of his, said to be older than the Greek tragedies themselves. And the painting above my bed, not unlike the one he sold to you. He had a knack for finding history's most *curious* treasures. My favorite, though?" His mouth curved faintly. "My shrunken head. Said to be the noggin of

Alexander Selkirk himself. You know the tale? Robinson Crusoe owes its birth to that man's survival."

He caught himself, waving a hand as though shooing away his own rambling. "Listen to me, drifting into stories again."

Adair laughed softly, but something in his words bothered her.

The painting above my bed, not unlike the one he sold to you.

She had never told him about the painting.

Neither of them had.

"Oh, my sweet girl."

Ian's voice cracked, his eyes brimming with unshed tears as he lifted a trembling hand toward her cheek.

"I truly wish you hadn't manifested."

The edges of the room blurred as cold realization surged through her veins. Her stomach dropped violently, the air rushing from her lungs as she spun.

"Ossian!" Her voice fractured. "He's working with the Order!"

The Irishman whipped around, eyes narrowing, hand darting toward his sword, but it was too late. Arms clamped around her from behind, and a low, familiar voice hissed in her ear.

"He can't save you this time, abomination."

"Nash!" Ossian's voice was a low snarl, his hand unsheathing the blade at his back.

Before he could fully draw it, another figure slipped silently into the room.

Éala's silver eyes were cold and calculated, her expression unreadable. She moved with a deadly grace, lifting one hand to conjure a barrier of air between them.

"I wouldn't," she warned, her tone emotionless. "Nash is still angry about his face."

"Shut the fuck up, Éala!" Nash snarled.

Adair's pulse kicked into a wild, erratic rhythm as the grip on her arm tightened, the bruising pressure forcing her closer against the man. She twisted, struggling to break free, but Nash was immovable.

"Let her go!" Ossian barked. His eyes locked on the intruders, his body coiled as though he was a heartbeat away from tearing them apart.

"Now, now," Nash drawled. "No need to get all worked up. We're only taking her for a little *chat*."

Adair forced herself to keep breathing, keep thinking, even as panic clawed at her throat. She caught Ossian's eyes and silently begged him not to be reckless. If he lunged now, Nash would snap her neck before he could reach her.

"She comes with us," Éala said coolly, her hand still raised, her gaze shifting briefly toward the Celt. "Unless you want this to get messy."

Ossian's jaw flexed, his knuckles bone-white around the hilt of his sword. "If you hurt her—"

"Spare me," Nash cut in with a snort. "We pinky promise not to euthanize your little *pet*."

The words made Adair flinch. The panic clawed higher now, scraping through her ribs.

Nash turned sharply. "The Chancellor is done waiting," he spat. "The Council moved the timeline forward."

Adair blinked, disoriented, until she realized Nash wasn't speaking to Éala.

The words crashed over as she stared at Ian, the man she thought she knew, her mind spinning, refusing to connect the pieces.

"Mr. Walmsley," Adair's voice shook. "Tell me he's lying."

Ian didn't answer right away. He simply exhaled a plume of smoke, his lined face quiet and unreadable.

"I am afraid," he said at last, "it is out of my hands, Miss Hanlon."

Adair shook her head, disbelief stinging her eyes.

"Why?" The single word cracked in her throat as her tears threatened to spill over.

Ian's eyes softened then, only briefly. He stepped closer, his hand landing heavy and father-like on her shoulder.

"It is what must be done," he said, regret threading through his words. "Despite my fondness for you, Adair, I will not betray the Order."

Her heart felt like it was tearing itself apart.

She couldn't breathe.

Betrayal sliced through her like glass, leaving her shaking in Nash's grip, fighting uselessly even as her strength bled out of her.

She turned toward Ossian, desperate for some kind of answer, some hint of defiance in the man who had always stood between her and the dark.

But he didn't move.

The Irishman stood with his arms crossed, his face carved from stone, watching it all unfold with no rage, no fear, no fight. When her panicked eyes locked on his, he only released an annoyed sigh, pushing himself slowly from the table where he leaned, and stepped forward to stand beside Ian.

Adair felt her entire world shatter in real time.

"Ossian?" Her voice was barely a whisper, a desperate plea.

He said nothing.

Not a single word.

"No," Adair whispered, shaking her head violently as tears broke free. "No, this isn't happening."

But there was no mistake.

No explanation was waiting to fall from his lips that would make sense of this.

There was only the finality of his silence as Nash yanked her backward, locking her in place.

Éala moved toward the doorway, her pale hands rising. The air warped, energy snapping through the space as the portal burst to life, its blue glow casting sharp light over everything.

Adair thrashed once, twice, her body frantic with refusal, but Nash's grip was iron, and Éala was quickly closing in on her other side. Together, they dragged her toward the threshold.

Adair's eyes clung to Ossian until the last possible moment, searching his face for the man who had once stood between her and the world.

She begged for even the slightest sign that she hadn't imagined it all. That the promises he had made meant... *something*.

But he never moved.

He only stood there, his jaw tight, his sea green eyes unreadable.

That was the last thing she saw before the galaxy swallowed her whole.

Epilogue

Uncertainty coiled tight in Ossian's gut as the portal snapped shut behind Adair, the faint glow snuffed out in an instant.

"You did the right thing, lad," Ian said, placing a hand on the Celt's shoulder.

Ossian shrugged him off and turned on him, anger simmering beneath the surface. "Did we? And what do you think Ainsworth will do if it proves true?"

The shopkeeper drew in a slow breath and puffed at his pipe, smoke curling lazily toward the ceiling. He rolled the stem between his teeth before speaking.

"If she *is* a Deity, then obviously she will be used to turn the tide of the war."

His tone was even, almost detached.

Ossian's fists clenched at his sides. He gave a stiff nod and turned to leave, though his steps felt heavier than before.

It was unlikely she was a Deity.

Her testing had been proof enough of that.

There was a higher chance she would be tagged and released, like every Creator before her.

"Your father would be proud of the work you've done, my boy."

The words froze him mid-step.

Ian spoke around the pipe between his lips. "You truly are bringing his dream to life."

Ian did not look up. He did not see the way Ossian's shoulders locked, or the way his jaw set in silent rage. The old man only leaned over the horn with the same infuriating calm he always carried, his expression unreadable through the faint haze of smoke.

Ossian said nothing.

Only clenched his fists tighter as he strode away from the scene of his betrayal.

PRONUNCIATION GUIDE

Adair - uh-DAIR
Nadia - NAH-dee-uh
Ossian - OSH-ən
MacCumhaill – Mi-COOL
Oísin - UH-sheen
Nash - N-a-SH
Eála - AY-la
Celtic - Kelt-ik
Slains - Slaynz
Takashi - tah-KAH-shee
Amelia - uh-MEE-lee-uh
Metamorphose - meh-tuh-MOR-fohz
Fiann - fy-on
Ogham - oh-um
Eta - EE-tuh
Sláinte - SLAHN-chə
Flahives - FLAH-hiv-s
Fianna - FEE-ə-nə
Alúine - al-oo-nyuh
Gaelic - gah-lik
Gaeilge - GAIL-guh
Carnyx - KAR-niks

ACKNOWLEDGEMENTS

This book could not have come to life without the patience, encouragement, and belief of so many extraordinary people.

First, to my anam caras—Laura and Lauren. Decades of friendship, countless conversations, and your unwavering belief in me have carried every word to these pages. Without your encouragement, none of my writing would have seen the light of day. Your sisterhood is stitched into these chapters and into the very fiber of who I am.

To my husband—thank you for loving me through late nights, scattered notes, and endless cups of coffee. You've always been my fiercest supporter. From helping me wrangle my "murder board" of story notes, to talking me through every stubborn plothole, you've believed in me even when I didn't believe in myself.

JW— Thank you for being such an amazing friend and love. You were the best storyteller and I hope I hold a candle to you. You are so missed.

Nyla and Khalid—thank you for your endless love, and for being the best Dadi and Dada to our kiddo. You and your family mean the world to us, and so much of this story carries your spirit.

Nadia and Omar—thank you for letting me steal your names for my characters, and for being the best Phuppo and Chacha to our little wolf.

Dad—thank you for teaching me the value of integrity and hard work. Your diligence is a quiet fire that pushes me to finish what I start.

Mom—thank you for teaching me the value of a good story. For those weekends at Books-A-Million, wandering the aisles and reading for hours. And for giving me my killer, dark sense of humor.

Luke and Matt—our stories, games, and roleplays live here between the lines. Peter Pan, the Lost Boys, and Neverland are here because of you.

Brenda and Rebecca—thank you from the bottom of my heart for taking the time out of your busy schedules to support us. You have been our biggest fans from day one and a constant throughout this journey.

Julia and Riley—those old notebooks full of roleplays and Myspace pages shaped me into the writer I am. I'm grateful for your friendship, your creativity, and every late-night scene we ever dreamed up.

To my online friends—Jazz, Tohma, and Tori—the wild Myspace roleplay days made me a better writer, and pieces of each of you are hidden in these characters.

To my writer friends—LeeAnn, Emily, Amalena, Taryn, Serena, Amanda, Nate, and Julia—you challenge me, inspire me, and push me to be braver with my words. I'm honored to write alongside such talent.

Syldryn— Thank you for fostering my love for Dungeons and Dragons and creating worlds with words with you. I will *always* be here for you, no matter what.

To the team at The Wild Mug coffee shop— To the owners, Fausto and Leia, thank you for opening your shop to me daily to provide me a comfortable writing environment, great food and amazing coffee. To my baristas, Abi, Annarella, Josey, Sebastien, and Vedha thank you for putting up with my antics and giving me even more great ideas to add to the series.

To the friends who kept me laughing when the words felt heavy, and walking forward when the road seemed long—you've been my anchor and my compass.

To the readers who take a chance on a new voice—thank you. You are the heartbeat of every story, and the thought of these characters finding a home in your imagination is the greatest gift I could ask for.

And to Rae Boylen—your guidance, insight, and kindness shaped this work more than you'll ever know. It has been one of my greatest honors to not only call you a partner in this but a friend. All the hours of revisions and collaboration led us here. Your love for these characters and this world means everything to me. Thank you for showing up even on the hard days, and for being my anam cara since high school. This story belongs to you as much as it does to me.

Finally, to those who live authentically, speak truth even when it shakes, and stand for what's right—you inspire every page I write.

TO THE ARTISTS

We want to give a heartfelt thank you to the incredible artists who helped bring this book to life.

Fen, your breathtaking cover art captured the soul of our story before a single page was even turned.

Marta, your gorgeous title page and internal artwork added beauty and depth to every chapter. We are endlessly grateful to you both for turning a spoken vision into a visual reality, and we can't wait to work with you again in the future!

Please show these two some love by liking and following them!

Cover Art by Fen
Instagram: @Rosdottir
Internal Art by Marta
Instagram: @Marta.intotheforest

ABOUT THE AUTHOR

Kelsey Wolfe is a loving mother, wife, and author. Having won her first award for writing in middle school, Kelsey has always aspired to further causes she believes in by broadening the reach of her stories. Based in Florida, she tends to her native garden and works from a local coffee shop. In her free time, she enjoys playing with her tiny human, husband, and Shih Tzu, Sir Galahad.

www.ingramcontent.com/pod-product-compliance
Ingram Content Group UK Ltd.
Pitfield, Milton Keynes, MK11 3LW, UK
UKHW040238250426
12048UKWH00043B/1574